Summer Angel

Books by Suzie O'Connell

NORTHSTAR
First Instinct
Mountain Angel
Summer Angel
Twice Shy
Once Burned
Mistletoe Kisses
Starlight Magic
Wild Angel
Forgotten Angel
Last Surrender

TWO-LANE WYOMING
The Road to Garrett

SEA GLASS COVE
The Abalone Shell
The Driftwood Promise

www.suzieoconnell.com

Summer Angel

A Northstar Novel

SUZIE O'CONNELL

ISBN-13: 978-1-950813-16-2

For my "Peanuts Gallery" buds:
Holly, Torrie, Tasmine, and Katie.
Friendship, not only laughter, is the best medicine.

One

WHEN THE CALL CAME over the radio about a possible drunk and disorderly near the Hood Canal Bridge, Ben wondered if it would be too late to call June when his shift ended in an hour. Probably, he thought and turned his patrol car north toward the bridge. He doubted she'd mind. Dinner with her and Aelissm last night had been wonderful—just like the old days before college and careers and distance had stolen so much time from them—and he looked forward to a repeat. June wouldn't be heading back to Montana for at least two weeks, and Aelissm had recently withdrawn from her summer classes in Seattle, and he fully intended to make the most of that.

He pushed his thoughts and memories aside as he pulled into the gas station. Sure enough, a plainly inebriated man staggered out of the convenience store, pausing momentarily to grip the metal edge of the glass door and regain his balance. Ben noted the unkempt brown hair, grimy white T-shirt, and ragged jeans. Ben guessed the man was in his mid-thirties, but he looked older; the wear and tear of a rough life distorted the youth of his face. He was a smallish man, standing only an inch or two over five-and-a-half feet with the kind of thin, ropy musculature that disguised a surprising strength that immediately became evident when he straightened and slammed the door with a bellowed curse.

Down on his luck? Ben wondered, swallowing the stab of pity. Unsnapping the leather guard on his holster, he stepped out of his car. Adrenaline trickled through his veins, heightening his senses.

"Evening," he called pleasantly to the man.

The man looked up at him with bloodshot brown eyes and snarled. The back of Ben's neck tingled as the trickle turned into a flood and primal instinct drove any thoughts but survival from his mind. His heart pounded, and seeing the flash of bright metal, he dove behind his patrol car just as the first shot whizzed by him. Another shot and another cracked in the still evening. Ben yanked his gun out of its holster and edged around to the passenger side. Carefully opening the door, he reached for his radio.

"Shots fired! Shots fired!" He relayed his information and location, then knelt beside his car, using it as a shield.

The man swayed drunkenly, glaring with his pistol shakily aimed in Ben's direction.

"Drop it!" Ben bellowed. "Get on the ground! Now! Face down on the ground!"

The shooter didn't seem to hear him.

Please don't make me shoot you!

The man fired again, and one of the convenience store windows shattered. The clerk inside screamed. Moments later, another shot boomed before the echoes of the last had died away, and the slug ricocheted with a zing off a concrete parking block before tearing across Ben's thigh. Ignorant of the pain, he braced his forearms on the hood of his car and trained his gun on the man.

"Drop it, goddammit! I *will* shoot you!"

For one long, agonizing moment, the man paused,

standing as still as a statue. Ben took aim at his leg, intending to disable him. Just as he squeezed the trigger and the gun bucked in his hands, the man stumbled.

Oh, God.

* * *

Ben flailed awake with the gunshot echoing in his mind. He stared blindly into the dark room and quivered, his skin damp with cold sweat. He sat helplessly paralyzed as the memory continued to unfold, and in horrifying detail, he saw the bullet slam into the man's chest, watched blood bloom on the dingy white t-shirt, and the gun slip from the man's hand as his legs folded beneath him. He was dead before he hit the pavement.

The only clear memory he had of what happened in the following hours and days was of later that night when he'd stood in Bill Granger's office staring at an eleven-year-old boy with blond hair and tears spilling from frightened blue eyes. That memory was the sharpest of them all and sliced him more deeply each time he recalled it. The horror of killing a man was nothing compared to the guilt that had crashed through him as Aelissm's uncle—a man Ben had known as a close family friend for years before he'd joined the sheriff's department—debriefed him. The man he'd shot was John McKindel, and the boy was his son. Now, because of Ben, the boy was no one's son.

Bill had conducted the investigation into the shooting and reported that Ben had acted well within his duties and the law, but that didn't matter. Ben absently traced his thumb over the smooth, four-inch-long white scar on his left thigh. The bullet had burned a shallow furrow across his leg a hand span above his knee, and he was lucky it was the only one that had struck him. But that didn't matter, either. Two weeks past his twenty-fifth birthday, with only three of the many years he'd hoped to serve as a sheriff's deputy behind him, he'd killed a man and—so much worse—destroyed a young boy's life.

Ben sagged back to the mattress and covered his face with his shaking hands. Luke Allen McKindel. He was tiny for an eleven-year-old, Ben had thought, barely four and a half feet tall, rail-thin, and pale. The boy had looked at Ben, and for the briefest moment, they had locked gazes. Even now, nearly five years later, Ben wanted to retch at the fear and uncertainty in those blue eyes.

He glanced at the obscenely perky green numbers of his bedside clock; it was half past four in the morning. With a grunt, he flipped back his blankets and pushed himself out of bed. His golden retriever lifted his head and whined softly. *Smart dog,* Ben thought. *You know when I'm down.* He patted the dog's head, and Casey thumped his tail slowly.

"I'll be okay, Case. Just another bad dream. Stay. Go back to sleep."

Casey put his head on his paws again, but Ben sensed those watchful brown eyes on his back as he walked away. He found his way into the kitchen and opened the refrigerator. He reached blindly for the jug of water in the painful light and fumbled with the cap. At last, he tipped the bottle back and let the frigid liquid slide down his throat.

"This has gotta stop," he muttered. He swallowed the rest of the water and closed the fridge. "That's three times in a month."

He wandered into the wide living room and turned on the lamp beside the couch. Despite the nausea that still churned in his gut, he smiled when he picked up the picture on the end table. His mother had taken it years ago at a picnic just after his graduation. Aelissm stood behind him giving him rabbit ears, and in his arms, he held a laughing June. He'd swept her off her feet, and the surprised smile on her face was one of his most cherished memories of that day.

There were other pictures of them scattered around his house, and he walked around, glancing from one to the next, allowing the fond memories to envelope him and chase away his nightmare.

Like a breath of cool wind on a stagnant summer day, understanding embraced him. He knew what he needed. He had to escape the constant reminders of what he'd done that night, and there was only one place he wanted to go—home to Northstar, Montana. He'd spent the first eight years of his life there, and though he'd been gone close to twenty-two years now, it was still the place his heart yearned to be. Besides, June and Aeli were in Northstar. The last time he'd seen them was that wonderful night before the shooting. No, that was wrong. He'd seen June briefly a week or so later, but he didn't think that counted because they hadn't spoken more than a handful of words, and he had turned away, afraid that he'd find his own assessment of what he'd done reflected in her laughing blue eyes. That would have destroyed him.

He'd missed her especially in the week since the last nightmare. He really could have used her friendship over the last four and a half years; she would have known what to say and do to help him see what everyone else had tried to tell him, that he shouldn't feel guilty for any of what had happened that night. He could have called her or visited her at any time, but that fear of her hating him had prevented him from picking up the phone. Now he wondered if there was anything left but to chance losing one of the best friends he'd ever had.

He shook his head to dispel the morbid musings. Climbing back into bed, he closed his eyes, determined to finish the night in peace. Keeping June's smiling face in his mind for reassurance, he spent the remainder of the small hours of the morning pondering his options. As dawn slowly lightened the world, he settled on a course of action, and there was a blissful lessening of the tension in his chest.

Maybe he'd just walk up to the manager of Donovan's Bar and Grill and give his two weeks' notice. So what if it seemed rash? The owner had thought the same three years ago when Ben had turned down a promotion to manager. To be honest, Ben hadn't planned to stay at the restaurant a year, let alone four.

He sat up, amazed it hadn't occurred to him sooner that he could just leave. Of course, there was still the chance that he wouldn't be able to stay in Montana. What if he couldn't find work? What if it wasn't what he expected? His sister did not regret moving back, but that didn't mean he wouldn't, so he'd be smart and keep up on his rent and bills. Just in case. Even as he thought it, it felt like a waste. He wouldn't be coming back. No matter what happened, he'd find a way to make it work.

Two weeks, he told himself. *In two weeks, I'll be home again.*

* * *

As the final bell rang, June smiled at her students and told them all to have a good weekend. When the last had filed out of the room laughing and talking, she sighed and gathered the towering stack of schoolwork she needed to take home with her. She had six class periods' worth of quizzes, vocabulary, end-of-chapter reviews, and labs to grade, and she wouldn't get to start on it until late tonight after she got off work at the Ramshorn. *And the kids think answering all of the end-of-chapter review questions is a lot of work.*

Normally, Marvin and Mary Struthers, who owned the Ramshorn, made sure she had Fridays off to get a jump on her grading, but that wasn't going to happen tonight because their new hire had decided to quit by not showing up to work. It was bound to be busy, too, and she doubted she'd have much opportunity to sneak in some grading between serving and cooking. The Marsh Ranch and the Crystal Peak Ranch were moving cows from winter pastures to spring allotments, so the ranch hands would likely be stopping in for dinner and coffee after. Then there was the large group arriving from Oregon for a rustic corporate retreat, and they would need to be checked in and fed as well. Of all the nights for someone to quit!

And where was her son? Glancing at the clock, she saw that ten minutes had already passed. He was usually here by now. Why'd he have to be late today?

Right then, he popped through the door, grinning, and her resentment vanished. It was rare that she could stay angry with him for more than thirty seconds—not that he ever gave her much reason. She wasn't mad at *him*, anyhow. That smile was so open and infectious and all the sweeter for having been so rare in the first months after he'd come to live with her.

"Sorry I'm late, Mom. Mrs. Ellsworth wanted to talk to me about my paper."

"What did she have to say?" Ruby Ellsworth was notoriously difficult to please, especially where Luke was concerned because he preferred science to her subject. By the way he was grinning, however, the English teacher must have said something good.

"I got an A on the paper. Best grade in the class. She said she was really impressed."

"About time," June muttered. She hugged her son. "What'd her prodigy get?"

"A-minus."

June indulged herself with a smug smile. "So, that means you have an A in her class now, right? Since you were only a percentage point below."

Luke nodded. "Yup. Straight A's, Mom."

She happily hugged him again. "I am so proud of you! But we'll have to be smug about it later because we need to get out of here. I have to work at the Ramshorn tonight."

"What? Why?"

"Mary called about an hour ago. Damon quit."

"That sucks. Need any help? I don't have much homework, and isn't that group coming in tonight? Besides, it's better than sitting around the cabin by myself."

"I'd appreciate it, and I'm sure Mary will be all right with that."

By the time they reached the cabin, it was already five o'clock. It took only a couple minutes for June to change and let Cheyenne out, though the golden retriever was not pleased to be left home alone again.

They made it to the lodge by five-thirty and were greeted by a harried but relieved Mary Struthers. The thickly lacquered log tables were empty at the moment, but the lull wouldn't last long.

"June, thank you so much. Marvin was going to give you a hand tonight, but he had to help Matt Carlyle unload. The cows he bought at the auction in Great Falls will be here tonight instead of tomorrow, and everyone else is enlisted to help elsewhere. So, Luke, if you wouldn't mind helping your mom—after you finish your homework, of course—we'd be very appreciative. Make sure you put your time down. Oh, the party from Oregon called a little bit ago. They should be here within an hour. I was running chicken-fried steak as the special, but if you want to do something else, you go right ahead."

"Chicken-fried steak is fine. Anything else?"

"I hate to ask, but would you mind doing a little dusting if you get a chance? I was going to earlier, but it was busy, and then I got side-tracked by book-work...."

"We've got it covered, Mary," June replied. "Go home."

"I'm so sorry to take your grading night, but—"

"It's okay, Mary. Go."

The pepper-haired older woman smiled gratefully, jotted down her time on the sheet behind the bar, grabbed her lightweight jacket, and zipped out the door.

June took the duster out from the storage closet and went to work, and Luke promptly took up residence on the couch to finish what little homework he hadn't gotten to during the ride home from Devyn.

She dusted her way efficiently around the lodge's dining area, making better time than she'd thought she would. Rustic was a fitting term for this place, which had first been imprinted in her mind the summer after her freshman year of high school. The walls were paneled with vertical, hand-peeled log halves, the carpet was a durable gray-blue, and the light fixtures were simple wrought-iron chandeliers with six lights each.

When she got around to the mantle over the fireplace, she paused to peruse the dozen photographs Mary had placed there to give the lodge a homey feel. There was a picture of her and Luke that the Ramshorn's owner had taken last year at the high school state championship game. Luke looked so handsome in his football pads and navy-and-gold home jersey with his blond hair mussed from his helmet and a brilliant smile igniting his entire face. He had his arm around her shoulders. In the photo, she'd still been a couple inches taller than Luke, but she wasn't anymore. In fact, he was beginning to make her feel rather short.

At the moment, Luke was still stretched out on the couch in front of the dark fireplace, diligently finishing his homework. Life had changed a lot with him around and definitely for the better. She leaned against the mantle and studied him for a moment with a frown furrowing her brows, wishing that having him in her life hadn't come with the price of losing a friend. Often, her musings about how she'd come to adopt Luke were entwined with thoughts of the man whose bullet had set the process in motion. *Ah, Ben.*

Half a decade removed, the grief and self-loathing in his face the last time she'd seen him—an hour or so before the initial meeting regarding Luke's fostering—still pained him, as did the memory of that moment he'd turned from her. As she'd watched him walk away, she realized she had to let him go, that nothing she could say would ease the guilt that engulfed him until he was ready to open his heart and forgive himself.

Sighing, she set her worries aside and went back to work, clinging to the fading hope that he'd someday find his way out of the darkness and come home. She finished the worst of the dusting and walked behind the bar to pull out the guest log and get the packets ready. Mary had left her notes about who was staying where and what activities to explain to them for their week stay; she was a little disappointed she couldn't go on the trail ride on Monday. Luke should be done with his homework by the time the party arrived and could show them to their lodgings.

No sooner had she put the guest log back in its place than seven people walked in the door for dinner. She glanced briefly out the window when she heard more vehicles and saw several Northstar ranch hands pull up. It was going to be a hectic evening, but she wouldn't trade it or anything in her life for the world.

"Welcome to the Ramshorn Lodge," she greeted the diners. "I'm June. Have a seat wherever you like and I'll bring over some menus."

And so it begins, June thought as she grabbed the menus from the bar.

* * *

Four years ago, JP had been certain his prize was lost when Adam Winters had strolled through the doors of the Bedspread Inn to confront Aelissm Davis and Patrick O'Neil. He'd spent a tense hour standing in the back corner of the dining room, waiting to be singled out as the events that had brought Winters to Montana simmered to a conclusion. Alternately shaking his head at Winters's spineless forfeit and praying the man would continue to ignore him, JP had finally found the opportunity to escape the crowded dining room. He'd spent the rest of the night in a cold sweat, fighting to maintain control. He couldn't shrink away like a coward again. If he did, he'd lie down and let his chance to claim his woman roll right past him like he had before. He was damned if he was going to let that happen again, but right then, there had been too many variables. So he'd stepped back to wait and assess the situation.

In the intervening years, he'd slowly come to realize there was no danger. Adam Winters had either forgotten about the man with whom he'd spent so many nights drinking in the lounge of the Paradise Motel in Devyn or had kept his promise. His deluded companion had since moved to Bozeman, married the young woman who'd diverted his attention from Aelissm, and if the rumors he'd heard were true, they'd recently added a little girl to their family. Perhaps things hadn't turned out so badly for Adam Winters. A wife and daughter were nothing to complain about, certainly.

But JP still thought Winters had taken the coward's way out by settling for Amber instead of fighting for Aelissm.

That was something JP refused to do. He wanted June Montana, and no one was going to stop him from getting her. Besides, there was no Amber for him. June was the only woman who could fill the gaping hole in his heart. For that all too brief time years ago, she had. He smiled at her as she brushed past on the way to the Ramshorn's kitchen, shivering a little inside when her lips curved in response. Taking another sip of his coffee, he watched her saunter out of sight around the corner into the kitchen. Damn, she was beautiful. Tall and graceful with an athletic build and slim, elegant curves. And oblivious of her appeal.

Beside him, Austin McGuire, a fellow Northstar ranch hand, shook his head and let out a low whistle. "If only I were a younger man," he said.

His son Shane lifted his brows in amusement. "Good thing you aren't. She's my best friend's mom!"

"So?"

"Luke'll pulverize me at football camp this summer if I don't defend her honor from my lecherous *old* father."

The other ranch hands sitting at the counter with

them chuckled in amusement. Austin's eyes glittered with laughter.

It wasn't long before JP's companions went back to their meals. From the corner of his vision, he watched June glide through the dining room to check on her customers.

When she'd seen to everyone, she settled behind the thick log bar and again picked up her schoolwork. Frowning, he turned his attention more fully to her. She was a dedicated, talented teacher. Even Shane, who hated science, loved her classes. The same qualities that made her such a great educator also made her difficult to get close to. JP tried not to sneer. She put her job and her students before all else, including—or especially—the few men she chose to date, and she'd told him as much, once.

Shaking his head, he corrected himself. There was one person who came before even teaching in June's life.

Her adopted son, Luke.

His gaze shifted to the young man now striding through the front door after showing the party from Oregon to their cabins. Luke McKindel, as he'd been *back then*, was now Luke Montana and had grown from a short, skinny, scared-of-his-own-shadow pre-teen to a tall, strong, and charismatic sixteen-year-old with far too much confidence. Everything else he had—June's undivided devotion, an athletic ability that made JP seethe with envy, and a sharp intelligence—was topped off with hair the color of late afternoon sunlight, laughing blue eyes, and a boyishly-handsome face. He had it all. And he deserved none of it. Not after he'd stolen June from JP.

It wasn't June's fault. She was only doing what came naturally to her. It was the boy who had turned her from him, and he deserved to suffer for it.

JP's fingers clenched around his coffee mug as mindless rage consumed him. Only by momentarily allowing his weaker side to flicker to the front was he able to swallow his hatred. As soon as his pulse slowed and his grip on the mug loosened, JP subverted that spineless part of him, effectively wrapping its fragile nature in a cocoon of sweet vengeance. His gentler half was pained by June's rejection and her declaration of loyalties but couldn't find the strength to right the wrongs anymore than it had been able to bear the horror of his brother's suicide, an event that had irreparably fractured him. JP, on the other hand, hadn't balked at the splatter of blood and brain matter on the walls of Paul's bedroom nor gagged at the gaping hole in his beloved sibling's skull, and he wouldn't hesitate to spill a little more blood to get his satisfaction, either.

He lifted the coffee mug to his lips and sipped. He couldn't let his anger get the best of him. Anger led to mistakes, and he couldn't afford any more mistakes.

"Well, c'mon, boys. We ought to get down to the C Diamond and see if Old Matt needs a little extra help before we head up to Andy's for poker," Austin said. He grabbed the check off the bar and paid. "June, thanks for the coffee and the grub."

She lifted her head and smiled. "You're welcome. Don't work or play too hard tonight, boys."

"Never," JP replied with a laugh.

Two

BEN'S BREATH LODGED in his throat and his chest constricted as he crested the hill. A blanket of sharp, deep golden light illuminated the familiar peaks of the eastern Northstar Mountains, but the valley itself was in the shadow of the lower western ridges. The sight of home was so much sweeter than he had imagined, more so because his memory of Northstar had been stunted by his many photographs of it; not even the most artistically framed among them gave an adequate sense of the scale. The mountains were so much higher and commanding than he recalled, the colors more vibrant, the light and shadows clearer. Those photos couldn't drum up the depth of sensory details, either, and he inhaled deeply the fresh, sagebrush-scented air that wafted through the truck cab through the open windows. There was something else they couldn't embody, something he felt with a deeper gratification than even his senses could comprehend—the freedom of open spaces.

It was so good to be back, he thought with a poignant smile. The valley, the mountains, the air. He'd missed it all much more than he'd realized, and in this moment, he felt almost whole again.

The sun drifted low in the western sky, nearly touching the horizon by the time he turned off the main highway into the Northstar Valley, and the uneven shadows of the western ridges climbed higher up the slopes of the eastern peaks as the light turned ruddy. It wasn't long before he left the pavement and bounced along on the packed dirt and gravel of the valley road. Even the washboard, which threatened to rattle his teeth loose, was a welcome pain.

He looked up towards the Bedspread Inn to see that the lights were on. Aelissm had started taking over operations of it from her grandparents when she'd moved back four years ago, and when he'd last spoken to her uncle four months ago, Bill had mentioned that Marge and Roger had begun the process of transferring ownership of it to her. He considered stopping in to say hi, but there would be time to catch up later. Seeing June again was more pressing, so he continued northward. It was a little after eight, so he hoped she'd still be down at the Ramshorn—when he'd called Marge and Roger earlier about taking them out to lunch tomorrow, they'd informed him she was working tonight.

Anticipation mingled with dread. She didn't know he was coming because he'd been too nervous to call her and tell her, figuring if she was going to reject him, he'd rather have it done to his face than over the phone. *For one last look*, he thought. *If it comes to that. Please, God, don't let it come to that.*

The air was surprisingly warm even in the forested area at the apex of the valley, but there was a crispness in it, too, that Ben hadn't felt in a long time. The touch of the silky, cool air on his exposed skin was heavenly. Casey window-surfed with his tail thumping lazily against the back of the seat. Ben chuckled at his dog's bafflement.

Not much had changed since he'd last visited. The driveway to the Ramshorn Hot Springs and Lodge was still dirt, and the entrance was marked by the same high, log gateway. As he pulled up in front of the lodge, he spotted two dirt bikes parked across the driveway from the lodge and tucked his truck in behind them. He told Casey to stay and stepped out into the blissful evening.

Off to the right, a creek ran through the darkness, and the soft breeze sighed in the trees. In the distance, he heard cattle and horses. Sounds he knew from long ago, sounds that lingered in his soul.

Ben frowned and glanced around. Above the natural sounds of the valley, he heard music. It came from the open doors of the lodge, and as he got closer, he heard snips of a familiar pop song by his niece's favorite boy band. When he climbed the stairs, the music got louder. He peered inside to find dining room empty with the tables cleared and the chairs placed neatly around them. The fireplace was dark, lending no flickering light to dance in the glass eyes of the big game trophies that adorned the walls of the room. The lodge looked exactly as he remembered. No, something had moved. The black bear that had once stood beside the grizzly was now by the door, greeting customers as they came in.

Movement caught his eye, and he turned to see a

teenaged boy stride out of the kitchen carrying a damp rag. If Becky hadn't called him and complained that her favorite group wasn't touring in Montana, he might have wondered if he was looking at one of its members. The boy had very similar facial features with the same golden blond hair in the same style—what was it called, a bowl cut?—about four inches long on top, short underneath, and no bangs. He was tall, probably a tad over six feet, and was dressed in blue jeans, a plain white t-shirt, a blue flannel with the sleeves rolled up, and hiking boots.

Ben stepped into the light, snagging the teenager's attention.

"Hi. Welcome to the Ramshorn," the boy said warmly. "What can I do for you?"

When Ben met the kid's gaze, he inhaled sharply. There was something familiar about those eyes, something that made his heart quicken, but he couldn't think of where he might have seen the boy before. Except in Becky's posters, though that wasn't enough to incite the odd flutter of nerves.

"I'm looking for June Montana. Is she here?"

"Yeah, just a minute."

The boy returned to the kitchen again, and Ben heard quiet, indecipherable voices. He looked around the lodge, his heart beating faster at the promise of seeing June again. Four and a half long years was a long time, and he wondered if it had changed her as much as it had him. Then, there she was, standing in the doorway of the kitchen wiping her hands on a dishtowel.

Ben lost his breath.

She wore jeans just tight enough to show off her long, graceful legs and a white t-shirt with a plum-colored flannel tied around her waist. Her blonde hair was pulled back in a simple ponytail. She was even sexier than he remembered, but her eyes were the same dusky blue, and in them, he saw elation. Relief washed away the trembling fear of rejection.

"You said I could show up on your doorstep anytime," he said cautiously. "Is that offer still open?"

"Of course it is, Ben. But… what are you doing here?"

"I'm coming home. Finally figured out this is where I need to be."

"About time." She ran to him and wrapped her arms tightly around his neck in a hug of welcome. "I can't believe you're here! It's so good to see you."

He brushed his lips across her cheek and returned her embrace, holding her as if she were an anchor.

Burying his face against her neck, he exhaled slowly as relief washed away apprehension. Doubt flickered momentarily, but the feel of her in his arms was too real to be a dream. He picked her up and swung her around, and her rich, delighted laughter elicited the brightest smile that had graced his face in a long time. "God, I've missed you."

She leaned back in his arms, and the glee in her eyes dimmed a bit as she read his face like she might a book. Unlike what he'd feared, he found no trace of disgust alongside the joy, only concern. When she spoke, her voice was startlingly gentle. "How are you?"

Knowing she'd see right through a lie, he took a deep breath and ignored his habit of responding with an evasive and uninformative *I'm fine.* "Better right now that I've been in a long time. I've been getting by but not well."

"I've worried about you a lot, and so have many others. Bill was quite upset when you resigned."

"I'm sure he was, but I couldn't do it anymore. I killed a man, June, and he had a son. A son I orphaned. How was I supposed to go back after that?" He paused in an attempt to subvert the bitterness. "I don't even know what happened to him. And while I'm sure Bill knows, I've never asked him."

"Why not?"

"I'm afraid of the answer—afraid he didn't make it."

"You shouldn't be." June glanced at the teenager, who was wiping down the tables. "I know what happened to that boy, and I can tell you, he's doing just fine."

He turned his gaze back to his friend. Her words did little to ease him, but he smiled anyhow, knowing she meant well. "So, June, does your teen-star-look-alike have a name?"

June glanced at the boy. "I guess I shouldn't be surprised you don't recognize him. He *has* changed a lot. Come on over, and I'll introduce you…. Properly, because I don't think that happened the last time."

Ben let himself be pulled over to where the teenager was working. June slid her hand across the boy's back. When the kid turned, Ben recognized the glint of keen observation in his eyes, so similar to the one June had worn in high school. *And the one she still has on today,* Ben mused. But observation wasn't all that he saw. He thought he caught a glimpse of flashing recognition in the boy's eyes.

"Ben, this is Luke Montana," June said quietly.

Montana? Was he a relative, then? There was

certainly a familial resemblance, both in their coloring and features. That would explain why he looked familiar. Maybe he was one of her nephews or a cousin, but he couldn't recall either of her brothers having a son, and the only male cousins he knew of were on her mother's side, not her father's.

"Formerly Luke McKindel."

Ben heard the name as if she'd shouted it in his ear. His heart stopped for a moment, and he stared at the boy. The guilt he'd managed to force down over the past few days came racing back at full force. He looked to June and saw from the expression on her face that she had more to say.

"He's my son now." Her voice was soft but tinged with possessiveness. "Bill called me the night of the shooting and asked me to foster him, and I almost said no, but when I met him the next morning, I knew I had to. The caseworker and judge agreed the arrangement was in his best interests, and eight months later, we made it permanent. Luke, I'd like you to meet my friend, Ben Conner."

Ben thought he might puke. He hunched over with his hands braced on his knees and sucked in a dozen shallow breaths, waiting for the nausea to pass. Before, the boy was just a name and a young face glimpsed briefly. Never in a million years would he have imagined he'd ever find himself face to face with the innocent victim of that day from hell, but his impulsive decision to return to Northstar had brought the past screaming into the present.

"I remember you," Luke remarked, his eyes narrowing. "I saw you with Uncle Bill in Silverdale the night my father was killed. You're the deputy who shot him."

What little warmth was left drained from Ben's body, and he straightened, waiting for the kid's reaction. Luke's face was unreadable, and his gaze was fixed on something only he could see. Then, his hand moved so quickly that Ben flinched. When he realized Luke had extended his hand in greeting, he absently shook it. His knees weakened with relief, and when the boy released his hand, he almost collapsed to the gray-blue carpet.

Luke grinned, but his eyes were cold and hard. "I'm glad to finally meet you."

"I thought you were going to punch me."

Part of him wished Luke *had* hit him, though he couldn't explain why. He looked away for a moment, unsettled by the knowledge in the boy's gaze. Luke was far too young to have that visage, and Ben swallowed hard against the surge of guilt. That trauma was his fault, and maybe that's why he would've preferred a fist to the jaw. "I remember seeing you that night. God, do I remember it. I guess you were a couple months shy of twelve back then, right? That means you should be sixteen, almost seventeen."

"Yeah." Luke smiled again, but it lacked any real mirth. "I like your friend, Mom."

Abruptly, he returned to his chore, but not before Ben saw the flash of pain in his eyes.

He winced and turned to June. "How can he like me? I shot his father."

"Maybe someday one of us will explain it," June replied. The flicker of heartache that passed over her face startled him, but she smiled reassuringly. "Have a seat on the couch. We'll be closing in a few minutes."

"Uh, before you do, I need to get a room for the night."

"No, you don't. You're coming home with us."

"June…."

"Don't argue."

Ben obediently plopped on the couch facing the fireplace to wait. The boy band sang on in the background with both June and Luke singing along, and he watched them work as he too hummed along with the song and tried to quell the ache of anxiety. Had he made a mistake in coming back? No. Something felt right, even after facing the orphaned son of John McKindel. Perhaps because of it.

The bell on the door jingled, and he looked up to see a man with dark hair and warm brown eyes flicking it with his finger. He was only an inch or so taller than June's five-foot-nine with a wiry frame and bowed legs. He flashed them all a friendly smile, and Ben noted how his gaze lingered for just a moment on June with longing and regret momentarily darkening his eyes.

"Evening, June, Luke," the man greeted, stepping inside. "For the second time. Looks like it slowed down for you."

"Hi, Pete," June replied. "It did, and you're just in time. Coffee?"

He nodded. "I need some for Andy and Jake, too."

"It's a little late for coffee, isn't it?"

"It's never too late. And I know that's exactly why you have a pot on."

There was a knock on the door, which was still open for ventilation. June looked up and rolled her eyes. Ben followed her gaze and saw another man, taller, with dark hair and shrewd brown eyes. He looked a bit like Pete, but there was an arrogance and a simmering anger about him that Ben instantly disliked. The scowl on June's beautiful face confirmed and strengthened his aversion.

"Pete'll be right out, Jake," June said flatly.

"I only came in to see how Lukie is doing."

"He's fine."

"Leave him alone, Jake," Pete muttered.

"But I wouldn't want him to feel unloved."

"Trust me, Jake, I feel quite loved when you're not around," Luke replied without looking up from his task.

"How's your father? Heard from him lately?"

Ben shot to his feet, horrified by the comment. Cold washed through him in wave upon wave of crashing guilt. He glanced between the two ranch hands, June, and Luke. The situation was so surreal that Ben wasn't sure if he was actually standing in the Ramshorn Lodge with his old friend and the son of the man he'd killed or if this was just a wild and brutally real dream.

"Jake…" June warned. "Leave him—"

"Go to hell, Jake," Luke said nonchalantly, "and ask him yourself." He finally raised his eyes. "Takes one to know one, as they say."

Tense though he was, the phrase he'd heard

uttered many a time by June's stepfather struck him as funny and made the scene that much more unreal. He had to be dreaming.

"What? No response?" Luke's lips twitched. "I'm disappointed, Jake."

Jake sputtered for a moment, clearly outwitted. Swearing, he stormed out. Despite the anxious memories Jake's comment wrought from him, Ben wondered why Luke would say such a thing about his father.

June scowled after him, pausing for a moment in her task. Then she shook her head and pulled three to-go cups out from under the bar.

"The night isn't getting any younger, Pete."

The familiar voice yanked Ben's gaze to the door. Striding inside with his well-worn black cowboy hat in its usual place on his head was Ben's brother-in-law, Andy Epperson. He was dressed as his companions were in stained tan Carhartt work pants, a white t-shirt, and roper boots. Married life had been good to him, Ben mused, noting that Andy's frame was thicker and more muscled than when he and Jane had first met. He was also glad to note that the injury that had almost ended Andy's career as a ranch hand was now only a barely noticeable limp. When the older man spotted him, he stopped midstride.

"Ben? What are you doing here?"

"Coming for a visit. Just got here."

"Well, I'll be damned. It's good to see you," Andy said laughingly. He walked over and embraced Ben. "Jane and Becky will be thrilled. Are you heading up to the house?"

"No, he's staying with us," June replied before Ben could.

"Are you sure?"

"I'm positive. I have more room than you do, and besides, it sounds like he's going to be staying a while, so you and Jane and Becky will have plenty of time with him."

Turning to Ben again, Andy asked, "How long are you staying?"

"If everything works out, I won't be leaving. It took me a long time to realize what my sister always knew, but better late than never, right?"

"I think you've always known it, but you got used to Poulsbo, so you stayed. That, and you're not as hardheaded as my wife. I'd love to stay and chat, but like I said, it's already getting late. Unless you'd care to join us for poker."

"It's been a long day and I'm wiped, but I

appreciate the offer. Tell my sister and niece that I love them and I'll be over to see them soon."

"Will do. Welcome home, Ben."

June interrupted their conversation when she re-appeared from the kitchen with three to-go cups of coffee. "On the house tonight, boys."

"Thanks, June," Pete replied. "Appreciate it."

"You're welcome."

Andy and Pete left, and June locked the door behind them, then flipped the open sign to closed.

"Who were those guys with Andy?" Ben inquired.

June sighed and rolled her eyes. "Pete Landers and Jake Sterling. I dated Pete for a while before Luke came to live with me and was stupid enough to let Jake take me on a date once. It's a longer story than I feel like telling right now, so if you'll excuse me, I'll get back to work so we can get out of here."

Luke finished wiping off the rest of the tables and closed and counted the register while June vacuumed the floor. They worked effortlessly as a team, and before Ben knew it, they were done.

"It's good to be back," he murmured, unable to pull his eyes away from June. He'd forgotten how naturally graceful she was and felt a bit like a dehydrated man drinking in the beauty and gentleness that radiated from her.

June smiled at him as she pulled a backpack up from behind the front desk and plopped it on the counter. She pulled the CD from the stereo before she turned it off, and once the disc was secure in its case, she stuffed it in her bag, then she reached behind the counter again and pulled out two helmets, one blue, one black. She tossed the blue one to Luke, who caught it and put it on. The other she jammed on her head.

"Uh, June, I brought my dog with me," Ben said. "That's not a problem is it?"

"Not so long as he gets along with our golden, Cheyenne." She turned to him as she tightened the helmet strap. One eyebrow was raised, and her lips twitched with amusement. "I take it you're planning on staying a while. Good. We have five years to catch up on."

* * *

June eyed Ben as she tightened the strap of her helmet, not quite able to believe he was here. He had changed some. His hair was darker, and he had definitely filled into his height since she'd seen him last, she noted appreciatively, but there were other differences, and they concerned her. His eyes were still the same intriguing gray she remembered, but they weren't quite as quick to smile, and a trace of weariness dimmed their brilliance. He had the look of a man struggling in a battle he knew he couldn't win.

She smiled sadly when he looked at her for a moment. The shooting had taken a toll on him, and she'd known it, but seeing the proof with her own eyes drove it home. He'd had been through counseling, but it hadn't helped, and she remembered too clearly when Bill had told her with tears thick in his voice that Ben had found it too difficult to continue what had been a promising career he loved in law enforcement. June's heart ached for him like it did for Luke when she saw things in his eyes that shouldn't be there, but perhaps meeting Luke and seeing that he'd come through that traumatic experience all right would do what nothing and no one else had been able.

She pushed Ben and Luke outside, shut off the lights and locked the door behind her. Luke was already starting his dirt bike by the time June got to hers. She inhaled, drawing the cooling air deep into her lungs.

When she had spent her first two weeks up at Aelissm's cabin with her family, everything she'd once wanted in life had shifted. She'd never had so much fun. She'd learned how to ride a dirt bike, hunted for crystals at Crystal Park, watched the talented Virginia City Players, hiked to Sawtooth Lake, and peeked into the old buildings of the nearby ghost towns. Ben and Aelissm had prepped her to love Northstar long before that summer, but she'd fallen irrevocably in love when she'd first glimpsed the Northstar Mountains, and she had understood what it was to be home, to be utterly complete in a way that still amazed her. That single moment had revealed everything about her.

Her parents had divorced when she was only four, and the tension that had plagued her since evaporated, and as that incredible peace settled over her, so had understanding. Everything in her life had led her here, to this point. Without her stepfather, Dan, she wouldn't have met his Navy buddy Bill Granger or Bill's niece Aelissm, and without her and her family, she probably wouldn't have ever had a reason to come to Northstar. And without that and Bill's meddling, she wouldn't have Luke. She glanced at the teenager, who waited patiently for her to get moving. He was, by far, the greatest thing in her life, and as much as she loved her home, she would give it all up in a moment for him.

"I assume you can follow us?" she called to Ben,

who nodded.

Untying her flannel and tugging it from her waist, she stuffed her arms into the sleeves. She and Luke buzzed along the gravel road, checking behind every so often to make sure Ben didn't mistakenly take one of many wrong turns. June's cabin was almost five miles up the side of Comet Mountain on a twisting, rock-pocked length of dirt road, and there were numerous, unmarked trails on which he could get lost. Fortunately, he kept pace, and they reached the gate to Aelissm's grandparents' property without incident. June pulled her bike to the side out of the way and swung the gate open.

"Follow Luke, and I'll catch up," June called over the dirt bikes and the low grumble of the truck.

Luke sped up the hill with Ben trundling along behind. After she closed the gate, June jumped on her dirt bike and took off up the road. When she got to her cabin, Luke had opened the door and let Ben in, and they stood in the living room. Cheyenne bounced outside, tail waving enthusiastically as she welcomed Luke home and greeted her masters' guest. June parked her dirt bike beside Luke's and trotted inside to find Ben staring up at the vaulted ceiling with an awed smile.

"It's beautiful, June," he said slowly.

She grinned. "Thank you. Aeli and I designed it ourselves. We did a lot of the building, too, with some help from a few locals."

Ben nodded and continued to gaze around. June followed the trail his eyes traveled, warmed by his obvious delight in her home. From the front door, the living room was on the left, occupying most of the front two-thirds of the first floor. The couches, which sat perpendicular to each other, gave the space a feeling of being its own room. Her office sat to the right and consisted of a log desk with a computer, printer, and stacks of papers. The kitchen took up the back third of the house with a snack bar and spiral stairs dividing it from the living room. The base of the stairs was in the kitchen, closer to the back door. Closer to Pat and Aeli's and modeled after their cabin. The dining room, such as it was, sat between the kitchen and office area. There were also two stools set at the snack bar under the shadow of the loft. There was a utility room through a sliding door to the right off the kitchen that housed her laundry room and bathroom.

"Very nice," Ben remarked, smiling over his shoulder at her. He dropped his sleeping bag and pillow on the longer of the couches. "Shall we introduce my mutt to Cheyenne?"

"Sure," June replied and stepped back outside.

Cheyenne was already beside Ben's truck, stretching her neck to sniff the dog leaning out the window. June smiled as she noted the pale blond feathers, reddish-gold overcoat and gentle but excited brown eyes of Ben's dog—another golden retriever, just a touch lighter in color than Cheyenne. "That's not a mutt, Ben. How dare you impugn his breeding," she remarked laughingly.

"I know he's not, and sometimes, I swear he let's it go to his head. Don't you, Casey?"

"He'll love it up here."

Casey leapt from the truck before Ben could fully open the door and stopped in his tracks. The two dogs spent a few moments getting to know each other, then stood perfectly still for half a dozen heartbeats before exploding into the woods, and June laughed as their excited barks resounded into the night. She let them play outside for a few minutes before calling them in for the night.

"Dogs are allowed on the beds and on the couches in this house," June told Ben, who was unrolling his sleeping bag. "I'm sure it won't be long before Cheyenne's bad habits start rubbing off on your dog, so I'm apologizing in advance."

"Likewise, but he sleeps on my bed at home… uh, in Washington."

June smiled. "It's hard not to call a place home after you've been there for a long time, regardless of whether or not it *is* home."

Ben grinned. "You haven't changed a bit, have you?" He paused, then asked, "Why didn't anyone tell me you took Luke?"

"We tried, Ben, but you wouldn't listen. You were inconsolable, like you *wanted* to hate yourself. Why did you shut me out?"

"I was afraid. Afraid that you'd hate me and turn away from me in disgust."

"I could never do that, Ben."

She glanced around and realized Luke had disappeared.

"It's great to see you again," Ben murmured, drawing her attention back to him.

She wrapped her arms around his neck. "It's been too long."

"I know, but I'm here now."

He laid his hand gently on her cheek, and she closed her eyes, leaning into his touch.

"I've missed you," he whispered. "So much."

"And I've missed you." She kissed his cheek. "Get

some rest. We'll talk more in the morning."

* * *

Luke sat with his arms around his knees and stared up at the star-spattered sky. The lodgepole pines stood black against the glittering indigo canvas, their branches swaying ever so gently with the cool breeze that whispered through the forest around him. Until he'd come to Northstar, he'd never seen a sky like that. The bright lights of Seattle polluted the night, and the stars, so brilliant and fiery here, could not compete. He took several deep breaths of the exquisitely clean mountain air to settle his mind.

He felt strange, sort of detached, and he couldn't quite grasp yet what the sudden appearance of June's friend meant to him. He had always known that there was a possibility that Ben would show up, or that he would meet him again because he was June's friend, but…. He buried a hand in his hair and propped his elbow on his knee.

The door creaked open, and June sat down beside him. She handed him one of the root beers in her hand and opened the other for herself.

"What's on your mind?" she asked softly.

Luke sighed. "I guess I never believed I'd actually meet him."

"Who? Ben?"

He nodded. "He was at the sheriff's department that night. Bill picked me up from my house and brought me in to tell me what'd happened. Since I was in the interrogation room, I couldn't hear what he said to Ben or the other deputies. I didn't know what was happening," he said. He stared at the can in his hand for a moment, turned it around and around, then opened it and took a long drink before continuing. "I thought I'd be thankful if I ever did meet him, but I'm not. Well, I am, I guess. It's kind of hard to explain. He was the one who made a second chance for me possible. Because of what he did, I've had the chance for a better life, but at the same time, all those memories come back."

June rubbed his back. For a while, they just sat there, quiet. Luke closed his eyes, enjoying the relief her simple gesture brought him. She always knew when he needed to talk or when he just needed to be reminded that he was loved.

"You've had a tough life, Luke, and you've made the best of it. I'm proud of you," she said. "You came to me a quiet, hurting boy, and before I met you, I wondered what Uncle Bill was getting me into. I figured, after I'd heard about your father's addictions and what you'd been through, that you would be the same… or at least on the way to becoming like him. But I was blessedly wrong."

"I saw what my father did to his life, and I wasn't about to do the same with mine."

He shrugged. His father was dead because of his addictions. From what Luke had learned, his father had started firing as soon as Ben had stepped out of his cruiser. John McKindel had died for a bottle of booze. And Luke had been cut adrift, but someone had been looking after him and looking out for him. He didn't remember Bill Granger picking him up and could only vaguely recall waking up on the ride to the sheriff's department and seeing Ben, the deputy whose single, fatal shot had slammed the door on the life Luke had known up to that point. It was all still so confused.

There were a few crystal-clear memories of those days after the shooting, like meeting June for the first time less than twelve hours after his father's death. She'd stepped through the front door of Bill and Mary Granger's Indianola home with the most gracious, welcoming smile he'd ever seen, and though he hadn't acted on the impulse, he'd wanted to run to her and throw his arms around her. They had bonded over breakfast with the Grangers. She had shared his love of science and hadn't pushed him to talk about anything he didn't want to. She'd told him about her job and where she lived, and he'd loved the way she talked about Northstar. When she had offered to foster him—asked him as if he had any say in the matter—he had jumped at the promise of peace, happiness, and love that came with being her son… however temporarily.

Eight months later, she'd asked him if she could adopt him, and it was then that he had realized he was home. He had never dreamed he could have what he did now. Coming from where he had, he knew that he should appreciate what he'd been given. And he did, so much.

"You know," Luke said, breaking the silence, "my life started out really bad, but I wouldn't change how it's turned out even if I could."

"I thought the same thing about *my* life just as we were leaving the lodge. If you want my opinion, you're a stronger person for everything you've been through," June remarked. She yawned. "Well, I'm going to bed. You might want to think about it, too, because we're chopping wood tomorrow."

"Mom?"

"Yeah?"

"Why does Jake hate me so much?"

"He's very insecure, and he can't stand it that, even after everything you've been through, you aren't. He's the kind of person who has to make everyone else feel small to make himself feel big and important. You haven't fallen under his criticism and he hates it."

Luke shook his head, pinching his brows together and wishing he could figure out how to make Jake leave him alone. June's subtle compliment eased his annoyance, and after a moment, his lips lifted in a faint smile. "Thanks, Mom, and I promise I'll go to bed in a minute."

Smiling, June stood, leaned down to kiss the top of his head, and went inside, leaving him to his thoughts. He wasn't a religious person, but he wouldn't be surprised if June was an angel. She'd helped him turn his life around, given him hope and love. Draining his root beer with one final gulp, he stood and went inside.

Only a single lantern burned dimly in the kitchen. Ben was sound asleep on the couch with his dog curled up on his feet. Cheyenne wagged her tail and approached Luke. He patted her head and went upstairs, setting the lantern on his dresser before blowing it out. He changed into his pajama pants and flopped on his bed, lying on his back with his fingers locked beneath his head. He stared out the window and tried to think about anything but the man sleeping downstairs on the couch and the last time they'd crossed paths so he could sleep.

It was probably three hours before he finally succeeded.

Three

MORNING WAS JUST BARELY edging its way past night when June slipped out of bed. She tip-toed to the window and looked out at the forest; three deer stood just down the hill from the cabin on the well-worn path to Pat and Aelissm's. For a while, she stared at them, shivering with the lingering cold of night. When the deer moved off, she left her bedroom and went to Luke's. Like the deer, she watched him for a while, leaning against the doorjamb with her arms folded tightly across her chest. The teenager was still asleep, and she wondered if his dreams had been pleasant.

With Ben's sudden and unexpected arrival, she had expected a nightmare to interrupt her son's slumber, but he'd slept through the night.

Almost five years, she thought. Five wonderful years she had watched him grow from an apprehensive eleven-year-old boy to a confident young man. If only Ben knew just how much she owed him for allowing this incredible person to be hers. Luke might not be her flesh and blood, but he was her son in every other way, though she wished his reason for being with her was different, that he hadn't known the traumas he had. It never ceased to amaze her, the bond they'd created in such a short time, especially because of the circumstances.

She sat gently on his bed and brushed a lock of hair out of his lightly closed eyes. He smiled.

"What time is it?" he mumbled.

"Early. Go back to sleep."

June sat a moment longer before she went downstairs to let the dogs out. For a moment, she stood beside the snack bar and gazed at Ben asleep on the couch. Yes, she had a lot to thank him for, though she didn't know if she'd ever tell him. He'd suffered too much from the shooting to understand what good she—and Luke—had gained from it.

June turned away and walked over to the sink, closing her eyes to take in the quiet of the cabin and the occasional bark of the dog. When she concentrated, she heard the first birds of morning begin their songs. There were no sounds of planes or cars, just purely natural music, and her lips curved. In this moment, everything was perfect. No one else could have made her any more whole than Ben and Luke. The latter she understood, but why Ben? Was it because she had finally seen for herself the damage the shooting had done? Or was it a hope that meeting Luke again, finding out that he was doing well would somehow heal Ben—heal them both?

She wondered how the five years since the shooting had changed them and their friendship. There was no point in pretending they hadn't because her priorities had shifted the day the judge had awarded her custody of Luke, and Ben… he certainly wasn't the same carefree, jubilant man he'd been prior to killing John McKindel.

Cheyenne barked at the back door, wanting in. June absently complied as she tried unsuccessfully to work through the mess of her thoughts. The dogs raced into the living room and pounced on Ben, who grunted and rolled over. June poured herself a bowl of cereal and sat down at the table to eat it. Before she'd finished, Luke thumped down the stairs, his eyes slanted with sleep and his blond hair mussed. He headed toward the bathroom, paused, staring at the two dogs and the unconscious lump of man on the couch, then shook his head and continued onward.

Ben at last gave in to the persistent nudges of the dogs and sat up, rubbed his eyes before he glanced at June with a groggy smile.

"Good morning," he mumbled.

"Good morning to you. Sleep all right?"

"Well enough, thanks. Which way to the bathroom again?"

"Through that door there, but you'll have to wait a minute. Luke beat you to it."

"Luke?" Ben asked, frowning. His eyes widened. "Oh, Luke. Right. How could I forget?"

Ben turned toward the bathroom just as Luke walked out, and for a moment, they stared at each other like two bears sizing each other up. When they flashed smiles at each other, June released the breath she'd been holding. Luke and Ben stood about the same height, six-one, and pride warmed her face. When she'd first met Luke, he'd been only four and a half feet tall, and there had been a hollow, gaunt look to his face and dark circles under his eyes. The memory chilled her, but he was healthy now, and strong with blessedly little remaining of that boy but the good things—his resilience, unshakeable sense of humor, and gentle heart.

"Why're you looking at me like that?" Luke asked, one eyebrow lifted.

"I was just wondering how tall you'll be when you finally stop growing."

Luke grinned. "I dunno. What's for breakfast?"

"You can wait a few minutes for bacon and eggs, or you can eat cereal."

He sat down beside June to wait, and she noticed that his gaze sidetracked frequently to the door of the utility room. Regardless of what he'd told Ben last night, the man's presence unsettled him, and though he had said he was grateful, June saw the memories in his eyes. Ben came back in, and she realized that he wore only in a pair of plaid boxer shorts. The view was magnificent, she thought, tracing his bare torso with her eyes. Oh yes, he had definitely filled out.

"I'll be back in a minute, and then I'll cook breakfast. Bacon and eggs all right?"

"Sounds delicious," Ben replied.

June drank the rest of the milk in her bowl and set

it in the sink before she went upstairs. She quickly pulled on a pair of cut-off jeans and rolled the frayed bottoms up. To that she added a black tank top and a worn blue flannel, then socks and her favorite pair of hiking boots. Before she descended the stairs, she listened for voices, but the kitchen was silent. Her heart sank`, and she could imagine them both standing in the kitchen, staring warily at one another. When she reached the bottom step, she saw that Ben had disappeared.

"He's in the bathroom shaving," Luke replied to her unasked question.

"Ah. Go get dressed if you want breakfast."

The teenager bounded up the stairs without further prompting.

"Same goes for you, Ben!" she called.

"What's that?" he asked, peering around the open doors. Half his face was still covered with foamy shaving cream.

"If you want breakfast, hurry up and get dressed. And take your bags upstairs for the time being. I don't care if you put them in Luke's room or mine, but they don't need to be in the middle of the living room."

"Yes, ma'am."

She grabbed the eggs out of the fridge and then

the bacon. Then she popped a CD in the stereo and turned the volume up. Her quiet morning hours were over, and it would be far less quiet on the mountainside with Ben here, but that was fine by her. While she was cooking, Ben hauled his bags upstairs, apologizing once or twice as he stepped across her path.

After she'd fried the bacon and drained the grease into a can, she scrambled the eggs and poured them into the pan. Just as she finished, she heard Ben ask what was planned for the day.

"I think June wants to chop wood," Luke replied. "Other than that… nothing."

"No homework?"

"Nope. Did it all yesterday."

June was pleased that they were talking, but there was a strain in both their voices. She scolded herself for worrying too much. Of course they'd be wary of each other for a while. A lot had happened to them both because of the shooting, and it would take time to adjust. *I just want everything to be all right between them.*

They came downstairs moments later, Ben on Luke's heels, and June watched them over her shoulder as she cooked. "Luke's right, you know, Ben. I'd planned to chop wood today. If you're going to stay with us, you're going to have to earn your keep. Since

I only have two axes, we'll flip a coin. Whoever wins, gets to stack."

"Fine with me. But I'm taking Marge and Roger out for lunch today. Do you two want to come?" Ben remarked.

"Sure. Where are we going?"

Ben shrugged. "The Ramshorn. Neither of you has to work today, right?"

"Nope, we're free for today," June replied.

He and Luke sat down at the table. June served them and then went over to the sink to wash the dishes. Long before she was through, both of them had cleared their plates and came to her aid. Luke usually helped, but she was surprised when Ben sidled up to the sink, allowing her to step back and watch him to her heart's content.

He was a sexy man with an easy grace she found irresistibly appealing. She couldn't recall being this attracted to him in high school. Sure, he'd always held a certain amount of physical intrigue for her—with that dark hair and those beautiful gray eyes, how could he not—and she'd counted him among her closest friends, but there was something different. Tilting her head to the side, she studied her old friend as he stood beside her son washing dishes. And then she realized.

She and Ben had grown up, apart. There was no longer any pretense of youthful ignorance. Ben glanced over his shoulder at her and smiled. Her breath caught in her throat. He went back to washing dishes with Luke, and although no one spoke, there was something complete about this moment.

Luke shifted to the side to stack dried dishes to put away, and Ben glanced at her again.

"Find us fascinating, June?" he asked.

"Mmm. I do. It's not every day I get to sit back and discover that the dishes still get washed."

Luke chuckled, and Ben glanced at him, cautious but smiling. She had no idea what Ben's plans were other than he intended to stay in Northstar this time, but she hoped he wasn't in any hurry to find a place to live because he and Luke needed to adjust to each other, and that would take time but less if they had to deal with each other on a daily basis. She stood by her belief that they needed something from each other; Ben needed to see that Luke was okay so he could forgive himself, and Luke needed to face the memories of his father and know once and for all that he was stronger than them, and having Ben hear undoubtedly brought those memories to the surface again.

Just so long as they don't end up hating each other, June

fretted. Then she straightened with a fresh pulse of determination. *I won't let that happen.*

* * *

"Hi, Grandma," June said as she gave Aelissm's grandmother a hug. "Are Aeli and Pat coming?"

"Of course. I figured Ben would want to see them," Marge answered. "Ben, it's so good to see you again. I wish you'd come out more often these last few years. It might have helped you, you know."

"I know now, but maybe the timing wasn't right."

"Well, we're glad you're here now." She turned to Luke. "How's school going?"

"Great. Straight A's."

"Good! I'm so proud of you."

Luke bent down so Marge could hug him. Ben couldn't help but watch, fascinated. He still couldn't quite believe that this tall, smiling young man was the same boy he'd seen at the sheriff's department. A lot could change in five years, especially kids, but damn. And yet, his eyes held a trace of the same sadness and uncertainty Ben remembered. Would Luke be the same boy he was now if he was still with his father? Would he be less watchful, less haunted? Ben couldn't answer the questions, and the teenager's comments last night—both to him and to that ranch hand Jake

Sterling—made him wonder. What had John McKindel done to earn such bitterness?

Just as guilt surged, Ben glanced at June and found her observing him with such tenderness that he was sure she'd been listening in on his thoughts. She reached over and squeezed his arm, and he returned her smile.

"I'm okay," he assured her.

"I hope so. Luke is doing well, Ben. If you want to blame yourself for anything, blame yourself for giving him a second chance at life."

He frowned and started to ask her what she meant, but the door of the Ramshorn Lodge swung open and Aelissm stepped through with a cloth-wrapped bundle in her arms. She smiled at June and Luke and gave her grandmother a hug. When Ben stepped out from behind Luke, she pressed the back of her hand to her forehead in a dramatic pose of faintness.

"My Gawd, is that Ben Conner? Has he finally come home?" she said in an exaggerated drawl.

"It's nice to see you too, Aeli," Ben said dryly.

She embraced him, and he saw at last that her bundle was a very young baby girl.

"Who's this?" he asked.

"My daughter, Iris. It's about time you came home, Ben. A lot's happened since we left you in dreary old Washington. I'm married, and June and I are both mothers." She winked at June and Luke, both of whom rolled their eyes, making them appear ever more like mother and son despite the mere twelve years' difference in age.

"Where're Pat and Ant?" June asked.

"They were right behind me, I swear."

The door opened again, and Ben stared. Could it really be Bill Granger's favorite detective who, as the rumors had it, had disappeared into the vast Montana wilderness? He looked like the Patrick O'Neil Ben remembered, though he appeared to be much improved from the last time Ben had seen him. With a lazy smile gracing his face and a young boy with his dark hair gripping his hand tightly, he was the picture of contentment.

"Pat?" Ben asked with a laugh. "It can't be."

"Ben Conner, this is a delightful surprise," the older man replied, shaking Ben's hand. "It's great to see you again."

"The feeling is mutual, my friend. Who is this handsome little guy?"

"My son, Antony. You can call him Ant." Pat

ruffled the dark red hair of the young boy at his side, then picked him up. "Ant, this is Ben. He's an old friend of your mom and Aunt June, and I used to work with him when I worked for Uncle Bill. Can you say hi?"

"Hi," the toddler said shyly.

"I hope Aeli introduced our daughter, Iris."

"She did. And you two are married? How did *that* come about?"

"We'll give you three guesses," Aeli answered, "but you're only gonna need one."

"Bill."

"Bill," Pat confirmed.

"Somehow I'm not surprised. I recall him mentioning a time or ten that you two would make a good match. I am, however, curious to know how he managed it."

"You remember what happened with Brent and Adam, don't you?" Aelissm asked.

"Some of it. Brent died from a burst aneurism, and Adam lost it. I know it's more complicated, but I never heard how it turned out, just that everything was resolved amicably. Bill told me Adam found himself a Montana girl to marry."

"He did," June said. "They have a daughter now,

and they live in Bozeman."

"Good for him. But how does that figure in to how you two getting involved?" Ben inquired, glancing between the spouses.

"Adam didn't get the idea that Aelissm wanted to be left alone when she moved back to Northstar, so Bill asked me to come over here to keep an eye on things. Weeks on end together in a cozy mountainside cabin…."

"He was helpless to resist my charms," Aelissm supplied.

"Yes, I was." Pat chuckled and wrapped his arms around his wife and daughter. Aeli smiled up at him, then kissed him rather passionately in front of their friends and family.

"It may be a little—or a lot—late, but congratulations. I mean that. Looks like Bill was right to think you'd be good together."

"He was indeed," June agreed fondly.

"All right, Ant," Ben said, turning to the toddler. "How old are you?"

"Two," the little boy replied, proudly holding up two fingers. "Wuke!" he cried upon spotting the teen. Luke picked him up and plopped him on his shoulders. The little boy grinned, revealing his pearly white teeth.

Ben looked away for a moment, then glanced back at the teen, who watched him with a curious frown. Luke seemed so happy, so at home here, and for a moment, Ben allowed himself to believe that maybe what he'd done wasn't so bad after all. Then their gazes met, and a shadow flickered across Luke's face.

"So, Ben, what have you been up to lately?" Pat asked.

Ben started. It took him a heartbeat to recover, and in that moment, the shadow was gone from Luke's eyes. "Not much. Waiting tables at Donovan's Bar and Grill, but that's done now."

"I still can't believe you resigned from the sheriff's department. Fool thing to do because you were a good cop."

"I couldn't do the job anymore, Pat. Not after…." Ben let his voice trail off as he glanced yet again at June's son.

Pat followed his gaze. "Ah. That's why you resigned. I didn't—"

"Shall we go get what we came here for?" Luke interrupted abruptly. "Or has everyone forgotten that we came for lunch?"

His expression was pinched, and no one present missed it, so the headed toward a table and sat down, dropping the matter of Ben's former occupation and his reason for leaving it.

They chatted about old times and caught up on all they had missed. Ben enjoyed every precious minute of it. It had been too long since he'd been able to indulge in the more pleasant memories of his life. The good old days, he thought, before the shooting. Before he'd taken a life. It was hard to rationalize it all when the boy he'd orphaned sat just a few feet away indulging Pat and Aeli's rambunctious toddler in a game of count-the-silverware. He had not only survived but also appeared to be thriving. Ben had shot in self-defense doing the job he'd been trained to do, and Luke—Ben's biggest reason for hating himself—hadn't fallen prey to the same trauma that had held Ben captive for half a decade.

"Hey, Ben. Wake up," Aelissm said, reaching across the table to prod him. "He's as bad as you were when you first came to Northstar, Pat."

"Hush up," her husband replied.

Ben glanced at Aeli, then at June and Pat. The three of them watched him quizzically, and he smiled. Pat and Aeli continued on with the conversation, but June didn't seem so easily convinced. God, she was beautiful. Those insightful blue eyes of hers were enough to take a man's breath away, and the elegant line of her jaw made him want to trace it first with his fingers, then with his lips. There was a gentleness about her but a toughness, too, that told him she could take care of herself.

June leaned over and whispered in his ear, "I hope you like what you see."

Ben's eyes widened, and his jaw dropped slightly before his lips curved upward with the promise of adventure before him. They hadn't seen each other in almost five years and hadn't gotten together nearly enough in the years after graduation. A lot could happen in that span of time, and he was anxious to find out where the time had taken them both. He pushed the thought aside. June was, first and foremost, his friend. He wouldn't jeopardize that, not when he'd just found her again because he'd needed her all along to tell him he wasn't a monster, that he was still loveable, and when he needed it, to smack him with the blunt truth that he was being an idiot.

The conversation stayed safely in the realms of their early adventures together before life had pulled them apart, and Ben felt like his old self for the first time in five years. God, it was good to be home, and a hundred times better to be home with friends.

* * *

Luke felt out of place, and as he observed them, he realized that Ben, June, and Aelissm had been friends for longer than he'd been alive. Pat had his children to dote on when the conversation switched to something he hadn't been a part of, and Marge and Roger launched in with updates for Ben, so Luke, with no one to talk to, quietly ate his cheeseburger. He was glad when it was all over.

On the ride home, June sat in the middle, Ben drove, and Luke stared out the window as June and Ben laughed about something that had happened in high school. Luke was glad Ben had come if only because June enjoyed catching up with her old friend. Her happiness was infectious, and even through the shroud of dismal memories that surrounded him, he felt it in the depths of his heart, a warm glow that kept him from completely being lost to his past.

What a strange world, he mused, shifting his gaze momentarily at Ben—the man who was one of his mother's best friends and the man who had pushed his life into a completely different direction.

As he stared again out the window and watched the flicker of blue sky above the lacy canopy of pine bows, Luke reminded himself how grateful he was for that change of course. He'd never belonged in Seattle, but out here, where the air was so fresh that his lungs rejoiced with every breath, he was home.

His eyes slid closed. This place had a different feeling to it, a freedom that was ingrained in every molecule. Everything was so clear, so intensely real. Colors seemed brighter, water colder, and the natural sounds of the wind and the birds were a symphony that never ceased and never annoyed. He'd know this place even if he lost his sight. But just as he would know this home, so too would he know his birthplace. Every time he went through Seattle on his way to visit June's mother and stepfather or drove past the road to that decaying trailer out by the Hood Canal Bridge, he went back and felt again the pain and hatred that were etched as deeply into his impression of those places as freedom and healing were woven here.

Luke felt June's hand on his arm and glanced at her. Her eyes were soft, and he knew she'd sensed the direction of his thoughts. He never needed to tell her when he was scared or lonely or sad. She just seemed to know. If Uncle Bill hadn't convinced the courts to trust her with his care, Luke wasn't sure what would have happened to him or if he'd even still be alive. Ben was partially to thank for that, too, and Luke really *was* grateful. The man probably thought Luke hadn't for-given him, which was true, but not for the reason Ben thought. There was nothing to forgive.

When they got home, they had the coin toss. June won, and she sat on the back porch for a while, feeding peanuts to the fearless local chipmunks. When there was enough wood chopped, she started stacking it in the woodshed that was carved into the side of the hill. It wasn't long before the heat and exertion drove Ben to take his shirt off to June's apparent pleasure. She watched him as she stacked, completely mesmerized as Luke had never seen her before. Ben, he noted, was oblivious. Luke rolled his eyes, set another log on the chopping block, and swung hard. The halves toppled away, and Ben glanced at him with surprise.

"You make me feel inadequate," he remarked. "I haven't chopped wood in a while."

Luke lifted a brow at the older man, then shrugged and went back to work.

"Get moving, Ben. Luke's way ahead of you."

"Oh, hush up. I'm out of practice."

Luke took his frustration out on the logs, and by the time the heap of logs had been diminished, the pile he'd split was considerably larger than Ben's. The real-ization did little to reduce his agitation. What the hell was bothering him? Jealousy? Over what? That Ben had appeared out of nowhere and taken a good portion of June's attention? Luke shook his head. No, that wasn't it, or at least not all of it. The emotions from years ago threaded their icy fingers around and through him, and he shivered. June wouldn't do that. She wouldn't shove him aside.

He didn't say a word all through dinner and went to bed early, just after sunset. After stripping down to his boxers and carefully stowing his dirty clothes in the hamper, he slid into bed and pulled the blankets up to his chin. Despite the warmth of the spring evening, he was cold. In the shadows of his room, he saw the glint of a belt buckle, staring at him like the eyes of a coiled snake, and got up to tuck it away in the closet. He curled up in his bed again, staring out the window at the darkening sky. He felt so utterly alone. But he wasn't, he reminded himself. June was just downstairs.

"Does he always go to bed this early?" he heard Ben ask.

"No, he doesn't. Something is really bothering him."

Her worried tone brought tears to his eyes; it reminded him that he was loved.

"June, I'm not sure it's a great idea, me staying

here. I should stay at my sister's until I find my own place."

"I know Jane would love to have you, but you're mine, mister. Jane's been able to talk to you over these past years. It's my turn now."

"Luke has every reason to hate me, and I don't want him to suffer just because I got a wild hair and decided I wanted to come see you."

"Luke doesn't hate you, Ben. You've been here a day, so I don't think you've given him or yourself the time to adjust. Did you think that maybe it isn't *you* he hates? I think you need to stay here. And hear me out on this one. You came home to put your guilt behind you, but if you want to *heal*, you can't run from it and simply put it behind you. You have to face it and let it go. Stay here. Please, Ben."

"I really don't think—"

"I want you here. I want to know that you'll be all right because I'm not so sure yet."

"June…."

"I have a spare bed, and if you don't want to share Luke's room, there's the couch until we can figure something else out for you."

There was silence again, and Luke pinched his eyes closed. He was so confused, stretched between the life he lived now and the one he'd left like the rope in a game of tug-of-war. He wanted to stay here, in this life, but the nightmares from his past kept pulling at him, trying to drag him back. Until last night, he'd thought he'd moved on. Until Ben had appeared in the doorway of the Ramshorn Lodge, he had thought his father was behind him.

He barely heard June come up the stairs and enter his room. Without a word, she came over and sat on his bed, brushed his hair back from his face. The tension eased out of his muscles as he concentrated on the gentle touch that meant so much. When he looked at her again, there was a light smile of affection on her face, an expression he'd been a stranger to until he'd met her. Then she frowned with concern.

"What's on your mind?" she asked.

Luke didn't reply.

"I haven't seen Ben in a long time, Luke. We were just catching up on old times. He doesn't mean to push you aside, and neither do I."

"That's not it."

"Then what's the problem?"

He shook his head. "I don't know. It's like…. I feel like I'm eleven again."

"Oh, sweetheart." She leaned down and hugged

him, then kissed his forehead. "I know it's going to take time, but maybe Ben coming here will be a good thing for you, too."

Luke nodded. She always had a way to comfort him without needing to know exactly what he was thinking, could brush away his fears and doubts just by being there. He smiled and she returned it. "Thank you."

"For what?"

"Everything."

"A mutual gain does not need thanks, Luke. I'm just glad I have you."

"So am I."

* * *

JP watched the boy walking along the well-worn trail beside the river. Mike Thompson spent a lot of time in this park, he'd noticed, since his long-time girl-friend had dumped him for JP's nemesis a year ago. He'd been pondering the wisdom of involving anyone else in his vengeance, especially a high school kid who happened to be, if not friends, at least teammates with his prey. Mike was a senior in high school, a year ahead of Luke Montana, and was the star quarterback. Luke was the star receiver. JP himself had never played foot-ball, but he knew about the bonds that formed between the players—he'd seen it firsthand time and again as his own friends had chosen their football buddies over him—but he also knew that his time was nearing, and he could not do some of the things he had planned.

From the shade of the park's tool shed, he watched Mike continue his listless walk, noted the picture that consumed his attention, saw the boy kick a rock with the toe of his tennis shoe, and listened to him curse his stupidity with a smirk. Debating the issue of involving the kid for a moment longer, JP finally made his decision and took a step forward.

"You still miss her, don't you?"

Mike flinched in startlement, but when he turned and saw who addressed him, he smiled. JP wondered if his young friend would be so quick to greet him if he had any idea what dark plans JP had in the works for Luke.

"How are ya, man?" Mike asked, shaking JP's offered hand.

"Good. You?"

The boy glanced at the picture he held, then tucked it away in his back pocket. I'm all right."

"I can help you get her back."

Mike regarded him skeptically. "Yeah? How?"

"Shouldn't you be asking why?"

"Okay. Why?"

"Because I like you. And I think you're a better match for Carol. You didn't deserve to be cast aside like that."

"Luke's not a bad guy," Mike replied, a little defensively.

JP again questioned the wisdom of involving Luke's teammate, but he needed someone to help him. More importantly, he needed someone with something to gain by helping him. That last requirement made Mike Thompson the only candidate.

"I didn't say he was. As for how, that's a decision Carol will have to make on her own. That's where I can help you."

"Okay…. How can I help?"

JP smiled.

Four

BEN DIDN'T QUITE RISE with the sun and hadn't managed to since arriving in Northstar a week ago, much to his disappointment. Of course, the mornings up here on the mountain were always peaceful, no matter how late he slept. June and Luke were usually gone by the time he got up, leaving only the dogs and the sounds of the forest to keep him company. He yawned and stretched, still snug in his sleeping bag. Frowning when he heard June and Luke talking quietly in the kitchen, he glanced at his watch. It was just after eight. What were they doing home? Ah, it was the weekend again.

When they laughed at something the dogs were doing, Ben decided it was nice to have them home. He wouldn't be alone today and he wouldn't be the only one doing chores. Not that June had given him many during the week. He'd had plenty of time to visit with Pat and Aeli and their family and with Marge and Roger and even Jessie Robinson, though he'd sadly seen very little of his sister and her husband, busy as they and the rest of the ranchers and ranch hands were. Even his niece had been so busy with end-of-the-year schoolwork that he hadn't seen much of her, either, but that was about to be rectified. June had invited her to spend the weekend with him here in her cabin.

With that promise in mind, Ben ambled into the bathroom and dressed quickly for the day. As he stepped into the kitchen, he saw that the dogs had been fed and that June had written out another list of chores. It was a short list, he noted smugly. At the moment, Luke was studying it. He picked out his own chores, leaving Ben to pick up the rest.

"Hey, that isn't fair!" Ben whined.

"Early bird gets the worm," June remarked, placing a bowl and spoon on the table for him. "Don't worry. You've only got two, and they're easy. But eat first."

As soon as he'd finished a bowl of cereal and a banana, he swept the front and back porches, then drove down to Ma Burns' to pick up some milk and sodas. When he returned, he decided to help June and Luke stack the wood he'd split during the week. Maybe it would earn him some brownie points with them both, particularly Luke.

"You're going to be late," June told him before they'd finished. "Go get Becky before she starts wondering if you've forgotten her."

"Yes, ma'am," he replied. "Luke, you wanna come?"

"Nah," the teen replied as he tossed another log on the stack. "But thanks."

Ben wondered what he was doing wrong because Luke still hadn't warmed to him much. If June was to be believed and Luke wasn't angry with *him*, what else could be on the teenager's mind? With a shrug, Ben decided that he wasn't going to find out unless Luke wanted him to. Over the past week, he'd been able to push aside some of his guilt, perhaps even lessened it permanently. And it was mostly, he realized, because he could finally see and believe that Luke was okay and because June wouldn't let him wallow in it anymore.

He glanced at her and caught her watching him. Ben blushed, feeling naked beneath her steady gaze. It was a little disturbing to be so intimately read and a little arousing as well.

"Well, I'm off then. I'll be back when I get back," Ben said and hopped in his truck. Casey and Cheyenne jumped in the cab with him, excited to be getting out of the house and going for a ride. They jockeyed for window position and finally decided to share.

He drove down the mountain, then headed north up the valley. He followed the road as it wound up the small pass, which remained dirt until it started down the other side into the higher Crystal Valley. Another fifteen minutes took him to the Royal R Ranch, where both Jane and Andy worked. The road changed back to gravel as he turned onto the ranch drive. About a quarter of a mile down that road, he turned left toward his sister's home. As the Eppersons' house came into view, he saw his niece sitting on the porch reading a book. Her dark hair was back in a tight braid. When he pulled to a stop and got out, Becky ran to him, wrapping her arms around him in an gleeful embrace. He marveled at how much she'd grown in the last year. She was as lanky as June had been at fourteen.

"Uncle Ben!" she grinned. Her gray eyes sparkled

in the late morning sunshine.

"You ready to get going?" Ben asked. "Where's your mom?"

He recalled the last time his sister had gotten time away from the ranch to bring Becky over to see him in Washington. He had taken them both, on Becky's insistence, to her favorite pop group's concert in Tacoma along with a Seattle Mariner's game. Jane had tried to convince him to take it easier on himself and to make sure he didn't lock himself away from the rest of the world, but at that time, he hadn't been able to obey her.

"Ben? What's taken you so long? She's been sitting on the front porch for the last hour waiting for you!" Jane scolded as she came out of the house. She trotted down the steps and hugged her brother. "You look good, Ben. Even better than you did three days ago."

"So do you, Jane. But I think that's because we didn't have long enough to get a good look at each other three days ago." He held her back and looked at her, taking his time, now that he had some. Like Ben and her daughter, she had the gray Conner eyes and their mother's black-brown hair. He tried to remember if she'd ever looked happier and decided not. Family and ranch life agreed with her. He smiled and hugged her again. "Sorry I'm late. June had me doing chores this morning."

"Good for her. A little honest work is good for you." Jane turned to her daughter. "Run in and grab your bag."

Becky immediately obeyed with an excited, "Okay!"

"You know she adopted a boy," Ben said quietly.

"Yeah, I know. Luke. Good kid."

He nodded. "You remember what I told you about John McKindel? That he had a son?"

"How could I forget, Ben? You've been killing yourself about it ever since. How many times do I have to tell—"

"Luke was his son."

Jane stepped back as if he'd slapped her. "They're one and the same?" Her eyebrows rose. "That's complicated. Wow. I knew his folks were dead and that he was from Seattle, but I never heard what his last name was before June adopted him. I didn't put the pieces together."

"I've spent all week wondering why you never told me Luke McKindel was here." Ben sighed. "He's a really great kid, and June says to give him a chance to get used to me, that it's not me or what I did that he hates, but how can I believe her when every time he looks at me…. Ah, hell. I don't know, Jane."

"Maybe you should listen to June. Luke is her son now."

"I know."

"Well, you look like you're doing better than you were last time I saw you."

"I am. It's so good to be home again."

Jane sighed. "I'd love to chat with you, Ben, and we will soon, but I need to get back to work. It's for the best, I'm sure, that you're staying with June. You never know. Maybe that little crush you both had on each other in high school will materialize into something more."

"What crush?"

"Oh, come on, Ben. Just because you never dated doesn't mean you weren't attracted beyond simple friendship. I'm your big sister. I know these things."

They chuckled, then Jane said again that she needed to be getting back. "You two have fun, and tell June I appreciate this. It's nice for Becky to spend time with her uncle." She gave her daughter a wink, a hug, and a kiss and sent her off to Ben's truck. "You be good."

"I will, Mama."

"I'll see you Monday afternoon?"

"Yeah. You're sure you don't mind her staying out of school?" he asked.

"Yes. She hasn't seen her uncle in a while. Good enough excuse. See you Monday," Jane replied, smiling at her daughter and tossing in another wink for good measure.

Ben looked at his niece with eyebrows lifted in suspicion. "What's with all the winking? Am I missing something?"

"Not really," Becky replied.

By her sheepish grin, he knew she was hiding something. He also knew that underneath the peaceful exterior she'd inherited from Andy, she could be as stubborn as her mother if she wanted. With a shrug, he opened the passenger side door for her. He had to shove the two wiggling golden retrievers out of the way so she could get in. She giggled as they tried to lick her.

"Hi, Casey," she said.

"Buckle up," Ben told her as he climbed in behind the wheel.

"I know," she replied with a roll of her eyes. She was already strapped in.

So there *was* a teenager in there somewhere, Ben

mused as he started the truck and pulled away from his sister's house. In the rearview mirror, he saw Jane waving from her front porch, and he stuck his arm out the window to wave back. He watched as she disappeared behind the trail of dust kicked up by his truck.

"So, kiddo, are you excited to spend the weekend with your old uncle?" he asked Becky as he turned onto the main ranch road.

"Yeah," she answered quietly.

Surprised by her meek response, he turned his head to stare at her for a moment. Her face was pale beneath the late-spring tan. "What? You were just bouncing around a couple minutes ago. Now you look almost… nervous. What are you so worried about? We're going to have a great time, like we always do."

She only nodded.

"June doesn't bite, Becky."

"I know. She's really nice. I have her for earth science."

Ben narrowed his eyes as he probed a little more. "Luke doesn't bite, either."

Her eyes rounded at the mention of his name. "Uncle Ben…."

"Ah. Why does spending the weekend with Luke make you nervous?"

She chewed on her bottom lip, and he could see the war between her stubbornness and her trust in her beloved uncle plainly in her eyes. "It's just…." The latter won out, and her worries all came spilling out so fast Ben barely caught them all. "He's so popular and smart, and he plays football, and I think he's nice, and all the girls like him, and he looks like… well, you know. And… and he's really cute."

Ben chuckled. "Is *that* all?"

"Uncle Ben!"

"What? You said he's nice, so what's the problem?"

"Well, he's popular, and everyone likes him."

"So?"

"I'm so *not* popular."

"And by the laws of adolescence, you can't talk to him. That's a bunch of nonsense I always thought you were too smart to give credit to."

She huffed out a sigh. "I didn't say I liked it."

He reached over and squeezed her shoulder reassuringly. "I don't think he does, either, if he's anything like June, and from what I've seen so far, he's a *lot* like her."

Becky smiled. "Thanks, Uncle Ben."

He laughed louder this time. "I think June's

rubbing off on me because I think I just said the right thing at the right time."

His niece laughed with him. "You've always said the right things to me."

When Ben pulled his truck to a stop in front of June's cabin, he spotted Luke putting gas in his dirt bike. The boy glanced up, and for the first time since Ben had arrived, he didn't see even a trace of wariness. Maybe they were finally beginning to make some progress. Or—more likely—Luke had reverted back to himself during Ben's brief absence. He looked over at Becky and found her staring up at the cabin, her hands buried in the thick coats of the two golden retrievers.

He turned the truck off and smiled at his niece. "Well, here we are. Welcome to June's cabin."

Becky grinned back, then grabbed her overnight bag and let the dogs out of the truck. She shut the door behind her, spotted Luke, and shyly ducked her head into her shoulders. She smiled timidly at the boy.

"Hi, Luke," she said. Her voice was so soft that Ben barely heard her.

Luke looked up and smiled. "Hi, Becky. I didn't know you were Ben's niece."

"I... I didn't know you were the son of... of the man he shot."

Ben flinched, expecting Luke's eyes to turn on him, cold and hard. They didn't. Instead, the teenager only nodded and finished filling the tank of his dirt bike. Ben and Becky continued forward and stepped inside the cabin. They found June standing at the kitchen sink, starting lunch. She turned and smiled at Becky.

"How are you, Becky? Welcome to my cabin, sweetheart."

"Thank you, Ms. Montana," the girl replied.

"We're not in a classroom, so please, call me June and make yourself at home. You'll be sleeping on that couch there, the longer one."

Becky blushed. She turned away and set her bag beside the longer couch. Just as Ben walked into the kitchen to help with lunch, the front door opened again. Becky whipped around as if she'd forgotten Luke lived there and stared. Ben smiled. She probably had a crush on him, he thought, and reviewing their conversation, he was not at all surprised.

"Hey, Mom?" Luke asked as he walked into the kitchen. He peeked over June's shoulder and snatched a piece of sandwich meat. She swatted at him. "Can I go for a ride?"

"Can you wait until after lunch?"

"Yeah."

"How many sandwiches?"

"Two, please."

"Becky?"

"Just one, thank you."

"Ben, you can give me a hand."

Ben grunted. "How come I get stuck helping?"

"Because it's your turn. Luke helped with dinner last night."

He pretended to pout, then stepped up to the counter beside her, startlingly aware of the light fragrance that emanated from her still-damp braid. It smelled of the lavender-scented shampoo she used and of her. He glanced sheepishly over his shoulder at Becky and Luke, who were chatting about something having to do with school, oblivious of the adults. As they talked, Becky began to relax and open up.

Ben sighed. It *was* getting easier, living here with June and Luke. June was a delightful distraction, and the longer he stayed beneath her roof, the harder he found it to keep his eyes—and his hands—off her. She was as beautiful as she was kind, as gracious as she was intriguing. It wasn't just her physical beauty that attracted him, but her quick mind as well, the way she said just the right thing at the right moment, a trait he'd always found appealing. What an amazing woman, he thought.

"Bill knew what he was doing," Ben murmured, glancing at Luke as he and Becky joined them in the kitchen. The boy kept trying to thieve a sandwich as June finished them. They both laughed, and Ben decided Luke was doing it more for fun than hunger.

"Quit, you bottomless pit," June laughed, swatting her son's hand away for the fourth time.

"But I'm cute," was Luke's beaming reply.

"Yes, you are. Now, get back before I stick a fork in you."

Luke chuckled and finally backed off. Ben found himself smiling. The kid was every bit as charismatic as June, and they were so comfortable with one another that he found it hard to believe Luke had been with June for less than five years.

June set the plate of sandwiches on the table, and the four of them gathered around to eat. Ben sat at the head of the table, and June across from him with her back to the window, Luke to her right, and Becky to her left. While they ate, Ben asked how Becky's first year of high school was going. She informed him that classes were going well, but made no mention of friends. When Ben glanced at June, he saw that she had noticed it, too. When he opened his mouth to say something, she shook her head. She was right. If Becky hadn't said anything, Ben knew she didn't want to talk about it, but it still hurt him to know that his charming niece was so lonely.

The rest of the meal was silent. Luke finished first, but waited patiently for the others to catch up. June finally told him he could go. He took his plate to the sink, then headed toward the front door.

"Why don't you call Carol? See if she wants to do something with us, since we have Monday off."

"All right." Luke snatched the cordless phone off the snack bar, called his girlfriend, and made arrangements for her visit before he grabbed his helmet from its hook beside the inner front door.

"That was your bike out there?" Becky asked with wide eyes.

He nodded. "Have you ever been on one?"

She shook her head. "No. Just four-wheelers."

"Maybe I'll take you out sometime. Not right now, though." Luke plopped his helmet on his head and fastened the straps. "I won't be gone too long."

Ben turned to June. "What do you mean 'we have Monday off?"

Becky smiled sheepishly. "That's why mom didn't

have a problem with me missing school. I can't miss it if there isn't any."

"So, I didn't get you out of a day of school. Darn. And I had so hoped I could play the good guy," Ben said with a false pout.

"You *are* the good guy, Uncle Ben." To prove her point, she gave him a big hug.

* * *

Carol Landers showed up early that afternoon, and Luke introduced her to Ben and Becky. She was only an inch or so taller than Becky and had a mane of red curls offset by deep green eyes. After the introductions were made, the two older teenagers took off on the dirt bikes and didn't return for nearly two hours, when they were running low on fuel. They checked in, filled the tanks, and were off again.

"So, does Carol go home or does she usually spend the night?" Ben inquired.

"Sometimes she stays over," June told him as she kneaded a ball of bread dough. "She sleeps on the couch. If they want to make like bunnies, they can do it out in the forest where no one will stumble upon them."

"You think they're having sex?" Ben asked, his eyes widening. "And that doesn't bother you?"

"I can't really stop him, now can I? I can just make sure he's *very* careful. I think you'll agree that I'm way too young to be a grandmother."

Ben nodded. When he'd been Luke's age, his parents had tried to stop him. The only thing it had done was make him a little more cautious. *Boys will be boys,* he thought with a sardonic smile.

As he stood beside June, helping where he could with dinner, he wrapped his arm around her shoulder and tilted his head down to kiss her cheek.

"Thank you," he whispered.

"For what?"

"For letting me stay here and for helping me through this."

She turned her face up to him and smiled. What an irresistible smile, he thought, one that made him want to do the same. But she'd always been like that, so enchanting and charismatic, and even though they were just friends, he couldn't deny that he was—and probably always had been—attracted. He took in all of her, from the golden hair that cascaded half-way down her back to the proud, graceful shoulders that were bare in her fitted black tank top, high, firm breasts, her trim waist, smooth hips, and long, shapely legs that stood bare below the folded bottoms of her cut-off jeans. She was beautiful far beyond the sexy body and elegant face and those insightful blue eyes, more stunning than her delicious, smiling mouth….

"You are most welcome, Ben. It's what friends are for, after all."

"You know, I don't think I realized just how much I missed you or needed you. I should have come back years ago, right after the shooting."

She reached up and touched his face. He closed his eyes, smiling as warmth rippled outward from her fingers. "You weren't ready to forgive yourself then, Ben, and I doubt you were ready to face Luke, and I know Luke wasn't ready for you, either."

Ben nodded. "You're right, as always."

"Of course I am."

* * *

June studied Ben as he stirred the noodles for the fettuccine alfredo, concerned and aroused at the same time. The way he'd slipped his arm around her earlier and kissed her cheek should have excited nothing more in her than friendship—which is what it was anyhow, a gesture of friendship—but she felt the tingles of something hotter still flickering along her nerve endings. What was he doing to her? The only time she'd ever felt like this was with David Finn back in high school, but even that paled in comparison. Ben was much more difficult to resist than any man she'd met, and she wondered why. Was it because of their long-standing friendship? Or maybe his battle with his memories and guilt from the shooting called to her innate desire to help.

"I think I've got dinner under control," Ben remarked. "Why don't you go out on the porch and feed the chippies? Take a load off. I promise I won't burn anything."

Smiling, June took a root beer from the fridge, the peanuts from the jar beside the hutch, and went out to the back porch. Absently alternating between feeding the multitude of chipmunks and taking a sip of her pop, June analyzed her more recent relationships with the few men she'd dated since adopting Luke. Pete had been a lot like Ben, wounded. He was generally a sweet, gentle man and had been her longest relationship in probably seven or eight years. They had dated for the better part of four months, but she had known from the start that it wouldn't last. Aside from their differences, Pete's issues were beyond her. It hadn't been like it was with Ben; she couldn't help Pete. He wouldn't let her. She harbored no bad thoughts toward the man. In fact, she still thought him a good person with a big heart and counted him among her friends.

Jake had been a disaster, and she'd known it even before their one, ruined date. When she'd agreed to go to dinner and a movie with him, she hadn't really known him, but she had sensed something about him when they'd first met that she didn't like. Her instincts had been proven right at dinner when one of her students had approached her to ask for help after school. Jake had snapped at the girl and told her to leave them alone. June might have been able to forgive that, but when he'd told her—after learning that she'd begun the process to adopt Luke—that she was too young to tie herself down to a "leech," she had backed out of the movie and walked the mile to the college campus where Aeli had been teaching class so she could catch a ride back to Northstar.

Three days later, Jake had come into the Ramshorn during her shift, and at first, he'd tried to apologize and convince her that he'd just had a couple beers too many at dinner, that he wasn't really like that. She'd almost been willing to at least forgive him, but then Luke had unintentionally interrupted by stepping out onto the porch of the lodge to ask for help with a math problem. Jake's temper had flared, but instead of taking his frustration out on June, he'd lashed out at Luke.

At the time, Luke had just started opening up, and the memory of him staring at Jake's red face with his eyes wide and terrified still infuriated June.

"Her man should come first, not some snot-nosed little brat," Jake had snarled.

"Luke will always come first, Jake," she'd replied as calmly as she could. Her voice had trembled despite her efforts. "Certainly before you."

Speechless, Jake had stormed from the lodge. Later that night, June's fury hadn't cooled much, and she'd wondered aloud if she was doomed to pick the worst men. Luke had sat on the couch beside her, tucked his tiny body against hers and said, "You'll always have me." She'd cried then, hugged him tightly, and replied, "Yes, I'll always have you."

It was then that she had truly realized how much Luke meant to her, that he was her son even though his adoption had not yet been finalized. It was an incredible thing, the bond between them.

From that night until a few months ago, she'd sworn off men completely, turned down a several offers for dates—some of them quite tempting. She'd broken her vow when the widowed Aaron Hammond had asked her out, claiming that he was ready to move on again after the tragic death of his wife, Erica. After seven dates, she'd realized he wasn't ready yet, and he'd agreed.

Now there was Ben. True, he was only her friend, but since he was living in her home, he could be considered the man in her life. And look at him. Nearly five years had passed since the shooting, and he when he'd arrived at the Ramshorn, he'd been as torn up by it as he had been when she'd seen him briefly a few days after.

"I really can pick them, can't I?" she murmured.

"Pick what?" Becky asked, walking around the corner of the cabin.

June smiled and patted the step beside her. "Have a seat."

"What can you pick?" the girl insisted.

"It's not important."

"You seemed pretty deep in thought."

June laughed. The girl was persistent and insightful, which made her lack of friends all the more heartbreaking. She was an intelligent young woman, and it was a pity people couldn't see it. "I could say the same for you, Becky. How are you liking the cabin so far? I'll bet it's nice to see your Uncle Ben again."

"Yeah. It is. He seems different now than the last time I saw him."

"How so?"

"I don't know…. Better. He doesn't seem quite so down. The last time we went to visit him in Washington, he took us places, yeah, but it just seemed like he didn't want to."

"I don't think it's that he didn't want to, Becky. I think it's more that he couldn't bring himself to enjoy it." June cocked her head to the side. "He does seem more relaxed now, though, doesn't he?"

"Yeah," Becky replied. "I haven't seen him smile so much in a long time."

Becky drew her knees up to her chest and wrapped her arms around them. For a long time, neither of them spoke. Over the soft sighing of the wind and the twittering of birds, chipmunks and squirrels, June heard Ben humming in the kitchen. From the sounds, she guessed he was probably setting the table while he cooked. She smiled. It was nice having him around. Luke cooked some nights, but usually because he was hungry and she was mired in grading papers. It was quite enjoyable to sit out on the back porch, feed the chipmunks, and close her eyes to better enjoy the soft fingers of the warm evening breeze on her cheeks, knowing dinner would be ready any moment. She tossed a peanut out to a squirrel.

"Whatcha thinking about?" June finally asked Becky.

Ben's niece hesitated, then blurted, "Luke seems really nice."

Laughing, June replied, "He is."

"A lot of girls I know have crushes on him." Pink brightened her cheeks. "He *is* cute."

June tried not to laugh, she did, but the giggles came spilling out. "I'm sorry, Becky, I'm not laughing at you. It just struck me as funny, especially the way you said it. A couple years ago, Luke made the comment that even if he wanted people to notice him, they didn't. And now…. He doesn't like it much, I can tell you."

Becky was soon laughing with her. "Please don't tell him I said that."

"I won't, I promise."

As if he'd sensed them talking about him, June heard the still-distant buzz of Luke's dirt bike. Then she heard the second bike, probably a bit behind. With another smile and a shake of her head, June pushed to her feet and offered a hand to Becky.

"Dinner should be about ready," she said, hauling the girl to her feet.

By the time Luke and Carol finally finished

washing their hands for dinner—a simple task drawn out because Luke kept flicking water at Carol, who retaliated by poking him in the side—the meal was finished and the table laid. June soaked up the noisy gathering, content to listen to the happy chatter. Even her most treasured moments of peacefulness didn't give her the same sense of family… or of completeness. It was perfect. No other word was enough to describe the joy in her heart. The tension that had been slowly slackening between Luke and Ben evaporated, if only for a little while, and she could imagine what life with the two of them could be like once they overcame their entwined memories.

Luke glanced at her and smiled in a way that told her he felt the same about this evening. She found herself watching him, a common distraction of hers, and couldn't help but be proud of him. He'd come a long way, she thought, but there was still more he had to overcome, and perhaps having Ben here would help him do that.

"Since I cooked dinner, that means I get out of dishes, right?" Ben asked.

"Carol and I can do them," Luke volunteered.

"I'll help, too," Becky asserted.

June grinned. Spending time with Luke and Carol

would be good for Ben's niece. Luke smiled at the girl and told her he'd love the extra help. Becky's cheeks pinkened. June told Ben to scoot outside and helped the teenagers clear the table before joining him out on the porch.

The air was so fresh balmy with the coming summer, and the narrow valley was colored prettily with the waning light of day. Ben was silent, but she could almost hear him thinking and saw the softness in his gray eyes. There was no shadow of guilt, only relaxed contentment. She rested her head on his shoulder.

"Whoever said home is where the heart is must have had a home like this," June murmured. "A place that's ingrained in your every cell with friends and family who love you unconditionally."

"There is no other home like this," Ben agreed. "Not for me."

"Nor me." June straightened, meeting Ben's gaze and holding it when he tried to look away. "What a great night."

Unexpectedly, his face split with a grin. "Indeed. Your son is a goofball, June."

"What else would you expect? I mean, come on. He's been living with me for five years with little influence from anyone outside of Northstar. How could he *not* be a character?"

"I've wondered since that day…. I didn't know what happened to him, if he'd even survive."

"Ben…."

"No, let me finish. That I killed a man was hard, and it took me a while to get over that, but the one thing I couldn't forgive myself for was Luke."

June's chest tightened and her heart ached for Ben. The pain in his voice cut her, but she didn't say anything. In a moment, he continued.

"I'd killed his last living relative, and it was my fault he'd be lost in the system, and then, without knowing him, I knew he wouldn't survive. You have no idea how much better I feel now knowing that he's thriving." Ben sighed. "I still have a lot of ground to cover before I can actually forgive myself, but I've made more progress in the short time I've been here than I managed in all the weeks and months and years since the shooting. So, you're right. I need to be here, with you, with Luke, because the best way—the only way—to forgive myself is to face what I did."

Unable to stop herself, she threw her arms around his neck. He hugged her back, shaking.

"I can't promise anything, June," he whispered. "I can't promise you I'll ever again be the man you think

I should be."

June didn't understand what he meant, but she did know that at this moment, she didn't dare let go of him. She couldn't for his sake, and she didn't want to for hers.

Five

TOO IMPATIENT TO WAIT for hot water, Luke braced himself and stuck his head under the icy stream in the kitchen sink. A nice, hot shower would have been preferable, but it seemed a waste since the plan of the day was to wallow in the dirt. He'd shower when they got home. However, his hair was out of control this morning, and if he didn't want to be fighting it all day, there was only one solution. So he endured the frigid water long enough to completely wet the mop.

Hearing a piercing squeal in the living room, he glanced under his arm just in time to see Becky's arms flail as she fought to maintain her balance. The thud as she crashed to the floor was muffled by her pillow and sleeping bag. Chuckling, Luke grabbed the towel he'd set on the counter beside the sink and tossed it over his shoulder. He quickly squeezed the water out of his hair and toweled it as he walked into the living room.

Becky was still on the floor, struggling to free herself from her tangled sleeping bag. When he squatted down beside her, she looked at him with wide eyes. A deep blush stained her cheeks as her gaze dipped momentarily to his bare chest, and Luke had to swallow another chuckle.

"Are you all right?" he asked.

"Umm… I think I'm stuck."

Luke glanced at her feet, which were still on the couch. The sleeping bag was twisted around her, and the bottom had somehow become wedged between the arm of the couch and the cushion, imprisoning her feet and legs.

"Here, let me help."

Gently grasping her arms, he pulled her free from the sleeping bag and set her back on the couch. Smiling at her in reassurance, he wondered if she'd ever stop blushing around him.

"What were you doing?" he inquired, curiosity

getting the best of him.

"Trying to see who was at the sink," she replied as a new wave of crimson spread across her face. "I thought it might have been Uncle Ben… but he isn't built quite like you."

Luke lifted his brow in question. Sometimes, it seemed like Becky couldn't help but announce her observations, no matter how embarrassed she was by even thinking them. Luke found that trait—that honesty—endearing.

"You've got a nice…." Blanching, she snapped her mouth closed. Her eyes darted wildly as she sought a way to salvage the situation. "You're very athletic. I wish I was."

"Thanks, Becky," he replied, trying not to offend her by laughing. "And you're a lot prettier than you think. Don't be so hard on yourself."

"I'm not pretty. Not like my… my friends in Devyn."

"You're far more beautiful than they are. Trust me. They're really not very impressive." This time he did laugh. "They sure think they're something, though."

Red once again colored Becky's face, and she lowered her gaze to the floor. "You don't have to be so nice to me, you know. It's okay. I'm used to being alone."

Luke narrowed his eyes and studied her for a moment. She had no idea how pretty she was with her dark hair and those innocent, honest gray eyes. She also had no idea how much he truly appreciated her personality. Unlike so many of the people he knew in high school, she wasn't afraid to be herself. There were no false fronts to muddle through. She was just Becky, and it might hurt that people didn't like that she didn't follow the rules of "normal," but that didn't stop her from being who she was.

He shook his head sadly. "I know I don't *have* to. I *want* to. Believe it or not, Becky, I really do like you. You're pretty cool."

And he meant it. From the first time he'd met Becky at the start of the school year, he'd known she was worth a lot more than she or anyone else thought. But she'd been too shy to approach him, even though they were both from Northstar, and whenever he'd tried to say hello, she'd only murmured a one-syllable response and blushed.

"Thanks," she finally replied.

"Good. Now that that's all settled, I should wake Carol up, or we'll never make it to Crystal Park today."

This time, she laughed softly. Openly. Luke walked over to the other couch where Carol was snoring lightly, oblivious of everything around her. At the moment he was grateful she was such a heavy sleeper because he doubted Becky would have been able to digest what he'd told her if faced with two older teens she thought herself too unpopular to associate with. What was popularity worth, anyhow? Not a damned thing, as far as Luke was concerned. From his experience with it, it was a hassle. Stares, whispers, false friendship. He'd take one friend like Becky—honest, loyal, and without pretenses—over a million "friends" he couldn't trust to tell him the correct time of day.

Pushing those thoughts away, he leaned over his girlfriend and kissed her awake.

"Mmm. Morning, sweetie," she mumbled.

"Time to rise and shine," he said. "Because the sun's already been up for a while."

She grumbled and tried to pull the blankets over her head, so Luke grabbed a handful and yanked.

"Luke!" she screeched.

"Time to get up," he repeated and dumped her blankets on Becky's couch. His new friend giggled conspiratorially.

Carol climbed groggily to her feet and growled

incoherently all the way to the bathroom. Luke chuck-led and made his way back into the kitchen where his brush was still waiting. After taming his hair, he headed upstairs to finish getting dressed. June was coming out of her room just as he reached the top of the steps. She lifted a brow at him.

"What was all the squealing about?" she asked, her voice mildly suspicious.

"Becky fell off the couch trying to find out who was in the kitchen and, I think, trying to get a better view. And Carol wouldn't get up, so I took her blankets. She wasn't too happy with me about it."

June laughed. "I imagine not." She glanced in the direction of the man sleeping on the air mattress at the other end of the loft. "Hmm. Ben's not up yet. Dibs."

She grinned mischievously, and Luke felt his face shift to match her expression. Sure enough, Ben was still sound asleep, which Luke considered something of a miracle, considering all the noise the girls had made downstairs. He stood back to watch with his arms folded across his chest, trying very hard not to laugh. He didn't want to ruin June's fun by waking Ben prematurely. With a wink, June curled her fingers around a fistful of blanket and jerked them off the bed. Ben, wearing only a pair of green plaid boxers, instinctively curled into a ball as the rush of cool morning air hit him.

"What the hell?!"

Luke couldn't contain it any longer, and he doubled over with laughter.

"Time to wake up, sleepy head," June said. Her voice shook with mirth.

Ben glared at them for a few moments as goose bumps rose on his bare skin, then joined them. He fit in well at the cabin, Luke mused. When you got past the melancholy, he seemed to have quite a marvelous sense of humor. It was easy to see why he and June had been such good friends and why she found him so appealing. No, more than appealing. He captured her attention every time he was in the room, and it was something more than their long-standing friendship had ignited.

Luke glanced at June and saw more than amusement in her eyes as she gazed at Ben. There was compassion there, something Luke was well acquainted with, but there was desire, as well, and that was meant for no one but Ben. Luke may have been only sixteen, but he wasn't blind. He'd seen it hundreds of times before… every time Pat and Aelissm looked at each other.

As unobtrusively as he could, Luke ducked into his room.

* * *

June sat back on the mound of dirt above her hole and tried to catch her breath, wondering if she'd spent more than five minutes all morning *not* laughing. At the moment, her face and lungs ached from the light-hearted squabble over who had rights to a thumb-sized, deep-hued amethyst. Ben's claim on the prize was that he'd been digging in the hole where it had been unearthed and had only momentarily left to borrow June's screen. Becky claimed she had continued digging—on a different side of the contested hole— and had been the one to unearth it. Luke claimed finders-keepers and stated that, as he was the first one to actually hold it, he should get it. He also pointed out that Becky hadn't seen the massive amethyst until he'd picked it up.

The whole battle had descended into one big dust bath.

"Stop!" June giggled. "Stop, stop, stop."

Carol, as prim as ever, had flitted beyond the cloud of dust. She watched the scene with a mixture of amusement and disdain, and June briefly—unfairly— wondered why she and Luke were still dating. How could two people so different find anything in common? But she knew exactly what they shared, and it was an unusual, hard-to-find commonality that created a powerful bond. Even if, at some point, they mutually decided they no longer wanted to be a couple, they'd probably remain friends because of it. Of course, if Carol chose to end it with Luke the way she'd ended her relationship with Mike Thompson, June highly doubted Luke would be able to trust her enough to remain friends, regardless of how strong the bond they shared now was.

"So, who wins?" Ben asked, his clothes mottled by the pale dust.

"Me," June replied. "Without my tools, none of you would've ever found it."

"Hey!" they chorused. "Not fair!"

"How about we have some poor tourist take a picture with all of us and the amethyst, and I'll have Aeli build a frame for both the picture and the rock."

"And who gets the frame?" Ben inquired.

"We'll hang it down at the Bedspread or the Ramshorn. Is that okay? And everyone can have a copy of the picture."

They grumbled an affirmative, and she beamed at them.

"Even me?" Carol asked. "I didn't help find it."

June tucked an arm around her shoulders. "Of course you get one. You're here with us, aren't you?"

The girl smiled, reassured.

June found someone to take the picture, glad everyone in their group would be included. The amethyst was front and center, of course, and she knew everyone was smiling if only because Luke was being his usual, goofy self, trying to give Ben and Becky bunny ears. The man trying to take the picture was laughing so hard he had to pause for a moment to wipe under his eyes.

When the photo shoot was over, everyone went back to digging. June plopped in her hole, but instead of getting back to work, she let herself be distracted by her haphazard family. Occasionally, one of them would pop up in their hole like a gopher, which made her chuckle. Becky seemed to have relaxed a lot and no longer seemed to be so conscious of her every move around the older teenagers. And Luke genuinely seemed to like her. Even Carol, who was usually a little more aloof, warmed to her.

And Ben… he was happier than he'd yet been since returning to Northstar. His laughter was rich and unrestrained, and the ever-present smile on his face was open and carefree. There wasn't a trace of the torturous emotions he'd been prisoner to for so long. Not even in his eyes. When he met her gaze, only peace and joy beamed at her from the gray depths. It was the same warmth she'd always associated with those eyes, whole and untarnished. She knew it wasn't permanent. Not yet. There was still a lot of work ahead of him before he was truly healed, but this moment, free of turmoil, was a sign that he was mending.

June leaned back against a tree root. She couldn't have asked for a more beautiful day. It was unseasonably warm, and though she worried about the coming fire season, it was nice that only a few ragged piles of crystalline snow remained. She could recall years when Crystal Park had still been inaccessible in mid-May. The pines were vibrantly green-black beneath the soothing heat of the sun, and the snow on the mountains contrasted brilliantly against the vivid blue sky. A dusting of upper level cirrus clouds made that expansive bowl seem so impossibly high, and as she gazed around her, she felt the long-familiar jolt of appreciation.

This was her heaven, the Crystal Valley, the Northstar Valley, and all the secret places tucked away in the arms of the Northstar Mountains. She'd be at peace here even with no one else around. But she wasn't alone. The spirited voices of her son and his girlfriend and Ben and his niece danced around her, woven with the elements of the day and the landscape to create absolute perfection. Why would she want to be anywhere else right now? Or with anyone else?

June went back to digging. She dumped a shovelfull of dirt into her screen and shook it to separate the loose dirt from the crystals. Poking through the pebbles of granite, she plucked out a handful of clear quartz, including one nearly as thick and long as her pinky. All in all, this seemed to be a good dig site, she mused as she added her latest gems to her nearly full quart jar. She had many others at home that she and Luke had filled over the years, and she'd given away crystals by the handful to customers of the Ramshorn or Bedspread Inn who hadn't been as lucky in their digs. She figured it was as much the fun of unearthing the crystals as the crystals themselves she enjoyed. With a smile, she recalled the first time she'd brought Luke here and explained the geology of the site, how he'd listened with rapt attention.

They continued their mining project for a few more hours, stopping for a while to eat lunch. They found several more amethysts—though none were as large or as dark as the first—a few rare scepters, and some sizeable, unclouded quartz. At last, as the sun tipped westward, they packed up their tools and treasures and made their way carefully through the dangerous, uneven terrain to the paved trail through the park.

"It looks like a minefield," June murmured to herself. "But it's a special place."

"Yes, it is," Ben whispered, close to her ear.

The gentle touch of his hand against the small of her back made her shiver. It wasn't shock or fear that coursed through her, and it certainly wasn't revulsion. She was hesitant to name it and unsure if she could, because the heat building was like nothing she'd ever felt before. And part of her, the part that was concerned solely for Ben's well-being, warned her against it. He was fragile, as odd as that description seemed to be for someone of his delicious build—June scolded herself for *that* adjective. Someday, maybe soon, he'd be stable enough to handle the kind of relationship she wanted, but right now, she couldn't let anything happen that might jeopardize the first tentative threads of peace that were stitching the wound in his heart.

Besides, he may not see her as anything more than a very good friend.

Yeah, right, she thought with a snort. *Just because I've never felt this doesn't mean I don't know the signs. But, whatever happens, I won't hurt him.*

It was a promise easier made than kept. There was no way to know what decisions she might be faced with. If it ever came down to a choice between hurting Luke and hurting Ben or herself, she'd protect Luke. *That* was the promise she'd made when she'd adopted him. The promise of a mother to her son.

"What's got you so peeved?" Ben asked, his eyes narrowed.

"Choices," she replied. "Like what to do with the rest of the afternoon."

"Well, you did tell Becky and Carol to bring their swimsuits."

"Ramshorn it is, then." She gave him a wide smile.

When they reached the trucks, Luke suggested that he and Becky ride with Ben and Carol ride with June and the dogs. June caught the brief scowl on Carol's face and frowned. She watched the two of them covertly as she loaded tools into the trucks with Becky's assistance. There was annoyance and worry flitting at the edges of Carol's expression. To anyone else, Luke would have appeared oblivious to it, but June knew better. The look on his face was too pristine, telling her that his outward lack of concern wasn't entirely genuine. Carol muttered something too quietly for June to hear, and Luke paused in his task to turn his attention fully to her.

"She doesn't have any good friends, Carol," he explained quietly. "She's a nice kid, and she's Ben's niece. I'm just trying to make her feel like she has someone else who cares besides her family. There's no reason for you to be jealous."

"Why would I be jealous of her?" Carol retorted, not quite as nonchalant as she probably wanted to sound.

"I don't know. Why are you?"

June was a little surprised by the edge to Luke's tone. He wasn't just being nice to Becky. He actually counted her as a friend and was defending her as such. June was glad to see it. Becky was the same kind of friend Luke was… loyal to the end. If Carol's method of dealing with her ex-boyfriend was any indication, she'd only be around as long as everything was happy and advantageous. June knew it was harsh of her to think that way about Luke's girlfriend, but she also understood that Carol Landers was a survivor. To live a normal life after the tragedy her family had suffered—and having Jake Sterling as an uncle, June added—she had to be.

June hoped Luke was smart enough to know it and wouldn't get his heart broken like Mike Thompson.

"You're doing it again," Ben remarked.

Startled, she spun around to face him. "Shit, Ben! Don't sneak up on me like that!"

He lifted his brows. "Normally, you're much harder to sneak up on. What are you thinking about now?"

"Luke and Carol," she answered. "I was wondering how much longer she'll stay."

"I take it you're not talking about when she's going home."

June shook her head. "She's a nice girl, and I *do* like her, but she and Luke are so different. Or maybe I'm just biased."

"Maybe, but I've been wondering about that a little myself. Luke's so fun-loving, and he doesn't mind playing in the dirt, and she's…"

"Prissy?" June supplied.

"Yeah. I wouldn't worry so much about him, June. He's a smart kid. I don't think he'll let her hurt him."

June nodded and hoped Ben was right. Either way, she needed to stop thinking about it. Carol had done nothing to hurt Luke so far and didn't deserve her animosity. Besides, she was having a marvelous day, and she refused to ruin it with such thoughts.

"All right, you filthy lot, if everything's packed up, let's take our loot and head home," June barked with amusement thick in her voice. "And then we'll all go swimming."

After they'd deposited their findings on the kitchen table, stowed all their tools in the appropriate places, and gathered their swimming gear, they piled into June's truck. The three teenagers climbed into the bed with the two dogs while June slid in behind the wheel, and Ben took the passenger seat. The rear window was open, and all the way down to the Ramshorn, they talked and laughed. Carol seemed to have gotten over her jealousy, June noted and finally let the matter drop.

Since they'd already had lunch and it wasn't quite time for dinner yet, June told everyone they'd swim now and eat later. As they wandered into the pool house, she waved hello to the young woman in the office. She was new to the Ramshorn staff and had been hired to replace the idiot geology student who'd quit the day Ben had arrived. So far, she was working out well. Not the greatest at waiting tables or cooking, the girl was great at keeping an eye on pool guests, and she didn't mind cleaning. Mary had mentioned looking for someone else since they were bound to start getting busier soon with the summer tourist season just around the corner. Perhaps it would be an opportunity for Ben, at least until he decided what else he might want to do with his life.

June changed into her sapphire blue bikini, checked her reflection in the full-length mirror and noted with feminine pride that she looked pretty darned good. A little winter-pale and maybe not as curvy in some places as she might like but attractive enough. She was normally not so image-conscious, but she wanted Ben to like what he saw.

Carol took her time changing, and impatient, June and Becky wandered out to the pools without her. The older teenager beat the boys out, however. June laughed as they both posed outrageously and did her best to ignore the flare of heat at the sight of Ben's toned upper body and legs. When they launched into the larger of the pools, water splashed everywhere, thoroughly drenching June, Carol, and Becky.

Having satisfied his apparent need to act like a kid, Ben swam over to where June was standing in the shallow end with her arms crossed.

"It's a good thing I wasn't planning to keep my hair dry," she muttered. "You two created quite a tidal wave with your cannon-balls."

The smile that curved his lips ignited his eyes, and June's heart skittered. "Don't be a spoil-sport."

Without warning, June dunked him. He came up sputtering and laughing.

Another wall of water washed over her as Luke picked Carol up out of the water and launched her skyward. Her screech of surprise reeled in half a dozen curious and amused glances from the other swimmers. In retaliation, she pulled him under. Ben and June backed away to watch as Becky joined Carol and the two girls stalked Luke across the pool. Once he figured out what was going on, he was careful to keep just out of their reach.

"I missed this, too," Ben murmured. "All of it. The pools, the aspen just leafing out just up there by the old cabin, the lodgepoles… the shrieking kids."

"It's an incredible place," June replied, tipping her head back to soak her hair properly. Blissful was the word that plopped in her mind. When she looked over at Ben, she smiled. "I'm glad you finally decided to come home."

"Me, too. I didn't have a chance to say it, but you

look damned sexy in that suit."

Her smile widened with satisfaction. Yep. All in all, it was a perfect day.

* * *

"I hope Becky had a good time."

Ben smiled at June as he hesitated just inside the front door. His niece was already in the truck, ready to head home. "I think she had a great time. Remind me to thank Luke and Carol, will you?"

"No thanks needed," Luke said, sliding past him in through the door. "Becky's really cool. And, no, I'm not being nice and just saying that. She's a lot of fun."

"I know she is," Ben agreed. "She's the one who doesn't believe it. But I really think you helped with that this weekend."

Luke grinned, but didn't say anything else. Ben watched the teenager stride through the kitchen and jog up the stairs. Sometimes it was hard to believe that he and the boy in the station that night were one and the same. He was so relaxed most of the time and so sure of himself that it was usually quite easy for Ben to follow June's advice and allow himself to let go of his guilt. Then he'd wonder if he was really letting go or if he was dealing with it at all.

"Don't forget to ask Jane and Andy about a dinner

date with us," June reminded him. "I haven't had much chance to catch up with them lately."

"Yes, ma'am."

She smiled and shooed him out the door.

All the way back to her house, Becky chattered excitedly about all the fun she'd had. Her face was as bright as the sun overhead as she regaled him with tales of the weekend's adventures as if Ben hadn't been a part of them all. He wasn't about to interrupt her to point that out, however. It had been too long since he'd seen his niece so openly animated about something. In the halo of her joy, it was hard not to feel the same, and Ben again sensed, as he had so many times in the last week, that he'd made the right decision. He also understood—finally—exactly why his sister had suddenly packed her bags and left her family behind in Washington right after graduation. Northstar was her home. It was Ben's, too, and he'd been a fool to believe Western Washington's rains could ever wash it out of his blood. The sagebrush, pines, dust, and granite mountains were as much a part of him as his gray Conner eyes.

"No wonder Dad's so miserable in Washington," he muttered.

"Huh?" Becky asked.

"Oh, nothing, Becky. I was just thinking out loud. Your grandfather really hates Washington, you know."

"Trust me, Uncle Ben. I know. He tells me almost every time I talk to him."

Ben laughed. "I'll bet he does. And I'll bet he gets all soft and mushy when he talks about Montana, doesn't he?"

"Yeah. Are they really coming back to Northstar?"

"Your mom would know more about that than I would, but I hope so."

"Me, too. Then we'll all be here."

Ben let the conversation drift away out the open window. He didn't want to think about having his family all together and happy again for the first time in over two decades because it was too much to deal with right now. And it seemed too much to hope for. Until he could truly forgive himself for killing Luke's father, he knew he couldn't be the son and brother he should be. Even as free as he was beginning to feel, he wasn't whole again. Not yet.

"Mom's actually home," Becky remarked.

With a start, Ben realized he'd pulled up in front of his sister's house and couldn't recall turning down her driveway. Sure enough, Jane was sitting on the porch with a glass of what appeared to be lemonade. There was an expression on her face that had been absent until she'd come back to Northstar. As he met her eyes through the windshield, his face lifted to match.

"You look happy, so I take it my daughter behaved herself well," Jane remarked.

Becky trotted up the stairs and bent down to hug her mother. Then she disappeared into the house to drop off her bags.

"You know she did, Jane," Ben replied. "She's always a good girl."

"And she looks like she had a good time, too."

"We all did. She really hit it off with Luke. Carol, too."

Jane's dark brows quirked upward. "Carol Landers?"

"That's the one. You sound surprised."

"Not about Luke. Like I said, he's a good kid. And June wouldn't let him be rude to Becky, even if he'd been inclined. Carol's something different, though."

Ben frowned and studied his sister, recalling the cryptic comments June had made about the girl yesterday. Luke and Carol seemed to really like each other, even if they were a little different, so why would June wonder how long Carol would stay around? And why had there been a stiffness about her, as if she were ready to spring to Luke's defense?

"Now, I'm curious," Ben finally said, unable to find anything suspicious with so little information.

"About what?"

"June told me yesterday she wondered how long Carol and Luke would stay together."

"Ah." Jane took a long drink of her lemonade. "It's not really my place to say and maybe it's a little cruel of me to think the way I do, but I have an idea why June would say something like that."

Ben waited a moment for her to add more, but when she remained silent, he scowled lightly and said, "Enlighten me, dear sister."

"She was dating Mike Thompson for two years, then up and dumped him when something better came along," Jane told him.

"By something better, you mean Luke. And if someone better than Luke comes along…."

Ben recalled the time he'd spent with the girl over the weekend and tried to find something about her that would hint at that sort of callousness. She'd been a little distant at times but not cold or mean. *Cautious* was the word that sprang to mind. "I don't see it."

"She doesn't do it to be cruel, but I don't think

she lets herself get too attached to anyone, either. She can't."

"And why would that be, dear sister? Give me the gory details."

Jane looked away and took a long drink of her lemonade before she answered. "Her father, Paul Landers, killed himself a few years ago… about six years, I think. He put a gun to his head and pulled the trigger."

Ben felt like he'd just been punched in the gut. It wasn't the horror and embarrassment that he'd phrased his question as he had that knocked the breath out of him because he couldn't have known what Jane would tell him. His blood chilled because he now understood why Luke and Carol had been together as long as they had with so few common interests. Losing a parent so tragically and at such a young age, no matter the circumstances, created a powerful bond of understanding. Few others could comprehend that kind of pain, let alone empathize with it. It was a pain Luke was no stranger to because of Ben.

"Why would he do that?" Ben heard himself ask.

"Caught his wife in bed with another man. Then his wife divorced him and was going to be granted custody of Carol. Cheryl swore she'd never let Paul see

Carol again, and I guess he just couldn't take that. Paul would've been the better choice for her. He was a good man. Cheryl and Carol were his world. He must've gotten that from his mother, because he sure as hell didn't get it from his father."

"Paul Landers? Any relation to Pete Landers?"

"And to Jake Sterling. They're all half-brothers with the same father. And I'm sure there are many more half-siblings out there. The man is a pig."

Ben tried to swallow the cold, swirling guilt by focusing on something else. "You said the way you thought of Carol was harsh. Why?"

Jane narrowed her eyes and studied him for a moment as if trying to decide the wisdom of answering his question. Dread folded in with the guilt as Ben held his sister's concerned gray gaze. Finally, she set her empty glass on the table and answered.

"It really sucks that she lost her father like she did and that her mother is too selfish to be bothered with her, but she doesn't have to do the same to others. Like poor Mike. I think he really loved her, and she walked all over him when she decided Luke would be a better choice. Just like her mother." Jane paused and looked out across the spring-green meadow that surrounded her comfortable little house. "I feel bad for thinking that way, but then I see Luke, who would sooner break his own arm than hurt someone else. That boy's got a heart of gold, Ben, and he's been through the same trauma, if not worse. At least Carol had her uncles and Pete's mother. Luke had no one. Not until he came here."

"Thank you for reminding me, Jane," Ben said through gritted teeth. He sat heavily in the chair beside her, unable to stand beneath the weight of shame that crashed down on him.

"Oh, get over yourself, little brother," Jane snapped. "He's far better off with June, I'll bet, than he would've been in Washington. Rather than thinking of what happened as something you should carry around with you like a dead weight—and yes, pun intended—maybe you should realize that what you did gave Luke a second chance. A chance to have a good life. I remember what he was like when he first came here. Pale, skinny, and half-terrified."

"He was half-terrified because his father was dead and he'd been ripped away from everything he ever knew."

"No, Ben. Whatever he was afraid of came from what he'd left behind not being torn away from it. He took to Northstar and everyone here like your dog takes to water. He's in his element here, and as soon as he realized it… Ben, it was like he'd never been happy before he came here. I don't know why, so don't ask me. You want to know, maybe you should try asking him."

With that, Jane picked up her glass, stood and went inside. Becky came out a moment later to say goodbye, and Ben promised he'd see her again very soon. He was walking down the steps out to his truck when he realized he hadn't invited Jane and Andy to dinner, as June had asked.

"Jane!" he called.

She reappeared moments later still looking rather annoyed with him. He smiled brightly, hoping she would accept the silent apology. When she shook her head and smiled back, he relaxed.

"I don't dare go back to June's without passing on her invitation," he told her. "She wants to have you and Andy and Becky over for dinner soon, whenever you get a break. She said something about not getting enough time to catch up with you anymore."

"Tell her we'd love to," Jane replied. "We should have a little break here in the next couple weeks once all the branding is done and the herds are moved up to the summer allotments. I'll call her when I know more."

"Great! I'd better be getting back."

"Yes, we wouldn't want you getting in trouble, now would we?"

He had just closed the door of his truck when Jane called his name. He looked at her expectantly.

"There's a reason why you came back to Northstar, and there's also a reason why it's best you're staying with June. Remember that!"

She was right, he knew. Just as he knew *why* it was good he was staying with June. Or did he? Maybe he'd been right in thinking he wasn't dealing with his guilt, and maybe it was time that he did. He'd start by finding out exactly what Jane had been talking about when she'd said Luke had brought his fear with him and shed it soon after arriving in Northstar.

Six

"LUKE, MAKE SURE BEN gets down to the Ramshorn on time, will you? I'd hate for him to not get the job because he got lost on one of the old logging spurs."

"I won't get lost," Ben retorted. "I've been here long enough and driven up and down this mountainside enough times."

"Luke?"

Luke laughed when Ben growled at June's playful lack of faith in his navigational skills and earned himself a rather dirty look.

"I'll make sure he gets there," he replied and flopped on the longer of the two couches with his math book and notebook. The sooner he finished what little homework he had tonight, the more of the evening he'd have left to enjoy.

"All right, boys, I'm off," June said as she jerked her helmet down on her head. "See you at the lodge at seven, Ben?"

"Seven sharp," Ben affirmed.

"You're sure you'll be all right by yourselves?"

"We'll be fine, June."

Luke felt her eyes on him and looked up to meet her gaze. The jolt of gratitude for her concern was something he'd felt more times than he could count in the last five years. This was the first time he and Ben would be alone together, and he was a little nervous June's friend would want to talk about pieces of the past Luke had no inclination to discuss. June knew his fears as if she could read his mind and was worried about how they affected him. It never ceased to amaze him that she could love him so much, and he hoped he'd never take it for granted. He smiled reassuringly and wondered, as he always did, how he'd gotten so lucky.

"See you at seven, Mom," he said when she

seemed hesitant to leave.

At last, she nodded and headed out the door. Luke waited until he heard the hum of her bike fade away into silence before he turned his attention to his books.

While Luke worked on his homework, Ben puttered around the house. Occasionally, Luke glanced up and listened for a moment, heard Ben playing outside with the dogs, and went back to his studies. Maybe Ben wasn't any more inclined to bring up the tender subject of Luke's father than Luke was. If not tonight, the topic would be broached sooner or later. He was sure of it. It was probably best that they got it out in the open, but Luke just wasn't ready to talk about it. Not yet. Not when he hadn't even told June about his father's darker secrets. He was sure she knew the truth—Uncle Bill was sure to have reached certain conclusions, and June wasn't stupid by the stretch of anyone's imagination—but it didn't seem right to not air it out with her first after all she'd done for him.

If Ben wanted to talk about John McKindel, it *would* be aired out. There was simply no other way to convince the man that what he'd done had given Luke a better life. Luke genuinely liked Ben and was of the opinion he didn't deserve to suffer for an hour over what had happened, let alone half a decade. Though he couldn't empathize with shooting someone, he understood that taking a life was bound to leave a mark. He was also aware, after getting to know Ben, that killing John McKindel was only drop in the bucket of guilt he'd been lugging around.

"If I keep thinking like this, I'll never get my homework done," Luke muttered and determinedly refocused his attention.

Once he forced himself to concentrate, he finished quickly. Stowing his book and notebook in his backpack for tomorrow, he stood and looked around the cabin for something to do. It was only a quarter to six, but that didn't really give him enough time to go for much of a ride on his dirt bike. He might've been inclined to split wood, but they'd already chopped everything that had been cut to length, so he grabbed the big jar of peanuts by the back door and went outside to feed the chipmunks.

Ben was throwing a ball for Casey and Cheyenne behind the cabin and turned to smile a greeting when the screen door slammed behind Luke. Luke returned the gesture and plopped on the steps of the deck. Even with two big dogs running around, the chipmunks were quick to realize it was snack time. Within minutes, he had five of the larger variety and at least eight of their smaller cousins skittering around him, chirping and squeaking for dinner.

As he fed the friendly rodents, he noticed that the afternoon sunlight was turning gold, and it tinted the forest around the cabin. The greens of the lodgepole pines and the delicate, alpine grass were fiery, if green could be described in such a way. The browns were more brilliant as well, and the first tentative spears of purple lupine glowed. Why would anyone want to live in a city when they could have this? Smog dulled the colors, but up here, where the air was so clear that it seemed to have the sharpness of a razor blade, color was as it should be, vibrant and undimmed.

And the smells… Luke's favorite smell, without a doubt, was the scent of the woods around the cabin. It was a cool, refreshing smell, infused with more than just the fragrance of the pines. There was also a hint of sagebrush in the air and an underlying spice of hay, livestock, and earth. He drew it deep into his lungs and sighed contentedly. Yep. Definitely his favorite smell in the world.

"You finished your homework already?" Ben asked. He sat beside Luke on the porch step.

"I didn't have much to do."

"Ah."

Since it appeared Ben was in Northstar to stay, Luke hoped their conversations would improve soon. The silences between them were awkward with a long way to go before they became even remotely comfortable. He glanced at the older man and found his companion staring with unfocused eyes in the direction of the dogs, whom he had apparently managed to wear out. Both golden retrievers were sprawled in the shade a few yards away, panting heavily with their tongues lolling out.

"I didn't know that was possible," Luke remarked, inclining his head at the exhausted dogs.

Ben gave a sniff of laughter, and for a moment, the tension left his face. "Neither did I."

One brief, meaningless exchange and the conversation crumbled again. Luke dug into the jar of peanuts and tossed a handful to the horde of waiting chipmunks. A few that were brave enough to dare the deck were rewarded with shelled peanuts out of his hand. Luke nearly laughed when one skittered over Casey's legs in its hurry to take a mouthful of nuts to its stash. The dog barely lifted his head to see what had interrupted his nap, but it was enough to make the little rodent chitter in angry surprise. With a grunt, Casey decided to ignore the animal's string of insults and flopped back down. After a few more moments of chirping and tail-twitching, the chipmunk bounded off.

A heavy sigh pulled Luke's attention back to Ben. Whatever was on the man's mind was no small thing, and as much as Luke dreaded what it might be, the tension between them was beginning to wear on his nerves. Sometimes it was best to just get it out. Whether or not either of them would be able to do it properly… they'd find out when they got there.

"You know, Ben, no matter how hard you stare at that log, it won't be able to help you figure out whatever's bugging you. Inanimate objects aren't properly equipped for problem-solving."

"Sometimes I really wish they were. It'd be easier."

"And what idiot ever said life was easy?"

"Do you have any idea how much you sound like June when you say things like that?" Ben asked, finally meeting Luke's gaze. There was amusement mixed with the strain in his gray eyes.

"I'm sure I sound a lot like her. Can't spend five years with her without having something rub off. She always knows what to say."

"And always has." Ben cleared his throat. "I've

been thinking."

"Uh-oh. That's dangerous."

This time, Ben laughed. "Now you're starting to sound like Aeli."

"She's pretty infectious, too." Without pausing too long to ponder the consequences, Luke asked, "But tell me, what have you been thinking about?"

"Something June said yesterday about Carol. I was curious enough that I asked my sister when I dropped Becky off. I'll admit that I'm sometimes more curious than I should be, but I can't help myself. Anyhow, what Jane told me makes it much easier to see what the two of you might have in common because from what I saw… I couldn't see much. Don't get me wrong, Luke, and please don't think I'm prying. Carol seems like a really nice girl. And I was sixteen once, so I know at least one reason why you're interested. She's good-looking."

Luke forced a smile at Ben's attempt to lighten the conversation. This wasn't what he'd expected, but the wrong word could push the conversation into danger-ous territory. "Yeah, she is. But she's got a good heart, too. And I can imagine what Mom had to say that would make you curious."

"She thinks Carol might up and break your heart

like she broke her last boyfriend's. Which again makes me curious. How did you two end up dating in the first place? You seem like the kind of person who'd be bothered by how she broke up with her old boyfriend."

"Well, I didn't know what happened until after she'd asked me out the second time. It bothered me a little when I first found out, but she'd apologized to Mike, and he was okay with that."

"She asked you out? Twice?"

Luke nodded. "I turned her down the first time. It was only two weeks after she and Mike broke up. I mean, c'mon. Mike Thompson's an all-star quarterback, and at the time, he was still a lot bigger than me." Mike's size hadn't played much of a role in his decision to tell Carol no, but it was a good point to use to diffuse some of the tension. Ben seemed to appreciate it, because he chuckled. "Plus, I actually like him. We're not really friends, but we get along pretty well, and you just don't screw your teammate like that. Not if you want to go to the state championship again."

"You play football? Any good?" Ben asked. There was a faint challenge in his voice.

"Good enough that I was nominated for the all-star award my sophomore year and awarded it this year."

"Wow. I played, but I was just okay. I was better at soccer. So, you turned Carol down."

"Yeah. But then Mike told me it was cool between them and that if I wanted to date her, he wouldn't mind. He had a new girlfriend by then, so I thought, why not? I liked her."

"And you had a rather unusual fact in common."

Luke silently begged Ben not to say it.

"You both lost a parent around the same age."

Dammit, Luke thought. "Technically, I'd lost two by that age. My mother overdosed when I was five after my little brother died from a heart defect no one knew about. It was nice to have someone to relate to, but that's not why Carol and I get along so well. Once you get to know her, there's a lot more to like than you might think. It just takes her a while to open up. The people she should have been able to trust and count on left her. Her father killed himself and her mother ran off with some globe-trotting writer-photographer."

"At least she had family left. You didn't."

"And I think I'm better off for that," Luke replied. He clenched his jaw, wincing when his teeth ground together. "I have June."

"That's what Jane said. And I'll agree that June is an incredible woman, but good God, Luke, I know it must've been horrible to be ripped away from your father like that. He was your *father*."

Luke thought he was going to be sick. Just the mention of his father sent chills through his entire body and set nausea to bubbling. Without a word, he stood and walked away, leaving Ben to stare after him in utter confusion. He could feel the man's gaze boring into his back like rods of ice-cold steel.

"Luke! Wait!"

"Leave me alone, Ben!" he called back without turning around. "Just let me go!"

He had to go somewhere. Anywhere. He just needed to walk it off or ride it off. He needed to be alone to think or to clear his head of all thought. He strode around the cabin, opened the front door and grabbed his motorcycle helmet and the key to his dirt bike. He'd go for a ride, maybe down into the Sheep Field or up toward Comet Ridge Road. Or maybe he'd take the logging road just below the gate and stop at the switch back to stare out over the valley. It didn't matter where he went as long as he got away. As if he could actually leave his father behind simply by hopping on his bike.

His hands shook when he inserted the key into the ignition. The sight of his trembling fingers nearly undid him. He was sixteen, for God's sake! He wasn't eleven anymore. There were nearly five years and seven hundred miles between him and his father. With anger and fear boiling together in a vicious acid in his stomach, he slammed his foot down on the kick-start and the dirt bike snarled to life. Jamming his helmet on his head, he sped off down the driveway, riding faster than was smart around the switchbacks.

Before he knew it, he was on the logging road and slowing down at the overlook. He killed the bike, put the kickstand down, and walked over to a rock beyond the edge of the road. Sitting heavily, he dropped his head onto his knees and bellowed into the fabric of his jeans. Why had he been stupid enough to get into a conversation that could so easily turn the way it had? And why the hell did the memories of his father still have so much power over him? John McKindel had been dead for almost half a decade, and yet he seemed determined to haunt his son and try to destroy the happiness Luke had found since that night.

None of his anger was directed at Ben, and he wished he could tell him that. But he couldn't without telling him why, and obviously, he still wasn't able to do that.

With tension aching in his shoulders, Luke forced his breathing to slow and regulate. Hysteria never solved anything. All it did was give him a headache. So, he lifted his head and focused his gaze on the land below him. The Northstar Valley widened as it swept southward, bordered to his left by the eastern Northstar Mountains. The foothills and ridges and the lower western Northstars to his right were thickly blanketed with lodgepole pine and the occasional groves of quaking aspen. Snaking its way through the center of the valley and bordered by a patchwork of ranches, hayfields, and acres of rolling sagebrush flats was the Northstar Creek. Its path and those of its tributaries were easily traceable by the willows that crowded the year-round sources of water.

How long he stared down at the valley, he didn't know, but it didn't seem like very long before he heard the quiet rumble of a truck heading down the mountain. He glanced over his shoulder but couldn't see who it was through the trees. It had to be Ben, on his way to his interview at the Ramshorn. Luke was glad Ben hadn't decided to try to find him first, but he was also ashamed because he knew June would worry. Maybe he should head back to the cabin and call her to let her know he was okay before Ben told her what had happened. That he was fine—at least emotionally—was a lie, and June would see through it, but he should tell her he was otherwise whole and unharmed.

He climbed on his dirt bike and rode slowly home.

The sound of June's voice on the other end of the phone line sent a rush of serenity through him. Since the caller ID showed who was calling, she didn't bother with the Ramshorn's greeting.

"Please tell me Ben is on his way down here," she said.

"Don't worry. He is. He should be there in a few." He tried to keep his voice light, but even to his ears, he sounded tired.

"Why are you still home?" June asked, a note of concern in her voice.

"I, uh, had to go for a ride. Ben and I got into a conversation that wasn't very comfortable for me."

"Oh, honey. Are you all right?"

"I'm getting there. I'll be fine, Mom. I just wanted to call you so you wouldn't worry when Ben got there and told you I took off on my bike."

"I'm glad you did. Go relax. I'll see you in a couple hours."

"Love you, Mom."

"Love you, too, Luke."

Since the evening was pretty well shot, Luke fixed himself dinner, read for a little while, and went to bed early. He stared out the window at the darkening sky, dreading the night to come. Even before his eyes drifted closed, he felt it coming. The old nightmare slipped into his mind like a wraith, as cold and stealthy as an icy fog. Before he knew it, he was wrapped in its grip and powerless to stop it. The last five years peeled away, and he was eleven years old again, and back in Seattle in that small, dingy apartment…

"Come here, you worthless little rat!" John McKindel bellowed. His words were slurred, and the stench of alcohol hung on him like a second, sickening skin. *"You little chicken shit."*

Luke cowered in the corner, shielding his eyes from the sight of his father. He didn't want to see the leather belt curled around John's fist or see his father's face contorted by rage and something close to thrill. Luke yelped as the leather belt snapped on his skin. He pushed himself farther into the corner, pressing his small body hard against the wall, trying to escape his father's wrath. He searched frantically to remember what he'd done this time, but as usual, couldn't think of anything. The belt came down on him again and again. He lost track of how many times it bit him. He made himself as small as he could and simply endured the beating. One lash cracked against his ear and he cried out in pain.

"*Stop!*" Luke screamed.

"C'mon, kid, wake up."

When a hand gripped his shoulder, he jerked away.

"Easy, Luke. I'm not going to hurt you."

He thrashed awake. His blankets were tangled around his legs, trapping him. His skin was damp with icy sweat, and he couldn't seem to breathe right. His breaths were far too fast and shallow, his heart pounded, and his head spun. For a moment, the panic overwhelmed him, left him disoriented, caught between the past and the present. Outside his window, the sky glowed with millions of stars. There were too many glittering in that stunning blue-black arch to be Seattle's light-polluted sky. He wasn't in Seattle or in Washington at all. He was in Montana.

"Take a deep breath," a man murmured beside him. "Slow and easy."

Ben. The man who'd put an end to his real-life nightmare. Luke tried to draw a deep breath but choked. It wasn't until he felt Ben's hand on his shoulder again and saw the concern in the man's eyes that he was finally able to subvert the worst of his terror. He gulped in air, struggling to subdue the lingering panic.

"Are you all right now?"

Unable to speak, Luke only nodded.

Ben stepped across the room and lowered himself onto the spare bed. Now that he could breathe again, Luke realized he couldn't remember hearing Ben or June come home and wondered how late it was. Ben had obviously been asleep because his eyes were slanted as if he'd just woken up. Luke flipped his damp hair out of his face and looked out the window again, shivering. Despite the chill of his skin, he opened the window and let the cherished scents of his home wash through him. He forced his breathing to slow and deepen, willed his heart to stop racing.

"What was it about?" Ben asked in a soothing voice.

Luke closed his eyes. Could he really tell someone the truth about his father? Could he tell Ben, barely more than a stranger to him, that his father had abused him? He hadn't even told June, but he had to tell someone. He couldn't keep the secret locked inside anymore. It wasn't healthy.

"My father… the night he died, he was drunk," he started.

"I know. Luke, I only shot in self-defense. I didn't mean to take him away from you."

"You don't get it, Ben."

"What don't I get?"

"You remember the night you got here, when you walked into the Ramshorn and I shook your hand? You thought I was going to punch you." Luke sucked in a breath, and it caught in his throat as tears threatened. "What I wanted to do was hug you."

"You're right," Ben said. "I don't get it."

"You didn't take him away from me. You helped me get away from him. He was an alcoholic and used drugs… I don't know which ones, and I really don't care. He used to take his leather belt to me, and if he couldn't find it, he laid into me with his fists. He told me that I deserved it, that I was worthless, and I believed it." As he spoke, Luke stared at the foot of his bed with unfocused eyes. "I used to cry myself to sleep, hoping I wouldn't wake up in the morning. If I were dead, I wouldn't have to feel like a failure. I tried to be a good son. I thought that maybe if I worked harder, stayed quiet, and minded my behavior, he would stop, but he didn't."

Tears slipped hotly down his face. Luke didn't care. He looked over at Ben, and even with his watery eyes, could read the written plainly thoughts on Ben's face.

How could any man do that to his son, his own flesh and blood?

"Now I understand." Ben shook his head. His expression slid from shock to anger. "What a low-life piece of shit."

Luke pulled his knees up to his chest, folded his arms around his legs and cried silently. The fear, the pain, and the shame he'd felt for so much of his young life eddied and flowed through him like a restless, murky tide. Perhaps he should have outgrown the need to be comforted by his mother by now, but he wanted June to hold him and chase it all away. He wanted to be reminded that he was a good son, worth her love, but he couldn't find his voice to call out for her. And even if he could, what would he see in her eyes? Pity? Anything but that. He never wanted to see pity in her gaze because the distance that came with it would destroy him.

* * *

Neither of them noticed June watching from the doorway. She stood with her hand covering her mouth and her eyes wide as she listened to Luke's story, fighting the instinct to rush to his side, gather him in her arms, and hold him until the nightmare faded away like she had so many times before. She had almost given in when she'd heard Luke cry out in his sleep, but Ben had already been at the teen's side, trying to wake him, and June had hesitated. Intuition told her that this was something Luke and Ben both needed to have out in the open.

When Luke folded his arms around his legs, she gave in to instinct and sat down next to him, pulling him into her arms as if he were a child of six instead of sixteen. He trembled and grabbed a handful of her flannel in his fist, and it was all she could do to keep her own tears from falling.

Luke had never told her about his father, but she knew. Before she'd met him, Bill had explained his suspicions, and she had seen the proof—the rainbow-hued, fading bruises on his back and arms and the healing cut on his cheek. She'd known, yes, but to hear him confirm it was like a bullet to her heart. Worse, it tore at her to know that he'd kept it all to himself because he'd been ashamed, that he'd believed the lie that he was worthless. Fury bubbled and seethed at how completely John McKindel had hurt her son. *My son*, she repeated to herself, wishing she could've somehow protected him from his father.

"Shh," she whispered in his ear. "I'm here. You're safe, and I love you. Go back to sleep, sweetheart."

As June combed her fingers through Luke's hair, she lifted her gaze to meet Ben's. There was anger and disgust burning in his eyes but not a trace of guilt or shame. Right at that moment, if given the opportunity, June believed he'd gladly kill John McKindel again.

She waited until she was sure Luke was asleep before gently laying him down and straightening his blankets. When she tucked them around him, she smiled a little, grateful that there was so much more of him to tuck in than there had been almost five years ago. Listening to him had brought the memories of his first weeks with her too close to the surface, and she shuddered to recall how small and fragile he'd been. She tried not to think about how much longer he would have survived in his father's house had fate not intervened.

"You heard everything, didn't you?" Ben asked.

"Every word."

"I think that judge made a wise decision when he entrusted you with Luke's care."

"She. And she almost didn't. She had reservations,

not so much about me but about sending Luke to Montana. Luke changed her mind when he said he wanted to stay with me. I was already licensed to be a foster parent, so the whole process was remarkably quick and smooth. That was July. I had only planned to foster him until a more permanent solution could be found, but as it turns out, this was the permanent solution."

"How long have you suspected he was abused? And don't tell me you didn't."

"Bill told me before I even met Luke that he suspected abuse. Back in May of that year, Bill was on a rare patrol and headed to Luke's house out by the bridge. Some neighbors had called in a noise complaint and a possible domestic dispute. Luke's scalp had been laid open with something sharp—my guess is a belt buckle." She ran her fingers through Luke's hair again and parted it to reveal the long, thick white scar an inch above his right ear. Ben's sharp intake of air was clearly audible in the quiet room. "It took twelve stitches. John needed three for a split lip, and his shoulder was dislocated. His story—and for whatever reason, Luke went along with it—was that they'd been roughhousing, and Luke had tripped and fallen into the glass coffee table. A social worker asked some questions, and

Bill kept an eye on them, but since Luke wouldn't talk about it, nothing was proven. I think John had the split lip and dislocated shoulder because Luke fought back. There were other clues pointing to abuse. Luke missed school a lot, but there were no medical records to say why. After Bill left the scene of the shooting, he went straight to Luke's house and found him unconscious on his bedroom floor. I saw for myself the bruises on his back and arms. There was also a cut on his cheek. When asked about that, Luke said he'd gotten into a fight at school."

"But there weren't any records of a fight, were there?"

"No." June narrowed her eyes and paused for a moment. "What do you remember about that night? About John McKindel?"

"I was thinking about calling you after my shift ended when the drunk and disorderly call came over the radio. He staggered out of the convenience store as I pulled up, and he pulled a gun on me when I got out to greet him. A ricochet grazed my leg."

Ben absently rubbed his thumb across the scar just above his knee. Even in the pale starlight, June could see it clearly and again cursed John McKindel.

"I aimed to disable him… and shot him in the

chest instead when he stumbled. After that... I remember seeing Luke at the station. I really remember *that* but very little else. I know Bill told me about McKindel, but I don't remember much of what he told me. Only about Luke being his son. And being an orphan because of what I'd done."

"It never occurred to you to ask why John McKindel had a gun on him? Or why he'd be stupid enough to use it?"

Ben frowned, shook his head. "I was too screwed up to think of anything past what I'd done."

"He was high. Bill had a rather long list of drugs they found in his system. That's what Luke knew until that night. Abuse, alcohol, and drugs. Not a happy picture, is it?"

"No. It's not."

"Do you understand now why you shouldn't regret what you did?"

Ben nodded slowly, smirking with what June thought looked like self-contempt. "It makes it easier, knowing I didn't kill a winner of the Father of the Year award."

"Luke is happy here, Ben. And I don't think happiness was an emotion he knew much about until he left Washington."

"No, I suppose not. Jane's right, then. Luke wasn't afraid of being torn away from everything he knew. He was afraid of what he knew."

"Exactly. What you did wasn't so bad, Ben. In fact, what you did might well have saved his life, so the next time you start thinking about how horrible a person you are for killing a man, maybe you should consider instead what good came of it. And I can tell you, Ben, a lot of good came from it. And not just for Luke. My life has been so much better for having him in it. I didn't give birth to him, but he *is* my son."

Ben's eyes glittered with relief and gratitude, and June decided that now he could finally begin to heal. Nearly five years of thinking he was a monster was going to be a hard habit to break, but he *would* break it.

"He's sleeping now, so I'm going back to bed," June said and returned to her room without waiting for his response.

As she slid under the covers of her bed, June allowed herself to give in to her emotions. She'd been strong for them both when they needed her, but now she had to let it out. Even she couldn't make everyone else's anguish go away without feeling the effects. She curled into a ball and cried. Her tears were for the pain Luke had endured and kept to himself, for the guilt

Ben had mired himself needlessly in for so long, and for the untarnished peace she knew could now begin to weave around them all.

Seven

BEN DIDN'T SLEEP well that night. But, for the first time in almost five years, it wasn't because nightmares about the shooting ravaged his slumbers. Instead of guilt and despair, anger churned his blood. Rather than return to the couch downstairs, Ben had climbed into the spare bed, as if his presence in the room would shield Luke from his nightmares. As he alternately stared out the window at the starlit night and watched the steady, peaceful rise and fall of Luke's chest as the boy slept, Ben tried to comprehend what he'd learned about John McKindel. The distorted, nightmarish blur that was his memory of the night of the shooting had suddenly popped clear as if the fog, which had allowed him to see only glimpses in any clarity, had vanished on a storm gale. He hadn't realized just how incorrect his recollection was.

John McKindel hadn't been the doting father Ben had imagined. Very far from it. When he considered what June and Luke had told him, he wondered how he'd ever come to such a conclusion about the man. Why on earth hadn't he bothered to ask himself why someone he'd assumed was—at the very least—a decent man had brought a gun on a simple errand? Not only brought a gun but used it with every intent to kill.

Ben knew exactly why he'd painted such a picture. Luke. He'd seen the terror and innocence in a young boy's blue eyes and assumed it was the result of grief, of staring into the face of a bleak, lonely, and uncertain future. He'd built his idea of John McKindel around that single, hideously false theory. And he'd wrapped that notion tightly around himself like a blindfold. Or a burial shroud. He'd been so consumed by his assumption that he'd been unable to see the truth, and the way he'd broken down and retreated into himself, he may as well have been dead because he certainly hadn't been living.

Five years of his life he'd wasted wallowing in unwarranted misery over a piece of garbage exactly like those he'd arrested on a regular basis. How had Luke survived all those years? Would the fear ever completely leave his eyes? Would that scar ever fade away? Ben felt sick to his stomach thinking about it.

Restless and edgy, Ben slid out of bed and padded out of the room. Pausing to look over the balcony, he noted that the cabin was still dark and wondered what time it was. He headed downstairs, deciding a glass of water was in order. He doubted it would wash the bitter taste out of his mouth, but it was worth a try.

Just as he reached the bottom step, light flooded the kitchen from the utility room, and he froze. His breath lodged in his throat when June stepped out of the bathroom, wrapped in a towel that revealed quite a lot of soft, damp skin. Rivulets ran tantalizingly down her back and chest, tempting Ben to follow their trails with his lips. God above, she was a beautiful woman. There was feminine grace and elegance and patient, enduring strength in every glorious line of her slim, athletic body. His fingers itched to trace a path from her finely angled jaw, down her graceful neck, and over her proud shoulders, or up her long, attractive legs, over that firm, well-shaped rear and up her gorgeous back.

He watched her from the shadows, too breathless and awestruck to move and too engrossed to avert his eyes. The voice telling him that this was his childhood friend was muted, nearly drowned out by another voice excitedly complimenting June's very grown-up physique. He'd seen more of her at the Ramshorn the other day, but this was more intimate. There was nothing but woman under that towel, which could easily fall open at any moment.

He stared at her as if he'd never seen a woman before, and his heart pounded as she walked toward him, flipping on the kitchen light as she made her way closer. She didn't see him until she was at the stairs. When she lifted her gaze and found him only inches away, her eyes popped wide and her hand went to her heart.

"You scared the shit out of me, Ben!" she hissed.

Her chest heaved in a most distracting way in her surprise, so Ben raised his gaze to her eyes… only to be swallowed by them. Her pupils dilated and became pools of black so large he could scarcely see the thread-thin rim of dusky-blue around them. What little of his brain that wasn't already consumed by her body was transfixed by the water droplets glittering in her lashes.

"Likewise, June," he murmured. He brushed away

a drop of water that slid down her cheek from a wayward lock of her hair, letting his hand linger against her cool skin.

June inhaled sharply but leaned into his touch. When she turned her face up to him, her eyes wide with innocent desire, Ben gave in to temptation. He took her mouth slowly and tenderly, first just touching his lips to hers. When she opened her mouth in surprise, he deepened the kiss. She tasted like heaven. As he curled his fingers around her neck, stroking her cheek with his thumb, she knitted her hands in his hair, offering the sweetest pleasure and asking for the same in return. The feel of her lithe body pressed against him was exquisite ecstasy, more powerful than he'd ever known. And it was only a taste, a mere hint of sensual oblivion.

Ben pulled away with a sudden understanding of what he was doing. June was his friend, and he couldn't take advantage of her like this, even though his body—and apparently hers—wanted him to. He wanted to take her in his arms, kiss her senseless, and spend the time to properly finish what they'd started, but he couldn't. He wouldn't jeopardize their friendship just for a few moments of thoughtless pleasure.

"I'm sorry. It won't happen again," he whispered.

"Unless you want it to."

"And if I do?"

Without warning, she yanked his head down and kissed him daringly. He'd never been kissed like that. She was bold and curious at the same time, awakening a passion Ben had never imagined existed. Every cell in his body was alive and singing with more than physical want. In those moments, all of him belonged to June, and he eagerly submitted to her will.

She pulled away slowly and brushed her fingertips gently along his jaw. Then she smiled and slipped past him up the stairs, leaving him shivering with raw desire and a wealth of emotions too new for him to name. New and wonderful. Whatever this feeling was, he wanted more of it.

After a moment, he followed her upstairs, intending to make the spare bed. There was no hope of finding sleep now. He paused outside Luke's room, hearing soft voices.

"Don't apologize, Luke. You have absolutely nothing to be sorry for."

"I should've told you."

"You didn't have to. I've always known, and I knew you'd tell me when you were ready. I'm just worried about you."

"I'm okay. Better, actually. I think talking about it—finally—helped."

"I'm glad. Now, get up, and I'll fix you breakfast. Ben can do the dishes."

Tender affection for them both lifted Ben's lips, disallowing any resentment he might have felt for being volunteered to do dishes. Something had changed since last night. Hearing the truth about Luke's father had somehow altered Ben's role in the situation. Rather than worrying over the teenager's uncertain fate, Ben now felt a strong protectiveness as if he was now obligated to continue what he'd started that night when he'd shot John McKindel, to ensure that Luke remained happy and safe.

His affection for June had always been there, since their friendship had first blossomed in childhood, but since his arrival in Northstar, new facets had been cut into their relationship. He could argue the matter until he was blue in the face, but she was no longer *just* his friend. The years *had* changed their friendship, but all those years of separation had not affected as much change as the time since he'd come home to Northstar… or as much as the last few hours. What had once been the comfortable familiarity of knowing nearly everything about one another had shifted, woven now with a newness that held such intrigue and potential of new memories to be made and a new comfort and familiarity to be found. What June was to him now and what she might become was something he'd dearly like to explore.

Ben cleared his throat. "If you're going to make breakfast on a weekday, June, I won't even complain about doing the dishes. But do I really have to get dressed?"

"I suppose you can lounge around in your boxers," she replied with a suggestive wiggle of her eyebrows.

Ben's faced warmed. Maybe he *should* get dressed. Breakfast would probably be awkward enough without throwing embarrassment into the mix. He snatched his flannel off the post of the headboard where he'd left it last night. As he headed back downstairs, he buttoned it, thinking again about what he'd learned. He sincerely hoped his relationship with Luke—such as it was— would not become more strained. He'd witnessed the boy at his most vulnerable and didn't know how Luke would feel around him now. If Luke didn't treat it like an invasion of privacy, they had a chance to create an open, honest friendship and an opportunity to help one another move past their interwoven traumas. Ben was a little surprised by how strongly he wanted that.

"So, Luke is feeling much lighter this morning," June said as she joined him in the kitchen. "How about you?"

"Pretty good. Better than I have since the shooting, actually."

It was the truth. He didn't feel so smothered anymore. "I've still got a long ways to go before I feel entirely like myself again, if I'm ever able to, but it's nice to be able to take a deep breath again."

June paused in her breakfast preparations to kiss his cheek. "It's about damned time."

She didn't add anything else, but she didn't need to. She couldn't have said anything truer or more appropriate, and her blunt statement had Ben smiling. Truly smiling, with his whole being.

When Luke all but bounced down the stairs into the kitchen moments later, it was clear to Ben that breakfast wasn't going to be awkward at all. Life on the mountain was going to be a lot more relaxed from now on.

* * *

By the time the day was over and Luke pulled up in front of the cabin, June was clinging to the lingering rush of heat and excitement Ben's kiss had stirred to keep the weariness at bay. She'd let Luke drive home so she could get a head start on her grading but thinking about the way Ben's lips had felt against hers and the way he'd submitted to her wants was even more distracting than the sleepiness that weighed down her eyelids. She'd been distracted by the memory all day. Not that there'd been much else to think about. Today, she considered that one of the downsides of finals. While the students were taking their tests, she'd had little else to do with her time but keep an eye out for cheating and try not to blush as she thought about kissing Ben… and all the other things she wanted to do to him.

The man so pervasively centered in her mind was waiting on the front porch, looking quite sexy in his worn blue jeans and plain white t-shirt. In the afternoon light, his dark hair shone with a touch of deep, red-brown highlights, and she had the urge to bury her fingers in it again. That could wait. It would have to because she had too much work to do, and if she was honest with herself, she was too wrung out from last night to be adding one more complication to the mix. A good roll in the sack or the woods or wherever might feel good—great, if their kisses this morning were any indication—but neither she nor Ben were the kind of people who could take sex so casually.

"How was school?" Ben greeted as she and Luke climbed out of the truck.

"Other than having to take tests all day… pretty good," Luke answered. "I think I aced my physics final. Biology and English, too. I'll have trig, geology and U.S. history tomorrow."

"Did I hear you right? Physics, biology, geology and trig?" Ben inquired.

"Yup."

"Are you trying to give yourself a stroke?"

Luke chuckled. "I'd rather push myself than let my brain sit at idle."

"Now, who does that sound like?" Ben's gaze settled on June, and the warmth in his eyes made her heart flutter deliciously. "And how was your day, June?"

"I have finals to grade tonight," she said sourly. She made a face and whimpered. "I'd ask Luke if he'd help, but he has to take his geology final tomorrow, and that's one I have to grade."

"Luke is in one of your classes?"

"Yes, I am," Luke rejoined. "Two actually. I'm also in her biology class."

"And he's my best student. I'm proud of him," June said, reaching up and tousling his hair. He ducked away from her hand with a chuckle and trotted into the cabin. She stared after him for a moment with a wistful smile. It never failed to amaze her how far he'd come, though his dramatic growth was an unmistakable reminder. The terror he'd lived through and the memories that continued to torment him broke her heart, but those shadows rarely darkened his eyes anymore, and that was something. The skittish, quiet boy was gone, replaced by an athletic, charming, and well-adjusted teenager with hope for a bright future.

"I take it this is the end of school?"

"Friday is the last day. The rest of my finals are tomorrow, so I get to relax the rest of the week. Once I get everything graded, that is."

"I got all the chores done. What do you want me to do next?"

June studied Ben for a moment. There was something about his expression that made her wonder if he'd been listening in on her thoughts. He held her gaze, almost begging her to step away from her distressing musings. "Take the rest of the day off, if you want."

"Or I could help grade the finals. Maybe I could correct the multiple choice if you have a key," Ben offered.

June sighed, grateful for both the offer and the distraction. "Sure. I'd love the help. Maybe, if we get done early, we'll have the O'Neils over for cards after dinner."

He nodded and followed her inside. Luke was sprawled on the floor with his schoolbooks in a semi-circle around him, poring over his notes. June dropped her work on the kitchen table and grabbed two root beers out of the refrigerator for Ben and herself. Next, she pulled out the geology exams and the matching key for the multiple choice, handing both to him.

"If it's wrong, put an X on the correct answer and a slash through the number of the question. It's that easy," June said as she sat down across from him with her back to the kitchen door. "I'll do the rest. When you're done with that, you can work on the biology exams." She pointed to the other pile she'd plopped on the table. The key was sitting on top.

How long it took them, June didn't know, but at some point Luke put a CD in the stereo. Shortly thereafter, June switched tests with Ben.

They were both surprised when they finished grading the finals by suppertime. It was only after the papers had been stored in June's bag that they got their first whiff of something delicious cooking. Ben stretched in the chair and looked over at the stove as if he expected to see dinner cooking itself. June nearly laughed at the shock on his face as Luke walked over to the table with a pot of spaghetti in one hand and a bowl of salad in the other.

"You two had your noses buried so deep in papers I thought you might completely forget dinner," Luke announced as he pulled the plates and silverware out and set the table. "And I wasn't about to let myself starve," he added. His lips quirked with amusement as he seated himself in the chair by the window.

"Yes, Ben, he knows how to cook," June said when Ben continued to stare at the teenager with his mouth hanging half open. "And he's pretty good at it, too."

After dinner, June and Ben did the dishes while Luke ran over to Pat and Aelissm's to invite them over for a card night. While she absently scrubbed a plate, June wondered if it was wise to play cards on a school night. She hadn't slept much last night, and though today hadn't been exactly strenuous, neither had it been a vacation. Tomorrow would be the same, and besides, Luke had finals to take. He didn't need to be staying up until the dark hours of the morning. On the other hand, after last night, she needed the release a card night with the O'Neils never failed to provide, and Luke could probably ace his finals in his sleep.

"You're frowning," Ben remarked as he put the last dish away.

June started attacking the splattering of spaghetti sauce on the stove before she answered. "It's a school night. Not only that, it's finals week, and instead of making sure Luke gets plenty of rest, I'm providing him with the permission and the means to stay up half the night."

Ben's lips curved upward and his eyes glittered. "Shame on you, June. I thought teachers were supposed to preach good study habits."

"I *do* preach them, but tonight, I'm choosing not to practice them." She turned to face him, but kept her gaze trained on the dishrag in her hand for a moment. Taking a deep breath, she lifted her eyes and found him watching her with contented amusement painted across his face. She didn't want to chase it away, but she needed to tell him something that would. "I've always known Luke was abused, but it was much harder to hear him say it than I would've thought. I want to thank you for helping him last night."

"I don't know that I helped much, June."

"You did. You cared enough to ask about the

nightmare." She inhaled deeply, irritated when her breath snagged in her throat. "I'm usually much better at handling things, but…."

"When someone you love hurts, you hurt, too."

His matter-of-fact statement helped wash away the anxiety, and she smiled gratefully.

"It's one of the traits I've always admired about you," Ben added. He laid a hand against he face and stroked her cheek with his thumb. "One of many."

June started when the back door opened. Ben looked over his shoulder but didn't move away.

"Well, well, well," Aelissm remarked as she stepped inside with her daughter in her arms and her husband a step behind her. "What's this we've interrupted?"

"A moment of weakness," June replied softly.

"So I see."

"Not *that* kind of weakness, Aeli." A faint smile tugged at her mouth. "Not really, anyhow."

"Uh-huh."

"Aeli, my love, you're a terror," Pat chided. He offered June a look of sympathy. "Luke told us about last night. So, you were right that he was abused."

June nodded. "But I can honestly say I wish I was wrong."

"So do I, June. But he has a warm, loving home now, and that's the best thing you could give him. I offered to listen if he ever wants to talk, but I don't think he needs it. He'll be just fine, thanks to you."

"Thank you, Pat," she whispered. She swallowed the lump in her throat and straightened her back. This was supposed to be a fun evening to help her forget last night, and she would not ruin it by crying. "Speaking of my son, where is he? And where's Ant?"

"They're coming. Ant wanted to show him the new bird feeder Aeli built."

June grabbed a deck of cards from a drawer in the snack bar, and they took their seats around the table. She divided the deck for euchre first since there were four of them and who knew how long it would take Ant to show off the new bird feeder. As they played, the tension began to slip out of June. The nagging exhaustion melted away with it, and she wallowed in the comfort of an evening spent with her closest friends.

They were just finishing up a second game of euchre when the back door opened again. Luke lifted Ant down from his shoulders before entering. He complimented Aelissm on her latest project—Ant's prized bird feeder—and joined them at the table. Ant promptly took his place in Luke's lap and looked at everyone expectantly.

"I gonna play," the toddler announced.

"How about you and I play together?" Luke asked. "I think I might need some help tonight."

"Okay!"

"So, who won?" Luke asked as he helped Pat and Ben distribute the chips for poker.

"Boys won the first game, we won the second," Aelissm replied, giving Iris to Pat. "Who wants what to drink?"

June added the rest of the cards to the deck, then got up to help Aelissm bring drinks and snacks to the table. She nearly laughed at the sight of Ben, Pat, and Luke making fools of themselves over Ant and Iris, crossing their eyes, sticking out their tongues, and uttering all sorts of odd noises in an attempt to get Iris to smile and make Ant laugh. June nudged Aeli and inclined her head at them.

"And they say women are fools over babies," she remarked.

"See, June, we're fools over babies," Aelissm responded. "Whereas they're just fools."

"Hey!" Pat, Ben, and Luke chorused.

"You're just jealous because Iris is smiling at us and not you," Pat retorted.

"That's my girl," Aelissm said with pride and affection thick in her voice. "Not quite two months old yet, and she's already got the three best-looking men in the valley wrapped around her finger."

"Aw, shucks, Aeli," Ben replied. "You're going to make us blush."

"And then she'll insult us about it," Luke said. "Won't you, Aunt Aeli?"

"I gotta get my licks in when I can," she agreed.

"You can lick me anytime, sweetheart," Pat teased.

Luke groaned and rolled his eyes. "You know, I have finals to take tomorrow, and I'd rather not be lying awake all night thinking about *that*, thank you. I still have nightmares about flute music and feathers."

June tried to hold it in but giggles spilled out when Aelissm and Pat both turned several very interesting shades of pink. When Ben turned a confused gaze on her, then looked between Pat, Aeli, and Luke, she collapsed into her chair, unable to stand in her fit of laughter.

"What am I missing?" Ben asked when no one explained.

"Pat and Aeli's first… romantic liaison. We'd all hiked up to Sawtooth Lake to spend the night. I'll spare you the details, but Luke and I woke up to find the feathers of Aelissm's pillow scattered all around our campsite."

Ben raised his eyebrows at the couple. "I'm guessing Luke saw a bit more than either of you intended. What about the flute music?"

"Pat plays the pan flute. That's what woke me up. To phrase it how Aunt Aeli might," Luke said, "they were making out like a couple of horny teenagers."

"Wow. Sawtooth seems to be the place for that," Ben remarked. "My parents mentioned something like that once. And my sister."

"Apparently, that's also where Will Hammond, Nick's son, was conceived," Aelissm added.

"Yep, there goes all hope of getting any sleep tonight," Luke muttered.

"Let's play cards," June suggested. She handed the deck to Aelissm. "You can deal."

Antes were tossed to the center of the table, the cards were dealt, and the game began.

"Starting bets anyone?" Pat asked. "Or did Aelissm deal another one of her infamous everyone-folds-hands?" He grunted when his wife elbowed him in the side, and he stuck his tongue out at her. When she grabbed him by the chin and kissed him firmly, his cheeks flared red.

Luke started the betting at ten, and while everyone met it, no one raised. Cards were exchanged and the heavy betting commenced. At thirty, June dropped out, at thirty-five, Aelissm and Pat called it quits, leaving Ben and Luke to fight it out. Ben called at seventy.

"Full house," Luke said, displaying his hand. "A triad of aces and a pair of twos."

"Two pair, queen high," Ben replied. "Good hand."

Ant squealed and clapped his hands.

"Wuke won! Wuke won!" he chanted.

The night continued on with Luke winning the majority of the hands. When he did lose, he didn't lose much. Ben was the first one out. June was next, then Pat. It was a while before Luke finally beat Aelissm in one big pot. By that time, both Ant and Iris were sound asleep, and it was edging toward early morning.

"Well, we'd better get these little monsters home," Aelissm said, taking Antony from Luke. "Good night, all."

June saw them to the door after telling Luke to get up to bed. After closing the door behind her friends, June returned to the table to help Ben clean up. Being alone with him in the kitchen brought the memories of their kisses racing back to the forefront of her mind. It was hard not to stand back and watch him move about her kitchen. Beautiful was not a word she often associated with men, but the easy grace and unconscious strength that radiated from him was exactly that.

"Good night, June," Ben said when everything had been stowed.

"Good night, Ben."

She was tempted to head upstairs without so much as a backward glance. The relaxing evening had gone a long way to settling her rattled heart, but she wasn't sure she was steady enough to handle a repeat of this morning, even though she really wanted one. The desire that had been her constant shadow throughout the day flared at the promise of kissing Ben again.

To hell with it, she thought. *If we always waited until we were ready, there'd be a lot that would never get accomplished. I wasn't ready to be a mother at twenty-four, but look how wonderfully that's turned out.*

She touched her lips lightly to Ben's, tentatively testing her composure. Then, as he stroked his fingers along her jaw, asking for more, she tucked her body against his and deepened the kiss. He released her hair from its confining bun and slid his fingers through it.

She moaned low in her throat when pleasure rippled from her scalp down her neck and shoulders.

"Sweet angel," he whispered against her lips. He leaned away for a moment and smiled gently. His eyes were so warm and so full of passion. Aelissm had told her, more than once, that there few aphrodisiacs in the world more powerful than seeing that primal hunger and being the reason for it. Until now, June had brushed it off, but she couldn't ignore the rising heat or the growing confidence and daring that came with.

She trailed her lips across his cheek. "Kiss me again," she whispered into his ear.

He claimed her mouth once again, starting with a blissful tenderness, and caressed her cheek with his thumb. He pulled away only to turn his gentle attentions to her neck, tracing a path down and around her jaw to the hollow of her throat. She arched against him, and he moved his hands to the small of her back to support her. He nuzzled her neck as he massaged her back, sliding his fingers up and down the ridge of her spine. She shuddered and kneaded his shoulders, grabbing fistfuls of his shirt as he sent her into ecstasy with his delicate touches.

By the time they broke apart, June was breathless and wide-eyed.

"You need sleep, June," he murmured. "And I'm losing control."

With a nod, she obeyed the unspoken command and stepped away. She ascended the stairs slowly, her heart pounding and her mind drifting with the stars. She absently undressed for bed and climbed under the covers with her senses reeling and Ben's kiss lingering on her lips. Just when she'd thought she'd recovered solid ground, she was trembling again but for an entirely different reason than last night. And she had no intention of fighting it.

* * *

In the morning, she woke early, feeling refreshed and oddly alive. The world outside the coziness of the cabin was dark, and above the canopy of lodgepole pines, the stars glimmered in the indigo arch of sky. Silently, she pulled on her flannel to defend herself against the chill of the early morning and crept down the stairs and out the back door. Cheyenne joined her. June said nothing to the dog but acknowledged her presence by burying her hand in the golden retriever's warm coat. She listened to the sounds of the forest as the nocturnal animals finished up their nightly rounds and returned to their roosts.

If she had been at her mother's house in Western

Washington, it wouldn't have been so quiet. The sounds of suburbia drowned out the natural sounds of even the wee hours of the morning. Out here, miles away from the closest town of any size, no mechanical or man-made sounds disturbed the peace.

Sensing a presence, she looked over her shoulder to see a bobbing globe of light coming down the stairs. It had to be Ben. Luke knew his way around the house well enough to go without a light, and he rarely got up in the middle of the night to snoop around. She puzzled over what Ben was doing up so early. Even she was up earlier than normal.

He stepped out onto the back porch, pulling on one of Luke's flannels. "I didn't think he'd mind," he said when June cast him an inquiring glance.

"That wasn't what I was thinking. I was wondering why you were out here. It's barely four in the morning," she said in a quiet voice. "We just got to bed a few hours ago."

"I woke up about an hour ago and couldn't sleep. I heard you get up, so I thought I'd come down and talk. You don't mind, do you?"

Part of her wanted to be alone with the serenity of the morning, but another section of her brain decided differently. "No, it's all right. You aren't interrupting anything."

He sat down beside her. "Are you sure? I remember how you used to sit outside by yourself if it was a sunny day, and if anyone bothered you, you either gave them the cold shoulder treatment or you told them in no uncertain terms that you wanted to think and they were disrupting that process."

"Did I really do that?"

"Yes. More than once, you told me to scoot. What changed your mind this time?"

"I honestly don't know."

He slid an arm around her shoulders, and she let herself be pulled into the warmth of his body. He said no more and asked no more questions, so the quiet of the hour returned once again and June was content to rest against him. She nodded off, utterly relaxed in his arms.

It seemed like only moments later when a gentle tap on her shoulder brought her back to consciousness. She looked up to see Luke standing above them with his arms folded across his chest. When she took stock of the situation and realized she was still wrapped in Ben's arms and that he was still asleep, her face flushed.

"Breakfast is ready," Luke said simply and went

back inside.

Was that a smile she'd seen on his face?

Eight

"YOU DIDN'T HAVE to bring me lunch, but thanks. I really appreciate it."

"Any time, kiddo," JP told his niece as she slid into the truck. He handed her the McDonalds's sack and the chocolate milkshake he'd bought her. "How're your tests going?"

"Ugh. I don't want to talk about it," she replied. "I just had to listen to Luke and Becky go on about how well they did. I'll be lucky if I get a C on my U.S. History final."

"I'm sure you'll do better than that."

"I hope so. I'd like to pass at least one class with an A."

They slipped into companionable silence as they ate their greasy cheeseburgers and fries. JP studied his niece for a few moments, deciding on the best way to broach a subject he was certain she was going to buck against. He needed her cooperation, and one wrong word would destroy any hope of success. She was a pretty girl with her mother's rich auburn curls and smooth, radiant skin and her father's kind green eyes. It wasn't really surprising that both Mike and Luke were smitten with her. Of course, her hair and skin weren't the only things she'd inherited from her whore of a mother, JP thought with disgust. She was also a heartbreaker, though at least she didn't enjoy causing pain like Cheryl did. JP frowned. She didn't set out to hurt people, but she certainly didn't choose to soothe someone else's heart when her own was in jeopardy. Mike was proof of that, and if JP could manage it, Luke would be, too.

The problem was, Carol was much more deeply involved with Luke than she'd ever been with Mike. JP wasn't sure if a survivor like her was capable of love, but if she was, he'd say she loved Luke. It was going to take a lot of smooth talking and coercion to make her dump him. Then there was the issue of her getting hurt. The weak side of him rebelled against the idea of bringing her harm, even temporary emotional anguish, but JP rationalized that it was a necessary cost. Besides, Paul was dead partially because of her. He'd loved his daughter so much that the thought of losing her had driven him to suicide.

She glanced out the window, frowning momentarily when her gaze fell on her boyfriend and Andy Epperson's daughter. JP wondered if convincing her wouldn't be easier than he'd suspected. Could it really be so simple? If she thought Luke was turning away from her in favor of someone else, it wouldn't be difficult at all to appeal to her instincts.

"Isn't that little Rebecca Epperson talking with Luke?"

"Yes." Under her breath, she muttered, "Not so little anymore, though."

JP thought he detected a thread of irritation in his niece's voice and nearly smiled. "I didn't know they were friends."

"They weren't until a few weeks ago. But they're just friends."

"Are you sure about that?"

She didn't answer. Instead, she reached for

another French fry and nibbled at it, all the while watching her boyfriend and his companion.

"They seem pretty… close." When she looked at him, he gave her a sympathetic smile. "I just don't want to see you get hurt, Carol. And I wouldn't put it past him to break your heart."

"He won't, Unkie."

She'd called him that since she was a small child, though she only used the term now when she was preoccupied or worried. Her use of the nickname nearly made him reconsider his plan., but he steeled his resolve and proceeded cautiously.

"I wouldn't be so sure, sweetie. That's what your father thought about your mother."

"My mother is a heartless slut."

"I just worry about you. It's my job." He paused. "I talked to Mike the other day. Seems he's still quite in love with you. I never worried about *him* hurting you."

"I know how you feel about Mike. I also know that you don't like Luke as much."

I don't like him at all, JP corrected. "I just think you should consider moving on before it's too late. It's high school, anyhow. You're too young to be tied down to one boy."

"But you'd have me go back to Mike."

"Well, I like him. And he's got a lot going for him." JP paused, his attention momentarily diverted by the scene that held his niece so enthralled. Austin McGuire's boy, Shane, had joined Luke and Becky. A delicious thought came into his head, and he nearly laughed at the genius of it. "There's also Shane McGuire. He's a good, hard-working boy, and I know he's always had a thing for you. And he's good looking, isn't he?"

She blushed, and he was a little surprised to learn that Shane had crossed her mind already. Wouldn't that be just perfect? He didn't have to imagine the pain of being dumped for one's best friend. It had happened to him in high school. The shock and the sense of betrayal had been a knife to the heart. He wished he'd thought about it sooner.

"Shane would never go out with me, Unkie, even if I wanted to go out with him. He's Luke's best friend."

"Ah, I forgot about that old rule." He patted her leg. "Just be careful and keep your eyes open. I'll bet you there's more between Luke and Becky than you think."

"You're wrong."

"Just promise me you'll be careful, just in case I'm not."

"All right, I will. I'd better go. Lunch is almost over. Thanks again, Unkie."

"Good luck with the rest of your tests."

He watched her join her boyfriend and noted with smug satisfaction the stiffness about her as Luke leaned down to kiss her cheek. The seeds of doubt had been planted, and with a few more careful words here and there, she'd start to see things his way. JP was fairly confident that his goal would be accomplished by Friday, the last day of school. Right on schedule. And to think, he'd been in a panic Monday when Carol had complained to him that it was finals week, fearing that his window of greatest opportunity was about to slam shut. Laughing softly, he pulled away from the high school.

* * *

Luke freely admitted that he liked school and took the ribbing about being a geek in stride, but even he was relieved summer vacation was finally within reach. It was Friday, the final day of his junior year, and though the day had only just begun minutes ago, he was in a splendid mood. As of this afternoon, he was free from tests and homework for three solid months and had every intention of spending that time hiking, riding his dirt bike, lazing around the cabin and working down at the Ramshorn.

"Oh, c'mon, Luke. You know you're gonna miss it," Shane remarked as they completed their final inspection of their shared locker. His brown eyes glinted with amusement.

"Yeah. It was a great locker," Luke replied. "Even if the door didn't want to open or shut most of the time."

"Hey, it's the golden boys of next year's team!"

Luke turned around at the sound of Mike Thompson's jubilant voice and smiled. "The golden boys?" he inquired with a lifted brow.

Mike reached up and ruffled both Luke's and Shane's hair. "Yup. Coach's two blond all-stars. You two better not let me down. I expect you to lead what's left of our great team to state again next year." The older boy headed off down the hall but paused to call over his shoulder, "I'll be watching!"

Luke watched him trot away for a moment before returning his attention to the locker.

"You think he's gonna miss the glory days?" Shane asked, still staring after Mike.

"With a full ride scholarship to play for the Griz?

No way."

From the corner of his vision, he spotted Carol and her best friend Nikki heading toward them, but before he could turn to face them, someone slammed into him, and he found himself wrapped in an enthusiastic hug. When he realized it was Becky, he hugged her back.

"Thank you!" she chirped. "I aced my general science test. You know, the one you helped me study for."

"You're welcome. And I'm glad to hear it."

Breathlessly, she released him and turned to Shane. "Mr. Banks told me to send you to his room if I saw you. I think it's good news."

"Really? Luke, if I actually pulled a B or better on that test…. Your mom's a genius, and I love her. Tell her that, will you, if I forget?"

"Sure," Luke replied, chuckling.

"I'd better go," Becky said, inclining her head in Carol's direction.

Luke glanced over his shoulder. Carol's brows were knitted together, and unless he was mistaken, it looked like she was fighting back tears. "Yeah. I'll see you later."

As Becky left him, Carol and Nikki started toward

him again. Something about the situation was decidedly unsettling, though Luke wasn't sure if it was Carol's anguished expression or something else. Nikki always unsettled him. She hadn't exactly made it a secret that if Carol hadn't gotten to him first she would've gotten her talons into him and not because she liked his personality. As appealing as some boys his age might find her aggressive tendencies, she reminded him too much of people he'd known before he'd come to Montana.

He greeted them both with a smile. Neither returned it and instead stared at him as if he'd been caught doing something he shouldn't.

"What's up?" he asked warily.

Carol took his hand and slapped a folded piece of paper in his upturned palm. Without a word and with tears spilling over, she turned on her heel and strode away.

"Carol!" he called and took a step after her.

Nikki stepped in his path and put a hand on his chest to stop him.

"Back off, Nikki," he growled.

"No, you back off, Luke. Don't make this any harder for her than it already is."

"What are you talking about?"

Without waiting for her answer, he unfolded the paper Carol had given him. He read the single sentence five times and still couldn't believe it.

I'm sorry, but I can't go out with you anymore.

That was it. No explanation, and in a handful of words, their relationship was severed.

"You know, I never figured you'd be such a piece of trash," Nikki spat.

"What are you talking about?" he asked, hoping she wasn't implying what he suspected. It was too absurd.

"What do you think?" she replied, nodding her head at someone behind him.

Glancing over his shoulder, he was nearly overcome by the incredible urge to slap Carol's friend. The only person in the hall was Becky, attending to her locker and glancing occasionally in his direction with protective concern flashing in her gray eyes.

"You've got to be joking. Becky is my *friend*, Nikki."

"Yeah. Sure."

She didn't give him any further opportunity to defend himself against the ridiculous accusation that there was something more between him and Becky than friendship. With a growl of frustration, he slammed the door of his now-empty locker, irritated all the more because it stayed closed. It seemed so inappropriate that it should latch now when it refused to obey when he tried to close it gently. He snagged his backpack and headed back to homeroom.

"Luke?" Becky asked tentatively as he passed her.

"Later," was all he could manage.

Since everyone was out clearing out lockers and attending to other end-of-year tasks, June was alone in her classroom when he entered. She was engrossed entering grades in her grade book and didn't notice that she was no longer alone. Luke slid quietly into his desk and unpeeled Carol's note. It didn't matter how many times he read it. The words she'd scrawled remained as sharply devastating and unreal as they'd been upon first glance. How could she believe he'd brush her aside so easily and without warning? Did she honestly think he was capable? Even if it were true that he felt more for Becky than a deep, open friendship, he was not a cheater. It simply wasn't in him to be so selfish or to hurt someone he loved. And he did love her. If he didn't, why did it feel as if his chest was in a vice? Slowly, methodically, he again crumpled the note, clenching it tightly. Then he slammed his fist on the desk.

June straightened like a shot and stared at him for a moment in confusion as if searching for an explanation.

"Luke? What's wrong?" she finally asked.

He opened his mouth to answer, but the bell rang.

"I'll tell you later, Mom."

He scooted out of her classroom before she could quiz him. Being the last day of school, there was nothing pressing going on, and he knew she'd excuse him from being tardy to his next class if he wanted to talk now, but there was no point. There was no way he'd be able to form the words of an explanation. He needed to talk to Carol first, but before he could attempt that, he needed to pull his head back together. Nothing would be accomplished if he couldn't keep himself under control, and at the moment, he felt a little like a bomb.

* * *

By lunchtime, June had still not had a chance to talk to Luke. He'd told her during second hour not to worry, and since he'd seemed much more like his usual, jovial self, she'd decided to heed his advice. It wasn't too difficult; the day thus far had been quite enjoyable and Ben had called to say he was bringing lunch. Even though she was expecting him, she was surprised as he slipped through the flood of students exiting her room with a grocery bag in hand. A wide and entirely unbidden smile curved her mouth.

"Happy to see me?" he asked, making his way toward her.

"Mmm-hmm."

After glancing behind him to make sure they were alone, he pressed a gentle, chaste kiss to her lips. She nearly moaned in disappointment when he turned away to set the bag on a desk. She wanted more, and she trembled against the ferocity of her hunger. Now was certainly not the time or place to indulge her desires. Wistfully, she admitted that it was probably for the best Ben was so firmly in control because she certainly wasn't.

"How's your day going so far?" he inquired, his voice distractingly husky.

"Good. Relaxing."

When Ben leaned down and kissed her neck, lingering to nuzzle her jaw, she wondered if he was as in control as she'd assumed. Pleasure tingled across her skin in delightful waves.

"Ben…" she warned.

"I know. I'm sorry."

Don't be sorry, June thought. *Just save it for later.*

She was shy enough that she didn't say it. They had restricted themselves to the occasional peck on the lips or cheek since those first kisses Tuesday morning. It hadn't been easy, and with each passing day, it was becoming more and more difficult to resist the growing desire. Ben's most fleeting, innocent touches sent the most incredible sensations racing through her and left her wanting more. How long would she be able to hold out against such a pervasive and relentless force? And, honestly, did she really want to?

That line of thought wasn't doing her any good, so she pushed it aside and concentrated on lunch. They pulled two desks together and sat down. Ben had brought homemade hoagie sandwiches, and the smell as he unwrapped one for her made her mouth water. She could happily get used to this, she decided, taking a bite of her sandwich. It was only bread, lunchmeat, lettuce, cheese, mustard, and mayo, but it was delicious. How much of her impression of the food was influenced by the company?

"Do you have any plans for tonight?" Ben asked.

There was something about the way he said it that made her lift her brows, a smugness that seemed out of place in such an ordinary, innocent inquiry.

What are you up to, Ben? She wondered. *Lunch more*

or less out of the blue and now that glimmer in your eye like you're the cat who ate the canary.

"I don't have any plans," she replied.

"Good."

He leaned across the desks and kissed her again, lingering a little longer this time. She smiled against his lips, pleased.

"I'm trying to soften you up for something. Is it working?"

"Mmm-hmm."

"Aelissm said she'd be ready for us by six. I thought dinner and maybe some dancing at the Bedspread would be a nice way to celebrate the start of summer. She mentioned something about enjoying a similar occasion with Pat when he first came to Northstar, so I thought… maybe you and I might have a good time, too."

June pulled away, a smile tugging at her lips and eyes. "Are you asking me on a date, Ben?"

"I am."

"And you felt you needed to soften me up before you could ask?" She leaned forward, took his face by the chin, and pulled him toward her for another kiss. "Foolish man."

"So you'll come?"

He sounded distinctly like a nervous, eager boy. Surely, after their kisses and taking into consideration their long-standing friendship, he wasn't afraid she'd turn him down. She laughed softly. All evidence pointed to the contrary. He searched her face as if looking for a sign of disinterest.

"Of course I will. You didn't need to soften me up at all, but thank you. I enjoyed it. The meal and the kisses."

Lunch was over far too quickly for June's liking, and before she was ready, he cleared the remnants of their meal and vanished out the door just as the first student arrived to check out of her next class.

"See you in a little while," he said over his shoulder.

June smiled and shook her head.

"Who was that, Ms. Montana?" the girl asked. "Your boyfriend?"

"Apparently so."

The memory of her pleasant lunch with Ben and the promise of tonight carried her through the rest of the day with a perpetual smile on her face. It was still firmly in place as she wished the last class of the day a happy summer vacation and bid goodbye for what was probably the last time to the newly graduated seniors who stopped in for a visit. Some she'd probably never see again, and it was impossible to not miss them after spending so much time with them over the past four school years. Still, she was happy for them, and proud, and wished them all the best in life.

She expected to see Luke within moments of the final bell, but it was almost fifteen minutes later when he finally strode through the door, scowling. Whatever it was that had sent him into an uncharacteristic display of anger that morning had apparently not been resolved. She watched as he dropped his bag beside a desk and sat down. He didn't look at her. He didn't seem to be aware of anything but his troubling thoughts. His eyes stared ahead unfocused, and he raked his hands through his hair. Strands of blond hair poked through his fingers as he curled them into fists. Swearing under his breath, he dropped his elbows to the desk with a *thunk* and glared at the tabletop.

"You want to tell me about it now?" June asked him, careful to keep her voice soothing and level. Concern for him shuddered through her, and the words nearly caught in her throat.

Luke leaned back in his chair, and his hands dropped into his lap. After a moment, he dug into his jeans pocket and pulled out a small piece of paper. He held it out for her to take. It had been crumpled so many times that it now had the texture of thin leather. Carefully, she unpeeled it and read the single, short sentence, and her heart sank as the meaning of those words trickled down through her brain. Returning her attention to her son, she found him watching her with his brows furrowed in anger. Not heartbreak, she noted, wondering what had happened between Luke and his now ex-girlfriend.

"She thinks I'm secretly dating Becky," he said. "Nikki called me a piece of trash."

June's brows lifted. "Wow. Did you talk to her?"

"I've been trying all day, but she's avoiding me."

"I'm so sorry, honey."

"How can she honestly believe I'd do something like that?"

"I don't know. Maybe because of what happened between her parents, she thinks anyone is capable. Even you."

"Maybe she never loved me enough to see I'm not. Look at Mike. She up and dumped him without warning, too. Maybe I shouldn't be surprised." He snorted. "Maybe—now that I think about it—I'm not."

His shoulders slumped as the anger drained out of

him. Sadness replaced the fury in his eyes, and he sighed. "She won't even give me the chance to explain. Do you think she'd believe me if I did?"

"Maybe someday, but probably not right now." She leaned down and hugged him. "I'd fix it if I could."

"I know you would," he murmured against her neck.

"Ready to go home?"

"Yeah. I just want today to be over."

June hated to see him hurting and know there was nothing she could really do to help him. Her only comfort lay in knowing that he was resilient and would bounce back from this trauma once he'd had a little time to grieve. They gathered their things and headed out to the parking lot. June spotted Carol standing with her friend Nikki across the parking lot. Carol bawled while Nikki talked animatedly. June didn't point them out to Luke and climbed into her truck hoping he wouldn't see them as they pulled away from the school. She couldn't help the spear of anger at Carol as the girl looked up and they briefly locked gazes. To break up with Luke over a fallacy was one thing, but to do it how she had and not give him even the benefit of the doubt was heartless. Just like her mother.

* * *

June looked rather angry pulling out of the high school parking lot. As much as he hated seeing that expression on her beautiful face, JP took it as a sign that her son was now without a girlfriend. He was relieved to know it, though a little surprised by how pathetically easy it had been to arrange. The despair on Luke's face was absolutely magnificent. JP had had only a momentary glance of the boy staring blindly out the windshield of June's truck, but it was an image he would relish for a long time. He was drunk on the pleasure of seeing the boy's pain.

The sight of his niece bawling on a bench near the parking lot did nothing to ease the dizziness. Instead, further proof of Luke's freshly broken heart nearly drove him over the edge into ecstatic oblivion. He fought against the delicious success because right now he had to play the concerned, doting uncle. He would have to review his victory later when he could afford to indulge.

Carol looked up and saw him pull into a parking space. She wiped furiously at her eyes as if that would stop the tears from coming. She made her way toward him with slumped shoulders, waved a listless good-bye to her friend Nikki, and climbed into his truck.

"Sorry I'm late, kiddo. I got held up at the parts

store." He paused to study his niece's tear-stained face as if he didn't know why she was crying. "Something happen between you and Luke?"

She laughed mirthlessly. "Oh, you could say that. You were right, Unkie. There's definitely something between him and Becky."

When she burst into a fresh round of tears, he pulled her across the seat and tucked her against him, all the while fighting to contain an irresistible, bubbling delight. "Hush now. My poor girl, I'm so sorry."

"I didn't want to believe you, but they were hugging in the hall… in front of me and everyone else, and he didn't even care that I was watching! He may as well have just plunged a knife right through my heart. It would've been kinder."

Her flare for melodrama was a trait that was singularly her mother's, he thought with a sneer. Maybe it was best Paul wasn't alive to see what his daughter was becoming.

"So I gave him a note and broke up with him," Carol continued. "I couldn't talk to him. I couldn't…."

JP spotted Mike walking out of the building and waved him over.

"Hey, Carol, I heard about you and Luke," the boy said, leaning in the open passenger window. "I can't believe he'd do that to you. I mean, I saw the signs… but I guess I didn't want to believe he could do something like that. He seemed like such a good guy."

You are such a natural liar, JP mused. Mike was fully aware that Luke and Becky were only friends, but that hadn't stopped him from dropping hints to Carol to the contrary. It was partly because of Mike's ability to manipulate Carol's perceptions—a talent he'd discovered since she'd broken up with him—that JP's plan had succeeded so spectacularly. Over the past three days, Mike's dedication to winning Carol back had eliminated nearly every reservation JP had about involving him. A few concerns still lingered, but if the situation began to slip out of JPs control, he was certain he could remedy the problem.

"How could he do this to me? I *loved* him!"

Mike opened his arms and beckoned Carol over. She curled into his embrace and sobbed against his chest. Mike met JP's gaze over her copper-haired head and smiled triumphantly.

"I'd never hurt you like that," the teenager said. "I hope you know that."

"I know," was Carol's muffled reply.

Mike was an unbelievable fool, JP thought later as he drove back to Northstar after dinner with his family.

Carol had already broken his heart once, but it had become staggeringly clear that he was so hopelessly in love with her that he would willingly betray a former teammate—who was, if not exactly a friend, someone Mike genuinely liked and respected—without a second thought. Logically, in JP's opinion, it was a stupid decision because Carol wouldn't hesitate to trample the poor kid's heart again if the mood took her. The more he thought about it, the more firmly he believed Carol wasn't capable of love.

She wasn't like June, who had broken JP's heart. June's problem was that she loved too much. And her love was wasted on the wrong person, he thought with a snarl.

"She can't help it," he muttered. "It's who she is."

Really, if she were a less caring person, he probably wouldn't find her so appealing. Need shuddered through him, and he sighed. The ache of wanting her never left him. He was not attracted only to her physical beauty. She had the purest soul of anyone he'd ever met, and he yearned to be the object of her devotion, to be her only love.

It was partially his own fault for driving her away; he'd foolishly misread her loyalties. She was blinded by Luke's disgusting charisma, and he hadn't realized that.

He knew it now, though, and he was going to show her just how thoroughly her defenses had been infiltrated. The kid was smart. From the first moment he'd come into June's care, he'd played the wounded bird, appealing to her gentle nature and her innate need to heal and protect. When all was said and done, and JP was satisfied Luke had adequately suffered for his con, June would know the truth about her golden boy. The best part about it? The truth walked hand in hand with vengeance. In this game, one would lead to the other.

The promise of triumph flowed through him, and the giddy laughter he'd managed to contain for hours now boiled free, filling the cab of his truck and drowning out the radio station with sounds of unbridled madness.

* * *

Ben offered to cancel his date with June when he learned what had happened to Luke, and was selfishly glad when June declined his offer. His own concern for Luke surprised him, and he hadn't offered to reschedule only for June's benefit; he wanted to help Luke, but June assured him the teenager needed time alone more than anything else right now. So, they'd changed and headed down for dinner.

When Ben and June arrived at the Bedspread Inn,

Aelissm was waiting for them just outside the double glass doors, clutching two menus.

"Good evening and welcome to the Bedspread Inn," she greeted. "Your table is right this way."

She led them to a table beside one of the big front windows so they could watch the sun color the mountains as it set. There was a vanilla pillar candle burning in the center of their table, and beside it lay a single red rose. Ben handed the rose to June. The shy warmth that spread over her face was something he'd never seen before, and it took his breath away. That look, so beautiful and full of coy desire, was entirely for him. There were no words to describe the pleasure and satisfaction it brought him… or the realization.

The invisible force that had drawn him home to June Montana was also telling him to stay. He was falling in love with her.

"This is beautiful, Aeli," June remarked. "Although, somehow, I get the feeling it was Ben's idea."

"It was. Entirely. You know roses aren't my style. And I know you don't need the menus, so what will you have tonight?"

They ordered, and Aelissm left them to tend to other customers. Ben reached across the table and took June's hand, rewarded when that shy, sweet smile returned.

"You are the most beautiful woman I've ever met, June." When her cheeks pinkened and she lowered her gaze, he added, "I don't think I fully realized that until recently. And, yes, I know you hate flattery, so it's a good thing I mean everything I say."

Laughter sparkled in her dusky blue eyes when she lifted them again. "I think, just this once, I may actually allow you to indulge me."

Ben's heart fluttered deliciously in his chest. Nerves, desire, and anticipation shuddered through him. He wanted to find the right words, but for a moment, he was caught up in her eyes, and any word that crossed his mind caught in his throat. Finally, he murmured, "You have the most incredible, compassionate eyes…. And your body, wow. Sometimes, I can't breathe around you. Like now. But I like it. It's the most incredible feeling, June." He paused for a moment to take a deep breath. "But all that—and I do mean *all*—is not what makes you the most beautiful woman I've ever met."

"Then what is?"

"Your heart."

June's eyes widened, but the smile didn't entirely fade away. Clearly, his response perplexed her but pleased her as well. Before Ben could elaborate, Aelissm returned with their dinner. The moment for compliments passed, and as they ate, they talked about easier, more familiar topics. Their discussion shifted effortlessly from fond high school memories to what had bonded them in the first place.

"I remember nights like this from when I was little," Ben remarked, gazing out the windows at the sunset-colored mountains. "I missed them so much for so long."

"It's good to be home again, isn't it?" June replied. "I remember the first time I ever saw the mountains like that. It was the first summer I came here with Aelissm. One evening, she and her brother and I rode the dirt bikes down here to call my mom and their dad, who didn't get to come. It was so much like tonight. The sun was setting on the mountains, the air was just barely warm with the touch of summer, and the sky was so blue… It was so beautiful. I've seen sunsets like this many times since, but that's the one that sticks in my mind the most."

He was enchanted by the contentment in her voice. Her love of this place dripped from every word and glowed brightly in her eyes. He'd heard her talk about Northstar dozens of times before, years ago, and though her fondness for the valley was as familiar to him as her smile, he heard it now from a new perspective. "Go on," he coaxed.

"I knew that very day what people meant when they'd gone somewhere and left their hearts behind. I think I did that when we had to go home."

"I know you did. You were different after that trip. Not only how you knew the places Aelissm and Jane and I talked about—and I doubt I saw it then or realized it—but it was like that quiet restlessness in you had settled." Ben chuckled. "At least, it settled whenever you were thinking about Northstar. I recall David Finn asking me once if it was weird that he was jealous of a place."

"Really? He actually asked that?" June laughed when Ben nodded. "I never knew that."

"I think he was right to be jealous. Especially since you *did* leave part of your heart here. That is, after all the most beautiful thing about you."

"Are you going to explain yourself, or are you going to tease me with that all night?"

"Hmm. I should tease you. It's not often I have the opportunity." Ben sobered. "Let me ask you something, June. How many twenty-four-year-old women you know would adopt an abused and orphaned pre-teen, no questions asked? Or be able to open her heart to the man who orphaned him?" When June opened her mouth to object, he held up a finger to interrupt her. "And not only open her heart to them both but refuse to allow either to remain a prisoner to his past? I don't know of anyone but you. And for that, my dear angel, I owe you more than I can ever repay."

June's brows had pinched together. For a long time, she didn't seem capable of speech. Then at last, she said, "You don't owe me anything, Ben."

Ben motioned Aelissm over. She came over, and with only a smug, knowing smile and a wink at Ben, cleared their plates. June frowned at her friend, then turned her gaze back on Ben.

"What is that all about?"

"You'll see," Ben replied.

Moments later, Aelissm turned the stereo on, cranked the volume, and sauntered back over. "Ben said he wanted to dance to make up for all the times he didn't ask in high school. Here's your music, so get dancing!"

The song was upbeat, so Ben stood and pulled June to her feet, spinning her first away and then into his arms. She fit so perfectly against him, and the feel of her body against his was intoxicating. He wondered how much he'd missed out on by not asking her to dance in high school or by foolishly never asking her out. Jane was right, and he could admit it now. He'd had a crush on June for a long, long time. Why hadn't he realized it then… before they'd grown apart and before he'd nearly destroyed himself after the shooting?

"Because it wasn't the right time. Because sometimes a friendship is too precious to risk. Take your pick."

Ben stopped dancing to stare at June, dumbfounded. "What?"

"You *were* wondering why you never asked me to dance before, weren't you?"

"Well, yes, but how the hell did you guess that?"

She wiggled her eyebrows. "I know everything. Besides, Aelissm said you wanted to make up for high school, and you had a rather… pained… look on your face."

"It's a good thing I didn't list sweet and demure among you're your attributes. You're evil."

"Not entirely evil. I saw you slipping."

"I was, a little. You're right."

"I'm always right."

"Modest, too."

They returned to dancing, and Ben tried to let go

of all the *what if* questions floating through his brain. Things might have turned out differently if he'd ever once asked June to dance or if he'd ever asked her on a date. But *if* hadn't happened, and somehow fate had brought June back into his life. The question now wasn't *what if*, it was *what now?*

"Ben, please tell your brain to shut up."

"Yes, ma'am."

Impatience began to gnaw at him the longer the other diners dallied over their meals. He wanted the room to himself. He recalled too well June's steadfast refusal to kiss in public and the longer he danced with her, the more he wanted to kiss her again. Aelissm was as close as family, so he doubted June would care if her best friend was witness to their passion. Besides, it wasn't like Aelissm wasn't already fully aware that something was happening between her two childhood friends. Better to have it out in the open, whatever *it* might be.

Ben untangled June's hair from the tight braid. He liked it down much better. He loved the cool, silky feel of it as he combed it with his fingers, and he loved how it framed her elegant face. He loved even more how she closed her eyes and smiled in pleasure at his touch. At last, the dining room was empty, and Ben sighed happily.

"I've been waiting all day to do this," he murmured.

Tilting June's face up, he lowered his head and slid his lips along the delicate, often proud line of her jaw, reveling in her tremors of passion. She melted into him, and he nibbled along her neck and shoulders before finally taking her mouth so swiftly and smoothly that she couldn't object. He drew her completely against him and shuddered when her exploring fingers slipped around the back of his neck. She trailed her fingers down his neck, over the muscle of his shoulders, and rested her palms for a moment on his chest before settling them in the back pockets of his jeans, locking their bodies in perfect, harmonious motion to the beat of the music.

"My God, June," Ben groaned. "You make me feel so… whole."

"You make me *feel*," was her whispered reply. "I've never felt like this, Ben."

He gripped her hips and touched his forehead to hers. Pinching his eyes closed, he focused on the feel of her in his arms and of being in her embrace. Never had he felt so in control of himself and yet so overpowered by his need. He wanted to make love to June, needed to, but this moment was too perfect to jeopardize. It fulfilled him even as it left him wanting more. What was she doing to him?

"When did this happen?" Ben heard a man ask quietly.

He looked up to see that Pat had arrived and was talking with his wife.

"I think it started happening a long time ago," Aelissm murmured with a gentleness Ben rarely associated with her. "Remind you of someone?"

"Mmm-hmm," Pat answered and took his wife in his arms.

Ben loosened his hold on June, and they went back to dancing, shyly watching the other couple. Ben thought Pat and Aeli had the perfect love, unconditional with all the heat and passion of their premarital romance growing stronger every day.

"I want that," Ben heard himself say. His voice was too quiet for his friends to hear, but June heard him. She turned a curious gaze on him, so he inclined his head at the dancing couple. "I didn't realize how much I wanted that until I came home."

June tightened her arms around him again, sensing perhaps that his thoughts had taken a dark turn.

"I wasn't kidding when I said you make me feel

whole, June. I see the happiness and love that Pat and Aeli have… and I want it, too. I want it with you.”

“But…?”

“I can't risk our friendship. What if *this* isn't *that?* I can't lose you as a friend, June. There would be no one left to mend my heart.”

He could see the same question in her eyes that plagued him. *What if it is?* She was too smart to ask it, however. Instead, she kissed him again. In a few rapid thuds of his heart, his worries were forgotten, and the fear was forced from his mind, replaced by promise. *What if it is?*

Nine

"I KNOW THE HIKE is four miles each way, but what's the elevation gain?" Ben asked, craning his neck to stare up at the granite outcrop that towered above the pines climbing its shoulders.

"I believe the lake sits at about eighty-five hundred feet. We're standing at just under seven thousand," June replied. She slipped her arms through the straps of her backpack. "So, we'll climb about sixteen hundred feet. I promise, it's not that bad. Not too steep, and the trail is *fairly* well maintained."

"So, this is your start-of-summer tradition?"

"Yep, since I started teaching. The first couple years, before Aelissm, Luke, and Pat came out here, I hiked with Nick and Beth Hammond."

"And apparently their son happened on one of those hikes?"

June laughed. "Thankfully, no. They both have more decency than some people I could name." She rummaged around for something in her truck. "Here we are. Shouldn't hike without this."

Ben's smile vanished in the rushing, icy chill that swept through him. Gunshots sounded in his head, and his body quaked. He couldn't tear his eyes from the pistol in June's hand, couldn't shake the memory of the night he'd killed a man with one so similar. He saw it all again, saw John McKindel stagger out of the convenience store as he pulled up, saw the bloodshot eyes try to focus as he drew and fired, saw him take a step and stumble. Helpless to stop what he'd done, Ben watched the blood pump from the bullet hole in the man's chest and blossom into a grotesque rose on the grimy T-shirt as he sank to the ground.

"It's for bears, Ben." June's voice was gentle to soothe his fear but firm and gave him an anchor that kept him from being swept away completely in the flood of nausea.

"Bears," he whispered.

"Yes, Ben. Bears."

June called Luke over from the trailhead sign, and Ben watched, still trembling, as the son of the man who'd died that night strapped on the homemade shoulder harness. The fluid movements of the teen's hands as he loaded the pistol, checked and re-checked the safety before holstering the gun reminded Ben of the identical ritual he'd performed hundreds of time as he prepared to go out on patrol. When Luke tugged his flannel over the gun, hiding it from sight, Ben lifted his eyes to the boy's face and locked gazes with him. There was compassion and worry in those blue eyes.

"Take a deep breath," Luke said quietly. "Slow and easy."

The very same words he'd murmured to Luke a little over a week ago stirred the fog of his daze like a pleasant wind. He inhaled deeply and let it out slowly. Better. He wasn't drowning in the memory anymore.

Luke turned away to let the dogs out of the back of the truck. June wrapped her arms around Ben's neck and the feel of her pressed against him was a heady distraction.

"Oh, honey, I thought you were doing so much better," she murmured in his ear.

"I was. It just… caught me by surprise." He took another deep breath. "I haven't looked at a gun since I quit the force. I couldn't, not after what happened the last time I used one."

He turned his gaze toward Luke. The teenager stood at the head of the trail, staring blankly at the sign as though he might be reading it. In the span of a few heartbeats, his expression slid from frowning irritation to shimmering sadness. The kid was nursing a broken heart, but he'd still found the sympathy to pull Ben out of the stupor. Despite everything John McKindel had done to convince Luke he was worthless, Ben knew better, and that strange protectiveness he'd felt when Luke told him about the abuse returned, stronger.

"I don't feel the guilt I did for what happened to Luke, but I took a life, June." He took her hand and gripped it for a moment before letting it fall. "We'd better get started if we want to get up to the lake before nightfall."

The scenery provided further and effective distraction from his memories as he followed June and Luke up the trail. On either side of him, towering cliffs of gray granite pointed the way up into the mountains. The rocky trail wound through a boulder-strewn forest, crossed over a narrow, glass-clear stream, and skirted the edge of a willow-choked flat where Saw-tooth Creek slowed and collected in a placid beaver pond. At the end of the willow valley, the trail crossed over another tiny brook. Here they stopped for a water break. The dogs bounded back, tails fanning the air, to lap up the pristine water.

Luke took the lead for a while, taking them through a grove of young pines. The forest floor was soft and springy with a thick blanket of brown needles. They were out of it quickly because Luke set a swift pace. Ben wondered if he wasn't taking a bit of his frustration with his ex-girlfriend out on the hike. Not that Ben blamed him. With each step he took up the trail, he imagined himself putting distance between himself and his momentary lapse back there at the trailhead.

The higher they hiked, the more frequently they saw patches of tired, crystallized snow. Just before the trail angled right to cross over Sawtooth Creek, there was a particularly large drift right across their path. Ben trudged through it, sinking up to his knees a few times. Once, June and Luke had to drag him out when he'd caved in a pocket of air where the snow had melted around a sapling. They laughed as he plopped on top of the drift to dig the snow crystals out of his boots.

"I'll remember this," he warned. When June

turned away and started forward again, he chucked a snowball at her back. It splattered satisfyingly just above the protection of her backpack.

Faster than he could comprehend what she was doing, she spun and hurled a snowball in retaliation. It hit him square in the chest.

"I was going to save this game for up at the lake, but you asked for it," she remarked and scooped up more snow.

Ben scrambled out of the drift and jogged ahead on the trail. The second snowball flew past his head just inches from his ear. June laughed breathlessly as she sprinted to overtake him. A third snowball pegged him on the shoulder, and he swiveled to find Luke a few yards behind him, grinning. Their hike deteriorated into an all-out snowball fight. Ben dove back into the drift for ammunition as dripping, icy projectiles soared by him.

Within minutes, all three of them were breathless with laughter and sporting wet splotches everywhere. It was a comfortably warm day, but the melting snow was cold, and Ben lurched out of it. He'd be warm enough again soon once they started hiking again. He stood at the edge of the drift and waited for June and Luke to crawl back onto the trail. It was good to see

Luke grinning again if only for a little while. June's smile was as bright and warm as the sun overhead, and Ben was enchanted. The cold snow and the exertion had coaxed a merry rosiness from her cheeks, and the snowball fight had left crystals of glittering ice in her golden hair. Clad in her usual boots, jeans, blue tank top, and blue-plaid flannel, she was an unusual and striking combination of comfort and beauty.

"What do you find so amusing, Ben?" she asked with her head tilted.

"You," he replied. "But not so much amusing as breathtaking."

He thought the pink in her cheeks spread just a little, and there was that precious coy smile he'd first seen last night on their date. It vanished too quickly when she tipped her head back to take a drink from her water bottle. Without another word, she took the lead and trotted up the trail.

A few yards beyond the snowdrift, the trail made another turn to the right and crossed over Sawtooth Creek. There was a bridge of sorts across it, a wide fallen tree that had been flattened out by time and perhaps an industrious hiker or two. The trail turned right again, toward the southwest for a bit, then made a hairpin turn back toward the northeast. There were two more switchbacks before the trail straightened and made the final curve to the right. At the crest of that last hill, Sawtooth Lake popped into view.

The clear waters rippled in the breeze that curled down from the peaks that formed the bowl of the lake. The sun sailed high in the sky, sending sparks of brilliant white light dancing on the water. The lake itself was the blue of a sapphire. The water was so clear that it was easy to spot several golden trout swimming lazily around the sunken logs near shore.

"Yet another jewel good old Montana has hidden from the rest of the world," Ben murmured.

"I love this lake," June agreed. "There's just something… magical about it."

The contentment Ben felt as he took in the span of the lake was mirrored on June's face and even Luke's. At the moment, as they soaked up the beauty of the lake, the mountains above it, the dark emerald forest that gathered along the shore, and the blinding patches of lingering snow, all their worries were forgotten and peace reigned. Magical indeed.

Moments later, the serene perfection of the lake was shattered when the two golden retrievers plowed gleefully into the water. They romped and splashed, pausing briefly now and again to drink, and kicked up clouds of silt in their play. Casey was the first out, and Cheyenne stood in the shallows, panting with her head cocked and staring at her companion questioningly.

"He's out of shape, Cheyenne," Ben remarked. "Give the poor guy a break."

Casey, as if retaliating against the insult to his prowess, pranced over to Ben and shook, showering him with icy droplets. June and Luke laughed, even when Cheyenne—in all her dripping glory—shook all over them. Both dogs were insufferably proud of themselves and flopped in the shade together with a distinct smugness in their brown eyes.

"And they say dogs don't smile," Ben remarked.

"That's because 'they' want to think we humans are so superior," June replied.

"The more I see of people, the more I like my dog," Luke said. He squatted beside the dogs and scratched under their collars. They rewarded him with licks. "A lot of people should take a few lessons from dogs about unconditional love."

"Are you sure you're only sixteen?" Ben asked jokingly.

"Yep. But, like Dan says, it's not the years, it's the hard miles."

"Tell me about it."

"Okay, boys, let's not bring any of that up, please," June interrupted. "The sun is up, the lake is gorgeous, and lunch is waiting."

"Yes, ma'am," Ben replied.

They ate their sandwiches just to the right of the top of the trail, perched on logs and rocks. Ben wondered what June and Luke usually did once they'd reached the lake. No one had mentioned swimming and he knew from his childhood that the alpine lakes in the Northstar Mountains were frigid even in August. Now, so early in the season, the last of the ice had only just melted away. They hadn't brought fishing poles, though he wished they had as he watched the brazen trout glide past him less than five feet from shore. Would June and Luke want to hike to the other side of the lake where a narrow meadow arched around the inlet stream? Ben wasn't sure he had enough energy left for that and the hike back. Then again, he didn't particularly feel like turning right around and heading back down the trail.

"Have you ever been swimming in this lake?" Ben asked.

"Yes," both June and Luke replied.

"And it hurts," June added. "Aeli and I managed almost a half hour in the water in late June once, back in high school. Well, I think we probably spent at least half of that time on that rock over there. See it? You can wade out to it—it's about hip-deep right there—but the bottom drops off sharply after that."

He spotted the boulder sitting about twenty feet from shore off a small point of land to their left. The image of the two friends perched on top of it brought a smile to his face. "I think I remember you telling me about it. That was the second summer you came up here, wasn't it?"

"Yeah. God, it was so cold. The polar bear swim at the Indianola dock in January wasn't even as cold as this lake was in June."

"Mom, are you going to eat your extra sandwich?" Luke asked.

"Still hungry?" When he nodded, June reached into her backpack for her sandwich and tossed it to him. "I should've known two wouldn't be enough for you. Good thing I wasn't all that hungry."

Luke smiled at her gentle teasing. "Thanks, Mom."

As the teenager walked out on a log overhanging the water, Ben noticed he'd taken off his boots to dip his feet in the lake and thought that was a fantastic idea. A few minutes later, he understood full well what June and Luke had meant by saying the cold hurt. The shock of it didn't fade away as his feet became accustomed to the cold but instead turned into an ache. As he pranced back on shore, June laughed.

"A little cold?"

"Freezing," he said as he dried his feet on his pant legs. "Maybe I won't be taking that swim after all. Luke, how can you stand it?"

Luke chuckled. "Just dip them in, a little at a time. That's why I'm on a log instead of standing in it like you."

"I hope you don't mind if I laugh if you fall in."

"If I fall in, I'll deserve it."

When Luke stretched out on the log, June took Ben's hand and led him across the outlet stream. She was careful to keep Luke in sight, he noted when he caught her glancing back toward her son until she found a spot where she could see him.

"Luke'll be all right, June," Ben said softly, standing beside her.

"I know he will be," she replied. "He's tough. He had to be to survive his father."

He liked the way she pulled him behind her and wrapped her arms around him. She was an independent woman, and yet it felt to him that she needed him somehow. As a shoulder to lean on, a lover, or a friend, he didn't know, but in whatever way, she wanted him to support her. He rested his cheek against hers and held her a little tighter.

The enticing, natural scent of her filled his lungs every time he breathed in, and he found himself tilting his head to nuzzle her graceful neck. She shivered and leaned back into him, inviting him to touch her. Her skin was silky beneath his lips and fingertips. She did not make a sound, but he didn't need a soft moan of pleasure to know she enjoyed his caress; she curled her fingers in his hair, turned her face to him, and kissed him soundly. When she rotated in his arms and pushed him back a step—out of Luke's line of sight behind a tree—then pressed her body against him, he melted, amazed and thrilled by her confidence.

"I think Sawtooth needs to be renamed," she whispered against his lips.

"Oh?"

"Mmm-hmm. Lovers' Lake."

She dragged her hands down and back up his chest, stroked her thumbs along his jaw and combed her fingers through his hair again. He would've ex-pected Aelissm to be so bold, but not June. Not his cool, reserved June. Something tickled his brain.

"June, we have to stop."

"Luke can't see."

"It's not… that."

She jerked back and anger momentarily pinched her brows together. Understanding smoothed her features again, but she wasn't happy. Without a word, she turned away and started back toward their picnic sight.

"June, please wait."

"I understand, Ben. You don't want to risk our friendship. I just…." She closed the distance between them, hesitated, and slid her hands up his chest. She studied his face for a moment, then touched her lips to his ever so softly. "I want you to be happy, Ben."

There was no heat in her voice and no irritation, only tenderness, and he wished he knew how she did it. How did she shove her own feelings and wants aside so effortlessly? As she walked away, leaping elegantly over Sawtooth Creek, he wondered if he was falling in love with her or if he'd always loved her. He thought about Pat and Aeli, about watching them dance last night and wanting what they had, but he was still afraid that whatever he felt for June wasn't the same. He tried to imagine loving someone the same way, of finding the energy to dance with his wife even after a wearisome workday, of raising a family with her, and of facing life's ups and downs together. Each scenario that played through his head had June at its center.

* * *

It had been a stunning day, the hike had pleasantly worn her out, and Luke didn't seem to be dwelling so much on Carol, so why was she so irritable? June knew exactly why. Unsatisfied desire was a pain in the backside, and Ben was an idiot if he thought he could keep kissing her like that without putting a strain on their friendship. She needed to stop thinking like this because she was only making matters—and her mood—worse. There was much today she should be grateful for, including the fact that Ben was back in her life.

She stood and glanced in the kitchen window. He and Luke were washing up the dishes from dinner, and they seemed to be having quite the time of it. The window was sprinkled with water. Both grinned, and their laughter spilled out the open back door, and that alone was something to be thankful for. The days and weeks of strained silence and forced, faltering conversations appeared to be over and observing the proof of that soothed her irritation. She loved them both dearly, and she supposed Ben was right because she wasn't entirely sure yet in what exact ways she loved him. He was still one of her dearest friends, but he was quickly

234

becoming more.

"Oh, for the love of God, June, knock it off," she muttered.

She dug a handful of peanuts out of the jar and tossed them out to the chipmunks and squirrels. Cheyenne and Casey were passed out on the deck beside her, and she knelt to stroke their soft golden coats. She figured, with all the racing ahead and doubling back, they'd probably hiked twenty miles. Factor in all the swimming they'd done, and it was no wonder they were exhausted. She was, too. Above her, the sky blossomed with sunset, and she guessed it was somewhere around nine, but she was ready for bed. No sooner had she thought it than a yawn seized her.

Grabbing the peanut jar, she whistled to the dogs and they pushed—slowly—to their feet to follow her inside. Ben and Luke were just finishing their chore.

"I don't know about you two, but I'm going to bed," she announced.

"I'm right on your heels," Ben said.

"I'll bet you're going to be really glad tonight that you decided to take the spare bed," Luke remarked. "But can you do me a favor?"

Ben lifted a brow in question.

"Try to keep the snoring to a minimum."

"I'll do my best."

"Good night, gentlemen," June said, shaking her head and smiling. "See you in the morning."

"Night, Mom."

"Night, June."

She could get used to that, she thought as she headed up to her bedroom. She *wanted* to get used to that. Ben was in Northstar to stay, though she knew he was keeping his rented house back in Poulsbo just in case. Now that he had the job at the Ramshorn—and Mary and Marvin seemed quite keen to have him stay on for as long as he wanted—she expected it wouldn't be long before he started looking for a place of his own. That was part of her dilemma. If she was completely honest with herself, she wanted *this* to be his place. Yes, she'd asked him to stay here, rather than with his sister, because she believed seeing for himself that Luke was flourishing would help him forgive himself, but she was beginning to find it rather difficult to imagine waking up without him here.

When she heard them coming up the stairs, she pushed her musings aside to listen.

"Yeah, I am feeling a little better, I guess. For now, at least. I don't get what she was thinking, but… what can I do about it?"

"I'm just sorry she even thinks it, Luke. You're a wonderful person. I mean that."

"Thanks, Ben. I appreciate it."

"I think I may just fall into bed. I am wiped. And watching you bounce up the stairs just now didn't help. I must be getting old."

"You're what, twenty-nine?"

"Almost thirty."

"That ain't old."

"Older than you."

"Yeah, but I'm only sixteen."

"Which makes me close to twice your age, so hush up, pup, and let me whine in peace."

"Whatever you say, old hound."

She could hear the amusement and camaraderie in their voices and wasn't sure if she wanted to laugh or cry with joy. Instead, she called, "Would you *both* be quiet? I'm tempted to come in there and smack you over the head with a pillow."

"Come on in and try it!" Ben retorted.

"You shouldn't have done that," Luke warned.

When June stepped into Luke's room, Ben stood beside his bed with his pillow in hand. First, June went after Luke, who ducked under his blankets, unarmed.

"Hey! I didn't ask to be a part of this!"

Next, she pounced on Ben, pushing him onto the bed and straddling his waist to pin him. He was already laughing too hard to defend himself, but she wailed on him with her pillow.

"Truce! Truce! You win!"

"I warned you," Luke said, peering at them.

"Hmm. This is kinda nice," June purred.

She leaned down, and taking his face in her hands, kissed him thoroughly.

"I don't want to see this," Luke muttered and pulled the blankets back over his head.

June ignored him and smoothed her hands over Ben's bare skin, enchanted by the feel of strong muscle beneath her palms. When she sat back a little to explore the lines and planes of him, she felt the bluntness of his arousal pressed against her, and her body's burst of heat and need shocked her. Abruptly, she rose to her feet.

"Good night, Ben," she whispered.

This time, the unquenched hunger was entirely her fault, but the realization did nothing to calm her irritation. As she climbed into her bed, she cursed her stupidity for so wantonly giving in to her desires because, despite her weariness, she doubted the ache of wanting Ben was going to fade anytime soon.

"Dammit," she muttered.

"Your mother is going to kill me," she heard Ben say with a groan.

"Ben?" Luke asked.

"Yeah?"

"I *really* do not need to know that."

They both laughed, and June grinned despite her annoyance, glad that her boys were getting along so easily now. *My boys,* she thought as her smile deepened.

Ten

"FORGET EVERYTHING I'VE ever said about you being an angel!" Ben yelled.

June laughed and opened the throttle a little more. She navigated the road with the skill of several years' practice, easily avoiding rock clusters and potholes, but Ben tightened his arms still more around her waist. He certainly wasn't feeling so cocky now, she mused. Recalling his piece-of-cake attitude about the dirt bikes back at her cabin, June rolled her right hand forward a bit more.

"You're a devil woman!" was Ben's response.

Becky's crow of excitement flew back to them on the wind, and June's smile widened. She was presented with endless possibilities for teasing Ben. Becky, who'd been a little nervous about learning to ride, was obviously relaxed now, while her uncle held on for dear life.

It wasn't long before they reached the flat, straight stretch in front of Betty Burns' store. Luke pulled into the parking area just ahead of June, and they shut the bikes down. Luke and Becky were off Luke's bike and had taken off their helmets and still Ben hadn't moved or loosened his grip.

"You can let go now, Ben," June said finally. "I need to breathe."

Despite her comment, June rather enjoyed having Ben's arms around her and was a little sorry when at last he let go and leaned back. The balmy late spring air felt cool where their bodies had been pressed together. Ben was always so warm, and the feel of his body against hers was so comforting… and also arousing.

"I thought you said you weren't scared to ride," June said as she unstrapped her helmet and pulled it off. *Better to tease you than tease myself with what might or might not be.*

"I wasn't! But you… are a crazy driver."

"Did we wreck?"

"No."

"Then I am actually a very *good* driver."

"C'mon, Uncle Ben," Becky piped up. "That was awesome! Can I try now?"

"In a minute," June replied. "I thought you all might like something cold to drink. And I need to catch my breath. Ben might need a few minutes to—"

"Don't say it."

"—regain his composure."

"You said it."

A shriek erupted from June's throat when Ben swept her off the dirt bike, tucked her against his chest, and bit her neck. The shriek tumbled into uncontrollable laughter as delight, pleasure, and need exploded. Waves of desire flooded her, and she dug her fingers into the meat of Ben's shoulders.

"Like that, do you?" he whispered. Abruptly, he set her on her feet.

"That's cold, Ben," she muttered.

"Payback's a b—"

She kissed him hard on the mouth, then promptly turned away and motioned for Luke and Becky to follow her inside. The teenagers wore matching expressions of amused curiosity. Both were also wise enough to keep any comments to themselves. Ben came in a few moments later, and June treated everyone to beverages. They chatted with Betty for a few minutes out on the covered porch about the doings of the valley. June's carnal wants subsided slowly, replaced by familiar contentment.

She decided to sit on the porch steps while Luke coached Ben and Becky on the dirt bikes. She sipped lazily on her lemonade and watched Ben and Becky make their first tentative runs back and forth on the flat stretch. June thought about what Ben had said almost two weeks ago on their date and about the mixed signals he'd been giving her since. She knew what she wanted. As a friend, lover, *and* husband, she wanted Ben.

He was worried about losing their friendship, but hadn't they nearly lost it in the eleven years between their high school graduation and the night he'd strolled unexpectedly into the Ramshorn a month and a half ago? A few letters, a couple phone calls, and a dinner or lunch here and there hardly resembled their childhood friendship, and in the years after the shooting, they hadn't spoken at all. What if he hadn't suddenly decided to come home to Northstar? Would their friendship have continued to fade until it was only fond memory?

Ben wasn't worried about their friendship fading away, however, and she knew that. He was afraid they would become lovers and it would somehow end badly. A friendship lost to time and distance could more easily be mended than one shattered by mistaken romance. June also knew that if this fire growing between them wasn't the same as what Pat and Aelissm had found, her friendship with Ben was already in danger of being scarred. Ben had taken that first step the first time he'd kissed her. He'd awakened her passion and stoked it each time he touched her. And each time he stopped, it irritated her anew.

"What was that all about?" Luke asked as he joined her on the steps.

"What was what about?" she asked moodily.

"The laughing and now the scowling."

"Am I scowling?"

He nodded, watching her with narrowed eyes.

"Sorry. It's another beautiful day. I should be smiling, shouldn't I?"

"You were. Smiling like you only smile around Ben." Luke turned his gaze on the pair of riders and watched them for a moment before returning his attention to June. "It's the same smile Aunt Aeli has only for Pat."

"You, young man, are far too insightful."

"And whose fault is that?"

June stared across the valley at the clear, shimmering blue sky above with unfocused eyes. "I don't know what's happening, Luke, and I don't know what to do about it." She wrapped her arms around him and pulled him close. "But whatever happens, you come first. I would never do anything if it made you unhappy. And if Ben's smart, he'll figure that one out and not do anything stupid."

Luke chuckled and hugged her back. "I love you, Mom, but what makes you happy makes me happy, too."

"You are truly the best son anyone could hope for."

"I do try." She felt him take a deep breath before he pulled back, and when he spoke, there was a forced carelessness in his voice. "If we plan to get to riding the mountain trails, we should probably put an end to their frolicking."

"Yes, we probably should."

At the moment, it appeared that Ben and Becky were racing each other. And, at the moment, June was grateful to them both. Ben had done his best to keep

Luke's mind occupied, and Becky's frequent presence over the past couple weeks had kept Luke from dwelling on Carol. He still hadn't managed to talk to her, so he still had no answers, but he'd already stopped asking questions. June had asked Pete if Carol had said anything, but the girl refused to talk about Luke.

"Dibs on first ride," June said, bouncing to her feet.

"Ah, Mom… do we have to wait? Becky's not exactly going to be patient about it."

"Tough."

"Make sure Ben doesn't wreck my bike."

"I will."

Half an hour later, Luke and Becky had been dropped—somewhat impatiently—at the cabin. June led the way back down the mountain. Down to Betty's again and back to the cabin, that's all June wanted for now. More than enjoyment of the ride, June wanted Ben entirely to herself somewhere she knew no one would interrupt. They hadn't had more than five minutes alone since their date, and she wanted to kiss him, to see if he would be as restrained when there was no one around to bother them. She hoped not.

The ride down was uneventful. June allowed the blissfully warm mountain air to soothe her worries and frustration, and by the time they started back toward the cabin, June felt downright mellow. Whatever would happen would happen, and it would probably be wise to let the cards fall where they would rather than force the issue and risk making a mess of everything. Ben wanted to be cautious, and maybe he was right. June didn't know *when* he'd become so careful—she had always been the cautious one of their trio—but maybe she should follow his lead, especially since she really had no idea what she was doing.

Then again, plunging recklessly ahead had turned out pretty well for Pat and Aelissm.

On a whim, June took the turn to the Sheep Field. The trail was well worn but much narrower than Wellman Creek Road, and even over her bike's motor, she could hear Ben swearing. Mercifully, the ride to the little clearing beside the creek was short. June stopped, shut her bike down, and hung her helmet from the handlebars. There was a bridge across the creek now, but the banks still showed signs of frequent travel.

"Take a walk with me," she told Ben, offering her hand.

He threaded his fingers through hers and allowed himself to be led across the narrow bridge.

"We built the bridge for Pat and Aeli's wedding,"

she remarked.

"They got married here?"

She nodded and pointed to the aspen grove that crowned the hill in front of them. "Right up there when the leaves were gold."

A faint breeze rustled the leaves in the grove, and the trees seemed to shiver. The touch of Ben's hand in hers brought all those questions fluttering through her again, and she trembled like the leaves on the trees. Memory of Pat and Aeli's wedding mingled with her desire, and June found it hard to swallow a plea to Ben to kiss her and hold her against him. She wasn't going to force him, she reminded herself.

"I wish I could've been here," Ben said. "I'm sure it was a beautiful wedding."

June only nodded, unable to speak. Finally, she found voice enough to say, "We'd better head back before Luke and Becky send out a search party. I know Becky is anxious to ride."

Disappointingly, Ben didn't argue. Nor did he move to kiss her or in any other way take advantage of the situation.

Back at the cabin, once again alone with Ben, June gave in to irritation. At the moment, Ben was brushing Casey and Cheyenne on the back porch. He was so engrossed in his task and looked so cute as he tried to duck the dogs' appreciative kisses that she hesitated. She doubted he knew how beautiful he was with such genuine serenity glittering in his gray eyes. How could something so mundane create such pull on her heart? And what, exactly, was that pull? Was it seeing him finally happy and untroubled again? Or was it something more?

"Ben."

He raised his gaze, and the faintest smile curved his lips.

"Can I ask a favor of you?"

"Of course."

"Would you *please* stop giving me these mixed signals?" *So much for not pushing the issue.*

"What do you—"

"I mean… don't kiss me senseless, then turn around and tell me we shouldn't be doing this because our friendship is too important. If you don't want to take a chance, I understand why, but—"

"What do *you* want, June?"

The question entirely ruined her line of thought. After taking a moment to collect the pieces, she dropped to her knees behind him on the deck, turned his face to hers, and kissed him tenderly. She slid her hand across his chest and let it rest over his racing heart.

"I want *this*," she murmured. "All of this."

"June…"

"I know." She rose to her feet and turned her back on him. "Keep in mind, Ben, that we almost lost our friendship once already."

Turning on her heel, she strode into the cabin to her desk and straightened the stack of photos she'd been sorting earlier, trying to pretend she was interested in her task. She felt more than heard Ben walk up beside her.

"June, look at me."

Slowly, she obeyed. All traces of irritation fled when she saw the vulnerability in his eyes. Then she began to truly understand his fears.

"I *am* keeping that in mind. That's why I'm so afraid now. I really needed you after the shooting, June." He looked at the gear on the table and his eyes locked on something. "You wouldn't have let me fall like that. You would've…."

This was something June knew she couldn't help. So she didn't try. Instead, she held him quietly and waited for his memories to pass. Just as she pulled away from him, she heard Luke and Becky returning from their ride.

"Why did I hear only one dirt bike?" Ben asked, frowning as he looked out the big windows. "Oh, god. Becky!"

* * *

"Pacing is not going to make them come back any faster," Luke remarked from the floor of the living room. He rolled on to his stomach and started his push-ups. "All you're going to do… is wear a path… in the carpet."

Becky stopped pacing just long enough to glare at him. "Sorry. I just really want to go for a ride. That was so much fun."

"I know it is."

Finally, she left the windows and sat on the arm of the couch. With folded arms, she watched him silently for a long while. Luke ignored her. There was something on her mind, something that had been bugging her since the end of school, but he'd been too preoccupied with his own issues to ask. Now that he had managed to put Carol's sudden and still-unresolved rejection behind him—or at least shoved it aside for the time being—he chided himself for not being a better friend to Becky. He had a suspicion about what was bothering her because Shane had mentioned something about her last week when they'd all gone swimming at the Ramshorn together.

"Coach Wells is putting you at quarterback this year, isn't he?"

"Yup."

Luke rolled over again and sat up, leaning back on his hands with his legs stretched out in front of him. Usually, she loved pestering him about football, but at the moment, she didn't have that gleam of curiosity in her eyes. Instead, she drooped a little and scowled.

"Jenny and Andrea will just *love* that," she muttered.

Luke lifted a brow in inquiry, but she wasn't looking at him. "What's up, Becky?"

"They need to keep their eyeballs in their heads."

He couldn't help but laugh. "Where did that come from? I thought Jenny and Andrea were your friends."

"They are."

"Uh-huh."

Becky opened her mouth, then closed it again. She took a deep breath and said, "Ever since Carol broke up with you, Jenny's been saying you should be her boyfriend. It's like she thinks it's her right because her brother was the starting quarterback and now you are. She said that if I was a real friend, I'd convince you to ask her out." She paused and dropped her gaze to her hands, which were busily pulling at the loose threads from a small hole in her jeans. The hole grew quickly.

"I've never been interested in Mike's little sister, and I am certainly not her property."

"I know that, Luke. I told her I wouldn't do it." Becky hesitated, lifted her gaze briefly to meet his and lowered her eyes again. "She also said that Carol and Mike are probably gonna start going out again. I told her to shut her mouth."

Hearing that stung a little, but Luke wasn't sure if he cared what Carol did anymore. If she could believe he could do to her what she herself had done to Mike, then she didn't love him enough to understand that he simply couldn't be that cruel. Whatever meanness he might have inherited from John McKindel had long since been washed out of him by June's love and kindness. And Pat O'Neil provided damned good example of what a man should be, and Luke fully intended to follow that example. He'd suffered too much pain to ever knowingly inflict it on someone he loved.

"What did they say to Shane?"

Becky blanched and slid backwards, letting her legs dangle over the arm of the couch. "I don't want to talk about it."

"Would it help if I told you he really didn't like whatever they said?"

"No."

"What if I said he thought whatever they told him was petty and completely untrue?"

She pushed herself up a little and stared at him. "He said that?"

"Yeah, he did. What did they say?"

"They told him I convinced Carol that you and I are dating so she would break up with you because secretly I wanted to go out with you. It isn't true, Luke."

"I know it isn't, Becky. No wonder Shane asked why you're still friends with them. If it makes you feel better, he doesn't believe anything they said. And—not that I'm trying to feed the crush you have on him—he thinks you're pretty cool."

She flopped back again and a quiet squeal escaped her. Luke rolled his eyes and went back to his exercises.

It wasn't long before the heard the dirt bikes. They were both on their feet and out the door with helmets on by the time June and Ben pulled up. With a hurried greeting, Luke and Becky hopped on the bikes and sped off. Luke fully intended to get as much riding in as he could in the hour or so left before he and June had to get ready to work at the Ramshorn. So, stubbornly, he refused to think about his conversation with Becky. Most of it, anyhow. He did come up with a solution to return Jenny and Andrea's insult.

On their last approach to the cabins, Luke stopped by the mine dumps at the bottom of the driveway. He shut his bike off and looked up toward the cabin, though he couldn't see it.

"Why'd you stop?" Becky asked after she shut her bike down.

"Invite Jenny and Andrea to dinner tonight."

"What? Why? Are you *insane?*"

"Possibly. But if they're going to act like jealous twits, I'll give them a real reason to be jealous."

Becky hesitated, and Luke glanced over to find her chewing on her bottom lip. Finally, she said, "But Carol already thinks you and I…. They'll just tell her it's true, even though it isn't."

"You know what, Becky? At this point, I don't really care what Carol thinks. She made her decision and she can deal with the consequences." He smiled coldly.

"Don't do that."

"Do what?"

"Smile like that. Don't let her do that to you."

"Sorry." This time, he offered her a genuine smile. "I'm mostly over it, I think, but sometimes, it still hurts. I don't want to hurt Carol, but I can't make her believe that unless she wants to. So, if she wants to believe I feel something for you other than friendship, it doesn't really matter what I do."

"Wow. We need to cheer up."

Luke chuckled and pushed the loose dust around with the toe of his boot. "Yeah, we do. It'll be a fun evening. Dinner with your folks and the O'Neils, maybe cards later…."

"Mmm. It *will* be fun. Hey! I know what'll cheer us up! We could pull a prank on Uncle Ben and June."

"What do you have in mind?"

"I dunno. Make them think one of us got hurt."

"It'd have to be you. I've been riding too long, and Mom would see right through it."

Luke's mind filled wonderfully with the possibilities. It wasn't often he was able to pull off a prank without June catching him at it, but maybe with Becky's help, he could do it this time. Ben, at least, would probably fall for it, so it was worth a try. "We could ride my bike up, and I could carry you into the cabin."

"Oh! And I could hold my leg like I broke it!"

"Sure. Hop on."

"How? If my leg's broken…."

"In front, with your legs on one side."

"Won't that be really awkward?"

"Just be very… very still."

To call riding up to the cabin carrying Becky awkward was an understatement. Leaving June's bike out of the way by the mine tailings at the bottom of the driveway, they started toward the cabin. The balance of the bike was off, but Becky stayed as still as she could, and Luke drove slowly and carefully up the hill so their prank didn't become a real accident. He decided to stop the bike several yards from the cabin so they could get hold of themselves. Laughter bubbled and Becky trembled with it. As cautiously as he could while trying to give the appearance of haste, Luke lifted Becky off the bike and started toward the cabin.

"Stop laughing," he hissed. "You're supposed to be in pain."

"I'm s… sorry," she replied.

She buried her face against his chest and laughed outright. Luke rolled his eyes and hoped Ben and June would think she was crying.

"Amateur," he muttered.

She giggled harder.

"Oh, my God! Becky!" Ben cried as he burst out the front door of the cabin. He bounded off the porch and raced over. "What the hell happened?"

"Ben, wait!" June called after him. She was smiling.

Busted, Luke thought.

Becky let her head fall back as she laughed uncontrollably. Luke grinned broadly, then gave up and laughed with her.

"What…?" Ben asked, dumbfounded. He glanced between Luke, Becky, and June. Then relief washed over his features and color returned quickly to his face. "You two… scared… the life out of me. Becky, I should send you straight back to your mother and ban you from ever coming back to June's cabin for nearly giving me a heart attack. I should, but I won't." Tuning to June, he sputtered, "And you! How did you know?"

"I know my son," June replied. "And Becky's clean. If she'd crashed, she'd be covered in dust."

Ben chuckled and shook his head in amusement. Altogether, it wasn't a reaction Luke would've expected. Now that he'd stopped dragging his guilt around like a lead brick, Ben was turning out to be a pretty cool guy. Luke genuinely liked him. Considering the way June and Ben had been acting around each other lately, that was probably a very good thing.

Becky might not be only his friend… soon, she

might be his cousin, too.

Before his mind had time to dwell on all the ramifications, Luke set Becky on her feet. "Mom, can I ask a favor?"

"After that?"

"Can Becky invite her two friends to dinner tonight?"

June raised an eyebrow in question.

"I have my reasons," Luke said in reply.

"Such as…?"

"They need to see that Becky is a true friend and that she deserves to be treated as such."

"If you want to put up with the pair of them, it's your choice."

"Call them," he told Becky.

After asking June if she could use the phone, Becky headed inside to make her calls. June slipped an arm around Luke's waist and around Ben's and pulled them close to her.

"You know I wouldn't normally condone what I'm sure you're planning, but those two need to learn that their feelings aren't the only ones that matter," June said after a moment.

He explained exactly what he was planning and why. The more he told, the more strongly he felt.

Becky was a great friend, and she didn't deserve to be treated as she had. Of course, he had another motive: self-preservation. The sooner Jenny and Andrea realized he was not remotely interested in them, the better.

"If I haven't said it recently, I'll tell you again, Luke," Ben remarked. "Thank you. For being Becky's friend. For standing up for her. She really needed that. A true friend."

"It's not a one-way street, Ben."

June cleared her throat. "I hate to interrupt this wonderful, mushy moment and I certainly don't like disrupting your male bonding, but Luke and I need to get ready for work." She pulled his head down and kissed his forehead, then kissed Ben's cheek and turned to face them. "I really do mean that. I'm beyond glad to see you two getting along so well."

They watched her disappear inside the cabin, silent.

"You and I may need to have a talk," Luke said to Ben without looking at him. He followed June without giving Ben the opportunity to question him.

* * *

Luke clipped a few more stems of wildflowers and added them to the already full basket. The brilliant red of the Indian paintbrush, sunny yellow of the arrowhead balsamroot, and the blue-purples of the flax, lupine, harebells, and larkspur created a nice palette of colors and textures. The question was, should he group them in multicolored bunches or should he segregate them so each table was unique?

"I think I'll take option C and let Mom figure it out."

He tucked the last handful gently in the basket and looked up just in time to see Mike Thompson's bright yellow Chevy extended cab—his graduation present— roll up the driveway of the Ramshorn. Luke watched from his vantage point on the hill beside the lodge, half-hidden behind a young subalpine fir as Mike stopped in front of the lodge to let Jenny and Andrea out before driving on to turn around in the parking area by the pools. When he continued down the driveway and out of sight, Luke felt a pang of unease. Should he think it odd that Mike hadn't even stopped in to say hello? It struck him as a little odd because his dirt bike was in plain sight in its usual spot across from the lodge. Then again... maybe Mike was feeling as awkward as Luke about this whole messed up situation with Carol.

With a shrug, Luke glanced at his watch. It was only five-thirty. Mike had dropped Jenny and Andrea off half an hour early. Great. He stood and carried the wildflowers to the lodge. The excited voices of Becky's friends met him as he strode across the covered porch to the front door, and he rolled his eyes, wishing he hadn't come up with this idiotic scheme. It was supposed to be a fun evening with his family and Becky's.

"Oh my God, Becky, I can't thank you enough!" came Jenny's voice.

"It was actually his idea."

"So, where is he?" Andrea inquired.

Luke swallowed his disgust, plastered a smile on his face, and tossed his head to flip his hair out of his eyes as he walked through the door.

"Out getting…. Oh, there he is," Becky said. "Hi, Luke."

"Hi, Becky." He inclined his head to the other girls. "Jenny. Andrea. Welcome to the Ramshorn."

"Hi, Luke," they chorused.

It was difficult to resist the urge to roll his eyes. Ben had retreated to the couch in front of the dark fireplace while Becky and her friends sat at the tables June and Luke had already pushed together for their dinner party. Three of the other tables were still occupied, and June had seated a family of three at a fourth. She was taking their order at the moment, so he waited to ask her about the flowers.

"Mom, how do you want me to arrange these?" he asked when she turned toward the kitchen.

"Oh, those are pretty. Nice variety. Just bunch them like that."

"Becky, would you mind giving me a hand?" Luke asked.

"Can we help?" Jenny asked.

"I think we can get it, but thanks," Luke replied and took the flowers to the sink behind the bar.

"Thank you again, Luke," Becky murmured. "That was amazing, with the smile and the flowers and the hair flip. You should be an actor."

"I'm glad you found it so amusing. Here. Mix a little sugar and vinegar with a lot of water in this jug and use the mix to fill the mason jars. It'll keep the flowers alive a little longer."

"Huh. Cool."

They made quick work of the flower arrangements and even quicker work setting them out. Luke checked on the diners and stepped into the kitchen to see what he could do to help June. He plated the food and carried it out to the waiting patrons, doing his best to ignore the stares and conspiratorial whispers of Becky's friends. He almost laughed when Becky caught his gaze and rolled her eyes.

Marvin and Mary Struthers walked in a few minutes before six to relieve June and Luke. Jane and Andy Epperson were just a few steps behind. They chatted with Ben and the girls while Luke and June finished their shift. When Luke had a moment between tables, he greeted the Eppersons. Andy shook his offered hand, but Jane gave him a hug.

"Thank you," she whispered in his ear.

"No thanks needed," he replied. "Have a seat. Mom and I will be off in a few minutes, and the O'Neils should be here any time."

Andy set his new straw cowboy hat on the table and pulled a chair out for his wife. She kissed his cheek before she sat. Luke could easily picture Ben and June doing the same and wasn't sure how he should feel about it. He liked Ben, more the longer he knew him, and June was happier—and a little more irritable at times—than he'd ever seen her. He was inclined to hope they'd fall the rest of the way in love, but it seemed somehow strange that he didn't feel much at all like the stereotypical son who didn't want to share his mother with a new man. Ben made her happy, and June's happiness made Luke happy, so why look for problems where there weren't any?

Pat and Aelissm's arrival with their boisterous son and wide-eyed daughter gave him the perfect excuse not to worry about it.

"Sorry we're a little late," Pat said, snatching his son around the waist and dangling the toddler upside down. Over the little boy's shrieks and giggles, he added, "Ant's being a bit of a pill pot."

"Pill pot!" Ant squealed.

"No worries, Pat," June replied from the cash register. "Luke, would you mind clearing that last table while I get these nice folks taken care of?"

He cleared the plates and wiped down the table after depositing the dishes in the kitchen. Marvin thanked him, and he nodded in reply. When he walked back into the dining room, Ben and Becky were telling everyone about their morning adventures.

"You wouldn't believe what your darling daughter did to me," Ben said to his sister and brother-in-law. "She decided that she would scare the daylights out of me by making me think she'd gotten hurt riding the dirt bikes."

"Rebecca Epperson, I don't believe you—"

"She didn't do it alone, Jane. My little hellion had an equal share in the prank," June remarked. "She couldn't have done it by herself, I assure you. She left my bike at the bottom of the driveway and rode up to the cabin in Luke's arms."

Luke watched Jenny's and Andrea's heads swivel simultaneously toward Becky with blatant disbelief and envy painted on their faces. Becky's face was a rather interesting shade of pink, but even her embarrassment couldn't dampen the smug grin.

"Trust me, Jane, when I say Luke can be a bit of a prankster. Becky didn't have to twist your arm, did she, Luke?"

"Uh, I need to write down my time for Mary," Luke said and stepped out of the spotlight.

The door on the bell jingled again, and Luke groaned when Jake Sterling strolled into the lodge. The cowhand's gaze skimmed the room as if looking for someone. Then he spotted Luke by the bar and Luke's grip tightened on the pencil in his hand when Jake's lips curled in a sneer.

"Well, well, well. What's this? A picnic?"

"Yes, and no one invited you," Luke replied.

"C'mon, Jake, shit or git," Pete muttered behind his brother.

Jake took another step into the dining room, his eyes still trained on Luke. Pete stepped around him, greeted everyone politely before heading to the bar.

"Can I get a cup of coffee?" he asked.

"Sure, Pete," Luke answered and went into the kitchen to pour a cup.

"Make it two, Lukie," Jake called.

Luke ground his teeth and forced himself to take a deep breath. The realization that Jake had more likely stopped in for the opportunity to harass him than for the coffee—or even to sneak a peek at June—sent a shudder of revulsion through him. This was not going to end well.

"You just can't leave well enough alone, can you Jake?" he heard Pete ask. "One of these days, that mouth is going to cost you."

"Whatever, Pete. I just want to make sure Lukie's doing okay."

Luke brought the coffee out, his jaw clenched to keep any smart remark to himself. It was going to be a pleasant evening, and he wasn't going to let Jake ruin it.

"Hey, Lukie, I just wanted to ask… has your daddy come back for you yet?"

Luke stopped in his tracks and glared at Jake, tense and ready to strike.

"Luke," June warned.

"My father's dead, and you goddamned well know

it, so stop asking."

"Oh, I'm sorry. I guess I must've forgotten that."

"Bullshit."

"Leave him alone, Jake," Pete snapped.

"Never."

Luke handed Pete one of the cups of coffee and looked thoughtfully at the other. "You want your coffee, Jake? Here you go!"

He tossed the hot liquid at Jake, who shot to his feet and lunged.

"You little son of a bitch!" he bellowed and grabbed Luke by the collar of his Ramshorn T-shirt.

Luke shoved hard against Jake's chest, pushing him back.

"Luke Allen Montana!"

Luke felt the sting of betrayal at June's words but obeyed her unspoken command. "Sorry," he muttered.

"Not yet," Jake snarled. Before he could attack, Ben and Pat wrestled him away. "I see you even have trained body guards! Too afraid to fight me yourself?"

"Not at all," Luke replied, following as Jake was hauled toward the door.

"Luke! Enough!" June barked. "Pete, you're welcome to stay, but Jake, I want you out of here now, and I don't want to see you back in here tonight."

"You're kicking *me* out? I'm not the piss-ant who threw the coffee."

"You came in here looking for trouble, and you found it, so get out."

Jake wrenched free of Ben and Pat and stalked outside. Pete drained his coffee quickly and followed Jake out without another word and without paying. Luke took his wallet out of his back pocket, snatched a dollar and slapped it down on the bar to pay for the two cups of coffee. Then, with all eyes on him, he went out onto the porch. Jake tore down the driveway, flipping Luke off as he went. Luke gripped the log railing so tightly that his knuckles turned white.

He shouldn't have done that and was more than a little ashamed that he had given in to Jake's taunts. He was better than that, he reminded himself, though it certainly didn't feel like it at the moment. More than nearly getting into a fistfight in front of everyone, it was the disappointment in June's eyes that bothered him. He'd let her down.

She joined him on the porch a few minutes later and studied his face for a while. He couldn't bring himself to look at her.

"I know you hate him, Luke, but that was uncalled for. We have guests."

"I'm sorry, Mom, I really am. I am just so tired of his crap."

"I know you are," she replied and tucked her arm around him for a moment before kissing his cheek. Then she tucked his dollar in his shirt pocket. "Mary said not to worry about paying for the coffee. She also said that if Jake wants to 'act like a complete and total ass' and harass one of her favorite employees, he is not welcome at the Ramshorn."

"Remind me to thank her," he said quietly. "I'm not sure I deserve her kindness right now."

"You always do, even right now. Everyone has a breaking point, Luke. And Jake has been prodding yours for a long time, so really, I should be proud it took you so long to throw coffee in his face. Come back in. Please."

"I will in a minute. I need to clear my head a bit first."

It wasn't thirty seconds after June went back inside before Jenny Thompson stepped outside.

"That guy's kind of a creep, huh?" she asked.

"He's something," Luke replied.

"I was really sorry to hear about you and Carol. I couldn't believe she did the same thing to you she did to my brother."

Luke shrugged. The last thing he wanted to talk about or think about right now was Carol Landers. There was still too much unresolved for him to contemplate it with a calm, rational mind, and at the moment, his mind was certainly neither calm nor rational.

"I don't want to be rude, Jenny, but I really am not in the mood to talk."

"Did Becky talk to you about—"

"About what, Jenny? About you telling Shane she convinced Carol to break up with me? Let me tell you something about being a real friend. Real friends, like Becky, have your back. They don't tear you down, especially for something as monumentally ridiculous as refusing to beg another friend to ask you out."

"W-what? I didn't—"

"Let's get something straight right now so it doesn't spoil the rest of the evening." He turned to face her fully, gratified by the pallor of her face. "I am not going to ask you out. I am not interested in girls who treat their friends like you treat Becky. I am also not interested in girls who only want to go out with me because I am the new quarterback and captain of the football team."

"Then why did you invite me to dinner?"

"To tell you that to your face so there would be

no doubt that I said it." Though she didn't deserve it, he added, "You're a pretty girl, Jenny, and smart, with a lot more going for you than I think you realize. And I bet, once you figure it out, you'll find someone you actually like for who he is and not his rank on the superficial popularity scale."

Luke didn't wait for her to gather the thoughts for a response. She would either think about what he'd said and realize he was right, or she'd continue following the herd and bemoan him for his cruelty. He really didn't care.

Dinner was a fun affair with a wealth of carefree smiles and infectious laughter. Jenny sulked for a while but gradually got over it, and Luke was glad to watch her and Andrea engage Becky in what appeared to be genuine, friendly chatter. After they'd finished eating, June turned on some music, and the adults danced. Luke kept an eye on Iris and shared his ice cream with Ant so their parents could indulge in a little marital flirtation. At one point, Pat picked Aeli up and swung her around, then planted a very passionate kiss on her lips.

"Have I told you yet today that I love you?" Aelissm said when they came up for air.

"At least fifty times, but you can tell me again," Pat replied.

"I love you."

"I love you, too."

Jane and Andy were no less engaged, Luke noted, pressed tightly together as they swayed to the slow song. Luke wondered if people elsewhere in the world danced like people in Northstar, at the spur of the moment, without a care in the world about who might be watching or what anyone else might be thinking. The other Ramshorn guests seemed amused, and though a few joined in the frolicking, they were a bit more reserved.

Luke danced with Becky a few times, and once each with Jenny, Andrea, Jane, and Aeli. June, it appeared, was too preoccupied with Ben to notice when they all switched partners. The others returned to the table for their dessert and to watch June and Ben. The matching smiles on their faces were for each other only and lit up the room.

"It's love, all right," Jane said. "She makes him so happy. Look at him."

"Mmm, yes. I'm not sure I've ever seen two people act so goofy," Aeli remarked, leaning back against her husband. She curled her fingers lovingly around the arms Pat wrapped around her.

"Oh, I have," Luke said. "You two."

"Busted," Pat murmured. "Although I think Jane and Andy could give us a run for our money."

"Probably so," Andy agreed.

"The only time I've seen June smile like that was when she adopted Luke," Pat said. "But her smiles are different… they're…."

"Hotter," Aeli finished.

"Are you all right with that, Luke?" Jane asked. "June hasn't exactly made it a secret that you come first in her heart, so I know she wouldn't do anything that would upset you."

Luke frowned and watched Ben and June for a while before he answered. He thought about what it would mean for him if June and Ben were to marry. A family. A mother and father who loved him and siblings he could spoil. Ben had already been living in the cabin long enough that it felt weird to imagine the cabin without him. He certainly hadn't made any plans to find his own place. Most importantly, Ben made June happy.

"I am just fine with that," he said at last.

Later, as he, June, and Ben stood at the front door of the cabin to say good night to Becky, her parents, Jenny, Andrea, and the O'Neils after a boisterous card party, Luke caught a glimpse of Ben giving June a peck on the lips from the corner of his gaze. Was he really okay with that? *No, I'm not just* okay *with them falling in love. I want it.*

Eleven

"YOU LIVED ON A RANCH, BEN," Luke said as he stepped over a log, "so you should know the basic operations of haying. Like how the beaverslide works."

"I was only eight when we left the ranch," Ben replied as he trod the well-worn path between June's cabin and the O'Neils'. "I was supposed to help the hay crew that summer."

"You watched, didn't you?"

"Well, yeah, of course."

"Then what are you worried about?"

Ben shrugged. They'd reached Pat and Aeli's

cabin anyhow, and June was out on the back steps rinsing out a blue and white cooler. When she lifted her head and spotted them, she smiled, and Ben's heart tripped a little. The rope of her braided blond hair hung over her shoulder, and the pure, rich happiness sparkling in her blue eyes stole his breath.

"Breathe, Ben," Luke said.

"Is it that obvious?"

"Uh, yeah. If you were trying to keep it a secret, I'm afraid you failed miserably."

"I guess this means we still need to have that talk."

"Yep. We'll see if you're up for it later. Haying will make the Sawtooth hike seem like a light afternoon stroll, so you might not be up for such a sensitive discussion."

There was amusement in Luke's voice and what Ben thought was a playful challenge. When he met the teen's gaze, he found bright mischief grinning back at him. Maybe he was getting ahead of himself or being too hopeful, but he felt like he had developed a true camaraderie with Luke. He didn't know how much of it was borne of their entwined experiences with John McKindel, how much was a result of June, or how much of it was built upon the compatibility of their personalities, but did it really matter?

"There you two are," June remarked when they reached her. "That hat looks good on you, Ben."

He swept off the black cowboy hat he'd borrowed from Andy and bowed. "Why, thank you, ma'am."

"I think Pat's about ready, if you boys want to head down to the Lazy H. Aeli and I still have a few more things to load up and then we'll be on our way."

Ben brushed his lips across June's cheek as he followed Luke into Pat and Aelissm's cabin. Casey and Cheyenne bounded over to greet them with a delighted little boy bouncing along behind.

"Hi!" Ant greeted, giving first Luke then Ben a giant hug.

"Hi, to you, too, Ant."

"Pway wiff doggies," Ant stated and trotted back into the living room. He patted his legs to call the dogs over, and the retrievers happily obeyed.

"You boys ready for this?" Pat asked, plucking his straw cowboy hat off the kitchen table.

"Ready as I'll ever be," Ben replied. "Luke seems rather enthusiastic, however."

"It's good exercise and an excuse to enjoy a beautiful day and the place and people I love," Luke retorted. "What's not to be enthusiastic about?"

"True enough," Pat said. "All right, Ant, can I

have a hug?"

Pat knelt on the living room floor, and the toddler threw his arms around his father's neck. Ben inhaled sharply with a twinge of envy at the adoration on Pat's face. Fatherhood suited him. He certainly deserved everything he had with Aelissm, and Ben *was* happy for his friend, but he couldn't deny that he wanted the same for himself. A wife. A family.

"Love you, Daddy," Ant said.

"Love you, too, Ant. You be good for your mom and Aunt June, okay?"

The little boy nodded, gave his dad another hug, and returned to the dogs.

"I cannot believe he's going to be three tomorrow."

"Three already," Ben said. "Wow. Are you sure you want to celebrate all our birthdays together tomorrow? Wouldn't Ant rather have his own party?"

"Ant is actually very excited about a triple birthday party."

"Three, thirty, and thirty-three," Luke remarked. "That's a lot of threes."

"Did you have to remind me that I'll be thirty in two days?" Ben groaned. "I'm sure I'll be feeling every one of those years and then some by the end of the day. It'd probably take a lot more than a couple hikes to get me into shape for haying."

"You'll be all right, Ben."

Luke was right about at least one thing. The day looked to be absolutely stunning with popcorn clouds drifting lazily across the azure skies and a light breeze to keep the day from becoming too hot. And, despite his self-mocking comments, Ben was looking forward to spending the day on the Hammonds' hay crew. He felt the same anticipation tingling in his gut that he had twenty-two years ago at the promise of being included in such an integral tradition of Northstar.

"And here we are," Pat said, parking beside Nick Hammond's pickup in front of the main house.

They climbed out of the truck just as John Hammond came out the front door. With strong shoulders, slightly bowed knees, and a lean frame dressed in jeans, blue and white striped button-up shirt, stained beige cowboy hat, and worn-soft boots, the patriarch of the Lazy H was the quintessential rancher. His blue eyes were keen but welcoming, and his smile was quick and friendly.

"Pat, Luke, Ben. Good to see you all again," John said when he reached them. He extended a hand in greeting and they each shook it in turn. "Thanks again for helping out today."

"That's what neighbors are for," Pat replied. "Aeli and June should be here shortly to help Tracie and Beth."

"Just think of how good those smoked ribs will be tonight for dinner," John said. "Looks like we're going to be a man short today unless Jake decides to get his lazy ass down here."

"Jake's not coming?" Luke said. "That doesn't break my heart at all. I'd do his share of the work just so I wouldn't have to deal with him."

John gave a bark of laughter. "I don't doubt it, Luke, and I don't doubt that you *could* do his share of the work." The rancher shook his head. "Man ain't worth a bucket of horse piss these days. If I didn't need the help, unreliable as it is, and if it weren't for Pete, Jake wouldn't have a job. You wouldn't be interested in filling his position for the summer, would you, Luke?"

"It's really tempting, Mr. Hammond. Mary's keeping me pretty busy at the Ramshorn, but I might be able to help out some here and there."

John clapped the teenager on the shoulder. "It's a deal."

They walked with John to the hayfield where the

beaverslide was already set up and the hay lay in long, neat windrows. The buck rakes and scatter rakes were tractor-driven, and the hoist was an old, modified pickup attached to the slide at a right angle by a cable that would lift basket up the beaverslide by way of a system of pulleys and cables.

"I've always loved watching these in action," Ben remarked. "I'm glad to see a few are still in use."

"The beaverslide was developed right here in Beaverhead County, so I figure a few of us should keep the heritage alive." John climbed into the driver seat of the hoist. "All right, let's get this show on the road. The hay isn't going to stack itself."

"The rookie is stacking," Nick Hammond added with a grin. "Sorry, Ben."

Ben glanced at the log-rail box made by the wings of the derek and the separate back panel. "Aw, c'mon, Hammond. Give a guy a break."

"Tradition is tradition," Nick replied. "Any volunteers to help him?"

"Sure," Luke said.

"Pat, you up for raking around the slide and keeping the pulleys clear?" John asked.

"Wherever you need me," was Pat's reply.

Luke and Ben grabbed their pitchforks and took

their places by the box. The others were assigned duties, and Ben watched with excitement bubbling in his blood as Nick drove the first load of hay onto the teeth of the basket. The basket hissed as John drove the hoist forward, sending the hay quickly up the derek. Ben turned his back to the box as the hay spilled over the top edge of the slide and cascaded into the box. The speed of the hoist sent the load into the rear of the box. Aaron Hammond pushed the second load onto the basket and John, driving the hoist a little slower, dropped it into the middle of the box. The third load he dropped into the front.

"Go time," Luke said, sliding between the rails and into the box. He slipped the tines of his pitchfork under a clump of hay and tossed it into a bare corner.

"Done this before?" Ben asked, following his example.

"I helped down here a lot before Mary hired me this past fall."

They finished leveling the hay and retreated just as Aaron pushed the fourth load onto the basket. It didn't take long for Luke and Ben to get into a good rhythm, and though he knew he'd be exhausted by the end of the day, Ben thoroughly enjoyed himself and the chance to work beside June's son. Should it be weird, he wondered, that he didn't think of Luke as June's *adopted* son? No, he decided. There was so much of June in him—from her intuition to her patience and compassion—that it was stranger to think of him as not being genetically related to her. He fully understood that a relationship with June included Luke, and take it or leave it, they were a single package. Could Ben live with that?

"So, you and June," Luke said. "How good of friends were you in high school?"

Ben glanced at the boy, startled. "We were just friends."

"You never dated?"

"No. I've been wondering—for a while now, I guess—what I've missed because I didn't ask her out when I had the chance."

"Then you've realized that you like her. A lot, it seems."

Ben chuckled. "You could say that."

"But you're torn. About what?"

"I don't want to lose her friendship if this isn't what it feels like."

"Can I give you a piece of advice?"

"Sure."

"Life doesn't often give you a second chance. If it

does—which it has, Ben—make the best of it while you can. I have."

"You're encouraging me to get involved with her?"

Luke pitched a clump of hay into a low spot and nodded.

"And what about you? How do you feel about it?"

"If I wasn't okay with it, I wouldn't be giving you the go ahead. I really do like you, Ben. Even if I didn't, after everything June has done for me, she deserves to be happy. From what I can see, you make her very happy. Now, that's my talk. Think about it. In the meantime, you might want to move."

Ben scrambled out of the way just as another load plummeted into the box. Hay swirled around him as sweet in smell as Luke's words were in meaning. The question was, did he want to keep June as only a good friend? Of course he wanted to keep her as a friend, but marriage to her and life with her promised more than mere friendship. It promised happiness and family, but was that what he really wanted? His eyes, unbidden, sought Luke, who stood across the box pitching hay, and the answer resounded in his brain. *Yes.*

* * *

They had already cleared almost half the field,

finished five stacks, moved the beaverslide again, and half-filled the box by the time Jake decided to show up. Luke stood on the horizontal rail halfway up the side panel of the box, scowling as Jake strutted across the field like he owned the ranch. So much for having a peaceful day haying. It was nearly lunchtime already, so why couldn't Jake just stay away for the other half of the day?

"Fan-friggin'-tastic," Luke muttered.

"Late again, Jake. The day's half over," John called. "I certainly hope you don't expect a full day's pay."

"I just got Pete's message," Jake replied. "I thought you were stacking tomorrow. Sorry, John."

"Late is late, and you're only getting paid for work you do."

"Fine. Hey, Lukie, give me your pitchfork, and I'll show you how a real man stacks hay."

"Jake, if you're a 'real man', I don't care to be one."

"That mouth is about to get you in trouble, punk. Or do you *want* to fight? Is that it?"

"No, Jake, I really just want you to leave me alone. We have work to do."

"I guess it's for the best. Living with June's made

you soft, so it wouldn't be much of a challenge to beat your ass."

Luke tightened his grip on the pitchfork and tried to get back to work. The last thing he needed right now was to get into a pointless and useless fistfight with Jake Sterling. There was still half of the day remaining, and it wouldn't do anything but waste energy better spent stacking hay. Jake continued to pipe out insults even as he set to work raking around the beaverslide.

"Do you ever shut up?" Luke finally snapped. "What is your problem with me, Jake?"

"I just don't like you."

"I'm sure he doesn't like you much either, Jake, but neither does he go out of his way to harass you," Ben remarked. "Come on, Luke. Don't let him get to you."

"Yeah, don't let me get to you, like I did last week. Of course, that stupid bitch isn't around to stop you now, is she?"

With a muttered curse, Luke stabbed his pitchfork into the hay and dropped the ten feet to the ground. "What did you just call her?"

"Don't do it, Luke," Ben called. "He's not worth it."

"No, he's not. But June is," Luke replied with his

eyes trained on Jake. "You were lucky to have one date with her, Jake, because she is way too good for a loser like you."

"She's a stuck-up whore who'd spread her legs for anything." Jake leaned on his rake, sneering. "Maybe even a little boy like you."

"Shut your god-damned mouth, you worthless, pansy-assed, piece of shit."

"Or you'll what? Shut it for me?"

Luke leaned forward, his nose inches from Jake's, and smirked. "Don't tempt me."

Jake took a swing and clipped Luke's cheek. Then he drove his fist into Luke's stomach, and Luke doubled over and backed out of reach.

"You see? I told you she made you soft. Guess I'm glad I never got a piece of that because I wouldn't want to end up like you. No wonder Carol dumped you. Smart girl, my niece."

Without a sound, Luke tackled Jake, pinned him in a pile of hay and pounded his adversary with his fists. Fury poured through him like fire or acid, blinding him and searing away every rational thought. He intended to beat the arrogance and disrespect out of Jake, but when he reached back for another blow, someone grabbed him under the arms and yanked him off Jake.

"Get off me!" he snarled, jerking violently against his captors. "Get the hell off me!"

"It's over, Luke. He's down. You made your point."

"What the hell is going on here?"

June's voice was like ice water, dousing the wild-fire and cooling the fight in him. He sagged in Ben's and Pat's arms and stared at the ground because he couldn't bring himself to meet June's furious gaze head on. The punch to the gut ached and his cheek and knuckles throbbed, but the forerunning thought in his mind was June's anger. He'd rarely seen her so mad, and the few times he had, he hadn't been the cause. Now he was, and he felt sick.

"He didn't do anything wrong, June," Ben said defensively.

"Didn't do anything wrong? He just beat the shit out of Jake, and you're telling me he didn't do anything wrong?"

"Okay, let me restate. He didn't do anything Jake didn't deserve."

"I don't care if Jake deserved it or not."

"God damn it, June! Luke has taken a lot of crap from this jackass and kept his anger in check, and he would have again today if Jake hadn't insulted you. And then added that Carol was a 'smart girl' for dumping him."

Luke lifted his eyes enough to see that everyone on the hay crew had gathered around them, and embarrassment churned in his stomach. He wanted to crawl under the haystack.

"He's better than this!" June said, jabbing her finger in the direction of Jake's groaning form.

"You're right. He *is* better than *that*," Ben retorted. "Luke didn't start it. He didn't even throw the first punch. Sure as hell finished it, though, and I'm sorry if you disagree, but Jake brought everything he got on himself."

June didn't answer, and Luke risked a glance at her face. A scowl pinched her features, and her arms were folded tightly across her chest, but her gaze was currently trained on Ben. It might be only his imagination, but Luke thought she seemed marginally less furious and silently thanked Ben for his support.

"I'm sorry, Mom," he murmured.

"I guess Jake finally pushed you too far," she said. Then she sighed, and when she spoke again, the anger slipped from her voice. "I'm sorry, too. I should've done something more about him long before now. No,

I never should have gone on that date."

"Go to hell," Jake snarled as climbed shakily out of the hay.

Luke couldn't look away from Jake, and despite the physical evidence of his bleeding knuckles, he found it difficult to believe the damage was of his doing. Jake's face was a mess. His bottom lip was split and swollen, his nose and several cuts seeped blood, and he'd most likely have a black eye by morning. Luke had never been a fight before in his life, excluding the failed attempt to defend himself from his father. The thought that he just might have inherited some of John's meanness made him shudder. *Please, God, don't let me be like him.*

"You're a hot piece of ass, June, but you're a first class bitch," Jake snarled.

"You've already had the shit kicked out of you by a sixteen-year-old," Ben remarked casually. "Keep running your mouth—"

"Ben, don't waste your energy," June interrupted. "He's not worth it."

Jake's lip curled in grotesque contempt. "You really are a—"

"Jake Sterling," John Hammond snapped. "I've heard more than enough out of you. Get off my ranch and don't ever come back. You no longer have a job here. I'm sorry, Pete. I know he's your brother, but I just can't use him."

"I understand, John," Pete said quietly.

Cursing and mumbling threats, Jake stomped away. Luke sank to the ground to watch him go and let out a breath of relief. He folded his arms loosely around his knees, wondering if Jake would leave him alone now or be even worse. Jake's taunts had escalated in the last year. The thought that it might have something to do with his dating Carol flitted through Luke's mind. Irritation twitched in his muscles at the thought of his ex-girlfriend.

"Well, now that a few appetites have likely been ruined, lunch is ready," June said. "Come on, Luke. Come get something to eat."

"I'm not hungry."

"Yes, you are."

Luke followed June and the rest of the hay crew back to the main house and sat down at the long picnic table in the back yard. The women—June, Aelissm, John's wife Tracie and Nick's wife Beth—served lunch. Despite the gnawing hunger and the delicious aroma of the homemade roast beef sub sandwiches, Luke didn't feel like eating. He stared at his lunch while the others discussed his fight with Jake. Maybe he should feel better that they all thought Jake deserved the beating and that Tracie and John were glad to have the excuse to fire him, but it just made him feel like crap.

"Here," June said.

He looked up to see her holding an ice pack. Grateful, he took it and pressed it to his cheek while she cleaned the cuts on his knuckles.

"Eat," she reminded him when she finished.

He did, and by the time he'd finished the first half of his sub, his hunger took over. June laughed when he asked for seconds.

The rest of the day passed pleasantly, the dinner of smoked baby back ribs and June's homemade barbecue sauce was mouthwatering—not surprisingly, there were no leftovers—and by the time the sun set in an explosion of yellows, pinks, oranges, and reds, Luke had put the fight behind him. They'd put up twelve stacks—the last one after dinner—and cleared the field despite being a man short. Luke was sweaty and tired and had hay in places he didn't want to think about, but he found the energy to laugh on the final ride down the derek.

"I am exhausted, filthy, and I'm already starting to

feel sore," Ben remarked, "but that was… fun."

Luke offered a smile in response but didn't say anything. All he wanted right then was to sit down. There was a peculiar bone-deep exhaustion in his legs, almost an ache in his shins. When he stepped off the basket and onto solid ground, his legs buckled. *That's not good,* he thought, frowning at his uncooperative limbs.

"You all right, kid?" Ben asked, offering a hand up.

"Yeah," Luke replied and let Ben help him up. "But I think it's going to be a long night."

"What do you mean? I'd think after today you'd be wiped out."

"I am. Let's just say I'll probably be taller than you by morning."

"Ah." Ben offered a sympathetic smile. "I really don't miss those days."

By the time they got home, the ache had intensified, confirming Luke's suspicions. Despite being just as tired, Ben generously gave him dibs on the shower. The hot water helped some, and though he knew it was only a temporary relief, it was nice to be clean again. His boxers and flannel were blissfully soft and comforting.

"Any hot water left?" Ben asked when Luke

stepped out of the bathroom.

"Yeah, there should be enough to wash the worst of the grime off. Sorry," he mumbled.

"Nothing to apologize for, Luke."

While Ben showered, Luke ate some left over casserole June reheated for him and sought any distraction from the returning and intensifying ache in his shins. When his eyes found his knuckles, he lifted his gaze. That wasn't a line of thought he felt like following right now. He was simply too exhausted to deal with it.

"It's nice having Ben here, isn't it?" he asked. He hoped it came out as lightly as he intended, but he doubted it.

"It is," June replied. She leaned against the sink, sipping at a glass of water, and watched him quizzically. "What are you thinking about?"

"You mean, besides how much my legs hurt?"

"Again?"

He nodded. "Why can't I be normal and grow just a little at a time like Shane? He never gets growing pains."

"I don't know, honey. Maybe because he didn't grow almost a foot in a year?"

Luke dropped his head to the table with a *thunk*.

"Ow."

June walked over and rubbed his back for a moment before saying, "Why don't you go upstairs and get what sleep you can? We'll talk about Ben later."

"It's really none of my business."

"It *is* your business, Luke, because you're my son."

Luke lifted his head and smiled at her over his shoulder. "I love you, Mom."

She kissed his cheek. "I love you, too, Luke. Go to bed. I promise, we'll talk."

As he stepped gingerly across the kitchen to the spiral stairs, he heard her mutter, "As soon as I figure out if there *is* anything to talk about."

Her comment brought his conversation with Ben—as brief as it had been—to his mind and a smile to his face. The smile was still in place when he slid into his bed despite his discomfort. *Don't worry, Mom. There's a lot to talk about.*

A few short moments later, Luke fell asleep with two warm, worried golden retrievers curled up beside him.

* * *

June listened to the quiet, familiar creaks of the floorboards above her and felt the usual pang of worry.

It was useless wishing she could help Luke because she knew full well there was nothing she could do to make the pain go away. After a few moments, curiosity wormed its way through her worry. From what Uncle Bill had learned about his parents, she wouldn't have expected him to be so tall… and he was still growing. His mother, Celia, had been only five foot four, and Luke was already five inches taller than John.

With a shrug, June tried to turn her thoughts to something less distressing only to have Ben land front and center in her brain. Again. Admittedly, her irritation with him had faded noticeably—and surprisingly—since he'd defended Luke this afternoon. He was right about Jake's taunts and right to stand up for Luke when she had been too angry to see the truth. She should have done something about Jake a long time ago, should never have let it come to the point that Luke finally had enough and dealt with it himself. Guilt prickled her, and she let her head hang. Luke was sorry for getting into a fight with Jake? She hugged herself tightly and knew without a doubt that she owed him an apology, not the other way around.

She hadn't seen what started the fight, but she *had* seen Jake punch Luke first in the cheek and then in the stomach. The others on the hay crew had dropped what they were doing and raced over, but as soon as it became clear that Luke could handle himself, they'd stood back and let him have it out until Jake stopped fighting back. Then Ben and Pat had dragged him off, and June was grateful. The last thing Luke needed was an assault charge. She could imagine what thoughts had run through his mind when he realized what he'd done and hoped he hadn't been too hard on himself.

Ben had fervently backed Luke when she had been too blinded by her anger to realize the fight was much more her fault than Luke's, and she appreciated it more than she would have imagined. Of course, it also made her wish he'd make up his mind. If he didn't want to be anything more than friends, she'd much prefer to know before her heart—and the rest of her— became any more entangled in this mess.

She was still leaning against the counter, reviewing the day and every day since Ben had first kissed her, when the man in question stepped through the door from the utility room with a dark blue towel wrapped around his waist and drops of water glittering… everywhere. The word beautiful floated through her mind. Masculine, graceful, and beautiful. He braced his forearms against the doorframe and leaned forward a little. When he caught her staring, he smiled, and her heart raced. It was amazing to see his smile fully ignite his gray eyes again, even though she knew he was probably ready to drop into bed.

There's a thought, she mused with a twitch of her lips.

"Why are you looking at me like that?" he asked.

"Do you have any idea how beautiful you are?"

"About as much of an idea as you have about how beautiful *you* are."

"It's good to see you smile like this again, Ben. For a while in there, I wasn't sure you ever would."

"That makes two of us," he replied and closed the distance between them. He hesitated a hand span away, frowning. "Kiss me, June."

"I thought you'd never ask," she murmured.

She combed her fingers through his dripping hair and tucked her arms around his neck before pressing her lips gently to his. Heat and gratification rushed through her when he slid his hands down her sides and over her hips to cup her butt. When he lifted her off the floor, she instinctively wrapped her legs around his waist.

"Mmm. This is nice," she said against his lips. "I like it."

"So do I. I can't seem to stay away from you even

though I know I probably should."

She dropped her head to his shoulder and tightened her arms around him. In response, he hugged her securely, and she found that she enjoyed the strength in the arms he wrapped around her as much as his kiss. She felt delicate and cherished. Protected. Needed.

I love you, Ben, she thought. She didn't say it out loud, but she felt it with such intensity that she had no reason to doubt it.

A groan from upstairs sliced through her, abruptly shoving every other thought out of her mind. She unhooked her ankles and set her feet back on the floor.

"Is there anything we can do to help him?" Ben asked.

The "we" tugged at her heart. His concern was a potent draw, and she nearly threw her arms around him again. Instead, she shook her head and went into the bathroom. She tapped a couple Tylenol into her palm and closed the medicine cabinet. Ben had already filled a glass with water and handed it to her as she walked by on her way upstairs.

"Will that actually help?" he asked, following.

"Not much," June replied.

Luke was awake, so she gave him the water and Tylenol.

"God, it hurts," he whimpered.

He squirmed against the pain, and even in dim light, June could see the glint of tears in his eyes. Helplessness constricted her chest. She sat with him for a while, combing his hair with her fingers. When she shifted her gaze to Ben, she saw the same restless worry in his pinched expression and gratitude for his supportive presence hit her like a sledgehammer.

June leaned down and kissed Luke's forehead. "Call me if you need me."

He only nodded as she rose to her feet. She took Ben's hand as she left Luke's room. She closed the door behind her before walking over to the loft railing and bracing her arms on the smooth, hand-peeled log. Ben joined her, and she tucked his offered arm around her.

"You may not want to hear this, Ben, but it's starting to really feel like you belong in this family," she whispered. "And right now, I am very glad you're here."

"I am, too," he agreed. "Luke and I had a talk this morning."

Curiosity needled her, but she couldn't find the energy to ask what they'd talked about. Besides, she didn't want to push Ben and ruin such a wonderfully tender moment.

"He told me to make the most of my second chance with you."

Relief drowned her curiosity, and she leaned against Ben as if her worry had held her up. She hadn't even realized how afraid she'd been that he and Luke would never be able to move far enough beyond the misery they had both suffered because of John McKindel. She had prayed, however deeply in her heart, that there was hope that they could all become a family. She had wanted it to be true, that Ben and Luke were developing a real bond, that it wasn't only some cruel trick of her imagination.

"I realized something this morning. First when I watched Pat with his son and again when Luke more or less gave me permission to get involved with you. I've thought for a long time that I didn't deserve a family because of what I'd done. Yet, here I am with the promise of a family right in front of me."

Say it. She squeezed her eyes shut. *Please, say it.*

"And I want it, June. I really do."

She should've been ecstatic to hear it, but his hesitation nearly broke her heart. There was something else coming, and she feared what that might be. He didn't love her. He wanted a more traditional family than she and Luke could ever be. He didn't want to be saddled with the very same boy who was—or had been—the crux of all his guilt and self-loathing. Finally, unable to stand the tension, she asked, "But?"

"I don't want to screw it up."

It was inappropriate, but she felt the odd urge to laugh as she thought, *That's it? That's all you're worried about?*

"I've made up my mind. Yes, our friendship is precious to me. But Luke's right. I have a second chance with you to find out if what I feel for you—and what you seem to feel for me—is really what Pat and Aelissm found with each other. I want to see where this takes us, and I'm willing to risk it."

"There's another 'but' in here, isn't there?"

"Go gently with me, June."

"Shouldn't I be the one saying that?"

He chuckled and curled his fingers around the back of her neck.

"No more kissing you and saying I shouldn't have. I'm tired of fighting something I'm not sure I *can* fight. But… I don't want to ruin whatever this is by forcing it."

"So, we'll just let it happen and see where it takes us?"

"Mmm-hmm."

With his thumb under her jaw, he tipped her head back and kissed her. Though he was tender, there was a subtle but powerful promise and an unspoken possessiveness that sent a tremor of thrill through her. She had no choice but to yield to him and no desire to push him away even if she were able. She was glad to be his, for as long as he wanted her.

Twelve

JUNE STRETCHED. No, she *tried* to stretch. With a frown of confusion, she opened her eyes and assessed the situation. She lay on top of the blankets of her bed, dressed in her favorite boxer shorts and flannel. And Ben's arm was tucked around her waist, pinning her against him with her back to his chest. He was under the blankets and still out cold. Her first thought, after deciding how nice it was to wake up with Ben wrapped around her, was, *How did this happen? Ah, that's right.*

After their talk—which June recalled with a pleased grin—she had invited him to take her bed for the night. With Luke tossing and turning, he wasn't likely to get any sleep in his bed, and besides, she'd likely be up all night with Luke, anyhow. But Luke had fallen asleep as the sky began to lighten with morning, and June had crawled onto her bed and followed her boys into dreams.

My boys, she thought. Her smile widened and softened, and she possessively clutched Ben's hand. She twisted beneath his arm to lie on her back. Her room was bright with full morning, and she glanced at her watch. It was after nine. She never slept in this late… although she wasn't sure it could be considered sleeping in since she'd fallen to sleep a scant four hours ago.

Luke appeared in the doorway. His hair was matted and strands stuck out in every direction as a testament to his rough night. There were dark circles under his eyes but amusement in them.

"Comfy?" he inquired.

"Yes, actually." She narrowed her eyes and studied him. "You still look exhausted. What are you doing up already?"

"Hungry," was the reply.

"Of course you are. Go back to bed, and I'll bring you some breakfast. What do you want?"

"Anything. Thanks, Mom."

June carefully and grudgingly lifted Ben's arm and slid off the bed. The dogs bounded out of Luke's room and raced downstairs ahead of her. She let them out while she fixed Luke some scrambled eggs, sausage, and toast. After she'd plated the food and let the dogs in, she poured a glass of milk, stuck a pencil and her measuring tape in the pocket of her flannel, and headed back upstairs.

"No point in begging, you two," she said to the dogs. "I highly doubt he's going to share."

A glance into her bedroom as she passed showed her Ben was still asleep on his side in the same position as she'd left him. She wanted to return to her bed and tuck herself back into his arms, but it was already getting late, and the O'Neils were supposed to stop by around eleven before they all headed to Devyn for Pat, Ben, and Ant's birthday lunch. She continued on to Luke's room and found her son sitting up in his bed by the window, leaning against the headboard with his head tipped back. His eyes were closed, and for a moment, she thought he might have fallen asleep again. Then he turned his eyes on her and yawned.

"Here you go," June said and set his breakfast on his nightstand. "Nothing still hurts, right?"

"Nope, other than a few sore muscles from

yesterday." He prodded his cheek. "That hurts a little, too. Otherwise, just really tired."

Taking the pencil and tape measure out of her pocket, she gestured to the doorframe. "You know the drill."

He obeyed and stood beside Ben's bed with his back to the wall. The piece of trim around the doorframe bore numerous pencil marks charting his growth since June had adopted him. The space from the lowest to the highest now spanned over a foot and a half, and June shook her head in disbelief.

"Stand up straight," she said.

"Sorry," Luke mumbled and straightened.

She made her mark and shooed him back to bed.

"What's the damage?" he asked around a mouthful of scrambled eggs.

"A tad over six-two."

"Yeah, that explains why it hurt so much last night and why I'm so hungry and tired now."

"It does indeed."

June went back to her room, pulled together her outfit for the day, and padded downstairs. She took her time in the shower and didn't get out until every inch of her skin was scrubbed soft and the water turned cold. Once she was dried, she slipped into her lacy undergarments—she didn't expect Ben to see them, but they made her feel sexy and feminine. The dress she'd chosen was one of only three she owned and was a lovely periwinkle a shade darker than her bra and panties. It was a simple cotton affair with a square neckline and narrow straps, a hem four inches above her knees, and a fit that was flirty but still innocent. She had not had an occasion to wear it since she'd impulsively purchased it on a shopping trip to Butte with Luke, Pat, and Aelissm. Aelissm had spotted it, drawn as she was to anything similar in color to her beautiful wedding ring, and when June had tried it on, both Pat and Luke had given the dress their enthusiastic approval. Now, as she stood in front of the full-length mirror on the back of the bathroom door, she hoped Ben found it as alluring.

By the time she blow-dried her hair, applied a little makeup, and slipped her feet into the strappy sandals she'd bought to go with the dress, it was a little past ten. She briefly debated pulling her hair back with some soft curls and decided against it.

"June? Are you in there? Because I need to…."

A feline smile lifted her lips as she opened the door to face Ben. He took a step back and raked his gaze over her with undisguised shock and approval.

His mouth worked as if he wanted to say something, but nothing came out. With her vanity piqued, she kissed him lightly and brushed past him. When she glanced over her shoulder, she discovered that he'd turned around and continued to stare in wordless awe. Without a drop of conceit, she knew she was attractive, and she wasn't completely oblivious to men's stares, but she couldn't recall ever leaving a man speechless before. She liked it.

"Tick tock, Ben," she said. "You have less than an hour to get ready."

"June… you look incredible. Wow."

"I clean up pretty nicely, don't I?"

"You're always beautiful, but… wow."

"You already said that, Ben."

"Sorry. My brain is having trouble responding. I was going to ask—before you so effectively drove the words out of my head—if it was just a really potent, really wonderful dream or if at some point last night you were asleep in my arms."

"Actually, it was this morning. Luke didn't fall asleep until around five." She glanced at her watch. "Better get a move on unless you want Aelissm to tease you for the next year about your moose-print boxers."

June didn't give Ben the opportunity to continue

the conversation. She checked on Luke again and collected the dishes. They could wait to be washed until later. The plan for the day began with lunch in Devyn, followed by cake, ice cream, and presents at Pat and Aeli's and possibly swimming at the Ramshorn after dinner. June knew Luke wanted to be part of the celebration, but he needed rest. Maybe if he stayed home and slept while they went to Devyn, he might be recovered enough to enjoy the rest of the day's festivities.

Ben, dressed in clean jeans and a royal blue button-up shirt, joined her at the table just as Pat and Aelissm arrived. Aelissm was dressed in a cute, moss green sundress, and Pat looked quite handsome in a dark green, short-sleeved button-up shirt and new jeans. Ant matched his father while Iris wore a pale aqua sundress. No pink for that girl, June mused.

"At least I'm not the only one who decided to go a little girly," Aeli remarked. "Where's Luke? That lazy boy still in bed?"

"Yes, Aeli, he is," June replied. "He had another rough night last night."

"What kind of rough night?"

"Let's just say he's rapidly closing in on Pat."

Aeli's golden eyebrow shot up. "How tall is he

now?"

"Six-two," Luke said, stepping down off the bottom stair. He took a seat at the table, and June winced when he dropped his head into his hand too tired to hold it up.

"Are you sure you're exactly six-two? Not a little under?"

"A little over, actually."

Pat's hazel eyes danced when he grinned and held out his hand to his wife.

"Dammit," Aelissm muttered. With Iris perched on her hip, she took her wallet out of her diaper bag and pulled out a one-hundred-dollar bill. She hesitated a moment before slapping it into her husband's upturned palm.

"Thank you, my love. I won't even gloat and say I told you so."

"You just did."

"That's what your bet was about?" June asked. "How tall Luke would be?"

Pat nodded and stepped away when his wife tried to elbow him. Ant giggled and bounced beside his parents.

"I think someone is excited to be a birthday boy," Ben remarked. "Shall we get this show on the road?"

"Luke? Are you coming?" Aeli asked. "Because you look terrible."

"Thanks, Aeli," he said flatly. "I really want to, but…."

"You should probably stay here and sleep," Pat finished. "I can sympathize with that."

"You're sure you don't mind if I don't come?"

"It won't be as much fun without you," Ben said. "Get some rest so you can enjoy the rest of the day's fun with us."

"I mind. You just cost me a hundred dollars," Aeli said. Then she hugged Luke. "You know I'm just teasing you, right?"

"I know," he answered with a weary smile and hugged her back.

"You got lucky with this one, June."

"I know I did," she replied. "He's an absolute sweetheart."

June hugged her son on the way out the door and promised herself that she wouldn't ruin lunch by worrying about him. This wasn't anything he hadn't gone through before. A few hours of sleep and he'd be back to his usual, energetic self. Then she smiled. Had she been the one to make the bet with Pat, she probably would have lost, too, but she wasn't in the least surprised Pat had won. At a tall six-foot-four, he had probably recognized the signs.

They piled into the O'Neils' newer black Suburban. Ant's car seat had been moved to the back seat so Ben and June could share the middle seat with Iris. The toddler was thrilled by the chance to sit all the way in the back, and June couldn't help but smile at his excited chatter. At almost every bump in the rocky road down the mountain, Ant clapped and cheered. Aelissm was a lucky woman, she mused, because Pat was a wonderful man, and they had a beautiful family.

Is that jealousy? June wondered. Yes, just a twinge of it. She was almost twenty-nine, and while she had Luke, he would be seventeen in September, and she had missed out on the first eleven—almost twelve—years of his life. She felt a bit cheated because she hadn't had the chance to experience the joys and frustrations of his early years. And honestly, she wished he had a sibling or two to spoil like he spoiled Ant and Iris. The pang of yearning that followed on the heels of that thought was strong enough to send a burst of heat to her core and a shock of icy despair to her heart. At the rate she was going, those siblings weren't likely to happen.

Iris shrieked happily in her car seat, and June

leaned over a little to smile at her.

"You're right, Iris. Nieces and nephews are wonderful, too, because when I'm done spoiling them rotten, I can send them home to their parents," she said softly. She stroked her hand gently over the baby's dusting of unbelievably silky, fine hair. "Hmm. Are you going to have blond hair like your mommy or dark auburn like your daddy?"

"Either way, she's going to be a heartbreaker," Ben replied.

He took June's hand and kissed her knuckles. The contact sent a ripple of delightful tingles up her arm and made her curse the redoubled, aching desire for her own family.

"I'm dreading the teenage years," Pat remarked from the driver's seat, "when that first boy asks to take my little girl out."

"You could always threaten him with a shotgun loaded with rock salt like Dan used to do with the boys June dated in high school," Ben suggested.

"Dads and their daughters," June said with a shake of her head. "Or, in my case, stepdads and their stepdaughters. And he never had to actually bring out the gun. He only said that if they thought about getting a little touchy-feely, he'd chase them down the street with it."

"Did that actually work?" Pat asked.

"She never let anything go far enough for him to have to make good," Aeli answered. "June's a very selective woman, and she knows what she wants. Always has."

Aelissm very pointedly turned around in her seat and looked at Ben.

"Here we are," Pat said, pulling into a parking spot.

"We're here already?" June asked. Had she been *that* lost in her thoughts?

"Papa T's!" Ben said, sounding nearly as excited as Ant. "I love this place."

"I should say that we remembered that," Aelissm said, "but we love it, too, which is actually why we picked it."

The restaurant was one long room with high ceilings paneled with the same vine-embossed tiles the builders had used nearly a century ago. The bar was in the back left corner, and arcade games and a couple of quarter operated merry-go-round rides stood on the right wall. June and Aelissm slid into one of the corner booths while the boys trotted off to play the games. As June watched Ben play with Pat and Aeli's son, she couldn't help but think of what a wonderful father he would be.

"So, has Ben finally decided to stop being an idiot?" Aelissm asked.

"If by that you mean has he finally decided to take a chance, then yes. At least, that's what he said last night. We'll see if he follows through."

"He will."

"I wish I could be so sure."

"Well, you could just dive in with the same to-hell-with-it attitude I had."

"I really want to, but Ben's not the same as he used to be. He's so cautious about everything now."

"All the more reason to slap—or kiss—some sense into him. If Pat could find the strength to try again after what Sara did to him, Ben can sure as hell get over his pity party."

"The circumstances and causes may be different, but the damage is very similar, Aelissm. Ben convinced himself that he's as worthless as Sara made Pat feel. He said last night that he thought he didn't deserve a family of his own because of the shooting."

"June, you're just proving my point."

"Maybe I am."

Aelissm wrapped her arm around June's

shoulders. "I'm sorry if I'm being pushy and nosy, but you're both my friends, and I want you to be as happy as I am with Pat. He made me forget about Brent, and loving him allowed me to forgive Adam. None of what happened in Seattle matters anymore because *he* is all that matters."

Maybe the passion in Aelissm's voice should have surprised her, but June had watched the change in her friend as it happened and had seen for herself the power of the love Aelissm shared with Pat. She sighed and wondered if she'd ever have the same with Ben. The potential was there, and he had come a long way already from the ashen horror she'd seen when he'd first been introduced to Luke.

"I know I need to be patient with him," June said at last. "But I don't want to be."

"Now who's the horny fiend?"

June raised her hand. "Guilty. I find myself in the peculiar situation of being the one to teach him to be spontaneous again. You and Ben were always the spontaneous ones, not me."

"Well then, you're screwed."

"I wish."

"June!"

Laughter spilled out of Aelissm, and though heat

blossomed in June's cheeks and she dropped her gaze to the table, she giggled, too. Ben and Pat turned their heads toward them, and June laughed harder.

"Don't think, June, just do. Just feel. Although, if your comment is any indication, I'd say you've already figured that out."

A man entered the restaurant, but June didn't pay him any attention. She was too distracted by the light, curious smile on Ben's face to notice anything else, so when the man put a hand on her shoulder, she nearly jumped out of her seat. She nearly didn't recognize him beneath the cuts and bruises.

"Jake! Get your hand off me," she snapped and swatted his hand away.

"Oh, come on, June. You're not still mad about yesterday, are you?"

"Why wouldn't I be?"

"You know I didn't mean what I said about you. It's just that boy. He rubs me the wrong way and makes me say things I don't mean."

"That *boy* is my son, Jake."

"What do you want?" Aelissm asked. "We're trying to have a nice family outing here, so say whatever it is you want to say and leave."

"I saw your Suburban across the street, so I

thought I'd come in and apologize to June for what I said yesterday."

"I don't need or want an apology for that, Jake. If you want to apologize, you can apologize for being an insufferable ass to Luke."

"And where is Lukie today? Where is your precious golden boy, June?"

The chill in his voice made June shiver. The sight of the ugly bruises and raw cuts on his face made her stomach convulse. It frightened and angered her that Luke had been furious enough to give in to Jake's harassment and so thoroughly defeat his opponent.

"Luke is none of your business," she said bitingly. "I'm going to tell you something right now, and I want you to pay attention so there won't be any confusion later. Are you listening? Good, because if you say so much as one more derogatory word to him, I will do what I should have done months ago and file a restraining order against you for harassment."

Jake opened his mouth, closed it, and stormed out of the restaurant. Ben, Pat, and Ant returned to the table moments later, and the irritation on both Pat's and Ben's faces was clear indication that they'd seen Jake.

"What was that about?" Ben asked.

"Jake came in to apologize for what he said about

me yesterday," June replied. "Which I couldn't care less about. I threatened him with a restraining order, something I should've done a long time ago. But enough of that. We're here for a good time and to celebrate the birthday boys."

"You're a good mom, June, so stop tearing yourself up about the fight." Ben leaned down and kissed her soundly.

"You can do that again," June purred.

She was surprised and thrilled when he sat beside her in the booth, pulled her into his lap, and kissed her again.

* * *

Somewhere in the woods, a bird sounded an alarm, letting everything in the forest know of his presence. JP paid little attention to it. He stepped carefully through the mess of broken logs and countless rocks as he made his way silently to the blue-roofed cabin. When he spied both the beige and the green trucks parked in the driveway, his heart skipped a beat. He paused in his trek to listen for voices coming from the cabin and heard only the stereo playing. The notes of a familiar country song drifted to his ears on the gentle midday breeze.

He sat on a log and stared at the green truck. It

belonged to Ben Conner, Jane Epperson's younger brother, who had been staying with June since he'd arrived back in Northstar in May. At first, JP hadn't been concerned, but in the last couple weeks, he'd begun to see signs of something brewing between the two old friends. Maybe it was nothing, but JP refused to let anything or anyone stand between him and June Montana. Still, he couldn't afford to let himself be distracted from his first goal.

Above him, the sky had become overcast, and he smelled rain on the wind. He continued on, moving cautiously down the slope, keeping well away from the area that had been carved out of the hillside for the cabin, where it would be impossible not to leave tracks and send a warning as clear as an air-raid siren that someone had been snooping. When it all came down to it, he really shouldn't have taken the hike up to the cabin in the first place, and he wasn't entirely sure why he'd felt the need. It was too chancy, especially since the two dogs were most likely in the cabin, but he couldn't resist the urge, nor could he deny himself the adrenaline rush. He made the final few strides to the cabin and peered through the kitchen window.

Inside, Luke was stretched out on the couch, with one hand buried in the golden fur of June's retriever.

The other dog lay on the couch at the boy's feet. Just seeing Luke's occasional smile as he read and the light of the lamp shining on his golden hair made JP's blood seethe. The hatred he felt in his heart toward the teenager was as frigid and bleak as a wintery midnight. Soon, Luke would know the pain and anguish and embarrassment JP had felt at the boy's hands. Vengeance would be his, and he smiled as he mused how sweet it would be. All that innocence was nothing more than a front, one he would rip away when the time came.

June's dog lifted her head and sniffed. When she turned her gaze toward the kitchen window, JP darted toward the woods behind the cabin. A chorus of alarmed barks sounded in the cabin as he circled around and raced for his truck. He tripped over a log and sprawled on the ground. Swearing under his breath at the twinge in his ankle and wrist, he rolled onto his back to lay low for a bit. After a short eternity, he heard the back door of the cabin open and lifted his head just a bit for a quick glance. Luke squatted on the back porch, holding the collars of the two dogs. He appeared to be alone.

JP stroked the grip of his pistol. He could take care of the problem right now and be done with it. Maybe he should. June would forever remember her golden boy as perfect, and that was a pity, but Luke would most certainly have paid for his deceit. Slowly, he slipped the gun from its holster and clicked the safety off. His heart raced, and the hand that gripped the pistol trembled with the thrill pulsing through his veins. He hadn't *really* considered killing Luke before, but with the opportunity right in front of him, he found it difficult to resist the powerful temptation.

No, he told himself. *This isn't right. June has to know the truth. Once she does… maybe I won't just send him back to Washington. Maybe I'll send him to join his father in hell.*

* * *

Luke had gone back to bed shortly after the birthday party had left for Devyn and didn't wake up until four hours later feeling a lot more like himself again. He fixed himself a couple of sandwiches and a bowl of soup and grabbed a book before taking up residence on the couch. Cheyenne and Casey, who had not left his side, sat beside him with their ears back and concern in their brown eyes.

"I'm okay," he assured them. He gave them both a few pats and scratches, and it seemed to appease them because as soon as he picked up his first sandwich, their ears perked. "Now you're just begging. It's pathetic, you know."

After he'd finished his lunch, Luke wondered how many more nights like the last he'd have to endure. While he wouldn't mind catching up to Pat, he really didn't want to be any taller than Aelissm's husband. He was glad that the football camp at the university in Devyn was still almost a week away. With Coach Wells putting him in as the starting quarterback, he wanted to do his best at the camp, and he probably wouldn't be up to it for a few days at least, if his past growth spurts were any indication.

"What's the deal with your dad, Casey?" he asked Ben's dog.

The retriever's response was a brief tilt of his head.

"Do you think he's going to stick around?"

Casey let out a soft woof.

"I hope so, too."

Luke opened his book to where he'd left off, but didn't get more than a few pages into it when fear prickled the back of his neck. Cheyenne, who had been sitting beside him with her head on his stomach while he absently stroked her ears, looked up with her ears and eyes alert. She sniffed, and her hackles rose when she looked into the kitchen. Then she was up and bounding toward the back door barking with Casey right behind her. Luke padded into the kitchen and peered out the window. There was movement up the hill and to the side of the cabin, a flash of tan. He watched for several minutes but didn't see it again. Had it been a deer? A mountain lion? Or someone's Carhartt work pants?

Against his better judgment, he walked to the back door, opened it, and stepped outside. He was careful to keep hold of both dogs because they seemed determined to go after whatever was out there in the trees. He squatted beside them and scanned the hillside. His eyes returned to the spot where he'd seen the movement, but there was nothing there now. At least, nothing he could see. The dogs' hackles were still raised, so he pulled them back inside and closed the door behind them. Then he turned the knob on the deadbolt and slid to the floor. The dogs were instantly beside him, licking his face and hands.

"Good dogs," he whispered to them.

The adrenaline quivering through him began to dissipate and he took several deep breaths. He wanted to believe it had only been a deer or even a mountain lion he'd seen, but Cheyenne had seen countless deer and a few mountain lions and had never reacted like that before. She was smart enough to know better than to go charging after cougars, and she treated deer as something exciting, not threatening. While trying to analyze the situation logically helped steady his nerves, it only firmed his belief that it had been a human—not an animal—stalking the house.

With that thought, he rose and went to the front door to lock it, too, then turned off the stereo and returned to the couch. He tried to get back into his book, but it was impossible. The dogs growled any time they heard a sound outside, even a woodpecker knocking on a hollow pole. When he heard Pat and Aelissm's Suburban pull up to the cabin, he barely resisted the urge to fly out the front door and throw his arms around June and Ben.

June laughed at something Aelissm said, but when she saw him standing in the doorway, the smile evaporated.

"Luke? You're pale. What's wrong?"

"I think someone was snooping around the cabin."

"When?"

"About twenty, maybe thirty minutes ago. The dogs went nuts. At first I thought it was a deer or maybe a mountain lion, but Cheyenne acted really strange. When I looked outside, I saw a flash of tan up there on the hill."

She jogged over to him and hugged him. Moments later, Aelissm had taken her children inside, and Luke joined Ben, Pat, and the dogs in a search for tracks.

"They're not bloodhounds, but they're loyal and protective," Pat remarked as the dogs picked up a trail right at the kitchen window.

The overcast sky eliminated the shadows that would make it easier to spot prints in the dirt, but they found a boot print that didn't match their treads. Luke shuddered at the proof that his suspicions were correct. He'd hoped he was wrong. Pat stepped into the house and returned a few moments later with June's pistol.

"Just in case," he said.

The dogs led them to the place where he'd seen movement, and the crushed grass hinted that someone had lain there. Cheyenne and Casey didn't need the "find it" command to keep sniffing out the trail. This wasn't a game of find the toy, Luke thought, trying to keep his fear subdued. It was probably just a lost hiker, who had taken off in fright when the dogs started barking. The accidental trespass did happen on rare occasions. He wanted to believe it, but he couldn't help thinking that people who accidentally trespassed usually apologized. They didn't stand at the kitchen window and look inside, then take off running.

Two hundred yards from the cabin, they found where a vehicle—most likely a truck—had pulled off to the side of Wellman Creek Road. The dogs paced the area, but found nothing else. Whoever had been snooping had parked here. Further evidence against the hiker theory.

"Could it have been a hiker?" Ben asked.

"Possible but doubtful," Pat answered and listed the reasons against it that Luke had considered.

"What about Jake? He still seemed a little pissed when he left the restaurant."

"Jake was at the restaurant?" Luke inquired.

"Yeah. He looked like hell," Ben replied with a smirk. "Maybe he was looking for a rematch and had second thoughts upon realizing he'd probably lose that, too."

Luke appreciated the unspoken support and pride, but he couldn't shake the trembling anxiety and doubt. "Maybe."

"Well, whoever it was, he's long gone," Pat said. "Hopefully, he won't be back. I'll talk to Aaron Hammond about it and see what he thinks."

They trekked back to June's cabin. Pat filled June and Aelissm in on what they'd found and what he thought. It was generally agreed that Jake had come looking for another fight and thought better of it when the dogs started barking. Luke had his doubts, and when he met Pat's concerned gaze, he saw that older man did, too. But it was supposed to be a fun evening in celebration of Ant's, Ben's and Pat's birthdays, so the subject was dropped for the time being, and they all headed over to the O'Neils' cabin for presents, cake, ice cream, and cards. It wasn't long before the infectious love and laughter convinced Luke that he had probably freaked out over nothing.

Thirteen

"THIS IS NICE," Ben remarked, resting his cheek on the top of June's head. No, he thought, nice was far too weak a word for the simple pleasure he took from the feel of her snuggled against him. She sat with her head on his shoulder, her arm around tucked around his torso, and her legs entwined with his. They hadn't yet turned on any lights, but the living room was mutedly illuminated by the rosy light of the glowing sunset.

"Mmm. It is."

They had worked down at the Ramshorn today, returned home for a lovely dinner together and had decided to round out the evening with a movie. All in all, it had been a very pleasant day and strangely all the more enjoyable for the routine simplicity of it. Something was missing, however, and Ben was amused to note how much Luke's absence impacted his sense of June's home. The teenager had departed for football camp that morning, and Ben sincerely missed the kid. June hadn't said anything, but he was certain she noticed how much emptier the cabin felt without him. He hugged her a little closer.

"You miss him, too, don't you?" she asked.

"I do."

"I'm really trying not to think about him going to college next August. This place is going to be so lonely."

He toyed with a lock of her silky blond hair. "It's nice to have you all to myself for a little while, though."

"Oh? And what do you plan to do with me?"

He tilted her head up and inhaled sharply when their eyes met. Curiosity and desire widened her eyes, dilating the pupils so that her irises were only a slender thread of blue encircling pools of black. He could drown in her eyes, he thought, and pressed a feather-light kiss to her lips. When she pressed her body closer, need sliced through him, and he groaned. He had been a fool to think he could fight this. It had been difficult enough to resist kissing and touching June before he'd made the decision to investigate the desire he'd kindled—or reawakened?—when he'd first kissed her. Now, it was damn near impossible.

Taking her face in his hands, he deepened the kiss, and she eagerly answered his demand. He trailed one hand down her neck to massage her breast. She moaned low in her throat and kissed him more fiercely. If there was any doubt in his mind about what she wanted, it vanished when she pivoted in his lap to straddle his waist.

"Good God, woman," he growled. "You're going to kill me."

"I hope not," she replied. Her voice was husky and unlike anything Ben had ever associated with her.

"Slow down, June."

"Why?"

"Because I want to do this right."

"How can this be wrong?"

He wished he could be so certain. Though his doubts were fading quickly and his list of excuses becoming shorter each time they kissed, his fear of losing something so precious as her friendship still lingered. When she sat back to study his face with a mixture of concern and desire brightening her eyes and flushing her cheeks, he reached to tuck her hair behind her ear. There was more to his hesitation than worry. He didn't want to fall into bed with her in a rush because that was just sex, and with June, it would never be *just sex*.

"It's not wrong," he said. "I want to take my time with you."

He wanted to explore every wonderful inch of her, to revel in the sensations and heat of each and every intoxicating touch.

The flare of bright white light in the dim living room of June's cabin was almost as effective at quelling his desire as ice water. Luke was supposed to be at football camp until the day after tomorrow, and they weren't expecting any visitors. June rose to her feet with a fluid grace that nearly had Ben begging her to return. She peeked outside.

"It's Aaron," she said and opened the door.

Dread poured through Ben, and he joined her at the door. The sunset had faded, but it was still bright enough that Ben could see Aaron's unworried expression. He sighed with relief.

"Evening, June, Ben. Sorry to stop by so late, but I just talked to Jake. Finally cornered him down at the Bedspread."

"Aaron, you didn't have to come all the way up here just to tell us that," June said as she stepped back to let the sheriff's deputy in. He wasn't in uniform, so he wasn't on duty. Not officially, anyhow. "That's what phones are for, you know."

He stepped through the front door, and when he glanced at June, Ben noted how his expression momentarily waxed remorseful, how he shifted his weight as if seeing Ben's arm draped around June's waist made him uncomfortable. Ben ignored the inexplicable spark of possessiveness, choosing instead to focus on the reason for Aaron's visit.

"What did Jake have to say?" June asked. "I assume you asked him about snooping around here."

Aaron nodded. "He claimed he didn't come back to the valley after he saw you in Devyn, which I know is a lie because he stopped by my parents' place about an hour after you said you'd talked to him."

"What did he want with your folks?" Ben inquired.

"He asked for his job back. When I asked him about that, he of course denied coming up here."

"It probably *was* him, then."

"Most likely, but you can be sure I'll be keeping my eyes and ears open for anything out of the ordinary.

Let me know if you notice anything suspicious."

"We will, of course," June said.

"All right. I'll get out of your hair. See you around."

After June closed the door behind Aaron, Ben took her hand and led her back to the couch. He tried not to dwell on the flicker of regret he'd seen on Aaron's face or his illogical gut reaction to it, but couldn't quell his curiosity. Now that he thought about it, he realized this wasn't the first time he'd seen the expression on the deputy's face. He'd seen it the day he'd helped on the Hammond's hay crew, at dinner, but hadn't given it much thought. He tried to reconcile that odd sadness with his earlier experiences with Aaron Hammond and couldn't. The Aaron he'd known as a boy and briefly as an adult on his trips to Northstar had been carefree and always laughing or smiling.

"June, can I ask you a question without you being offended?"

"When you start by saying that… I can't make any promises, but go for it."

"Why did Aaron look at you with regret just now?"

Her expression softened with compassion. "We went on a handful of dates a few months ago. His wife,

Erica, was shot and killed two years ago, and he thought he was ready to move on."

"But he wasn't."

June shook her head. "It was a tragic accident. The man who shot her was just trying to scare Aaron—Aaron had arrested his brother in connection with a rather large drug bust a few days before. The man didn't mean to shoot anyone but ended up killing Erica and then himself."

"I can't imagine…. I'm glad Aaron didn't resign like I did."

"He almost did." June frowned. "You're… not jealous… are you?"

"I might have felt a tiny prickle of envy."

She took him by the chin and kissed him. When she pulled away, she was smiling. "You silly fool. You're the only man I want."

"What if I hadn't come back to Northstar?"

"Then I might've waited until Aaron was ready. He's a good man." She embraced him tightly and when she spoke again, the teasing tone had vanished from her voice. "So are you, Ben Conner. And whether you want to be or not, you're mine." Leaning back, she combed her hands back through his hair. Then she kissed him again. "And for as long as you want me, however you want me, I am yours."

"What if I want your friendship?"

"You've always had that, and you always will."

He stroked his hands down her neck, over her breasts and sides to grip her hips. "And your body?"

"Yours, too. Right now, if you want it."

With a chuckle, he replied, "I want it, but I wasn't kidding when I said I wanted to take my time."

And what if I want your heart? He didn't ask, but the fact that he wanted to surely meant that something incredible was happening. Before he could test his theory, the phone rang, and June jumped up to answer it. Ben joined her beside the snack bar. The caller ID showed a Devyn number, so June hit the speaker phone button before threading herself around him.

"Don't tell me you're just finishing for the night," June remarked by way of greeting.

"Hi, Mom. Yeah. We had dinner earlier, and we've been watching film since."

"How is the camp so far?" Ben asked.

"Hi, Ben. It's a lot of fun. It's great to get back out on the field, but I am wiped. Coach Wells wanted to try a bunch of new drills and plays… so we ran them again… and again. My brain is more tired than the rest of me, I think. Anyhow, are you still planning a camping trip up to Sawtooth tomorrow?"

"Yes, we are," June replied. "If we have the energy after work."

"Then I won't call. Hey, Shane wants to call his dad, so I should go."

"All right. Love you, Luke."

"Love you, too. Night, Mom. Night Ben."

June ended the call, but didn't step away. He was grateful because she was his anchor in the swirl of new and unexpected emotions. Was this what it felt like to be a husband and father, this overwhelming concoction of pride, desire, and love? Whatever it was, he liked it.

"Well, since the movie is over and since we have to get up fairly early tomorrow, we should probably go to bed," June remarked. She turned in his arms and pressed her body against his. "Join me?"

Somewhere, in the farthest reaches of his mind, a tiny voice warned him against taking June up on her offer, but its reasons were flimsy and drowned out by his need to be close to her. She slipped her hand into his, and he let her pull him upstairs. Once he'd changed into his favorite pair of flannel boxer shorts, he rejoined June in her bedroom. He climbed into bed beside her, curled around her with his knees fitted like a jigsaw puzzle piece behind hers and wrapped his arm around her waist. Maybe it was corny to think it, but lying beside her felt right.

"I think I'm falling in love with you, June," he whispered.

"I hope so," she replied. "Because I know I'm falling in love with you."

"How can you be so sure?"

"Because I trust my heart. Maybe you should try listening to yours."

* * *

June glanced at the clock again as yet another group strolled through the door of the Ramshorn Lodge. Only twenty-five minutes left until she and Ben could escape. It had been a long, busy day, but she still had energy to burn. Ben had seen to that shortly after sunrise, when he'd kissed her awake… and then disappeared downstairs, leaving her aching for more and irritated because he wanted to take his time. She had managed to swallow her irritation, but now, after hours of catching Ben's shy smiles and enduring the renewed burn of desire every time he touched her hand or her shoulder, she was beginning to feel the nudges of annoyance again. So, she stepped outside for a quick breather.

When Ben joined her, her fingers curled around the porch railing. She let him kiss her and pointedly ignored the flare of heat.

"Is this all we're ever going to do?" she asked when he pulled away. He regarded her with a frown. "I want more, Ben. What do I have to do to make you understand that? Prance naked in front of you?"

"June…."

"Tonight, Ben." She rocked her hips against him and slid her hands up his chest. "At the lake beneath the stars."

He sighed and touched his forehead to hers. "Are you sure?"

"Absolutely. I've been patient, waiting for you to realize that this is not a mistake, trying to understand why you're still trying to fight this. I know it isn't because you don't want me. Are you afraid—"

He clamped his mouth over hers in a kiss that was forceful and demanding and left no room for argument. "You are certainly right that I want you. So, you win. Tonight."

For the first time, June saw a spark of the Ben she remembered. The caution and sadness she'd become so familiar with since he'd returned to Northstar disappeared, replaced by confidence and hunger. The combination sent a kick of desire straight to her core. When he went back inside, she stayed on the porch, quivering with need.

"There you are, Ben," she whispered with a smile. "I've missed you."

June got back to work, anxious for the last minutes of her shift to be behind her. They dragged by without a single customer to distract her. *Figures*, she thought with a scowl. Finally, Mary and Marvin Struthers arrived to relieve her and Ben. She wrote down their hours, bid the owners farewell, and was dragging Ben out the door when the phone rang.

"I'll get it," she called. "Ramshorn Hot Springs and Lodge. This is June."

"Ah, June, just the woman I wanted to talk to."

"What can I do for you?" she asked.

"Actually, my dear, there is something I can do for you."

She frowned as a shiver coursed along her spine. There was something indefinably unsettling about the caller's voice. It struck her as familiar, but she couldn't place it. "And what is that?"

"You will find out tomorrow when you check your mail. There will be a letter from me."

"Who is this?"

The click of disconnection stuck her nerves like a shot. *What the hell was that?* she wondered.

"June? You're pale." Ben closed the distance between them in three long strides and gathered her in his arms. "What's wrong, honey? Who was that?"

"I… I don't know." She let herself be comforted while she tried to figure out why she needed his strength in the first place. "It was a man. He said there was something he could do for me and that I'll find out what when I check the mail tomorrow."

"And that spooked you?"

She stepped back and tried to analyze why a phone call that had lasted less than a minute had so unnerved her. There was nothing conspicuously threatening about the call. In fact, other than hanging up on her, the caller had been rather polite. So why was she shaking?

"After what happened a few days ago… yes, I'm spooked."

"I'm sure it's nothing. Just a weird coincidence."

She wanted to believe him, but she had her doubts. If the narrowed eyes and stiff posture were any indications, Ben had doubts as well. Thoughts of the terror Adam Winters had put Aelissm through sprang to mind. No, it was ridiculous to think like that. What proof did she have beyond her racing pulse and a queasy feeling in her gut? She was overreacting. Aelissm's experience was bound to make her more jumpy about strange calls and trespassers.

"Let's get out of here," June said. "I'm really looking forward to that hike right now."

Without giving Ben the opportunity to suggest he drive, June hopped in behind the wheel of her truck. She hoped the need to concentrate on the road would prevent her worrisome thoughts from breeding. She drummed her thumbs on the steering wheel as she drove, tapping out an inconsistent beat that matched the tempo of her anxiety. Why couldn't she believe that these two startling incidences were unrelated? As long and tiring as the day had been, she couldn't wait to start up the trail to Sawtooth. Maybe the exertion would chase the nagging fear away.

She didn't bother shutting the truck down when she reached her cabin. Because she and Ben had packed for their campout the day before, getting ready for the hike to Sawtooth was only a matter of adding the perishable items—hot dogs, by tradition—to the packs and loading Cheyenne and Casey in the back of the truck. In less than ten minutes, she was back in the truck—passenger seat this time—and heading down to the trailhead.

"I'll take the gun this time," Ben said.

"What?" she asked. She glanced around. They were at the trailhead already?

"It's for bears, June. Remember?"

Unbidden but very welcome, a smile lifted her lips. If Ben had any lingering anxiety about holding a firearm, it didn't show, and that simple, powerful realization did a lot to draw June from her dread. "Right. Bears. Are you ready to shoot it yet?"

"We'll see."

The hike up to the lake did exactly what June hoped, and by the time she and Ben had crossed the outlet stream and picked out a campsite under the trees beside the meadow on the opposite shore, she had finally pushed the phone call from her mind. She had far more important, exciting things to consider. Letting her pack drop unceremoniously to the ground, she twined her arms around Ben's neck and kissed him hungrily. Then, abruptly, she stepped away, leaving him staring after her with his mouth hanging open. She watched him for a moment, marveling when a sly, predatory grin spread over his handsome face. He stalked her across the packed dirt of the camping area and out into the meadow. Laughing, June pranced out of reach again and again until at last he snagged her around the waist and dragged her down in the lush, spongy grass. They collapsed together in a heap, and she reveled in the breathless joy of it. This was definitely the Ben she remembered.

Ben propped himself on his elbow and gazed down at her. His expression softened into adoration, and when he kissed her, June understood what it was to be cherished. He was tender and considerate, giving and attentive. She could've stayed there, lying in the meadow with Ben's undivided attention all night, but Cheyenne and Casey had other plans. Seeing their people at such a perfect level for licking was too much to resist, and they bounded over. June squealed as the dogs lavished her with kisses.

"All right, all right!" she said, rising to her feet. "Dinner and fetch it is. Get us a couple willow sticks so we can roast the hot dogs."

As she gathered enough kindling and firewood for a small campfire, she wondered if Aelissm had felt the flutter of butterflies that night she'd lost her virginity or if she and Pat had simply gone with the moment without any forethought at all. June took a deep breath. Was she nervous? Or excited? Both, and a lot more. Once she had a nice bed of coals, she broke out the hot dogs, buns, and condiment packets. While they toasted their hot dogs over the fire, they talked about the weather, the dogs, fishing, and so many other mundane topics that June began to wonder if Ben was trying to keep her mind off the phone call or what she had planned for the night.

"So, tell me again. How long until the trip to Washington?" Ben asked.

"About ten days now."

"I guess I should clean my stuff out of the house in Poulsbo while we're there."

"You're really going to stay in Northstar?"

"I really am. There are too many reasons to stay."

"Such as…?"

He didn't answer. Instead, he curled his fingers around the back of her head and kissed her. Her eyelids slid closed, and she leaned into him. When he pulled away, there was the faintest, most beautiful smile on his face.

"Your hot dog's turning black."

Ben lifted his willow poker and glared at the black-crusted hot dog. "Crap."

"Since Luke isn't here, we have plenty more," June replied with a laugh. "I'm sure the dogs would love that one."

After dinner, they finished setting up their tent and zipped the two sleeping bags together, then journeyed out across the meadow. June sat on the log across the delta of the inlet stream with her feet in the icy water while Ben threw a stick for the dogs. The stream was so clear that she could count the individual, coarse grains of granite sand and gravel and watch the minnows darting through the lazy current. She lifted her gaze to watch Ben and the dogs. Though he chucked the stick over the meadow, Casey and Cheyenne still found their way into the water, bounding through the stream or darting past Ben and barreling into the lake.

"Well, I was trying to keep them dry," he remarked as he joined her on the log.

"If there is water within a quarter mile, Cheyenne will find it."

"Casey's just as bad. Water dogs."

Ben tucked June into his side and wrapped his arms around her. Together, they watched the sun color the scattered clouds with gold, orange, and crimson, and June was glad for the warmth of Ben's body as the temperature dropped. Dew gathered around them, glistening in the failing light, and the first stars glittered faintly in the twilight sky. The dogs, exhausted, sprawled nearby on the grassy bank of the stream. June pulled her numb feet out of the water, kicked the water off, and tucked them up on the log. There were few things in the world more right or more perfect than sitting with Ben, watching the day bow to night. When she dropped her head to Ben's shoulder and he tightened his arm around her, her nerves settled and a pure, blissful calm settled over her. It was the same healing peace she'd felt when she'd first come to Northstar all those years ago and confirmed what her heart had known all along. She loved Ben the way best friends, lovers and old married couples loved.

Without a word, she took Ben's hand, rose to her feet with a grace and balance aided by the utter tranquility she felt in her heart, and helped him up. Their campfire was now only a dimly glowing bed of coals, so the brief thought to sit up for a while longer and bask in the warmth of the flames faded away. She dragged the sleeping bag out of the tent and spread it out just beyond the edge of the forested camping area. The ground was springy and surprisingly soft—much softer than the packed dirt of the camping area—and above her, the darkening sky was flooded with sparkling stars.

Ben spoke her name with hesitation in his voice.

"Are you a virgin?"

She glanced at him and away again as shyness twined with embarrassment. "Why does that matter?"

"It doesn't, really. But I'm curious as to why because you're a beautiful woman, and I imagine you've had your fair share of men to choose from."

"Maybe, but that doesn't mean I trusted any of them enough to let them get that close to me—physically or emotionally." She stared out across the lake and chewed on her lips for a moment before continuing. "Then I adopted Luke, and that further upped the level of trust I needed to feel for a man because it wasn't just about me anymore. I had to trust any man I dated with *him*. Aaron was the only one I felt enough for and trusted enough, but he's still grieving, and honestly, what I felt for him is *nothing* compared to how I feel for you."

Ben was quiet for a long while, and she hoped she hadn't ruined the moment, but she needed to be completely open with him so he would understand the depth of her commitment to them. At last, he squeezed his arm around her.

"I admire your selflessness, but it's okay to put yourself and your wants first on occasion."

"What do you think I'm doing?" she asked, trying

to be playful but certain there was still too much self-consciousness in her voice to pull it off. "Does it turn you off that I'm a twenty-nine-year-old virgin?"

"Good God, no. I can't explain what it makes me feel. Flattered. Special to be the one."

"The only one."

She beckoned him to join her on the sleeping bag. When the dogs bounded over, only half-dry after their swim, June tried to scold them but only laughed.

"Bugger off, you two. Go on, git!"

The golden retrievers obeyed, walked a few paces away, and settled down with very audible grunts. June turned her attention back to Ben. She pulled his t-shirt over his head and trailed her hands over his shoulders, chest, and stomach, enjoying the feel of soft skin and firm muscle beneath her palms. He'd never let her play like this before, she realized, and she wanted to take in and memorize every precious line of him. He was so beautiful, she thought, with his toned body bathed in pale starlight, and his dark hair limned with silver moonlight.

"Aelissm was right," she whispered. "This really is the most romantic way to make love."

"Maybe not for everyone," Ben replied. His voice had a sexy hoarseness that made her shiver with pleasure. "But for us… it's perfect."

"Before you go diving in, here." She pulled one of the foil-wrapped condoms out of her back pocket. With a smirk, she added, "It's pack in, pack out up here, you know. Don't want you to go plunging in unprepared like Pat did."

Ben tipped his head back and laughed. "Way more than I needed to know. And here I always thought Aelissm was the shameless one."

"She is, but I have my moments."

She trailed her lips and her teeth from Ben's jaw to his shoulder, pleased when goose bumps rose on his skin. Slowly, teasingly, he removed her shirt. The cool night air hit her skin, and she shivered, but Ben's warm hands quickly chased away the chill. At first, he was gentle and curious, caressing her with feather-light touches and kisses. Then his hands and lips became more aggressive, driven by the same urgency pounding through June's veins. The rest of their clothes were discarded in a rush. He stroked her to aching need until she writhed against him, pleading with her body for more because she could not find the words. She sat in his lap and a whole new heat ignited when she felt him hard and ready against her.

"Are you sure?" he asked.

"There are very few things I've been more sure of, Ben."

"I just don't want you to regret this in the morning."

"I won't."

He laid her down, and the intensity of his kisses and touches reminded her deliciously of the man he'd been before the shooting. There was no hesitation in him, no cautious restraint, and no more excuses. There was only exquisite hunger.

"Tell me you want me," she whispered.

"I want you," he replied. His breath was hot against her neck. "I need you."

Those words were a heady aphrodisiac. The exhilaration of being the center of his attention and his desire was more thrilling than June had ever imagined. He sat back for a moment to roll the condom on, then pulled her into his arms again. She knitted her hands together behind his head and pressed her body against his chest. They sat locked together like that for a few moments before Ben pulled away so they could crawl into the sleeping bag. Warmth folded around her like a cocoon.

Ben nipped at her ear and whispered, "I love you."

Then, with a thrust, he was inside her, and she

inhaled sharply and tensed at the spear of pain. Ben moved gently and slowly, and soon pleasure overcame the pain. She clung to him, digging her nails into his back as they moved together, racing toward the climax. Her love for him built with it, consuming her with a resolute assurance that this was right and that she loved him with every beat of her racing heart. The orgasm broke over them with shattering intensity, saturating her with pleasure and devotion. Ben panted as he held her, and she trembled in his arms.

"I'm sorry, June," he whispered. "I couldn't control myself."

"Don't apologize. That was… wow." She snuggled against him, and as her heart rate slowed, contentment filtered through her. "Well worth the wait."

"Definitely." He was silent for a moment, then said, "I forgot how beautiful they are."

She tilted her head up to see him staring at the sky with the glimmer of a smile playing on his face. She followed his gaze to the glittering tapestry above them and her love for this magical place was renewed tenfold. Back in Washington, the night sky was black and only the brighter stars could pierce the light pollution of Seattle, but out here, miles away from any city, the sky was a rich, glowing arch of sapphire blue.

"I've looked at the stars since I've been back but not like this. I haven't really stopped to appreciate them."

"Maybe tonight is just more special."

"It is *much* more special. Stargazing will never be the same."

A soft laughter escaped her, almost a purr. She couldn't imagine a more perfect time or place to give herself completely to Ben. "Hmm. There's the Big Dipper… and the Little Dipper," she said, pointing to the constellations. "And Polaris, the North Star. Guiding us home."

"We are home."

"We?"

"Yes, June. We." Ben nuzzled her neck.

She rested her hand over his heart, felt the steady rhythm and knew that every beat belonged to her now. "Show me again."

This time, Ben held himself in check, driving her to the edge and pulling her back time and again until, finally, she couldn't stand it, and he pushed her over the edge. She clung to him, panting and quivering with the force of her climax. It was several minutes later when she finally regained enough sense and breath to whisper his name.

"I love you, too, Ben Conner."

Fourteen

BEN OPENED HIS EYES, fully lucid and wonderfully refreshed though he had been sleeping soundly just moments ago. He looked through the mesh skylights of the tents. The sky was bright with coming day, but the forest canopy was still in the shadow of the mountain peaks. A glance around the interior of the tent showed both dogs curled up together on the other side of June. When his gaze fell on his lover, memories of last night saturated his brain with sweet intensity, and tendrils of need curled through him. He never would have thought that the quietly observant girl he'd known in high school would be so eager and so willing, though perhaps he should have had an idea from the way she kissed. She was an enthralling mixture of confidence and innocence, demanding one moment and yielding in the next. She was… everything.

She lay on her side, facing him, with one hand beneath her head and the other curled against her chest, and she was the most beautiful thing he'd ever seen. He tucked her hair behind her ear. Last night had changed their friendship. No, *changed* was the wrong word. She was still his best friend. The weeks living with her here in Northstar—especially last night—had added several new, breathtaking facets to their friendship.

He understood now. He had loved June—and not only as a friend—for a very long time, though he had no hope of pinpointing the moment he'd first fallen for her. As his mind wandered back over the weeks since his return to Northstar and farther back through high school, he felt a stab of guilt that it had taken sex to make him see the truth… or at least to admit it. Although, honestly, it wasn't their lovemaking, as spectacular as it had been, that had opened his eyes. It was what June had given him and what she had said. He was *the only one,* and there were few things she was more sure of than loving him. Perhaps she had referred only to the physical act, but June didn't give only part of herself, and when she gave her heart, she gave it all. Luke was proof enough of that.

Thought of her son made Ben smile. What he felt for the boy was more than simple fondness derived from June's love, more than a feeling of responsibility to see to Luke's welfare because of the shooting. He hesitated to put a name to that particular emotion, unsure if it was real. Luke had condoned Ben's relationship with June, but would he really be able to open his heart and accept Ben in the role of his father? Could Ben forgive himself—finally and completely—for creating that void? He understood that a family with June and Luke was what he wanted, but was it possible?

June shifted a little and she opened her eyes. "You're awake early."

"So are you," Ben replied.

"I always wake up early."

"I might have to start waking earlier from now on." He gently kissed her brow and though he could easily—and very much wanted to—make love to her again, he resisted. He wanted to savor the memories of last night for a while longer before he added more to them. "What's the plan for the day?"

"Well, since we have to be to work by noon, we should probably pack up camp and head back down the mountain. I know it's early," she said, trailing a finger down his chest. "But it usually takes an hour and a half to hike down, and I would rather have some time to eat and rest… and maybe do something else… before work."

"Something else, huh?"

"If we're lucky."

"There's that 'we' again."

"It has such a nice ring to it, doesn't it?"

"Mmm-hmm. And as much as I would like to explore this we thing again, *we* should probably get on down the trail."

It did wonders for his ego and his heart to see her so unwilling to crawl out of the sleeping bag. Judging by the way she curled around him and stroked her hands over his body, it wasn't the chill in the morning air that made her hesitate.

"June…."

"All right, all right. I'm up."

Yup, chilly, he thought as a draft of cold air flowed into the sleeping bag when she crawled out. Then again, that was probably for the best because June was gloriously naked. Last night, there had not been enough light to fully appreciate the sight of her, but in the brightening morning, his eyes were able to take in every smooth, elegant line and curve. *I am one lucky man.*

"Well, come on, lazy bones. Get up."

June was efficient at breaking down camp, and within fifteen minutes after they'd dressed and eaten a light snack of breakfast bars, they completed their final check of the campsite and meadow. Ben glanced around and knew that this would forever be a very special place. With a sigh, he turned away and followed her along the narrow trail back to the main trail.

When they arrived at the cabin, they quickly stowed their gear and June wasted no time stripping out of her clothes.

"Mind if I join you?" Ben asked.

"Please do."

What started out as June's polite offer to scrub Ben's back quickly spiraled out of control, until Ben had her pinned against the rough stone of the shower wall with her legs wrapped tightly around him. The need to claim her was so overpowering that he nearly forgot the condom. Impatient and annoyed by the delay, he allowed June to sheath him, then kissed her forcefully and gripped her hips, hoisting her off the ground. With a thrust, he was inside her, and a guttural growl rumbled in his throat as he gave his desire free reign. This wasn't the tender, considerate lovemaking as before, but heart-pounding, feral sexuality. She clenched her legs and arms around him, digging her fingers into the meat of his back and matching his driving pace with eager abandon. The orgasm slammed through him with such intensity that he cried out. They sank to the floor of the shower, panting and trembling together, and let the steaming water pour over them.

"Is it always like this?" June asked a few minutes later, still breathless.

"No. Not until you."

"That was… incredible. Untamed."

"Yes," was all he could find breath to say.

By the time they'd recovered, the water was beginning to cool, and they had to rush to finish their shower. Ben stepped out as the water turned icy so June could finish rinsing the lavender-scented conditioner out of her hair. He pulled his towel off the rack and wrapped it around his waist, then grabbed June's. When she stepped out of the shower, he held it open, and she turned her back to him so he could fold it around her. With his arms around her, he lowered his head and kissed her neck. He brushed his hands over her bare shoulders with the tenderness their joining had lacked, and she leaned back against him. She seemed so content to be held now when only minutes ago she had been consumed by the throes of passion. The complexity of her was humbling, and Ben imagined a life spent with her would be the most exciting, fulfilling adventure.

Looks like Luke and I may need to have another talk, Ben thought. Reluctantly, he let go of June and headed upstairs to dress.

"Since we've crossed the line between good friends and lovers, you may as well sleep with me," June remarked, standing in the doorway of Luke's bedroom with a playful smirk and her arms folded across her chest.

"Shouldn't we make sure Luke is really okay with this whole situation first?"

"I'm sure he'll be fine with it. I'm also sure he'd appreciate having his room back. Besides, I kinda like waking up with you beside me."

"I like it, too. All right. You win again." He grinned. "Although, it could be fun sneaking around like a pair of naughty teenagers."

She rolled her eyes and retreated to her room. *Their* room now, it appeared. He got dressed and moved his belongings out of Luke's room while June cooked breakfast.

They lingered over a tasty meal of scrambled eggs, bacon, and toast, and as Ben watched the time tick toward eleven-thirty when they would have to head down to the Ramshorn, he began to wonder if June was intentionally cutting it close so she wouldn't have to check the mail or if she had forgotten about the strange call yesterday. He hoped it was the latter. He hoped, too, that there wouldn't be anything in the mail from the caller.

* * *

June didn't see much of Ben after they started their shift. Almost immediately after they'd arrived, the large group from Great Falls arrived for their week-long wedding party. June was kept busy getting them checked in and showing them to the cabins while an unusually crowded dining room kept Ben and the new waiter occupied in the lodge. It was probably for the best because it was easier to do her job—a job she usually enjoyed—when she wasn't distracted by Ben's sexy physique or turning red as memories of their lovemaking spun through her mind.

Shaking her head, she refocused on the task at hand and smiled at the forty-five people gathered around her with their bags piled beside them. She gestured at the six cabins tucked into the trees at the edge of the circular clearing. "Here are your homes away from home for the next week. All of the cabins have at least one full bathroom except the Moose, which has only a half bath. Swimming is included with your cabins, and the pools are open from eight in the morning until ten at night. If you need fresh towels, just ask at the desk in the pool house. Your meals are also included in the package, and the lodge is open from eight A.M. until nine P.M. I'll give you a few minutes to get settled before we all meet back right here to go over the itinerary."

She watched as the guests briefly discussed who would take which cabins and dispersed. What a fun idea for a wedding, she thought. The couple would be married in an outdoor ceremony right there in the clearing in two days. The activities for the rest of the week included a barbecue reception put on by the Ramshorn, hiking, no doubt a lot of swimming in the hot springs, a trail ride to Sawtooth Lake—June cursed the shimmer of heat she felt at the mere thought of the lake—and crystal digging at Crystal Park. It was her kind of wedding and honeymoon. And it was good business for the Ramshorn. June made a mental note to look into creating a wedding package and advertising it.

It was more than an hour later before June made it back to help Ben and the new waiter. The dining room was still busy, and they were both beginning to look a little harried. She helped the waiter get caught up, then sent him outside for a short break. Next she relieved Ben.

Before she realized the passage of time, it was already after four o'clock, and her stomach growled. She hadn't eaten anything since her late breakfast. There was finally a lull, so she fixed herself and Ben cheeseburgers. Mary walked in just as June plated the burgers and took over the two occupied tables so June and Ben could enjoy their food.

"Everything go all right with the wedding party?" Mary asked, joining them for a moment.

"Yes. I was thinking… if this party goes well, we should look into offering a wedding package."

"That would be a good idea. Maybe some other types of party packages, as well." Mary smiled. "So, how was your camping trip to Sawtooth last night?"

June nearly choked on her burger, and her cheeks flushed hotly.

"Oh, my dears," Mary said. Laughter tinted her voice. "You had a lovely time, I see. Sawtooth does seem to be the place for that."

"Apparently so," June muttered. "I'm beginning to think at least half the couples in Northstar have, uh, had a 'lovely time' there."

"Ben, honey, I do believe you have managed to catch our sweet June. Congratulations."

"Thank you, Mary," Ben replied.

"She's a picky one, but only because she knows what she wants."

"I've always admired that about her."

"Okay," June asserted. "New topic."

"How is Luke doing with all this?"

"Quite well. Encouraging, actually," Ben replied. "Which surprises the hell out of me, after everything he's been through because of me."

"Ah, well, there's a lot of June in him, so I'm not surprised at all."

June straightened. "Ben Conner, I swear… if you try to take the blame for what his father did to him or fall back into that pit of guilt and self-loathing, I will slap you. Yesterday, I finally saw something of the man you used to be before the shooting. Don't you dare bury him again."

"Yes, ma'am," was Ben's quick reply. Then he leaned over and kissed her rather passionately in front of Mary and the lingering diners.

If she hadn't worked for Mary since her freshman year of college and if she hadn't been so surprised, she might have added a few more shades of red to the canvas of embarrassment. Instead, she smiled against his lips. "That's more like it."

"All right, you two, finish your lunch and get back to work," Mary said with a chuckle and excused herself to check on the diners.

"Speaking of Luke, when is he supposed to be back?" Ben asked.

"Well, the camp was supposed to be over by four. So… five-ish." She glanced at her watch. "Wow, it's almost five already."

"It's been a busy day."

June finished her burger and took their plates in to the kitchen while Ben washed his hands in the sink behind the bar and went to take menus to the party of four who had just arrived. The phone rang as June left the kitchen, and she stepped behind the bar to answer it. She held the cordless to her ear with her shoulder and took down the reservation for two more cabins.

"Well, the cabins are all booked for the next three nights," June called into the kitchen.

"Wonderful!" Mary replied.

A family of five walked in the open door of the lodge, and June was about to take them menus when the phone rang again. "Have a seat where ever you like, and Ben will be with you in just a moment," she told them before picking up the cordless phone she had just set down. "Ramshorn Hot Springs and Lodge, this is June."

"Good evening, June."

She felt as if someone had poured ice water into her veins. "You. What do you want?" she asked. Her voice trembled as a heavy ball of dread settled in her stomach. How could she have so completely forgotten about the call yesterday?

"You didn't check your mail today."

"I haven't had time. I've been swamped all day."

"Do you know where your golden boy is? I do."

For the second time, the man hung up on her. Fear drove a shard of ice through her heart. "Luke," she breathed.

Ben strolled by, and his grin evaporated when he met her gaze. "June, you're white as a ghost," he said and walked around the bar to gather her in his arms. His firm, steady embrace made her realize that she was shaking.

"He called again."

"Who?"

"The man. The man who called yesterday and told me to check the mail today. I forgot. He asked me if I knew where my 'golden boy' was, then said he knew. What the hell does that mean?"

"I don't know, honey."

"I wish Luke was here. What if—"

"No, June. Don't think it. Don't think anything like it. I'm sure Luke is fine. Probably on his way here right now."

She tried not to dwell on the call or the threat the caller had insinuated if not stated, but as the minutes crawled more slowly as each one passed, June grew sick with worry. At five-thirty, Mary finally told her to sit down on the couch for a few minutes. Sitting just made it worse and within two minutes, she was back on her feet, trying to distract herself by doing her job and trying unsuccessfully to not glance out the window every time a car pulled up or drove past to the pool house.

Five forty-five came and went, and still Luke had not arrived. Panic clawed at her.

"Where the hell is he?"

"He just pulled up," Ben remarked.

June raced out the door and threw her arms

around Luke's neck as he crested the six steep steps from the driveway. She clung to him, and the feel of her son safe and whole in her arms left her weak and saturated with relief. "Thank God you're all right!"

"Hey, I'm here and I'm fine," he replied soothingly and hugged her back. "Would someone please tell me what I missed?"

June looked up to see both Ben and Mary standing behind her on the porch. Ben explained about the two calls, and Luke tightened his arms reassuringly.

"That would explain this. There's no return address and no postmark. Grandma says someone left it on the counter sometime last night after she closed or this morning before Tracie Hammond opened the post office."

Ben snatched the envelope before June could grab it and held it out of her reach. "Oh no you don't. I want you to sit down, June, and take about twenty deep breaths before I give this to you."

June obeyed and sat down on the bench beside the door but didn't let go of Luke's hand. She closed her eyes and inhaled as slowly and deeply as her lungs allowed and let it out. Luke was safe, she told herself, which meant she was overreacting again. She felt the tickle of a small smile. The bastard could threaten Luke all he wanted, but if he tried to hurt her son, she'd put a bullet between his eyes without flinching.

"That is a frightening smile, June," Mary remarked. "And I don't have to ask to know what you're thinking, Mama Bear. I've got to go back in, but you let me know if you need anything."

"Thank you, Mary." She shifted her attention to her lover. "I'm calm, Ben. Give me the letter."

When he handed it over, June finally let go of Luke and carefully, deliberately opened the envelope. The letter was typed.

My dearest June, please do not be alarmed, she read. Her lip curled in snarl. A snowball had a better chance surviving in hell than the writer had of her not being alarmed. *I do not wish to hurt you, but I cannot continue to sit by and see you deceived because you are too generous and selfless to understand that you are being used. I am afraid the time has come for me to prove to you that Luke McKindel is not the innocent golden boy you believe him to be.*

June nearly crumpled the letter in disbelief. Anger flared, hot and acidic, and burned away the last traces of her fear. She took another deep breath and forced herself to keep reading.

He is cold, cruel and entirely selfish.

"Bullshit," she muttered.

What he did to Carol should be proof enough of that. He claimed to love her but betrayed her without a thought. And you. How many times has he stood in the way of your happiness? He is a jealous beast, and if you think he will share your love with anyone else, you are sadly mistaken. I know it all too well. He deserves to suffer for the anguish he has caused so many others. I will make him suffer, and though I know the truth will bring you pain, I must protect you from his lies. I cannot take the coward's way like Adam Winters. I will not. I am yours always.

She felt the need to let out a searing string of expletives, but her voice was paralyzed by the most vicious, seething fury she'd ever felt. Every muscle tensed with it, and it was only when Ben sat beside her and put a gentle hand on her shoulder that she noticed she was shaking again. Luke squatted in front of her and the sight of his concerned blue eyes brought a low, animal snarl from her throat. How could anyone look into those eyes and believe Luke was anything but big-hearted?

She looked at the letter again. All at once, the curses flooded from her mouth with such ferocity that even Ben leaned back in surprise. It turned into a river of gibberish when she tried to repeat what was in the letter. Finally, she thrust it at Ben, too irate to form coherent speech. After he'd read it, she saw the same boiling rage darken the features of his handsome face, though he was able to contain it better. He briefly wrapped his arm around her shoulders and squeezed, then kissed her cheek and stood.

"Here," he said and handed the letter to Luke. "I'll be right back."

Luke sat where Ben had just moments before and scanned the letter. The only outward sign of his reaction was the twitch of the muscle in his jaw.

"Apparently I'm cold, cruel, and entirely selfless and I deserve to suffer for it," he said. His voice broke on *suffer*. He took a deep breath, seemed to collect himself, and smiled at her. "I've been called a lot worse before. It's weird to see McKindel again. It feels like that was a different life."

"It was," June replied. Her anger receded and tears blurred her vision, but she refused to cry. She wasn't going let this man—whoever he was—do this to her. She'd already given him too much.

Ben stepped back outside. He glanced between Luke and June before asking, "Luke, are you all right?"

"Yeah."

"Good. Take your mom home. I'll be home as soon as it slows down."

"I can finish my shift."

"I might believe you if you weren't shaking like a leaf again. Go home, June."

He kissed her so tenderly that she couldn't refuse him. And, honestly, she didn't feel like plastering a fake smile on her face for the next two hours while she battled the sickening, shifting tides of anger and worry.

"I called Aaron about the letter," Ben added. "He'll probably beat you home."

June nodded and allowed herself to be pulled to her feet. Ben hugged her tightly before promising to be home as soon as he could get away. She wanted to tell him that she didn't want to be even two feet away from him—or Luke—let alone twelve miles, but Mary needed the help. She felt guilty for leaving early, but Ben was right. She needed to go home. In all likelihood, there was probably nothing to be worried about, anyhow, besides a very strange, deluded man.

Luke drove Ben's truck since his bags were in the bed, leaving June's parked across the driveway from the lodge. June asked him about the football camp, and the change in topic did wonders for them both. It wasn't long before his stories about the practical jokes had her laughing.

"I'm looking forward to watching the games… and watching you and the team take state again."

"We'll see. We've got this untested new quarter-back."

"Untested? Yeah, right. I seem to recall Coach Wells putting you in at quarterback a few times… like last year when Mike thought he'd sprained his ankle."

"Yeah, but that was only for a couple of plays."

"Quit being so humble. You'll do great."

"Sorry, can't help it. It's in my nature."

Aaron's truck was parked in front of the cabin when they arrived, but he was just pulling his three-year-old daughter out of her car seat, so he hadn't been there long. Luke parked the truck and shut it down. June climbed out and greeted Aaron and his little girl.

"This makes twice in three days that I've ruined your evening at home," she remarked.

"You haven't ever ruined my evening, June." He cleared his throat. "Ben tells me you received two concerning phone calls and a letter."

She nodded. "Luke has the letter. Come on inside, and I'll get you and Jessie something to drink."

She let the dogs out and stepped inside with Aaron following a step behind. Luke took up the rear with his bag slung over his shoulder. He dropped his bag in the laundry room, then pulled the letter out of his back pocket and gave it to Aaron.

"Do you mind if I take a shower before we sit down and discuss that? I only got a quick one after practice, and I still feel filthy."

"Help yourself," June said.

While Aaron sat on the couch and read the letter, she went into the kitchen to get him a glass of ice water and Jessie a glass of milk.

"Jessie! No, sweetheart. This isn't our house. Put that back, please."

June glanced under the cupboards over the snack bar. Jessie had pulled a DVD off the rack and now waved it at her father, trying to get him to put it on.

"Moomie," she said.

"No movie," Aaron replied. "Put it back, please."

June watched them for a moment. Aaron absolutely adored his daughter, and when he was with her, he looked happy again. Feeling like she was spying, she took the drinks in to her guests and sat on the loveseat.

"You're a good dad," she remarked quietly.

"I hope so. Most days I feel like I don't do enough for her."

"I think that's a feeling most parents have. Is she starting to talk a little more?"

Aaron frowned and watched his daughter carefully return the DVD to its place on the shelf. "Good job, Jessie. Thank you."

The toddler beamed and raced over, slamming into him at full force. With a shy smile at June, she crawled into her father's lap and snuggled up to him.

"She's picked up a few more words. I get the feeling she can say more than she does. She listens well and seems to understand just about everything I ask of her. I should really start scheduling more play dates with Ant for her."

"I'm sure he'd love it."

A faint frown darkened his features when he looked at her, and she noted the same flicker of regret she'd become familiar with since their last date. Until Ben had showed up so unexpectedly, she'd wished Aaron had been ready to start dating again. He was, as she'd told Ben, a good man. Maybe he'd been a little wild for her tastes when they'd first met in college, but marriage to Erica had given him focus and calmed the restlessness in him.

"My window of opportunity is closed, isn't it."

"I'm afraid it is."

"I figured as much the first time I saw you and Ben together. I'm happy for you, June."

"I'm happy for me, too, for as long as it lasts. Nothing's been set in glittering stone yet, but…."

"It will be soon enough. Just wait. So, anyhow, about this letter."

June suppressed a shudder. "I haven't even tried to figure out who wrote it yet. All I can say is that the caller sounded familiar. I can't place the voice, but I've heard it before."

"I have a question. Adam Winters? As in the man who put Aelissm through hell four years ago?"

"And then fell for another woman while he was trying to find her. Yeah. As far as I can guess. He's the only Adam Winters I know."

"That may be somewhere to start. I'll have to get his number from Aelissm."

"I have it."

She went to her desk and retrieved her address book. She flipped it to W, found Adam and Amber Winters' information, and passed the book to Aaron. He jotted the phone number down in the spiral notebook he'd brought in. She should probably call Adam herself, but the thought of dredging up those dark months of his life made her decide to leave it up to Aaron.

"I'll give him a call tomorrow. Next question. What exactly happened between Luke and Carol?"

"Carol got it in her head that Luke and Becky

Epperson are more than just friends, which they're not. She broke up with him in a short, to-the-point note without giving him the opportunity to deny it. From what I've gathered, she didn't say his friendship with Becky was the reason she broke up with him, but her friend Nikki insinuated it. Luke hasn't spoken to Carol since."

"Luke wouldn't ever do that to Carol." He shook his head. He scribbled more notes in his notebook, un-bothered by having to reach around his daughter to write. "Between that and this letter… someone really has a skewed opinion of him."

"I think your daughter's asleep."

Aaron looked down at the little girl curled against him, and a gentle smile graced his features. "Doesn't surprise me. She's been fighting the naps lately, and she hasn't had one today. Which means getting her to go to bed tonight is going to be a royal pain. Anyhow, back on track."

"The calls and the letter are very personal, but they aren't specifically threatening beyond saying he will make Luke suffer for the pain he's *supposedly* caused." June took a deep breath to slow her increasing pulse. "After the trespasser, I was already a little on edge."

"Understandably so. It's too much of a coincidence for me to believe they're unrelated. Calling you his 'dearest June' and wanting to protect you points to someone who has a thing for you, someone who is jealous of your bond with Luke. Can you make me a list of the men you've dated since adopting him?"

"Besides you and Ben, the only men I've dated are Pete Landers and Jake Sterling."

"Jake's always been an ass but more so lately. He didn't use to slack work, and we all know how he feels about Luke, but I don't think he would write something so eloquent. Pete… he's got a little college under his belt, but I've never heard him talk like that."

"Some people write far better than they speak."

"True enough. He's been a little off lately, too, but I guess his mother has been ill."

"I don't want to believe it's Pete. He likes Luke. And if you strip the letter down to its basic meaning, it sounds exactly like Jake."

"Jake does make a more believable suspect, doesn't he? The mention of Carol makes them both more suspicious because she's their niece. I don't want to limit the field to just the two of them, and until I have a little more to go on, I think it's wise to be very, very careful. I'd watch what you say about this to anyone outside your family and trusted friends. If this man and the trespasser are one and the same, he's someone who knows you well enough to be able to find your cabin."

"And it may turn out to be nothing more than empty threats."

"I really hope that's the case. Either way, maybe it's a good thing you guys are heading to Washington in a few days. It'll be a nice distraction for you."

June heard the shower turn off. "It will. Do you still want to talk to Luke about this?"

"Not tonight. You guys have been through enough for one day."

"Thank you."

Luke stepped out of the utility room with a towel around his waist. As he climbed the stairs, he said, "I'll be down in a minute."

"No need to hurry," Aaron replied. "I think we've figured out all that we can with so little information."

Luke nodded briefly. June watched him cross the balcony and disappear into his bedroom. Somehow, a sliver of discomfiture made its way through the distressing thoughts cluttering her mind. It would take Luke all of about a second to notice that Ben's things were no longer in his room. When he came back out of his room comfortably dressed in plaid pajama pants, he met her gaze and uttered a knowing *huh*.

Busted, she thought. Willing her face to stay cool and not betray her, she turned back to Aaron. "Are you hungry? I can fix you something to eat."

"That's not necessary, June. I don't want to impose."

"I have to feed Luke, anyhow."

"In that case, sure."

Barking at the back door alerted her to the dogs' desire to be let in, so she went into the kitchen and opened the door. The two golden retrievers bounded in the door and made a beeline for Aaron and Jessie.

"Cheyenne! Casey!" she hissed. "Shh!"

Abruptly, the dogs stopped, looking back at her questioningly. She pulled a couple of dog cookies out for them and made them lie in the living room while she cooked. Luke joined Aaron in the kitchen, and they talked about football. Luke expressed a desire to help Aaron any way he could, but even from the kitchen June could see the relief in his posture when Aaron assured him the subject had already been covered well enough for now.

When Ben arrived just as she was putting dinner on the table, she was in a much calmer state of mind.

For some inexplicable reason, the sight of him strolling through the front door as if he were already a permanent piece of her home made her feel like everything was going to be all right. He greeted Aaron and Luke and looked at June. The worry on his face drifted away when he saw the welcoming smile on hers.

"All right, boys, dinner is served."

Aaron gently slid out from under his daughter, paused to make sure she was still asleep, and followed Luke to the table. Ben stepped over to June and planted a quick kiss on her lips.

"Hi, honey," she said. "Hungry?"

With a twitch of his lips, he threaded his arms around her and replied, "Yep."

Luke glanced between them with one brow lifted. "There's a question I wanted to ask, but I'm pretty sure I already know the answer."

"I'd say the answer is pretty blatantly obvious," Aaron agreed. "And I don't even know the question."

"Yes, Ben, my smarty-pants son is too smart for our own good."

"Luke, I think you and I need to have another talk," Ben said.

"Probably so."

After dinner, Aaron took his daughter home, and

June changed into her flannel and boxer shorts and settled onto the couch to watch a movie with Ben on one side of her, Luke on the other, and the dogs curled up at their feet. She held her boys close to her, soothed by the simple love between them. They had both been there for her today, her beacons of strength when she'd needed it most. Exhausted and lulled by the warmth of them, she dozed off with her head on Ben's shoulder.

Quiet voices roused her some time later, but she was too comfortable to open her eyes, so she listened.

"I've never seen her like that," Luke said. "She's always so strong and so in control of her emotions. To see her lose it like that…. It scared the crap out of me."

"Like Mary said. Mama bear defending her cub," Ben replied. "How are *you* doing?"

"I'm all right. More pissed than anything right now. It's not what he said about me. I know who I am. 'Don't be alarmed', he said. Why wouldn't Mom be alarmed by someone threatening to make me suffer? And after seeing what Aunt Aeli went through with Adam, of course she's going to be alarmed! He has to know that because he obviously knows what Adam did!" Luke paused for a moment. "Sorry, but being angry is better than being terrified."

"Maybe so. I felt my fair share of both today. June wasn't the only one afraid something had happened when you didn't show up when she thought you would."

"I appreciate that, Ben. You know, I'm glad you seem to have made up your mind about her. I don't remember ever having a happy family, so I can't even begin to explain what it's like to have one now."

They fell into companionable silence, and June nearly fell asleep again, but Ben shifted beside her. When he lifted her into his arms, she curled instinctively into him.

"Time for bed, love," he whispered.

He carried her upstairs and settled her into bed with infinite tenderness, then slid under the blankets and tucked her against him. Enveloped by his warmth and quiet strength, she slipped easily back into a peaceful sleep.

Fifteen

LUKE OPENED HIS EYES and groggily looked around. He lay on the couch with his book lying open on his chest. The cabin was quiet, which meant that June and Ben hadn't returned with Becky. He reached up to rub the sleep out of his eyes, then covered his face with his hands for a moment. The tension that had grown steadily in the week since the letter had arrived now tightened the muscles in his neck, shoulders, and back. There had been no other word from the man—who, if it was the same man Adam Winters remembered, called himself JP—and maybe Luke should have relaxed a little. No news was good news, right? But he couldn't suppress the nagging worry that a man who had been fixated enough on June four years ago that Adam Winters would remember him like it was this morning would give up so quickly after just beginning to implement whatever it was he had in mind. It was probably JP's intent to give Luke time to dwell on it.

He closed his book and set it on the coffee table, then let his eyes drift closed. It seemed like only moments later that he heard June's voice in the kitchen.

"I hate to wake him, but we should probably haul the bags out to the trucks."

"I'll wake him up," Becky volunteered cheerfully.

"I'm awake," he said, hoping to prevent whatever rude awakening Becky surely had in mind.

"Darn," she muttered.

He sat up, swung his legs around to set his feet on the floor, and stepped on two warm, furry bodies. Casey and Cheyenne lifted their heads and glared at him accusingly. He apologized by vigorously scratching under their collars, and he knew he was forgiven when they laid their heads on his knees. "Good dogs."

With a yawn, he walked into the kitchen where June and Becky were gathering food for the long drive to Washington tomorrow. He helped Ben take the bags out to the trucks while June and Becky finished the snacks. He wished they could leave tonight, anxious to see if a little time away from Northstar might help him forget JP's letter. Luke snarled. The fact that he wanted to get away from his home made him angrier. He was always glad to visit his grandparents, but had always left the Northstar Valley with a twinge of reluctance.

After everything for the trip had been taken out to the trucks, Luke sat at the kitchen table while June and Ben double-checked the cabin to make sure they'd packed everything they wanted. Becky sat down across from him, frowning. She didn't know about the letter or the calls because Ben hadn't wanted to worry her or his sister, but Becky was smart, and she sensed something out of place.

Luke pushed to his feet, restless and hungry. A glance in the fridge reminded him that they hadn't been grocery shopping because of the trip. There were a couple of apples that hadn't been packed for the trip, so he grabbed one and offered the other to Becky. She nodded, so he tossed it to her. The apple did little to slake his appetite and did nothing to calm the agitation. When he realized he was pacing around the kitchen like a cornered mountain lion, he forced himself to stand still at the kitchen sink. He braced his hands on the lip of the sink and stared blindly out the window. His stomach growled, and the strain and anger crashed down on him. He took a swipe at the dish drainer and sent it flying. The silverware scattered in a cacophony of metallic clings and clangs, and the single glass shattered against the corner of the woodstove. He felt something warm and wet trickle down his fingers and stared at his hand in disbelief. Blood streamed from a gash on his thumb. He watched a drop splatter on the floor.

"Dammit!" he bellowed.

June jumped off the second stair with Ben half a step behind. She slid to a halt when she saw his hand. "What happened?"

Luke couldn't speak. He was too angry about the letter, too frustrated about the lack of something filling to eat, and too vexed at his own stupidity to form an explanation. He just stood there, dripping blood onto the floor and clenching his teeth to keep any further outbursts locked inside.

June turned the faucet on, snatched his hand and pulled it under the stream of frigid water. "Ben or Becky, can you get me the first aid kit out of the bathroom?"

Ben retrieved the kit while Becky stared at Luke with wide eyes. Ben held the kit open for June. Shaking her head, she plucked out the necessary supplies, and Luke let her doctor his hand without saying a word. It wasn't as bad as it had looked and wouldn't need stitches.

"Now, would you mind telling me what you're pissed at?" June remarked when she finished.

"The world."

"That's a broad topic. Can you narrow it down a little?"

"The letter, mostly. And I'm hungry."

"Maybe we should head down to the Bedspread now instead of waiting until six. I could eat, too."

"What letter?" Becky asked. "What's going on? And don't tell me 'nothing', because I know something's wrong. We're going on a fun trip tomorrow, but no one's excited."

Ben sighed. "I think it's time to bring her into the loop. And probably Pat and Aelissm, too."

"Ben, we talked about that."

"I know we did, and I don't want to bring up Aelissm's bad memories, either, but as I recall, Pat was a pretty gifted detective. We could probably use his input."

"Fine, whatever."

Luke walked outside and sat on the steps of the back deck while June cleaned up the silverware and broken glass and Ben filled Becky in about JP's calls and letters. A few minutes later, June called him in to get ready to head down to the Bedspread. June, Ben, and Becky piled into June's truck, but Luke grabbed his helmet and hopped on his dirt bike. He took off down the mountain, willing his stressful thoughts to stay behind him in the dust. Aelissm was on the deck of the Bedspread Inn when he arrived.

"Hi, Aunt Aeli," he greeted.

"Hi, Luke. You're here early. Or are you just out for a ride."

He shook his head. "Mom, Ben, and Becky are following in the truck. I felt like riding."

"You guys all packed and ready for tomorrow?"

"Yup. You?"

"Almost. What happened to your hand?"

"I got into a fight with a knife in the dish drainer and lost."

His aunt raised an eyebrow but didn't voice her question. He took a seat in one of the woven willow chairs to wait for the rest of his family to arrive. "So,

Aunt Aeli, do you want a chance to recoup that hundred dollars you lost in your bet with Pat?"

"That depends. What are you thinking?"

"A new bet."

"About what?"

"How long until Ben proposes to Mom."

She tossed her head back and laughed. "I'm not taking that bet. You have the unfair advantage of front row seats."

"And you've known them both a lot longer."

"Not gonna happen, Luke. I learned my lesson on the last bet, thank you. But I will say this. Judging by the changes in them both since their overnight stay up at Sawtooth, it'll be soon."

At last, June, Ben, and Becky arrived. Instead of taking a table inside, they opted to dine at one of the picnic tables on the deck. Ben asked Aeli to go inside and bring Pat out. She frowned, but did as he asked, and moments later, Pat strolled out the glass doors of the dining room. Ben fetched JP's letter—now safely sealed in a Ziploc bag—and put it on the table.

"What's this?" Pat asked, turning it so he and Aelissm could read it.

June and Ben took turns filling Pat and Aeli in on what had happened nine days ago, including the talk with Aaron Hammond and what little Adam Winters had been able to tell. June's worry that the letter would dig up painful memories for Aelissm seemed to be misplaced as it wasn't fear but sympathetic worry that flashed in her friend's eyes.

"Why didn't you tell us about this sooner?" she asked, hugging June.

"We didn't want to bring up those memories," June replied.

"That shouldn't have stopped you," Pat remarked. "We're your friends, and we would've done our best to help you regardless of what we felt."

"I know that, Pat."

"Good. Next time, don't wait nine days."

"So, this is why you got into a fight with a knife," Aeli said to Luke. "Don't believe a damned word this JP says. We all know who you are, and *you* know who you are. Don't let him win, Luke."

She leaned down and hugged him tightly. He closed his eyes and thanked God for his family. Whatever happened, he had them, and with their love, he could get through anything. Whatever sick game JP was playing, he wouldn't win.

* * *

June stepped out of her truck in front of her

parents' Keyport home and inhaled deeply. The smells were so different here than in Northstar, but the fragrances of the riotous flowers in her mother's garden and the faint, permeating mixture of saltwater, cedar, fir, and damp earth never failed to yank her back to her childhood. The American flag drifted with the light breeze beside the front door of the two-story, rectangular house. She stretched, grunting as the muscles stiffened by hours in the car pulled loose, and looked up to see her mother step out onto the front stoop. Calling Cheyenne out of the truck, she led Luke up the cement steps and walk to the stoop.

"Welcome home!" Trisha Blue said, opening her arms. "How was the drive?"

June hugged her mother. "It wasn't too bad," she replied. "We played musical drivers."

"That's good. And Luke, honey, how are you?"

"Good, Grandma. It's good to see you."

"Get up here and give me a hug."

When Luke ascended the steps and leaned down to hug her, she laughed.

"You, young man, must have grown half a foot since I saw you at Christmas!"

"Pretty close," he replied.

"Come in, come in. Dan's upstairs waiting to see

you."

Trisha reheated some dinner for them, and after, Dan and Luke bid everyone good night. June sat at the dining room table with her mom as night fell, with her hands curled around a glass of ice water. She closed her eyes to better enjoy the cool breeze wafting in through the open sliding glass door. For a while, they sat in companionable silence. Since June talked to her mother at least a couple times a week, Trisha was up to date on pretty much everything in June's life except the letter, but Pat had talked her into telling her family and Bill at the big barbecue they had planned for the last night of the vacation. June certainly didn't want to pile that on her mother this late at night, and besides, that wasn't what was keeping sleep at bay. Tonight would be the first time since Ben's return to Northstar that he wouldn't be sleeping under the same roof with her.

"It feels… really strange that Ben isn't here," she finally said.

"I imagine it does. This will be the first night you've spent apart in weeks." Trisha paused, then said, "You know Ben has my full support, and Dan's. He's always had it. You just be sure to give us enough time to make arrangements to get to Montana for the wedding."

"If there is a wedding, you know I'll make sure you can be there. Dan has to give me away after all."

"He'll love that. I'm glad to see you sound a little more sure there *will be* a wedding."

June laughed softly. "I'm still not sure of it, but I'm hopeful."

"That boy's loved you—and you him—a lot longer than I think either of you realize. After all, if you didn't love him, why did you wait for him?" Trisha finished her glass of wine and stood. "With that, I'm going to bed. It's good to have you home, honey."

"It's good to be home," June replied, rising to hug her mother.

She stood the dining room for a while longer and let the warm tones of her mother's recently remodeled kitchen and dining area wash over her. The house was starting to look very different from her childhood memories, but her mother's touch was everywhere. The outer wall was painted an accent color—a rich red sponged with a darker shade—while the others were a gentle tan. The wood tones were a medium red-gold, not too dark or too light. Tiffany-style lampshades and bowls added a few splashes of blues and greens. No, June thought, it didn't look much like her childhood home, but no matter how much her mother altered and improved, it would always feel like her first home.

June drank the rest of her water and set the glass in the sink before heading downstairs. Luke was asleep in the spare bedroom with Cheyenne snoring at his feet. Turning away, she tiptoed into her old room, which, like the kitchen, had been repainted and redecorated with a touch of Tuscany. The changes struck a chord of longing in her, and she wished Ben had taken up the offer to stay here instead of at his house in Poulsbo.

She changed into her sleepwear and climbed under the blankets, trying not to reach for him. Everyone else seemed so certain that they were falling in love—had already fallen. She had been so certain of it herself, but the feel of cool sheets where she'd become accustomed to Ben's warmth made her doubt. She had been so sure of what she felt. What if Ben's hesitation to get involved with her and his fear that their friendship might suffer wasn't him just being cautious? What if he really didn't feel the same for her that she felt for him?

Ben planned to move out of his house in Poulsbo this week, and he'd said he'd found his home with her, that he loved her, but that didn't mean he wanted to marry her. Maybe she'd imagined a lasting love where there was only a brief wildfire of passion.

You're being stupid, she chastised. But when she shuddered, it wasn't with the perpetual infusion of cool damp in the air.

* * *

It took Ben only two days to pack all his belongings and clean his Poulsbo house. His things fit in the back of his truck; the furniture stayed with the house. He stood just inside the front door with Luke, staring at the space he'd called home only a couple months ago. Though it was a fully furnished house, it no longer looked inhabited. All the personal touches were gone, packed away in the boxes in the back of his pickup. As he walked outside and locked the door, Ben did not feel a single twinge of regret.

"I thought you said you needed my help," Luke remarked.

"I do, but not here."

"Then where?"

"Shopping."

"Shopping?"

"Yep."

"For what?"

Ben smiled and climbed in behind the wheel of his truck. He'd return the keys to Mrs. Miller later. As soon as Luke was buckled in, Ben turned the key in the ignition and pulled out of the driveway for the last time. He drove down around the end of Liberty Bay, then up to the freeway. As he took the southbound on-ramp, he glanced north, his gaze habitually drawn in the direction of the gas station where he'd killed John McKindel. Instead of the crashing waves of guilt, he felt only a passing moment of remorse. He forced his gaze back to the road in front of him.

"Is it hard for you, coming back here?" he asked Luke.

The teenager frowned thoughtfully, gazing out the window at the tall evergreens and pink-blossomed native rhododendrons gliding past. "It's getting easier every time I come back. Though, sometimes I still want to gag when I drive past the road to my old house."

"You and me both. The couple times I went over to the Olympic Peninsula, I actually drove around to Port Gamble to get to the bridge."

"I can't begin to explain why, but hearing you say that makes me realize that we are both so much better than him. He wasn't worth either of us getting sick over him."

"You're damned right about that."

The rest of the drive to Silverdale was pleasant, with the conversation light and joking, but as he parked his truck near the main entrance of the Kitsap Mall, Ben began to feel the tickle of nerves. It wasn't that he doubted his decision. He didn't. He doubted his ability to find exactly what he was looking for, which is why he wanted June's son's advice. He also wanted to be absolutely certain Luke was okay with it before he spent hundreds of dollars, and this excursion should prove that beyond a doubt.

As they strolled into the mall, a wall of tantalizing aromas crashed over them, and Ben's stomach growled. In an unspoken agreement, they made their way to the line for the Chinese eatery across the food court. When Luke pulled out his wallet, Ben shook his head.

"Oh, no you don't. I'm buying. It's the least I can offer in return for dragging you shopping. I'm sure you'd much rather be doing something—okay, anything—else."

"Actually, I have a feeling this will be *far* more interesting."

Once they had their food, they found a table toward the edge of the food court and located in prime people-watching territory. As they ate, they watched the shoppers milling and meandering in and out of the brilliant rectangles of sunlight streaming through the peaked skylights. The constant thrum of conversation had a positive tone, and Ben smiled. Groups of teenagers loitered around the tiled planter boxes or dragged each other laughingly from store to store. Luke seemed to be particularly drawn to a trio of boys who stood apart but almost huddled together. Ben thought they looked like the stereotypical outcasts. Their clothes were dingy and colorless; tattered t-shirts of gray, faded black, and army-green and well-worn cargo pants. All three sported longish, greasy hair, and their skin had a pale, sallow tinge. He didn't want to call them grungy because that wasn't quite right. Neglected or forgotten seemed more accurate.

"Do you know them?" Ben asked.

"We were all in the same class second semester of sixth grade. Since I'd just moved from Seattle—and then moved to Montana before the next school year—I don't know if you would call us friends. I try to say hi and talk to them whenever I see them, but we don't have much in common anymore." Luke frowned. "Jared's not with them. That's weird."

When the trio glanced in Ben and Luke's direction, Luke waved. They walked over but didn't smile.

"Hey, Luke," said the boy with the dark hair.

"Hey. Have a seat. Ben, these guys are Kevin, Matt, and Jory. Guys, this is Ben, Mom's boyfriend. Where's Jared?"

"He's dead, man," replied the same boy. "Died a couple weeks after we saw you over Christmas break."

Luke sat back like he'd been struck, and for several moments, seemed incapable of speech. Finally, the shock gave way to regret. "What happened?"

"His old man finally pushed him too far one night. He locked himself in the garage and started the car while his dad was passed out drunk."

"Ah, damn." Luke shook his head. "I don't even know what to say."

The dark-haired Kevin shrugged.

The thought of what might have happened to Luke had fate not intervened hit Ben straight in the chest with the force of a cannon ball. If John hadn't died, would these boys instead be mourning Luke's death? His heart tripped sickeningly, and he tried to erase the idea.

"Wow," Luke said. He gathered his and Ben's empty trays and stood.

"Christ, Luke, ya friggin' giant," the one named Matt said, craning his neck.

"Oh, come on. I am not *that* tall."

"Well, no one's gonna tease you about being short anymore. You still playing football?"

"Yep. Starting quarterback this year."

"Man, back in sixth grade, no one woulda believed you'd be a jock. You sure John was your dad? 'Cause I remember him being kinda short."

Jory inclined his head at Ben. "You look more like him."

"Funny you should say that," Luke said with a smirk. "Because I'm pretty sure we're here so he can complete the second part of the application to be my new dad. Speaking of which, rumor has it that this endeavor might take a while, so we should probably get started. Take care of yourselves."

Ben politely excused himself and walked with Luke to the first jewelry store. Luke declined his offer to stay and chat with his old friends, claiming more interest in Ben's quest. The length of the teenager's strides and the set of his jaw spoke more of an escape. Not that he could blame the kid. It must be heartbreaking to learn that his friend was dead at only sixteen—maybe seventeen—because he'd had so little hope for a better future that he'd felt the only way out was suicide.

"I'm really sorry about your friend, Luke."

"Me, too. Jared was a good kid, but his dad was a lot like John. Too much like him. Just drives home that I got lucky." Luke's voice cracked. "Jared didn't."

"Please don't take this the wrong way, Luke, but I couldn't help think what might've happened if you hadn't gotten lucky. It scared the hell out of me."

Luke turned and hugged him. "Thanks, *Dad*."

Maybe Luke was joking, but there was something urgent in his expression that reminded Ben of a frightened animal.

"Dad?" Ben was careful to keep his tone light but soothing.

"Better get used to it if you really want to marry June because you being 'Dad' is my stipulation on letting you marry her."

It was Ben's turn to hug Luke. The gut-wrenching jolt of fear made him understand that, however strange it should probably seem, he loved Luke like a son… not only June's son but *their* son. "Do you really mean that?"

"Yes, I do. So, let's go find that ring. That *is* why we're here, isn't it?"

This was the first time Ben and Luke had really spent quality time together without June around, and

Ben thoroughly enjoyed it. Luke was a charming young man, and they had enough in common that their conversation continued on a steady stream. Ben was relieved and encouraged that Luke agreed with his thoughts regarding June's ring, though they couldn't seem to find what they were looking for. After they'd browsed the offerings in stock at four of the five jewelry stores in the mall, Ben wondered if he'd have to expand his shopping range. He'd looked through a few catalogues and had found a couple rings that might do but nothing that jumped out at him.

"Well, this is the last store," Ben remarked, staring up at the glowing storefront sign before stepping inside.

"The Butte Plaza Mall has a great family-owned jewelry store that has a lot of great rings. That's where Pat went for Aelissm's wedding set."

"Yeah, but didn't he design her ring?"

"That's my point. If we don't find the right one, we can design it and have them make it."

"It's a thought. But, honestly, I was hoping to propose to June at Bill's barbecue."

"Ah. Are you nervous?"

"Surprisingly, I am not. Once I realized this was something I couldn't and shouldn't fight, it's been quite natural and easy.”

“Told you.”

“So did she. Repeatedly. At one point, she asked if she should strip and prance naked in front of me to prove it.”

“Ben, I really, really did *not* need to know that.”

“Sorry, kid. Hey, take a look at that one.”

Luke joined him beside a glass case. Ben pointed to a ring with a square-cut diamond flanked by two triangular diamonds. Rectangular sapphires threw blue sparks in the channels on both sides of the band. Ben asked to see it, and the saleswoman took it out of the case. The platinum band, when viewed from the side, was graced with tiny arches that reminded him of a bridge. The matching wedding ring was a channel band set with rectangular diamonds.

“Can the wedding band be ordered with rubies instead of diamonds?” Luke asked.

“Rubies?” Ben inquired.

“Yeah. Your birthstone. You wanted sapphires because they’re Mom’s birthstone and mine, right? Well, why shouldn’t yours be part of the set? Three diamonds for the three of us, and all of our birthstones. It’s perfect.”

Ben continued to turn and admire the ring, his

eyes blurring a little as the glitter of it mesmerized him. Luke was right. It *was* perfect. He cringed when he glanced at the price tag, not because he couldn't afford it—he had plenty in his savings to cover it—but because June would not like the idea of him spending so much on jewelry.

"In answer to your question, sir, yes, I can order a band set with rubies," the saleswoman remarked.

"How much more will that cost?" Ben asked.

"Let me check for you."

The woman stepped to the side to her computer and told him the price would be the same. Ben pulled out his wallet.

"Well, Luke, speak now or forever hold your peace."

Luke wrapped an arm around his shoulders. "Welcome to the family, Dad."

"Thanks. Just don't tell your mom how much this cost."

* * *

As Ben folded her into his arms and kissed her soundly in front of her son, her stepfather, and Becky, June felt a little foolish for questioning his feelings for her. He'd spent quite a bit of time with his parents—more in this one week, he said, than he had in any six-month stretch since the shooting—but he'd declined their invitation to stay with them and had decided instead to stay with June. There was a futon upstairs in the Blues' computer room, but no one had questioned his desire to sleep in the same bed with June. Tonight, being the last night of their trip, the futon would be occupied by Becky, anyhow.

"What are you thinking about, love?" Ben asked her.

"Sleeping arrangements."

"Not happy with them?"

"I'm very happy with them."

"So Luke wasn't kidding when he said you were moping when I was staying at my old house."

She turned a playful scowl on her son. "Traitor."

"I'd tell you two to get a room," Luke remarked, "but then we might miss the fun at Indianola Days."

"Yeah, and I want to see the sand castles," Becky replied. "And get my face painted."

"And roll an egg across the sand with your nose," Luke added, nudging Becky with his elbow.

"That's really one of the games?"

"Yup."

"All right, all right," June said and pulled reluctantly out of Ben's arms. "Finish getting ready, then, so we can head out to Indianola as soon as Mom gets back from the post office. Probably ought to bring your swimsuits, too."

Luke headed downstairs while Becky went into the computer room to finish getting ready. Trisha walked in the door moments later.

"June, there's a letter here for you," she said. "That doesn't happen often."

"Who's it from?" June asked. She didn't want to hear the answer, but she was pretty sure she knew what it would be.

"There's no return address."

"JP," Ben whispered.

June nodded. Her mother crested the stairs and handed her the letter before heading to the dining room table to go through the rest of the mail. June's hands trembled as she opened the envelope. The note inside was short but to the point.

Running away to Washington won't end this.

"Waste of a stamp," she muttered.

"It's another clue, though. This JP—if this is the same man Adam remembers—knows you well enough to know your parents' address."

"Or he's someone who's very thorough."

"Try not to think about it. It's supposed to be a

fun day of games and then Bill's barbecue, and it's the last day of vacation."

She nodded but didn't make any promises. Honestly, how could she *not* think about it? She was certain that was JP's intent, to keep his game fresh in her mind. Though she hadn't forgotten it over the past week, she'd been able to push it to the back of her mind. Now, the helpless confusion and fear was once again front and center in the spotlight of her attention. Damn him.

Ben took the note downstairs to put it with the other while June gathered their swimsuits and towels and went out to Ben's truck. Everyone else came out of the house, and there was a brief discussion about who would ride in which vehicle. Luke volunteered to ride with his grandparents, and June almost begged him to ride with her. Only the thought of how foolish her desire was kept her from giving voice to it. Whoever was sending these letters—threatening him—was in Montana. He was safe enough for the time being, but she selfishly wanted him close.

On the ride to Indianola, she listened to Ben and Becky talk about the festivities in store and their preparations for their departure for home. It was Becky's off-handed remark about being ready to go home that sent a shock of anger pulsing through June.

For the first time, she didn't want to leave Washington to go home to Northstar.

This JP, whoever he might be, was most likely someone she knew, someone from Northstar. Someone she considered a friend. She felt… hollow and betrayed. The place she called home was shadowed by a sense of fear and distrust. Behind which treasured face would she find a predator?

When Ben parked in front of Bill and Mary Granger's house behind her parents' car, she was surprised, unable to recall much of the ride. She climbed out and retrieved her swimming gear from the back even though she no longer felt like swimming or playing games. She let the dogs out. It was a testament to her state of mind that both golden retrievers stayed close to her instead of racing between their people. As she walked up to the front door with Ben on one side of her and Luke on the other, she tucked her towel and swimsuit under her arm and took both their hands.

Bill and Mary met them at the door and greeted everyone with hugs.

"We assumed everyone would want to head down to the beach or over to the street fair to partake in the festivities, so we planned dinner for around five," Mary said. "The sand castle judging is almost over, but the games are about to begin."

They walked through the house and out onto the deck. The Grangers' house perched atop the bluff with a commanding view of the expansive sand spit, the long, retired ferry pier, Agate Pass, and Bainbridge Island. Down the long flight of wooden steps was a small yard segregated from the beach by an ivy hedge. It frequently doubled as a volleyball court and June noted that the net had already been strung between the two poles.

She leaned on the deck railing and took in the sights while the others debated what to do first. The tide was out—Indianola Days celebrated the lowest tide of the summer—and the sand was dotted with beachgoers and sandcastles. Almost directly in front of Bill and Mary's house, people were gathering for the games. Kids of all ages and numerous dogs ran around the beach in merriment, and laughter filled the air. June had always loved this particular festival and always tried to plan her summer trip to Washington around it.

"Remember that year you and Aelissm painted faces?" Bill asked, joining her at the railing.

"I'll never forget it. I still can't believe we made over a hundred and fifty bucks."

"I don't think any of the kids since have done as well." He cleared his throat. "Pat and Aeli tell me there's been a little trouble recently."

"Of course they told you already."

"Ah, so you weren't planning on keeping it a secret. Good. I don't know how much help I can be from here, but I hope you know I'll do whatever I can."

"I *do* know that, Uncle Bill. We would've told you sooner, but we didn't want to ruin everyone's vacation. And, honestly, I wanted to forget about it for a little bit."

"I don't blame you. So, forget about it for a few more hours by having some fun in the sand and sun with your family, and we'll talk about it at dinner."

"Thanks, Unk."

"So, you and Ben."

"Yes, Uncle Bill. Me and Ben."

"Can't say as I'm surprised… but I *can* say it makes me happy."

"So far, it makes us happy, too."

"Luke, too, I hear."

June smiled. "Thank you for asking me to foster him."

"Don't thank me. I'm just glad it's worked out so well. Kid deserved a chance."

They rejoined the rest of their families and headed down to the beach. Despite Bill's subtle attempt to reassure and distract her, June couldn't find quite the same enjoyment as her companions. Luke unwittingly garnered most of her attention. He hadn't been told about the second letter from JP, and she didn't intend to break the news until she had to. *Let him enjoy a few more hours of peace*, she thought.

She allowed herself to be dragged into competing in the balloon toss, partnering up with Ben. When she dropped the water balloon on the fifth toss—standing only five feet from him—he gave her a quizzical look but said nothing. Not that she could've heard him over the exuberant shouts and laughter. Luke and Becky took second place, much to their delight. Next came the egg roll, and June decided to watch instead of participate. It was such a comical thing to watch so many people get down on their hands and knees in the sand and roll an egg twenty feet with their noses. Becky, despite her initial doubt about the game, proved her skills when she was the first to cross the finish line.

"I think the egg roll might be my favorite," Aelissm remarked. "It is certainly the funniest to watch."

By the end of the games, June's group had amassed several ribbons, and June had managed to subdue the worst of her anxiety. Even if she didn't feel entirely like herself, it made her happy to watch her friends and family enjoy themselves. They wandered across the vast beach, looking at the dozens upon dozens of sand castles. Some were as simple in design as an upturned bucket of wet sand while others were elaborate, multi-towered behemoths. There were the traditional castles, sea monsters, mermaids, dragons, pirate ships, and even a pair of lovers embracing.

"This is so neat," Becky remarked.

"It is," June agreed.

They climbed the main stairs beside the dock and browsed the tables and booths of the street fair. Becky, Luke, and Ant had their faces painted. After, they sat in the shade of the picnic area across from the town's clubhouse and enjoyed the live music, then headed back to Bill and Mary's for a volleyball game before dinner.

As the clock ticked toward five, June felt her restlessness growing again. She didn't want to spoil the pleasant air or the carefree smile on Luke's face by bringing up the second letter. She didn't want to talk about any of it. What would they be able to figure out that hadn't already been brought up?

"June! Look out!"

The volleyball smacked into her face, and she stepped to the side to catch her balance. She stared at the offending ball and rubbed her stinging cheek.

"Oh, June, I'm so sorry!" Becky said.

"Was that your serve?" June asked.

"Yeah. Jeez, I really am sorry."

"Guess I should pay attention, huh?"

"Are you all right?" Ben inquired. He turned her head gently to inspect the damage.

"I'll be fine."

"I'm not talking about your face. I'm sure you had a lot worse when you played soccer."

She met his gaze and saw plainly that she hadn't fooled him. When she spoke, she kept her voice soft so only he could hear. "No, I'm not all right."

"I didn't think so."

He gathered her into his arms and started to say something but was interrupted by Bill announcing dinner. June drew a deep breath and held it for a few moments before letting it out. She let Ben lead her up the stairs to the Grangers' deck where Mary, Trisha and Aelissm's mother Gail had set the picnic tables with quite a spread. There were salads, a veggie tray, a pasta dish, corn on the cob, baked beans, barbecue pulled pork, barbecued chicken, and steaks—more than enough food for their party of fourteen. It all smelled delicious, and June was hungry, but she didn't feel like eating.

"Are you going to do it or not, Dad?"

Luke whispered those words to Ben so quietly that June wasn't sure she'd heard right. Had he called Ben *Dad?* She turned her head toward Ben and found him watching her with narrowed eyes.

"It's not the right time," he replied.

"What do you mean? I thought—"

"A second letter came in the mail today."

"What? *Here?* What did it say?"

"Running away to Washington won't end this," June answered. Even to her ears, her voice sounded flat and lifeless.

"What letters?" Trisha asked.

"Go ahead and tell them, Ben. I can't do it."

She barely resisted the urge to cover her ears as Ben detailed the phone calls and the letters and what they and Aaron Hammond had figured out so far. She listened to the explosion of disbelief, worry, and sympathy with burning eyes.

"All right, Bill. You're the detective. What do you think?" Ben inquired.

"I think Aaron's right that whoever this JP

character is, he's got a thing for June. I believe he's right not to narrow the list down to only men June has dated, too. It's impossible to know who else might harbor feelings for her and against Luke. What about the initials JP?"

"Jake and Pete are both JPs. Jacob Philip and Joshua Peter," June replied.

"The initials might not mean a damned thing," Ben said. "What about Mike Thompson?"

"I really doubt it," Luke said. "He and Carol are back together, and I don't even want to think about him having a 'thing' for Mom."

"You're probably right," Bill said, "but I'm going to keep him on the list."

The conversation continued with little said. Everyone voiced the hope that this was nothing more than a sadistic hoax, but June couldn't believe it.

"Pat, you've been strangely quiet," she said quietly.

"I've been taking it all in. And, besides, it's been a few years. My instincts are a little rusty."

"You may not wear the badge anymore, but instincts are instincts," Bill said.

"I think we can rule out anyone who doesn't know June fairly well. While it's possible someone determined could find Dan and Trisha's mailing address, it's not so easy to find the cabins."

"Assuming the trespassing and these letters are not merely coincidence."

"We followed the trail, Bill." Pat paused for a moment and glanced between June and Luke. "Adam finally called me back this morning, and we had a good, long talk. From what he told me, I do believe this man is the same one he remembers. Even four years ago, JP was fixated on June and Luke. Adam described him as being physically not very memorable—brown hair, brown eyes, between five-ten and six-foot, average build, which could be either Jake or Pete."

"But there was obviously something very memorable about him," June supplied. She held Pat's gaze for a long while, hoping to find something in his eyes that would allay her fears. She wanted to feel the heat of anger, not the chill of dread, but she found nothing reassuring staring back at her. Finally, she forced herself to ask, "What else is your gut telling you, Pat?"

That this isn't a hoax. He didn't have to say it. The concern etched in his expression was all the answer June needed.

Sixteen

JP STOOD ON THE COVERED front deck of his house, leaning against the post with a steaming cup of coffee nearly forgotten in his hand. June had returned from Washington three days ago, but he hadn't yet seen her. He hoped his note had arrived at her parents' house in time. He'd been so caught up in his preparations that he hadn't even known she'd left until he realized she hadn't been to work at the Ramshorn in four days.

Absently, he took a sip of his coffee and let his eyes roam. His home was a small, one-bedroom log cabin, and it sat a quarter mile off the main road on the slope of a south-facing hill. From his porch, he could see the sweep of the valley below, the patchwork of pastures, hayfields, stands of quaking aspen, sagebrush hills, and the imposing line of granite peaks above the forest-cloaked foothills. His gaze drifted north along the flanks of the Northstar Mountains to the three meadows below Comet Mountain. June's cabin was tucked into the woods just below and south of those meadows. He shivered with longing at the thought of her.

He'd see her soon. This afternoon was the annual Hay Fever Potluck and Barbecue, and June, he knew, was helping the O'Neils put it on at the Bedspread.

"Do you kids want something to eat before you head down to the Bedspread, or do you want to wait until the potluck?" he asked, turning his gaze to his bench where his niece and Mike Thompson sat silently.

"I could eat," Carol replied.

"Yeah, I could, too," Mike agreed.

"Turkey sandwiches okay?"

"Yeah, that'd be great. Thanks, Unkie."

"All right."

He drained his coffee, turned, and went inside. He

threw some sandwiches together, piled them on a plate, and set the plate gently on his kitchen table before stepping silently to the front window. The curtains were closed, so they wouldn't see him, but the window was open just a crack, and he would be able to hear them.

"I guess Coach Wells is putting Luke in at quarterback this year," Carol was saying.

"Oh my God, Carol, will you ever shut up about him?"

"I'm sorry, Mike. I just…. I'm sorry."

"Yeah, so am I. Sorry I was stupid enough to think you really wanted me back. I can't do this anymore, Carol. I'm not going to put myself out there just so you can have a backup plan."

"W-what are you saying?"

"I'm done. We're done."

"But—"

"Go crawling back to Luke. Maybe he'll take you back, but I doubt it."

"But he's with Becky. Even your sister said—"

"Listen to you. I just broke up with you, and you're worried about Luke. Get it through your head, Carol. He's not with Becky. He was never with Becky. They are just friends."

Tread carefully, Mike, JP thought. His hands curled into fists.

"What do you mean? You said—"

"I lied, Carol. I thought I loved you, so I lied. I made it up."

"No. Maybe you lied, but you're not the only one who saw things. Unkie pointed out how—"

"And you trust your uncle, right?"

"Of course I do. Why wouldn't I?"

"He's off his rocker, Carol."

JP snarled. *Oh, you stupid boy.*

"What do you mean?"

"I mean… I think he's losing it. Look, I'm not going to talk about it here. Take a walk with me."

Time to put an end to this conversation. JP forced his expression to relax and his jaw to unclench. He stepped out onto the porch and smiled at Mike and Carol. Mike regarded him with unveiled wariness, but Carol's eyes were red-rimmed as she fought back tears. She was such a drama queen. "Lunch is on the table, kids."

"I'm not hungry anymore," his niece said and scooted past him. Though she tried to hide her face, he saw the tears streaming down her cheeks.

When Mike tried to walk past him, JP put a hand

on his chest. There was something distinctly satisfying about seeing the dark terror dilating Mike's olivine eyes. The kid was a good four inches taller, heavier, and probably stronger, but he feared JP. JP's lips curled into a poisonous smile. "I think you and I need to have a talk."

* * *

"Hey, Luke! Do you and Shane want to take a break from food prep for a few minutes?" Aelissm called. "I could use some help unloading and setting up."

He looked up from the large pile of corn and saw that Nick Hammond had returned with a flatbed trailer loaded with eight more picnic tables. Luke and Shane gladly dropped the ears of corn they were shucking and raced each other down to the grassy lawn in the center of the Bedspread Inn's looped driveway. Ben, Pat, and Aaron and Henry Hammond arrived to help unload. With two men to a table, it took a disappointingly short time to get all eight off the trailer.

"Well, guess it's back to shucking corn and stirring barbecue sauce," Luke remarked grumpily.

"Oh, no you don't," Aelissm said. "We need to level these."

She sent Shane into the back of Nick's truck for

the two-by-six planks. Luke lifted the end of the first table so Aelissm could slide a couple of boards under the legs.

"Carol's here," Shane remarked as he brought another plank over.

Luke glanced over his shoulder and watched his ex-girlfriend's silver-blue car pull into the driveway. Then he determinedly turned his attention back to what he was doing. It was pointless. Even without looking, he knew that she parked in front of the dining room and felt her eyes on him as she walked toward the smoker where June was currently checking on the pig.

"Great," he muttered.

He and Shane helped Aelissm level the rest of the picnic tables and headed back to their food prep duties.

"Hey, Luke, can I talk to you for a minute?"

Luke stopped in his tracks, surprised to find a teenaged girl jogging over. It took him a moment to collect his wits and put a name to the sun-streaked brown hair and pretty face. Heather Brown. Right. Her parents had bought the Rocking A Ranch a couple years ago. "Um, yeah, I guess."

Shane grinned and kept walking.

"Would you go out with me?" Heather asked.

Luke's mouth fell open, and he snapped it shut. His mind raced, searching for a reply that wouldn't make him sound like a total jerk. "I'm flattered, Heather, but I'm just not ready for anything yet."

"Wow. She did a number on you, huh?" Heather looked at Carol with a sneer. "Well, if you change your mind…."

She sauntered off, purposefully striding past Carol. Luke thought he heard a hissed insult, and Carol winced. When Heather's back was turned, Carol flipped her off with a smug gleam in her green eyes, then headed directly toward Luke as if emboldened by his rejection of Heather. He deftly sidestepped her and returned to his corn-shucking station.

"Luke, please, I need to talk to you."

"I have work to do, Carol."

She stalked away, but Luke had the distinct and unsettling suspicion that he'd be spending a lot of his time today avoiding her. Fantastic. He hadn't seen her or talked to her since she'd broken up with him, and with everything he'd had on his mind lately, he had no desire to talk to her today. He grabbed an ear of corn and yanked the husk off. Why were both she and Heather Brown here two hours early? His question was answered moments later when Aeli thanked them both for coming and immediately put them to work. Luke rolled his eyes and growled as he jerked the husk off another ear of corn.

When the band arrived from Devyn, Luke volunteered to help them set up. After that, he helped June arrange the wildflowers for each table. Next, he busied himself setting up the brightly-colored canopies over each of the twenty picnic tables. As people started arriving, it became easier for him to find ways of avoiding Carol without it seeming so much like he *was* avoiding her. Twenty tables weren't going to be enough, Luke thought as he watched the lawn fill with the residents of Northstar. Aelissm and Pat had put up flyers in Devyn and put an ad in the Devynite Daily for the barbecue to attract more tourists and Devynites. Their advertising had apparently worked because there were numerous faces he didn't recognize. The dining room was probably going to be packed, too.

He ran a plate of food and a bottle of water down to Austin McGuire, who was stationed at the driveway entrance collecting the five-dollar cover charge. Entry was free for anyone bringing a dish—it was still a potluck, after all—and for those who helped set up. Luke thought it was brilliant.

"Thanks, Luke," Austin said, taking the offered

refreshments. "This was a good idea your mom and Aeli came up with. Mmm, that smells delicious."

"It does," Luke agreed. "And tonight should be a lot of fun."

"It should indeed."

Luke trotted back up to the main gathering to find something else to keep him occupied.

The heavy-duty triangle Aelissm had borrowed from the Royal R Ranch jangled out the call to come eat, and the barbecue officially began. Luke stepped up to help June, Ben, Pat, and Aelissm serve the items the Bedspread was offering—pulled pork, baby back ribs, steaks, burgers and hot dogs—and tried not to search the faces of the people he knew for some sign that JP lurked behind the familiar features. With dinner under-way, Aelissm stepped away for a moment to switch off the stereo. Moments later, the band took up an upbeat country song.

"There are more tables inside," Aelissm began telling guests as the picnic tables filled up.

Luke stood beside his family after everyone had been served and watched. Some people finished early and got up to dance, while others seemed more in-clined to linger over their meals. They couldn't have asked for a more beautiful day. The sky was a deep sapphire littered with fluffy clouds, the temperature was a comfortable seventy-five or so, and there was a light breeze to keep the mosquitoes away. Horseflies and deerflies were still an irritation, but if that was all anyone had to complain about, it was a magnificent afternoon.

"Is it possible to have a street dance without a street?" Luke inquired.

"Apparently so," Aelissm answered. "Hey, Luke, would you run inside and grab the horseshoes out of the basement?"

"Sure, Aunt Aeli."

"And check on everyone inside, too, will you? I know Janice is inside, but she may need a hand, so see if anyone needs anything."

"Will do."

As soon as he brought out the horseshoes, a line formed of people wanting to play. Luke told Shane to help them set up so he could go back into the inn to see if Aeli's waitress needed help. When he finally stepped back outside, Carol was standing on the deck. He glanced at her and started toward the steps.

"You don't have work to do now, so can I please talk to you?" she asked, grabbing his arm to stop him from walking away.

"I haven't eaten yet, and I'm hungry."

"Please, Luke."

"Fine." He tugged his arm free. "Talk."

"I'm so, so sorry," she said. "I was wrong. I love you."

She threw herself against him. He didn't lift his arms to embrace her, and after a moment, she stepped back with tears glittering in her eyes, undoubtedly realizing that an apology wasn't going to be so simple.

"I know you and Becky never…. I know you're just friends with her, but Mike and Unkie said—"

"Mike? What about him? I thought you two were back together."

"He broke up with me this morning because he says I'm not over you. And he's right. I'm not."

"This morning. Wow, Carol, you really do get around."

Luke looked away and closed his eyes. He hadn't meant to say that. They'd both been virgins not so long ago, and even if she'd slept with Mike since breaking up with Luke…. He shook his head, unwilling to judge her as she'd judged him. "I'm sorry. That came out wrong."

"You're still the only one I've been with, Luke."

They sat on the top step of the deck, and Luke

waited silently for Carol to say whatever it was she thought would change his mind.

"Mike said things that made me think you were drifting away from me, that you were getting close with Becky. He pointed out how you two were always hanging out and how you hugged her a lot. He lied to me to break us up, and he doesn't really even want me. Not anymore. I shouldn't have listened. I love you, Luke. I want you back."

"How can you say you love me and believe I could do that to you?" He pushed to his feet and turned to face her. "If you can come up with a real answer to that—one that doesn't push the blame off on someone else—I *might* consider taking you back."

He went back down to the party, wondering how stupid he would have to be to actually get involved with her again. Ben dished him a plate of food, and together they walked to where June, the O'Neils, the Eppersons, and Aelissm's grandparents had spread out a blanket. He sank cross-legged onto the ground, determined to enjoy his meal. It was difficult as his gaze seemed drawn to the deck where Shane and Carol sat talking, watching him.

Not a minute after he'd finished eating and had taken his empty paper plate to the garbage can,

Heather Brown was at his side. "I know you're not ready for a relationship, but would you at least dance with me?"

Unbidden, his gaze again returned to Carol. Her eyes were locked on him, and even from the distance, it was too easy to see that she was crying. Luke's chest constricted, but a cold voice in his mind wondered how much of it was real. Carol was such a talented manipulator that she usually didn't even know when she was doing it. When she ran for her car and peeled out of the driveway, Luke realized that for once, her tears were sincere.

"Thanks for the offer, Heather, but I really shouldn't."

"Suit yourself," she replied with a shrug.

"Real smooth, Montana," Shane snapped as he strode past on his way to his truck.

"Stay out of it, Shane!" Luke called.

Shane either didn't hear him or chose not to listen, and Luke let his head fall back, clamping his jaws shut to keep the bellow locked inside. So much for a fun evening.

* * *

"I really don't miss being a teenager," June said, watching the drama unfold between Luke, Carol,

Shane, and Heather. She didn't have to hear what was said to know what transpired.

"It sucks," Becky said. "I never thought I'd say this, but I am so glad I'm not popular."

"I hate seeing him so distraught," June murmured.

"So do I," Ben said. "But I think I know how to cheer him up. Or, at the very least, distract him."

Without a word of explanation, he stood and walked away. June frowned and watched him go first to his truck, then to Luke. At first, Luke's distressed expression remained firmly in place as Ben placed a comforting hand on his shoulder. For a few moments, Ben talked, most likely telling Luke something along the lines of "everything will work out in the end," if Luke's dispassionate nods were any indication. Then Ben smiled and said something else that fully seized Luke's attention. Within a few seconds, the teen's whole countenance changed. The gloom lifted, and in its place was June's favorite, heartwarming smile. Together, Ben and Luke rejoined their party, and both of them were beaming. They sat down on either side of her.

"All right, you two, what are you up to?" she asked, swiveling her head from one to the other.

"Well, we'd planned this for Bill's barbecue, but

after the second letter arrived, it just didn't feel right. You had a lot on your mind that night."

"Get to the point, Ben."

"Yes, ma'am."

He rose up on his knees and turned her to face him. Then he kissed her, slowly and tenderly, trailing his fingers along the line of her jaw. She melted into his touch, and for a moment, she didn't care that everyone was watching, or that Ben still hadn't satisfactorily answered her question.

"You know I love you, right?" he asked.

"Mmm-hmm."

He kissed her again. "And that I love your wonderful, charming son?"

"I'm beginning to understand that."

"I want a family, June. With you and with Luke. Will you marry me?"

June sat back, dumbstruck. She stared at him, searching his face for some sign that this was a joke or a dream, but all she saw was the purest adoration and love. Then she lowered her gaze and realized he was holding something in his fingers. Platinum, diamonds, and sapphires glinted in the golden evening sunlight. The ring was exquisite. She raised her eyes and met Ben's gaze, speechless. The sweetest joy she'd ever felt pulsed through her, more potent with each pounding beat of her heart. Unable to speak even to utter the answer resounding in her mind, June clasped his face and kissed him.

"Yes," she whispered against his lips. She said it firmly, without a doubt in her mind that it was right.

Cheers and clapping erupted, not only from their friends and family sitting with them but from everyone close enough to hear Ben's proposal. She felt dizzy in the most spectacular, giddy way.

"All right, June, let the man breathe," Aelissm remarked. "Because I get the feeling he has more to say."

"Actually, the rest is Luke's to tell."

June dazedly turned her attention to her son, who was still grinning, perhaps more widely than before.

"I know it doesn't make much sense, since I'll be seventeen in a couple months, but Ben agreed to adopt me when you get married. So we can be a real family."

It was a good thing June hadn't promised herself she wouldn't cry because the tears flowed unrestrained as she gathered Luke and Ben to her. A real family. It was the most perfect moment, and she doubted even heaven could offer more than what she had right then.

"Congratulations, you three," Pat said, raising his plastic cup of lemonade in a toast. "To your friendship and your love. And your family."

Ben slipped the ring on her finger and tucked her against him while she admired it. He couldn't have chosen a more beautiful piece. She loved the splash of color the sapphires added.

"Like it?"

"I love it."

"Luke helped me pick it, you know."

"So that's what you two were up to that day we girls went to the movie. Ring shopping. And here I thought you were just doing a little male bonding."

"We were. But you're the heart of that bond, June."

"I love you both so much." She wiped under her eyes with her thumb and laughed. "Now, cut the mush so I can stop crying."

She sat on the blanket, wrapped in Ben's warm embrace, and watched as the sun turned a deeper gold and drenched her beloved Northstar Mountains with vibrant light and sharp shadows. The restlessness that had plagued her over the past couple of weeks stilled, unable to compete against the beauty of her home and the power of her love for Ben and Luke. They were already a real family, she thought.

"Aaron."

At the sound of Marvin Struthers' voice, June lifted her head to see the owner of the Ramshorn striding across the driveway toward the sheriff's deputy.

"Pull up a patch of grass and have a bite," Aaron replied.

"Thanks, but I can't stay. I'm just on my way back to the Ramshorn, but I wanted to stop to tell you there's a truck parked out by the junction. Looks like someone may be passed out inside."

"Who's truck?"

"I didn't recognize it."

"Dammit, I'm not on duty tonight. I specifically requested tonight off."

"I know, Aaron, and I'm sorry, but I thought you should know."

Marvin excused himself and jogged back to his truck. Aaron stared after him, frowning.

"Ah, crap," he muttered. "I'd better go check it out."

Aaron pushed to his feet and tracked down his daughter, who was currently entertaining her grandparents. June watched him give Jessie a quick hug and a kiss, then stride away with a strained expression as he ignored her cries. She couldn't explain the shiver of dread, but she felt it all the same.

"Anyone else remember Aaron being pulled away from a potluck?" she asked.

"Yeah," Aelissm replied. "And with neither of the prime suspects present or accounted for, it makes me a little nervous. But we're not going to think dreadful thoughts tonight. We have something beautiful to celebrate. My best friends are engaged!"

The brief flicker of unease blew away in the gale of excitement. June spent the remainder of the evening dancing with her fiancé—how new and wonderful *that* sounded—her son, and Pat, playing a few games of horseshoes, and enjoying the gorgeous July evening. As the sunlight turned ruddy, the guests began to leave and clean up began. June tried not to notice that Aaron had not yet returned. With a large crew of helpers, it didn't take long to bag the garbage, wash the dishes, take down the canopies, and return the tablecloths, flower vases, and horseshoes to storage. Nick would pick up the picnic tables in the morning.

June leaned on the railing of the deck with Aelissm beside her, gazing at the Northstar Mountains as the light on the peaks deepened to ruby while Pat, Ben, and Luke finished cleaning up the kitchen.

"I'll never tire of that," she murmured.

"We are very lucky women, aren't we?" Aelissm

said. She dropped her gaze from the stunning view and took June's hand, lifting it to better admire the new jewelry. "It's beautiful, June. I imagine they put a lot of thought into it."

"I know they did. I have been smiling so much over the last couple hours that my face actually hurts."

"Feels good, doesn't it?"

She nodded. "Add another perfect Northstar night to our long list of them."

"It was definitely a big success. We'll have to do it again. Hey, I just thought of something. You remember that old dream we had, of getting married and raising our kids together at the end of Wellman Creek Road?"

"Old? I don't know about you, but it's still my dream."

"But it's not a dream anymore, June. It's happening."

June hugged her friend. In the last five years, that dream had nearly died more than once. First when Aelissm had moved back to Washington to pursue her master's degree, it had looked like she would settle permanently in Seattle. Then, after Brent's death, she had returned to Northstar to escape Adam's obsession, and things had finally started going right for Aeli; she'd fallen in love with Pat, they'd gotten married, and nine months later, Ant had arrived to make Aelissm's side of the dream come true. In the years since, June had begun to wonder if the rest would happen. Hope had flickered again when she'd dated Aaron until she realized that he wasn't ready to let go of his wife. Now… Ben had stepped back into her life, and all the pieces were coming together seamlessly.

"I'm not entirely sure I believe it. It's all still too new." She glanced over her shoulder when she heard the doors open. "All done?"

Pat nodded. "No sign of Aaron?"

Aelissm shook her head.

"No news is good news," Ben suggested.

"Maybe," Pat said, "but the last time it took this long to get news, it wasn't good."

"Pat, I am trying really hard not to think about that because I am having one of the most wonderful days of my life."

"My apologies, June. Congratulations, again."

June, Ben, and Luke bid the O'Neils good night and climbed into June's truck. They rode up to the cabin with the windows down, content to enjoy a peaceful silence. Shouldn't a quiet evening at home feel anticlimactic after all the excitement of the day?

Because it didn't. They arrived home and settled on the couch together and just… talked. It was mundane, but the feeling of rightness was powerful. Curled up nearly in Ben's lap with Luke sitting on the other side of her and both golden retrievers below her, June was wholly enraptured. She could spend every night of her life just like this and never tire of it.

They watched a movie, but June was too dazed by this exquisite new feeling to pay it any attention. Time slipped by unnoticed until the low rumble of a vehicle coming up the driveway followed by the glow of headlights sliced through June's daydream. She glanced at the clock. It was after ten. Luke was on his feet and heading to the window before she even registered the thought to do the same, so she stayed where she was.

"It's Aaron," Luke said, peeking out the curtains.

"If he's here this late, it's bad news."

Luke opened the door for the elder Hammond twin, and the first thought that popped into June's mind was that he looked like hell. His dark blond hair was disheveled, and there was a haunted look in his eyes that reminded her sharply of the days and weeks after Erica's tragic death. Icy dread slithered into her belly, and she braced herself.

"What happened?" she asked.

"It's Mike Thompson. It was his pickup at the junction. He's dead."

443

Seventeen

BRIGHT MORNING SUNLIGHT illuminated the kitchen and the forest outside the window, but Ben paid little attention to it. He took three coffee mugs out of the cupboard, grabbed the coffee pot and joined Pat and Aaron at the kitchen table. At the moment, they were frowning over Mike Thompson's suicide note, so he poured for them. He sat back, sipped his coffee, and listened to their discussion.

"So, June is pretty sure this isn't Mike's handwriting?" Aaron asked.

"She's been grading his papers for four years," Pat

said. "Heard anything about the second print on the gun yet?"

"No match."

"What's the ruling on his death?" Ben asked.

"Everyone seems inclined to believe it's a suicide. Am I looking for something that isn't there because seeing him with a hole in his chest reminded me of what happened to Erica?"

"I don't think so," Pat said with a shake of his head. "You're an intuitive cop, Aaron, with good instincts."

"Thanks, Pat."

"Mike was shot in the chest—a little unusual, in my experience—and there's the issue that the gun appeared to have been hastily cleaned *after* it was discharged. Factor in the second print, and you have enough to make me doubt that it's a suicide… without taking into account that Mike was not remotely suicidal."

"Hard be anything but excited when you're going to play for the Griz *and* earn a fully-paid degree in the process."

"May I see the note again?" Ben asked. Aaron slid the copy to him—the real note was at the sheriff's department in Devyn—and he read it again. "Here's what

I don't get. Luke said Carol told him Mike broke up with her that morning, but in the letter, he says—someone says—that he couldn't live without her and would always love her."

"Seems a little contradictory," Pat observed. "And, honestly, it's a little melodramatic for a boy who—more than once, according to several people who knew him—put football before his girlfriends."

"The only thing that rings remotely true is the line blaming Luke for tearing Mike and Carol apart, and even that…. Carol asked Luke out twice before he said yes, and he only agreed after Mike said he was okay with it. I know it's circumstantial—most of this is—but I have no reason to doubt Luke."

"Neither do we," Aaron said.

The gentle tone of the other man's voice made Ben aware that his own had become noticeably defensive. He stood and paced the kitchen, though he didn't expect the physical movement would actually do anything to relieve the nagging sense of helplessness. Somehow, Mike's death was tied to JP's yet-undisclosed plot. Was it honestly that big a leap to think it? No matter how flawed JP's beliefs about Luke were, he wanted the teenager to suffer. Ben mulled over the two days since Mike had been found dead behind the wheel of his parked truck with a suspicious suicide note lying beside him on the passenger seat.

June, who had taught Mike for four years, was naturally stunned by his death. She couldn't believe a kid with so much going for him would end his life over a broken relationship. Frankly, no one could believe it. She tried to keep her emotions under control for Luke's sake, but Ben had heard her crying softly at night when she thought he was asleep. He'd pulled her into his arms and held her, wishing there was something he could do to make it all go away.

Luke was a different story. The shock of his teammate's death had settled over him like a shroud of silence. The teenager had barely spoken since Aaron had delivered the news, and he walked around with a perpetually distant expression. It hurt to see the frequent shine of tears in his eyes, to know that he was suffering exactly as JP wanted.

"What did the sheriff say about this crap with JP?" Pat inquired.

Ben was relieved to know he wasn't the only one thinking there was a link, though he didn't say it.

"He thinks a connection between Mike's death—if it *is* a homicide—and the calls and letters June received is far-fetched. He of course said June should take precautions to protect herself and Luke, but otherwise, he doesn't seem too concerned that someone is being threatened." Aaron leaned back in his chair and dragged his hands down over his face. "Sorry. It pisses me off."

Pat chuckled. "You're in good company there, Aaron."

"So I am." He glanced at his watch. "I should probably go so I'm not late for work."

Ben and Pat walked to the front door with him.

"Thanks for your help, Aaron," Ben said.

"Hey, it's my job. But, more than that, June and Luke are my friends. If anything happens or if you notice anything suspicious, do me a favor and call it in."

"We will."

Aaron bid them farewell, and they stood on the front deck of June's cabin to watch him drive away. Ben's gaze roamed around the pine-covered ridges that sheltered the cabins and inhaled deeply of the fresh mountain air. Beneath the turmoil of the last two days—the past couple of weeks, really—and ignoring the raging, primal need to protect his family, Ben was surprisingly at ease.

"Someday soon," Pat said, waving his hand in a sweeping gesture at the surrounding ridges, "all this will be yours."

"That right there is an incredible thought. I couldn't think of or hope for a more wonderful place to call home."

"There is something truly special about Northstar, isn't there?"

Ben glanced covertly at his friend. Pat might not be a Northstar native, but he belonged here every bit as much as Ben, June, and Aelissm. He tried to remember Pat as he'd been for much of their overlapping time with the Kitsap County Sheriff's Department and found it difficult to recall the man with haunted eyes. Though Aelissm was mostly responsible for Pat's recovery, Northstar itself had given Pat the peace necessary to begin rebuilding his heart.

Northstar had somehow healed them all. The breathtaking natural beauty and loving residents had calmed the restlessness in June by providing the home her compassionate heart needed, had helped Luke learn to trust and love, and had given Aelissm the courage to face her fears. Now, Northstar—and June's patience and Luke's forgiveness—had drawn Ben from his pit of shame and self-loathing.

"I feel... whole," Ben said after a moment. "I didn't know it was possible to feel so complete. May I ask you something, Pat?"

"Anything."

"Do you ever miss being a detective?"

"Sometimes. It breaks my heart, what June and Luke are facing right now, and Mike Thompson's death is tragic no matter how you look at it, but it does feel good to use that part of my brain again."

"Do you ever regret your choice to give it up for Aelissm?"

"Never. It was the best choice I've ever made. I have the most incredible wife, and without her love, I might never have healed. I have two beautiful children. I have a home I treasure… and I have all this. No career is worth more than what I have with Aelissm."

Pat settled his insightful gaze on Ben, narrowing his eyes briefly. "You're not having second thoughts about asking June to marry you, are you?"

"Not one. But I keep wondering if I *should* have a few doubts. I'm not even worried that adopting Luke is a mistake after everything we've both been through."

"You're worried about not being worried?"

"More curious and amused than worried."

Pat chuckled. "Then I'll tell you what you should do. Thank God every day for what you have and don't ever take it for granted because it is very special."

* * *

"How are you doing?" June asked her son as he walked into the kitchen of the Ramshorn.

Luke leaned against the sink and folded his arms across his chest. He seemed to be dealing with his teammate's death a little better today, but the shadows under his eyes were darker. June didn't need that visible sign to know that he hadn't been sleeping well. Neither she nor Ben had been sleeping any better.

"A little better, I guess," he replied quietly.

"Are you sure you don't want to take a couple days off?"

"I'm sure. I need something to do." He met her eyes, and she winced to see the bright pain in his eyes. "Half the time, I can't believe he's dead."

"Neither can I. Such a waste."

"That's two people now I knew—two friends— who've died this year." Luke hesitantly took her hand and touched her ring with his thumb. "At least we all have something to look forward to."

"Yes, we do."

June kept that thought in her mind as she arranged lettuce, tomatoes, onion slices, and pickles on the plates for their last table of the afternoon. She and Ben hadn't yet discussed a wedding date, and for now, it was enough to be engaged. Luke finished plating the burgers for her and took them out to the dining room.

Mary zipped into the kitchen like a whirlwind.

"Sorry I'm late, June," she said. "I got caught up talking to Tracie at the post office. Sounds like the memorial for Mike Thompson will be next week. Are you and Luke going to attend the service?"

"Mike's parents asked us to. It's nice to know they don't believe the note, either. I wish everyone else felt the same. Luke wants to go, but I don't know if it's the best idea. I think he should go to say goodbye, but I'm worried someone might get it in their heads to attack Luke for what happened." June felt the sting of tears and closed her eyes. Grief lodged in her throat, for the pain in her son's eyes that she couldn't erase and for the terrible loss of a bright, gifted young man. "Mike was one of the few seniors I had thought I would see again as he went on to bigger and better things. What the hell happened?"

"I don't have any answers, either, June, but I know in my heart he didn't kill himself, just like I know this business between him, Luke, and Carol is nothing more than typical teenaged turmoil that someone is twisting out of proportion. I just hope to God Mike didn't die for this sick bastard's pleasure."

"That's what I'm afraid of. If his goal is to make Luke suffer, he's doing a damned fine job of it."

Mary laid a soothing hand on her cheek. "Shh. Don't let this JP win. And you tell Luke not to let him win, either. Go home, kick back, and start planning your wedding and remember that if you need help with anything—*anything*—we're here for you."

"Thank you, Mary."

June wrote down her time and Luke's, grabbed their helmets, and led the way out to the dirt bikes. She imagined her worries drifting away on the wind as they rode home, though she doubted it would really be so easy. Thoughts of her impending wedding were a better distraction. She had really loved Pat and Aelissm's outdoor autumn wedding, but that didn't give much time to plan—barely more than two months—and besides, she didn't want to copy her best friend. Summer was her next choice, but Ben and Luke didn't want to wait that long because by next summer, there *really* wouldn't be much point in the adoption. Which left spring or winter. Spring meant heavy, wet snow and mud. Winter, then. An image of the Northstar Mountains as a snow-covered backdrop bloomed in her mind's eye. It would be nothing short of spectacular with either cloudless sapphire skies or soft, feathery flakes drifting down from pewter clouds.

"What do you think about a winter wedding?" she asked Luke after they'd parked the dirt bikes back at the cabin.

"I think it would be gorgeous. What are you thinking?"

"Having the ceremony on the deck of the Bedspread, if Pat and Aeli are willing."

"You know they will be."

June was rewarded with the first genuine smile from Luke in two days. If she'd had any doubts about his approval of her marrying Ben, that radiant grin in the midst of tragedy cured her of it. The promise of a family brought him as much peace and happiness as it brought June and Ben, and that was something to celebrate.

She stepped into her cabin to find Ben in the kitchen prepping for dinner and added the sight of him wielding a sharp knife against an onion to the growing list of things she wanted to get used to. Because he apparently hadn't heard them come in, she tiptoed into the kitchen, slipped her arms around his waist, and laid her cheek on his back.

"I love you," she murmured.

"I love you, too," he replied. He set the knife

down and turned to face her. His lips curved but not before she caught the frown of concern. He brushed his thumb across her cheek, and his eyes waxed remorseful. "It's good to see you smile again."

She sensed a 'but' behind his words. The regret in his eyes dampened the anticipation, and her smile slipped away, too quickly replaced by a frown. "What's happened now?"

"Another letter," he said quietly. "It came in the mail today."

"Where is it?"

"Upstairs on your dresser. I thought you might want to read it before you decided whether or not to show it to Luke."

"Whatever's in it, he has a right to know."

She pressed a kiss to his lips, very tempted to linger, but she needed to know what was in the letter. With a glance over her shoulder to see that Luke was occupied helping Ben with dinner, she went upstairs. Ben had already sealed the letter in a plastic Ziploc like the others and set it on top of June's dresser. Her hands trembled a little as she picked it up, and she took a deep breath to steady herself before reading it.

My dearest June, there have been a few developments you need to be aware of. You have, I am sure, heard about Mike

Thompson's tragic suicide. I must implore you to open your eyes. Your golden boy, through his self-serving manipulations, tore a loving couple apart and drove one of this community's brightest stars to end his life. Some good has come of this heartbreak. Carol has at last realized Luke is not worth any more tears. On the night Mike died, Carol wisely moved on to Shane McGuire, a boy I know will be far more careful with her heart than Luke has been. I can only hope your golden boy feels even a glimmer of the pain he has inflicted when he learns that Carol slept with Shane that night.

You tell Aaron Hammond and Pat O'Neil to keep their noses out of my business. If you do not comply, if you allow them to continue digging, you will not like the consequences. I know this hurts you, June, and I want you to know that the last thing I ever wanted to do was cause you pain. When this is all over, and you finally realize the truth, I will reveal myself to you, and you will be gratefully mine.

June sat hard on her bed and the letter fluttered to the floor. Nausea bubbled in her stomach, and her head spun. She lifted her shaking hands and stared at them for a moment. She couldn't decipher the emotions flooding her brain, couldn't begin to analyze the letter. The only thought that stood clearly in her mind was that she didn't want Luke to see this. She still believed he had a right to know, but she wanted to protect him as best she could from further heartache. He'd already been through too much.

"Mom? Are you all right?"

She looked up to see him standing in the doorway of her bedroom with worried eyes.

"Another letter came."

"May I see it?"

She almost said no. "We were finally starting to relax a little."

"Well, that's already ruined. What does it say?"

"He blames you for Mike's death."

"He already said that in Mike's suicide note."

It relieved her to know that Luke didn't believe Mike had killed himself anymore than did anyone else who knew Mike.

"What else?"

Again, she hesitated. "He claims that Carol slept with Shane the night Mike died."

Luke's eyes slid closed, and he clenched his teeth. Without a word, he spun on his heal, walked into his room, and slammed the door. June flinched. Moments later, she heard his muffled bellow, and her vision wavered with the tears that swarmed to her eyes. Why was this happening to them? What had she or Luke ever done to deserve JP's obsession? When she heard

Luke's door open again, she walked out to the balcony. He offered her a lop-sided smile, and though it didn't reach his eyes, any smile at all was better than none.

"Sorry. I figured it would be better to get it out instead of trying to contain it. Would you mind if I chop some of that firewood we cut the other day?"

"Help yourself."

She followed him downstairs and joined Ben at the kitchen sink. They watched Luke for a few minutes as the teenager took his frustration out on the firewood.

"We should have thought of that before now," Ben remarked. "Maybe he'll actually sleep tonight."

"We can hope. I can hope, too, that JP is lying and that this won't destroy his friendship with Shane. I could honestly kill this bastard and not regret it for even a moment. Luke has never done anything to anyone to deserve *any* of this."

"I know, beloved."

Ben tucked her against his side and kissed her cheek. Several minutes passed before the anger receded and she stopped trembling.

To distract herself, she helped Ben with dinner. She would've thought beef stroganoff would be too heavy a meal for such a warm day, but it was one of her favorite comfort foods. A little flirtation while they cooked did wonders to restore her sanity, and by the time Luke came in from his firewood-splitting therapy just as June drained the egg noodles, she was able to greet him with an honest smile. His lips curved in response, and his eyes warmed.

"I made a decision. He can't screw with my head if I don't let him. Even if it's true...." He shrugged and stepped over to the sink to wash up for dinner. "So, Ben, Mom and I were talking about a winter wedding. What do you think?"

"That... sounds wonderful."

* * *

Luke's resolution lasted him through that evening and all the way through his eight-hour shift at the Ramshorn the next day. Each time he felt a thought of Mike or Carol or Shane tickling the edge of his thoughts, he ignored them, focusing instead on his job. It wasn't hard. The cabins and lodge were all booked for another wedding, so there was plenty of cleaning and stocking to be done before the party arrived on the morrow. It wasn't Luke's ideal task, but the physicality provided a good outlet for nervous energy.

He stepped out of the small, very rustic Moose cabin and locked the door. Ben stepped out of the cabin right next to the Moose.

"Last ones," he said.

"Perfect timing," Luke replied. "Only fifteen minutes left on our shift."

"If we take our time walking back to the lodge…."

"I don't feel like crawling. How 'bout I race you back?"

"Like this old dog stands a chance."

Ben took off at a sprint along the trail through the forest, and Luke scrambled after him. They pounded across the bridge over the gurgling Ramshorn Creek and bounded up the earthen steps to the main drive-way with Luke trailing a few steps behind Ben. Even though Ben had only a couple seconds' head start, Luke didn't catch him until they were only ten yards from the lodge and tagged the railing of the stairs only a breath before his opponent. Ben doubled over for a moment, but when he straightened, he grinned. They were both panting.

"That was fun," he said. "I needed that."

"You're lucky I didn't trip and break something," Luke remarked. "Coach Wells would be after you like flies on stink for jeopardizing his starting quarterback."

"My football coach would've said the same—"

"Excuse us."

Luke glanced up to see Jake and Pete descending the stairs, and his heart began pounding in a way that had nothing to do with his brief spurt of physical exertion. They nodded briefly to Ben as they passed, but both ignored Luke as if he hadn't moments ago been blocking their path. A shiver of dread coursed down his spine. He could be looking at Mike's killer, the man who had, for a couple of weeks that felt more like an eternity, been playing destructive mind games with him.

"That was cold," Ben murmured. He frowned as he watched the brothers walk toward the pools where Pete's truck was parked.

"Yeah, but even in the off chance neither of them is JP, they both knew Mike well. Jake, at least, liked Mike better than me, and if they know what Mike's note said…. Well, a cold shoulder is the least I would expect. Especially from Jake."

"You okay, kid?"

"Surprisingly so. Like I've been told by all the people who matter, I know who I am. I know I'm not what JP says."

Ben clapped him on the back. "I can't tell you how proud it makes me to know that JP is an idiot to think he can break you."

"Thanks, Dad."

"You know, I really like that."

"I know you do."

They climbed the stairs, and Ben took the brunt of June's questions about their eventless run-in with the two main JP suspects while Luke spent the last ten minutes of his shift sweeping the porch. He stubbornly refused to think about anything but his task and how much he loved the sigh of the wind through the boughs of the pines and the sweet, damp scent of impending rain. Peeking out from under the porch roof, he noted the thickening clouds. The forecast said a slow-moving cold front would be pushing through the area, which meant a few thunderstorms were possible tonight and tomorrow, but the weather was supposed to settle again in time for the guests' wedding.

A low grumble of distant thunder momentarily drowned out the swish of his broom, and he paused to listen.

"Yeah, I love this place," he whispered to himself.

A familiar car rolled up the driveway, and he leaned on the porch railing to watch his copper-haired ex-girlfriend park and climb out. She lifted her gaze and flinched when she saw him watching her.

"Hi, Luke," she said shyly.

"Hi."

"Can we talk?"

He shrugged, so she crossed the driveway and crested the stairs. He turned around and leaned on the railing with his arms folded and his ankles crossed. She took one sweeping look at his defensive posture, and instead of trying to hug him again, she took a chair at the nearest table. For several long moments, she didn't try to talk, just sat there, wringing her hands and fidgeting in her seat. Her vibrant green eyes were red-rimmed, and Luke briefly wondered how many hours in the last three days she'd spent crying. Part of him ached at her obvious grief, but a larger part of him coldly knew she'd brought a lot of it on herself. Not Mike's death—even if he hated her with every ounce of his heart, he would *never* believe either of them was responsible for that.

"This is such a mess," she mumbled at last.

"Yeah, it is." He thought *mess* was a bit of an understatement, but he kept the comment to himself. He took a deep breath to quell his mounting irritation and vowed to be supportive because he wasn't the only one hurting. "What did you want to talk about?"

"I don't even know. I can't believe he's gone."

"Neither can I."

They lapsed into silence again. He studied her as she stared blindly at the scarred tabletop and couldn't make sense of his tangled emotions. Instinct told him he should comfort her, but the unproven possibility that—despite claiming she wanted Luke back—she had slept with Shane left a bitter taste in his mouth. It wasn't the act itself that bothered him. It was the lie.

"May I ask you a question, Carol?"

She lifted her gaze and nodded hesitantly.

"Did you sleep with Shane the night Mike died?"

The answer was plain in her eyes, though she did not speak to either confirm or deny. Tears welled, making her green irises contrast more sharply against the red of her lids.

"You said you loved me, but how can I believe that now? How can I trust anything you say?"

The tears spilled over as she met his gaze. "I'm so sorry, Luke. For everything I've done to you and for everything I did to Mike. I don't deserve either of you." She tried unsuccessfully to choke back the sobs. "I'll never be able to tell him that. I don't understand it at all.… Why did he kill himself?"

"I don't think he did," Luke said matter-of-factly.

"What, you're saying someone killed him? He left a goddamned note, Luke! Blaming us."

No, blaming me, he thought.

"He said he only *thought* he loved me, but in the note—"

"The note's a fake, Carol. He didn't write it."

"W-what?"

"Someone killed him and wrote the note to make it look like a suicide."

"That's insane. How can you even—"

"Would you rather believe Mike—star athlete with a full-ride scholarship to the school of his dreams—killed himself because of us?"

The color vanished from Carol's face, leaving her skin sickly pale. "Oh, God."

She was on her feet and running for her car too fast for Luke to react. By the time he recovered from her hasty departure, she was already racing away in her car. An inkling of something very out of place wormed its way into his brain. Why had she looked so terrified? Shaking his head to dispel questions to which he had no answers, he took the broom inside.

"Porch all swept?" Marvin asked. When Luke nodded, he said, "Thanks, Luke. I wish every kid your age was willing to work as hard as you do."

"Thanks, Marvin."

He joined June and Ben behind the bar to clock

out.

"Was that Carol?" June asked.

He only nodded.

"She seemed upset."

"JP wasn't lying," he said. "I know you're both curious, so there you go."

They stopped at the cabin only long enough to collect the dogs before setting off on the trail over to Pat and Aelissm's. Luke tried to arrange the questions he wanted to ask Pat and to formulate his theories into something the former detective might be able to use. He waited until after dinner to broach the subject, partly because he didn't want to disrupt the pleasant time with his family and partly because he was still putting pieces together.

Aelissm brought out the cards while Pat finished up the dishes.

"It has to be Jake or Pete," Luke said.

"What has to…. Never mind." Aelissm held up her hand. "Stupid question."

"Why do you say that?"

"Who else would even care who Carol dated let alone know the details of what all has transpired between her, Mike, and me?" He hesitated before adding the fourth person to the list. "And now Shane. And who else besides her uncles would feel the right to approve or not approve her choice for a boyfriend?"

"I'm willing to agree, but what makes you so sure?" Pat inquired. He divvied up the chips for poker.

"Well, he knew why Carol broke up with me and knows she slept with Shane. There's something else that's been bugging me since the Hay Fever barbecue. Carol said Mike and 'Unkie' made her believe Becky and I were more than just friends so she would break up with me. She only mentioned 'Unkie' once, but it stuck in my head. Maybe because of the fight with Jake. I don't know. Maybe I'm imagining it."

"No, I think you're on to something," Pat said.

Luke dealt the cards. "She stopped by the Ramshorn to talk this afternoon just before we got off work. When I asked about Shane… she didn't say anything, but she didn't have to. I told her the suicide note was a fake, that someone killed Mike… she looked *afraid*. Like she'd just realized something and it scared her. She took off before I could stop her."

"Did you ask who she told about Shane?" Ben questioned.

Luke hung his head. "I didn't even think about it."

"Why don't you call her, and Shane, too? If we can find out who they told, that will really help us narrow it down."

Luke stood and grabbed the cordless. As he dialed Shane's number, he walked out onto the back steps.

"Hello?"

"Shane? It's Luke."

"Oh, hey, Luke. What's up?"

"I need to ask you something. And please, just give me a straight, simple answer."

"Okay, shoot."

"Who did you tell about you and Carol?"

"Ah, Jesus, Luke." The regret was thick in Shane's voice. "I'm so sorry. I didn't mean for it to happen. I wish it hadn't. After she left the barbecue crying, I went to talk to her, because she's *my* friend, too. Then Jake stopped by to say Mike had killed himself, and she started crying again, and one thing led—"

"Shane. I don't want the details. Who did you tell?"

"No one."

"Well, someone found out."

"I swear to God, Luke, I didn't tell anyone. Not even my dad."

"You're sure?"

"Positive. Luke, I really am sorry. How can I—"

"I gotta go."

"Luke, wait!"

He ended the call before the obscenities and accusations came spilling out of his mouth. Without giving himself time to dwell on his brief conversation with Shane, he called Pete Landers. The sound of Pete's voice sent a wave of cold through him. He would need to be very careful about what he said.

"Pete, it's Luke. Is Carol there?"

"No, she's not. I haven't seen her since this morning, and she was supposed to eat dinner with me before heading back into Devyn."

"Well, if you see her, will you tell her to call me?"

"I don't think that's a good idea, Luke. She's having a really hard time right now."

"I know she is. Look, when you see her, will you tell her something for me?"

There was a pause and for a moment, Luke wondered if Pete was still on the other end of the line.

"What do you want me to tell her?"

"That I'm sorry, too. And that it isn't her fault. She'll know what I mean."

"If I see her, I'll tell her."

"Okay, thanks."

Next, Luke tried Jake's number. There was no answer. Lastly, he tried Pete's mother in Devyn, praying

Carol had ditched dinner with Pete and gone straight home to Tammy's. When the answering machine picked up, Luke asked Carol to call him at Aelissm's in the next couple of hours or at home if she didn't get the message before then. He disconnected the call and stared at the cordless for a while before turning around and heading back inside.

"Couldn't get hold of Carol?" June asked.

He shook his head. "And Shane says he didn't tell anyone."

"Who would Carol tell?" Ben asked.

"Her uncles, maybe Pete's mom. Probably Nikki, but she won't be back from Hawaii until next week."

"So, Jake or Pete." Pat leaned back in his chair. "Pretty much what we've been thinking since the first letter arrived. Still…. Because so much of this is speculation, I want you both to continue to take precautions. Keep a gun handy when you can and keep your eyes and ears open."

"And somehow try to get on with our lives in the process," June added.

"Well, planning a wedding should help with that," Aelissm remarked. "So, have you set a date *yet?*"

"What did you do to her, Pat?" Ben asked. "Weddings and kids and barbecues. Wow. I never thought

I'd see the day."

"Ben, do not make me embarrass you in front of your fiancée."

"She's known me for twenty-some years, and she's seen me naked. Do your worst, Aeli."

"You aren't supposed to call my bluff." Aelissm turned to June. "I guess this means we have our Ben back."

"We do, indeed." June took Ben by the chin and kissed him. "Shall we tell her the date, or shall we make her guess?"

"December eighteenth, on the deck of the Bedspread," Luke said. "Now, before this conversation takes the usual detour into territory I really don't want to know about, may we *please* play our cards instead of staring at them?"

His comment was met with laughter. So long as he had his family, he promised himself he would make it through whatever JP threw at him. In the years before June had adopted him, he had never known this kind of love, and now that he had it, he would not let a delusional nutcase ruin it.

Eighteen

HE STARED AT HER tear-stained face and wondered if any of it was real. He doubted it. She was as manipulative as her whore of a mother and as capable an actress. When she met his gaze, he glimpsed raw fear in her eyes. *That*, at least, was authentic and a very appropriate emotion. He had thought twenty-four hours tied onto that chair with no food, very little to drink, and only two bathroom breaks would cure her stubbornness, but when he reached to take the tape off her mouth, anger flashed in her gaze. He backhanded her, knocking the resentment right out of her. Her eyes filled *again*, and he sat in the chair across from her.

"This is your last chance, Carol. I'm going to take that tape off, and you are going to tell me what you told him."

He yanked the tape off. She choked out a cry of pain and pressed the side of her face to her shoulder as if she could rub away the sting. Then she turned accusing eyes on him.

"What is wrong with you?!" she croaked.

"You don't get to ask the questions, little slut. You really are like your mother, aren't you? Although I guess I shouldn't complain too much right now, since your tryst with Shane McGuire served me quite well."

"I hate you."

"I'm sure you do."

"Did you kill Mike?"

JP smirked but didn't reply.

"Luke said it wasn't a suicide, that Mike was murdered. Did you kill him, Unkie? Are you going to kill Luke, too?"

"Not until he has felt every stab of agony his lies have inflicted on me."

"What did he ever do to you?"

"I thought I said you didn't get to ask the questions."

"It's June, isn't it? You've never gotten over her." Carol straightened. "She never would've married you."

He clenched his hands into fists behind his back. He wouldn't strike her again.

"She's too smart, and she would've eventually seen the evil inside you. You *are* evil."

If he was evil, Carol and her mother and Luke *McKindel* had made him so. Carol and Cheryl had taken away everything that mattered most to his beloved brother, and with no hope of happiness, Paul had blown his own brains out. The image of Paul sprawled on the bedroom floor of his house in Devyn with a puddle of blood around his head like an inky red halo and bits of brain clinging to the wall nearly made JP gag. If he could make Cheryl pay for the agony she'd caused Paul, he would, but she was out of his reach, and it was far too late to help Paul. It wasn't too late to help June or himself, so he leaned forward and sneered.

"I will ask you again and warn you to consider your answer carefully. What did you tell Luke?"

"Nothing," she said. Defiance radiated from her like heat from the earth in the height of summer.

"I don't believe you." He hit her again, unable to stop himself. "What did you tell him?"

"I only apologized for what I'd done to him and Mike. I didn't tell him anything. How could I?"

Slap.

"I didn't tell him anything! I didn't know! Please… please stop."

For a moment, his vision dimmed, and all he could see was the one thing he wanted in life slipping away from him. June was engaged. Another man had already claimed her, and even if she never found out he was behind the letters and the calls and the fear she undoubtedly felt, she was lost to him. When his vision cleared again, he looked at the girl sitting in front of him, and though somewhere in the back of his mind he knew who she was, but he didn't recognize her face, her fearful emerald eyes, or her mane of soft red waves.

He rose slowly to his feet, drained of all emotion, even anger. He untied the girl he vaguely knew was his niece—the girl he could no longer recall helping raise—and jerked her off the chair. She scrambled to get her legs under her and regarded him with barely-veiled terror. He pulled his handkerchief from his back pocket and tied it around her eyes.

"What are you doing?"

"We're going for a little ride, and I don't want you to see where we're going until we get there."

Then he taped her mouth shut again and half-led, half-dragged her out to his pickup and buckled her in with her hands still tied behind her back. He felt nothing as he drove up the mountain. No fiery hatred, no remorse for what he had done and what he was about to do, only a cold, single-minded determination to finish what he'd started.

* * *

"Becky, you keep working like this around here, and you'll have a guaranteed job when you turn sixteen," Luke said as Becky folded the last towel and plopped it on top of the stack.

"Well, I'd rather be doing something to pass the time than sitting around letting it drag by," she replied.

"There we go. All clean, all folded, and all ready for swimmers."

"Great. So, you're shift is over now, right?"

"Yep."

"I know you just spent the last eight hours here, but doesn't a swim sound good?"

"It does, actually."

They walked down the hill from the pool house to the lodge to ask Ben and June if they could run up to the cabin to get their swimming gear. The dining room, when they walked through the door, was

476

packed. Every table was occupied, and a couple of ranch hands—Austin McGuire and two new hands Luke hadn't met—sat at the bar eating an early dinner. Ben and June bustled between tables, and Marvin and Mary were both busy in the kitchen. The new waiter appeared to have arrived only moments ago and was transitioning into his shift so June and Ben could leave.

"Hey, Mom, do you mind if Becky and I ride up to the cabin and get all our swimsuits and towels to so we can all go swimming before dinner?" Luke asked as he helped June deliver plates to the largest table.

"A swim sounds great right now, but would you mind waiting until Ben and I can come with you? No one's home, and I don't want you up there alone right now."

"It'll only be up and back. We won't be long. That way you can help a little longer until this place settles down."

June glanced around the crowded room and for a moment, he thought she would say no. "Fine. Straight up and straight back, no lollygagging and no detours."

He gave her a quick kiss on the cheek and swung around behind the bar to jot down his time and grab his and June's helmets. He tossed the latter to Becky and scooted out the door before June could change her mind. Or before he allowed himself be volunteered to wait tables until the rush calmed down. Normally, he wouldn't mind, but today, he just wasn't in the mood. He wanted to go for a ride, take a swim in the hot springs, and enjoy some worry-free time with Becky. She had spent much of the last three days with Jenny Thompson—being a far better friend than Jenny had ever been to her—and had stated in firm terms that she was game for anything that didn't involve thinking too much. A long, invigorating ride on any one of the numerous Forest Service roads and trails would've been ideal, but June's edict killed that plan. So, they'd have to settle for a ride to the cabin and back and some horseplay in the hot springs.

"So, just up and back? Bummer," Becky said as she plunked June's helmet on her head and fastened the strap.

"I know, but it's better than nothing."

"Race you to the cabin."

"I've created a monster," he muttered. He stood on the kick-start, and his dirt bike growled to life. With his helmet securely fastened, he shot off down the driveway of the Ramshorn and out onto the main road with Becky right behind him. They obeyed the posted speed limit. Barely.

The cold front had stalled just east of Northstar, leaving the air almost chilly after the past few days of near-eighty-degree weather—the temperature was only in the upper fifties. The sky was flat and gray. The cool wind smelled of rain, though the clouds were holding on to the moisture for the time being, and Luke let the hint of autumn wash through his senses and soothe him. Only a few months after arriving in Northstar, he'd found it difficult to imagine living anywhere else, and now, after five years… it was impossible.

He wasn't foolish enough to disobey June's sensible command, so instead of stopping in at Ma Burns' to say hello, when he spotted Betty on the front porch of her store, he only waved and rode on. He let Becky shoot past him on the straightaway but caught her shortly after turning right on Clark Creek Road. The dust on the turns through the sage hills was getting deep and a cloud of it billowed out behind them. He smiled when he heard his friend's excited whoop over the buzz of the bikes. Yep, this was the life.

The air in the trees was a couple degrees cooler, and the wildlife seemed to be taking advantage of it. He saw at least two-dozen deer, and on the side of the hill just above Clark Creek, a cow moose and her calf. A mile later, he and Becky paused for a few moments to let a small band of six bull elk—all summer-sleek spikes—cross the road. The animals froze, and their heads turned as one up the mountain, away from Luke and Becky. Then something startled the elk back to life, and they took off at a flat run. Luke watched them disappear over the top of the ridge to the west, amazed. The fact that this was not an unusual occurrence made it all the more incredible. With a shake of his head, he continued on.

He stopped at the gate, flipped the kickstand down with the heel of his boot, killed the motor and leaned the bike on the stand. He strode up to the gate and reached up into the bell-shaped housing that protected the lock from the elements. As he unlocked it by feel, the hairs on the back of his neck stood on end. He snapped his head up and looked around, unable to explain the sudden, gut-wrenching anxiety. Every sense sharpened as something unnamable and subliminal triggered a flood of adrenaline. Something was wrong. Every instinct screamed at him to turn around and flee, but since nothing else seemed obviously out of place, he swung the gate open… and left it open. They'd only be up at the cabin for fifteen minutes at most, so there was no point in closing it until their trip down even if the voice in the back of his mind weren't demanding he keep that means of escape open.

He climbed back on his bike and proceeded forward with as much caution as his racing pulse allowed. Becky started to zip past him, but he held a hand up, motioning her to stay back. She frowned at him in inquiry, but heeded his unspoken warning. They crested the hill, and just ahead, the driveway to June's cabin forked off to the right. Across from it were the pale yellow, sulfurous mine tailings and it was to them that Luke's gaze was inexplicably drawn.

In his distraction, he lost control of his bike. It tipped to the left, and he overcorrected, pitching himself over the handlebars. The bike crashed into the side of the old log cabin ruins at the bottom of the driveway. Luke lay sprawled in the dust on his back with the wind knocked out of him and his eyes locked on the top of the mine dumps. Becky was beside him in a moment, asking if he was okay, but he couldn't answer. Even after his lungs started working again, he couldn't find his voice. He couldn't tear his eyes away. At last, she followed his gaze. Then she screamed.

Time seemed to slow as Luke took in the figure tied to the post at the top of the mound. The head, hanging with the chin touching the chest, was covered with long waves of shimmering copper hair. She still wore the same dark green tank top and jeans she'd worn yesterday. He couldn't see most of her face beneath the loose-hanging hair, but he didn't need to.

"Oh… my… God…. Is that… is that *Carol?*"

A gust of wind shifted the red hair, and he saw for the first time the small hole and dark black stain on her shirt. Right over her heart.

"Is she… dead?"

He rolled onto his feet and stepped cautiously closer so he could see the eyes. They were open, staring blankly and glassed over. Lifeless.

"Luke?"

He lowered his gaze and noticed an inky red stain that seeped into the mine dumps. The stain grew as he stared, and fear shot through him, kicking him into action.

"We have to go. Now."

A glance at his bike showed him that the bead was popped on the front tire, so he climbed on June's bike. Becky jumped on behind him and wrapped her arms around his waist.

"Oh God, oh God, oh God," she chanted. "Who could do this?"

JP, Luke knew. He sped down the hill as if their lives depended on it. Their lives *did* depend on it.

* * *

June was glad the Ramshorn was so busy these days, but she was also glad to see the dining room clearing. She and Ben were already almost an hour over on their shifts, and she was really looking forward to that swim. A soft rain had started to fall, which would make the hot water feel even better. She tried not to worry about Luke and Becky riding up to the cabin on their own and thought it was ridiculous that she had any reason to worry. Luke had ridden the twelve-mile stretch between the Ramshorn and the cabin solo more times than she could count, but it wasn't worry about an accident that set her nerves to fluttering.

"Quick, let's sneak outside and sit on the porch to wait before more customers show up," Ben said, grabbing her hand and dragging her outside.

She giggled as they took up residence on the bench against the outside wall of the lodge just as a group of seven walked up the steps. When Ben tilted her face toward him and claimed her mouth, she let her eyes slide closed. She felt a little like a teenager sneaking around and admitted that it was fun. Then Ben turned from her mouth to her neck, whispering how much he loved her as he trailed kisses from her jaw to her shoulder, and she felt something much hotter and much more lasting than teenaged lust.

"I love you," she murmured, tucking her face against his neck.

"Mmm. I'd like to show you just how much I love you, too."

"Uh-huh. I don't think that's going to happen tonight."

The distant hum of a dirt bike put thoughts of a late night seduction on hold. She sat up, thinking it seemed a little early for Luke and Becky to be returning. She listened for the sound of the second bike but continued to hear only one.

"They can't possibly think I'm going to fall for that one again," Ben remarked.

When the dirt bike came into view, June smiled. Luke drove her bike with Becky behind with her arms wrapped tightly around him. "Apparently they do."

There was something about the sight that triggered an alarm in her head. If they were going to pull a prank, wouldn't they have used Luke's bike? Also, Luke was going far too fast. And even from this distance, June saw that his clothes were smudged with dirt.

"It's not a prank," she breathed and ran out to meet them. "Something's wrong."

Luke skidded to a stop only a few feet from June. His face and what she could see of Becky's—the girl had her right cheek pressed against Luke's back—was pale. He lifted his gaze, and worry jolted her when she saw the terror in his eyes.

"Luke, what happened?" Ben asked.

"The elk… they stopped in the road… then ran…. Something scared them. I shouldn't have gone past the gate… and then there she was, and I crashed—my bike's wrecked. I couldn't look away. She's dead. He killed her. On the mine dumps. Still bleeding, but dead. We turned and—oh, God, the dogs!"

The words spilled out of him so fast, June barely caught them. His eyes darted wildly, seemingly unable to focus on anything. She glanced at Becky, who quietly chanted something unintelligible.

"The dogs will be fine, Luke. Who's dead?" June asked.

"Her eyes were just… blank. He tied her up there for me to find."

She grabbed his face and forced him to look her in the eye. "Luke!"

He took in the sight of her face and sagged against the handlebars for a moment. Then he started to breathe more slowly in and out as got hold of himself. When he spoke again, his voice was firm and angry. "Carol. She's dead. He killed her and left her on the mine dumps for us to find."

Ben swore and ran inside.

"Becky, honey, you're okay," June cooed. She gently encircled Ben's trembling niece and helped her off the bike. As soon as Becky let go of Luke, she turned and latched on to June. "Shh, Becky. Take a deep breath."

June held out an arm for Luke, too, and he let himself be tucked against her. Adrenaline throbbed through her as surely as it did through the two teenagers clinging to her. She couldn't begin to imagine what they had seen or think of anything beyond her gratitude that they were safe. Clearly traumatized but safe.

"Luke, are you all right?"

"No."

"Are you hurt?" When he shook his head, she wondered if he even knew yet. "Let's go inside. You're both wet from the rain, and the lodge is warm and almost empty now."

Becky seemed incapable of moving, so Luke picked her up and carried her inside. Ben was on the phone, giving directions quickly and quietly to someone June presumed was the 911 dispatcher, so she escorted Luke and Becky to the couch by the dark fireplace.

"I feel sick," Becky murmured as Luke carefully lowered her onto the couch.

"Deep breaths will help. Kevin, when you get a moment, would you bring us two glasses of water?"

The new waiter nodded and quickly complied. June nodded her thanks as she took the waters and gave them to Luke and Becky. For a long time, she sat with them, refusing to think about anything but their comfort. Slowly, Becky's shaking stopped, and she began to relax, though she remained tightly tucked between June and Luke on the couch. Luke was harder to gauge. Outwardly, he appeared remarkably calm, though she knew a torrent of questions and thoughts crowded his mind. She asked again if he was hurt, and again, he shook his head.

"Might have a few bruises," he said quietly, "but nothing major."

He stared at the empty fireplace, and June watched helplessly as tears welled in his unblinking eyes until they spilled over.

"Sorry, Mom. We didn't make it up to the cabin."

"Why are you apologizing for that? After what

you saw...."

"I feel like I have to apologize for something. I won't ever be able to tell Carol that I'm sorry for the mean things I said. Or to Mike for screwing up his relationship with Carol."

"Oh, honey." She reached over and hugged him as tightly as she could leaning over Becky. "None of that is your fault, so don't you dare blame yourself for any of it."

He tipped his head back, closed his eyes, and slumped down into the couch cushions.

"I called Aaron first," Ben murmured as she joined them. He squatted in front of them, frowning as he studied the teenagers. "He should be up there by now. And the sheriff and a couple more deputies are on their way. I tried to call Jane, too, but she and Andy weren't home."

"I really wish we had the swimsuits now. They could probably use a long, hot soak while we wait."

"Actually, we still have the ones we took to Washington in the back of my truck. Thought of that while I was talking to Aaron."

"Wonderful. Luke, Becky, you still up for that swim?"

Both nodded mutely and stood. Seeing movement

from the corner of her vision, June glanced toward the kitchen. Mary stood in the doorway, leaning against the wall with her hand covering her mouth. June stepped away for a moment to talk to her.

"Is it true?" she asked in a bare whisper. "Carol Landers, too?"

"I think so."

"You don't think Pete or Jake would…?"

"At this point, Mary, I don't know what to think." She briefly embraced her boss. "I hope we'll know more soon."

Mary shook her head as June trotted away. June blocked the scenarios and questions prodding her, unwilling to give in to the fear and sadness. As long as she focused on helping Luke and Becky, she wouldn't fall apart. She grabbed the bag with the swimsuits out of the back of Ben's truck and jogged up the driveway to catch up with Luke, Becky, and Ben.

"Aaron said he'd come down to get us once they've removed the body," Ben whispered, "but it'll probably be a couple hours. He also said he'd check on the dogs for us and let them out."

"But we locked the doors."

"I gave him the spare key the other day."

"Ah."

June really wanted to bury her hands and face in Cheyenne's and Casey's warm blond coats right then. She wanted the assurance that they were okay as much as the therapy they never failed to provide.

At the pool house, they pulled out their swimsuits, grabbed four of the towels Luke and Becky had finished folding only an hour ago, and went into the changing rooms.

"Are you going to be all right, Becky?" June asked. "You're looking a little steadier, at least."

"Yeah. I think I'm heading toward disbelief at last. I didn't see her at first... I saw Luke crash, and I was shocked because Luke doesn't crash."

"You don't have to talk about it right now, Becky. I'd rather you forget about it for a while, if you can. There will be too much thinking about it before long, so take the chance and relax for a bit before it all starts."

"Thanks, Aunt June." She smiled. "Is it okay if I call you that now?"

"Of course it is."

They spent much of the next two hours in the hot springs, mostly just sitting on the steps of the smaller, warmer pool. June steadfastly refused to let them talk about Carol or Mike or JP, and gradually, Luke and

Becky began to unwind. After, they returned to the lodge for something to eat, though no one was very hungry. Aaron arrived just as the new waiter Kevin cleared their half-eaten meals.

"It's all cleaned up if you want to go home tonight," he said.

"Thank you, Aaron." June frowned at him. "You look exhausted."

"I *am* exhausted. Anyhow, Sheriff Rogers is still on scene if you want to talk to him." Aaron snorted. "He's concerned now."

June pulled him aside, out of Luke's and Becky's hearing. "I haven't asked them because I don't want them to think about it any more than they already are. What happened? Is it really Carol?"

"It is. She was tied to that post on top of the mine dumps and executed. One shot to the chest from point-blank range. Her face…. It looks like she was struck a few times, and there's sticky residue around her mouth like it had been taped shut. I found a shell casing with prints on it, so hopefully we'll be able to make a concrete connection with Mike's death. Here's something interesting for you. Tammy Landers—Pete's mother—called the sheriff's department late this morning, worried about Carol and Pete because she couldn't get hold of either of them. Or Jake. As much as I don't want to believe either of them is capable of any of it, this is so far beyond messed up that I'm not sure anything would surprise me right now. Oh, almost forgot. Your dogs are safe and sound. I let them out, then locked them back in the cabin."

June thanked him and gathered her family to go home. Since they hadn't heard from Jane or Andy, they headed to the Royal R Ranch first. Aaron would meet them back at the cabin. Ben's sister and brother-in-law met them in the driveway of their house.

"We just got your message and called the Ramshorn," Jane said, hugging her daughter and Luke together. "Marvin said you'd already left to bring Becky home. Is everyone all right?"

"As much as we can be, considering the circumstances," Ben replied. "Give me a hug, kiddo."

Becky threw her arms around Ben's neck. "Be careful, Uncle Ben."

"You know I will. Take it easy tonight, huh?"

"I'll try."

"We'll get the details later," Andy said. "Although I'm not sure I really want to know."

They bid farewell, and Ben drove home. As they passed the mine dumps, June looked for any sign of the horrible tragedy that had happened there, but the sheriff and his deputies had thoroughly cleaned the scene, and even dug up the bloody dirt. Someone—Aaron, most likely—had picked up Luke's dirt bike and taken it up to the cabin, but she could see where he'd crashed. Luke stared as they drove past as if wondering if he'd imagined it all. June wished he had.

The sheriff and Aaron were sitting on the front steps, frowning over what looked like notes. They looked up when Ben shut down the truck. Luke went inside without saying a word to anyone.

"Aaron. Sheriff Rogers," June said by way of greeting.

"Sheriff Rogers will be handling the investigation."

"I'd feel a lot better if you were on the case."

"He is," the sheriff replied. "I need to ask Luke a few questions, if that is all right with you, Ms. Montana."

June shook her head. "Not tonight, Sheriff Rogers. Tomorrow will have to be soon enough. I think you will agree when I say he has been traumatized enough for one day. I apologize for being rude, but—"

"I fully understand, Ms. Montana. Would eight be

too early?"

Anything sooner than never would be too early, but June didn't voice her thoughts. She smiled and nodded. "We'll see you then, unless you would like to come in for coffee."

"I'd best be heading back into Devyn. I have some paperwork to file and evidence to catalogue."

"Aaron?"

"Coffee sounds great. I'll see you in the morning, Sheriff."

"Just remember, you're off duty."

"Don't worry, boss. June won't let me talk about anything tonight. I'm staying as a friend only."

The older man nodded and started for his SUV. Aaron followed June and Ben inside and locked the door behind them.

"I'm surprised the sheriff didn't warn us to be careful tonight," Ben remarked, "even though the killer is 'probably miles away by now'."

"He knows well enough that people up here can take care of themselves without being told, and the look on June's face right now almost makes me hope the bastard is stupid enough to come waltzing up to the front door. Case'd be closed right quick."

June smirked.

Nineteen

IT AMUSED JP to no end that, for two days now, the men crawling all over the mine deposits—scavenging for minute clues about Carol Landers' killer—had not thought to look up. If they had, someone might have spotted him watching from the ridge west of them. Less than two hundred yards away, as the crows flew. He had been hiding out in the mountains, too afraid to return to his cabin. Afraid was perhaps the wrong word because, if he were honest with himself, he hadn't been feeling much of anything lately. Not fear, not anticipation, not even hate. Where there had once been a raging flood of wild emotion there was now a void. He knew there was no redemption for what he'd done, and he longed to feel remorse for his niece's necessary death, but he felt nothing. Even his amusement was hollow, something he knew he *should* feel.

Luke would pay for that, too.

He lifted his high-powered binoculars, squinting against the brilliant sunlight reflecting off the mine tailings. Aaron Hammond had found the single shell casing before anyone else had arrived and had dusted it for prints on scene. Whether or not he had found a print, JP hadn't a clue, but he *did* know he hadn't cleaned Mike Thompson's pistol well enough because the nosy sheriff's deputy *had* found a print on that. If Aaron put two and two together… the world would know Mike hadn't committed suicide. More was the pity because the blame would be shifted off Luke. Then again, maybe the seed of doubt had already germinated and even a murder ruling wouldn't be able to kill it.

He continued to watch the investigation of the mine dumps and realized that some small part of him wished they would find something and catch him before he hurt someone else he loved. JP understood on some level that it was his weaker personality that wanted this, but since he'd shot his own niece in the chest and killed her, it had become increasingly more difficult to suppress that pathetic, spineless fool. The memory of her pleading, hating green eyes haunted him. He'd taped her mouth shut to keep her quiet, but the accusation and defiance in her eyes still echoed more loudly than any scream. A fist to the side of the head had dazed her, making the task of carrying her up to the top of the mine dump and securing her to the post fairly easy. She had regained full lucidity just in time to realize with certainty that she was about to die, and the unspoken plea for her life had left her gaze, replaced by pure insolence. His hands had trembled as he'd raised the pistol. He'd resisted the urge to close his eyes when he pulled the trigger and had seen the life leave Carol's eyes as the blood spilled from her ruined heart.

A single shot and now his niece was gone forever. JP nearly blacked out for a moment and struggled to remain in control. He wasn't about to give up now when he was so close to achieving his goal. What part of it he *could* still accomplish.

Shifting his binoculars up and left to June's cabin, he found the object of his now-dead fantasies standing on her front deck. The distance was too great for him to make out the details of her, but he didn't need them to know it was her. He'd seen the glittering confirmation of his suspicions—that she had given herself, body and heart, to the dark-haired, too-good-looking ex-cop from Washington—three days ago, when he and his brother had last stopped by the Ramshorn. Well, that was one more wrong he intended to rectify. She'd broken his heart once already, and he wouldn't stand for her trampling all over what little was left of it.

She *was* beautiful, though. Her hair, hanging loose, shone brightly in the midday sunlight, and the jeans and tank top she wore nicely showed off her trim figure. Somewhere in the deep recesses of his frozen heart, he felt something stir… a faint longing. He squashed it instantly. She'd given herself to Ben Conner up at Sawtooth Lake, if the rumors were true, and the thought of another man touching her and taking her was more than that fragile yearning could bear. However, the knowledge that he would never claim her for his own did not mean he couldn't make her pay for the heartache she'd caused him. He didn't want to hurt her, not like he wanted to hurt Luke. He only wanted her to realize the pain she'd inadvertently caused him when she'd chosen her precious golden boy over him. No man deserved to be cast aside as he had.

Luke sat on the front steps, and when JP focused on him, he felt another vague stirring of emotion, though it was too weak to be true hate. Even the guilt-tinged sadness that hung about the teenager like a fog could not incite the triumphant glee JP knew he should feel. He began to doubt if even the culmination of his plan would restore any sensation within the emptiness. After today, he would know. It would all end, one way or another.

He glanced at his watch. June and Luke would be heading down to the Ramshorn for work soon, so he tucked his binoculars in their case, stood, and headed down the mountain to set the rest of his plan in motion.

* * *

June stepped out onto the front deck and stood beside Luke for a moment to admire the beauty that surrounded her and wonder if she should still be able to find such joy in her home after Carol's horrible death just down the hill. She leaned down and squeezed Luke's shoulder.

"We should probably get ready for work," she murmured.

"Yeah," he replied and stood.

The mine tailings were out of sight down the hill and around to the south, but she could hear the occasional shouts of the sheriff and his deputies, and once or twice, she heard Pat and Ben. The sound of their voices made her smile. She knew Pat occasionally missed his career as a detective, and apparently at least a part of Ben missed being a sheriff's deputy, too.

There had been two fingerprints on the shell casing Aaron had found, and they'd matched the second print on the gun in Mike Thompson's car, so the sheriff was now calling the teen's death a homicide. Two homicides now. June couldn't wrap her head around it.

Nothing much else in the way of evidence had been found, other than a couple of tracks that hadn't been washed away by the rain and were made by worn cowboy boots. Many of the men who lived and worked in the valley wore that style of boot, including the two main suspects Jake Sterling and Pete Landers, both of whom seemed to have vanished. No one had seen either of them since the afternoon before Carol died, not even Pete's mother Tammy. She had only been able to say that both men had been acting secretively of late.

With a sigh, June turned and followed Luke inside. After the endless stream of questions and speculations, she was looking forward to work. She and Luke both needed a break from the investigation. Luke especially. The vacant, dead look in his eyes was worse than even the pain and fear, and she worried that JP was succeeding. She had hoped he would give Shane another chance or attempt to reconcile their friendship, but so far, Luke hadn't been able to bring himself to even answer Shane's phone calls. It was one more heartbreak, one more win for JP. At least when Luke was at work, he seemed a little more alert and animated.

"Like I'm doing any better," she murmured.

She had lost two students in the last week, and even though she didn't like what Carol had done to both Luke and Mike, she still liked and cared for the girl. If either Jake or Pete was behind her death.... June shook her head, unable to imagine either of them killing her. They both doted on her. Then again, whoever JP was, there was obviously something very wrong with him. Most of the time, she found it difficult to believe either Carol or Mike were gone.

"Stop thinking about it, June," she muttered.

That was easier said than done, but she managed to finish getting ready for work. While she waited for Luke, she went out to her truck to check the .357 pistol she'd been keeping under the seat. It was loaded and the safety was on, so she slipped it back into its hiding place.

"I wish school was here already," Luke said. He slid into the passenger seat. "It'd be a better distraction than work."

"It would," June said. "Ready?"

"Very."

She drove down the driveway and stopped to say hi to Ben. Her fiancé—she really liked thinking of him with that particular term attached, though *husband* would be even better—leaned in the open window to give her a quick kiss on the cheek.

"You have the gun, right?" he asked.

She showed it to him. "Of course."

"I'll be heading up to the cabin in a few minutes. Call me when you get to the Ramshorn."

"Will do."

"All right. See you both in a few hours. Be careful."

"We will. Love you."

"Love you, too."

She didn't voice her hope that they would figure out who had plunged her family and her tranquil community into a spiral of fear and grief, nor did she ask when she and Luke would be able to breathe freely again without worrying some deranged beast might jump out of the shadows and end their lives as quickly and ruthlessly as he had killed Mike Thompson and Carol Landers. Surely, it couldn't be long. If his intent was to hurt Luke, what more could he do before her son reached the tipping point and numbed to the pain or broke under it?

"This is where the elk crossed. We should've turned around when they spooked."

June glanced at Luke, then took in the lay of the land. They were about a mile down from the cabin, in one of the open bowls between the two trails that led down into the Sheep Field. It was a well-used thoroughfare for wildlife. She had seen elk, deer, and moose here dozens of times and enough predators like bear and mountain lions frequented the area that she wouldn't have thought much of the elk spooking from something higher up.

Since she couldn't think of anything to say that hadn't already been said, she reached over and squeezed his hand. She wished he and Becky hadn't been the ones to find Carol's body, but she was beyond relieved that they had made it back to the Ramshorn safely. It chilled her to think that JP had been so close to them, that he might've taken a shot at them. At the same time, anger flared. There was no justification for any of it.

Her dark thoughts plagued her all the way to the intersection with Clark Creek Road. She slammed on her brakes, and her truck slid to a stop in the loose gravel and dust.

"Why is there a tree across the road?" Luke asked.

June stared at it. A large Douglas fir had fallen—or been felled—diagonally across intersection, blocking her from continuing down on Clark Creek Road. The tree was dead but still wore red needles, and there had been no wind to knock it over. She couldn't see it's base through the saplings, but instinctively she knew it had been cut.

She sat for a moment, frozen in indecision. There wasn't room to turn around in the intersection, and it struck her as stupid in the extreme to turn around at the trailhead even though that would be easier than backing up until she found a place to turn around. Twenty or so yards back up Wellman Creek Road was a short but steep incline choked with loose rock, and she didn't know if she'd be able to get enough of a run at it to make it up in reverse. She popped her truck into four-wheel drive and shifted into reverse, ignoring the unsettling pulse of adrenaline.

"It's too late for that, June."

Instinctively at the sound of his voice, she stomped on the gas. The tires spun, spraying dust and gravel into the air, and the truck lurched back. When she reached the incline, the tires just dug down into the loose rock.

"Shit!"

She looked up and stepped on the brake. He stood in the middle of the road, swathed in a cloud of dust with a pistol leveled at her and Luke. She recognized his face—though not the arrogant hatred on it—and her disbelief withered in the face of undeniable evidence.

Pete Landers had indeed killed his own, beloved niece.

"No sudden moves, now, June," he said, walking slowly toward the truck.

Could she hit him hard enough to kill him? Probably not. She thought about grabbing the gun, but when she moved to get it, he called a warning.

"Move over, Luke."

Luke scooted over, and Pete climbed in without once lowering his gun.

"Now, June, if you don't want his brains decorating this cab, you will do exactly as I say."

She met his gaze, bit back her fury, and nodded once.

"Good. Drive to the trailhead."

With a white-knuckled grip on the steering wheel, she did as he asked and didn't question him. There had to be a way out of this, though at the moment, she couldn't imagine what it might be. His truck was nowhere to be seen, but she didn't bother wasting energy trying to figure out where he might have left it.

"Park there, by the sign, then shut the engine down and get out. Make sure you both move very slowly. We're going for a little hike."

June continued to follow his instructions, but Luke sat stubbornly in the cab. Finally, Pete prodded him with the barrel of the pistol, hard enough to push him over. Or did Luke fake it? His hand shot out as if to stop his fall, but when he lifted it and slid across the seat, June caught a glimpse of her pistol in his hand before he tucked it in the waistband of his jeans. He tugged his flannel over it and fastened a button in such a seamless move that June wondered if she had really seen him do it. Hope flared in her heart when they locked gazes and the corner of his lips lifted just a bit. He was not beaten. Not even close.

"You won't win, Pete," Luke said in a low, level

voice.

"Pete's not here, but yes, I will win. Now, get moving."

* * *

Ben watched June's truck disappear around the corner and turned to Pat. Aaron touched his shoulder and pointed in the direction of June's cabin.

"Steve, we're gonna head up to the cabin to wait for Becky," Aaron called to the sheriff.

Steve Rogers looked up from his squat and nodded. He didn't look too pleased that Aaron was handling all the questioning of Luke and Becky, but Ben, June, Jane, and Andy had requested it. Ben liked the sheriff well enough, but he tended to be a little pushy. Besides, both Luke and Becky were more comfortable with Aaron, whom they knew well. Right now, they were both in a fragile state of mind and were much more inclined to open up and revisit their gruesome find with the people they were certain they could trust. Sheriff Rogers hadn't helped himself any by momentarily insinuating that Luke had in his mind been—very briefly—a person of interest. That still rankled Ben.

"They're not going to find anything else down there," Pat remarked as they hiked up to the cabin.

"No, and I doubt there's anything else we can

learn from Becky, either," Aaron said. "I'd feel a lot better if I knew where Pete and Jake were."

"June doesn't want to believe either of them could kill Carol," Ben said. "But who else would know so much about what went on between her, Mike, and Luke? Or her and Shane?"

"I certainly don't want to believe it, either. I don't want to believe anyone from this valley could be doing this."

They fell into silence as they stepped over and around fallen logs and rocks. Ben picked up the pace, anxious to get back to the cabin to make sure he received June's call. He would rather have been with her and Luke and would have volunteered to work a shift at the Ramshorn for free if Sheriff Rogers hadn't decided he wanted Becky to clarify a couple of points for him. A sneer curled his lips. There was nothing to clarify. She had given the exact same, detailed recollection four times already.

Just as he stepped onto the front deck, he heard a vehicle approaching and turned to see his brother-in-law's truck roll around the bend in the driveway. He waited as Andy parked and climbed out.

"You're a bit earlier than I was expecting."

"I wanted to get here fast to ask you something.

June and Luke are working at the Ramshorn today, right?"

"Yeah, why?"

"I didn't think anyone would be stupid enough to let them go hiking right now," Jane said as she joined Ben on the deck. "We saw her truck heading toward the Sawtooth Trailhead."

Ben felt as if he'd been punched in the chest. "No, that's not right."

"I'm glad I still had the chainsaw in the back of the truck, because there was a tree across the road," Andy said. "Took us almost fifteen minutes to clear it. We drove up to the trailhead, and her truck was there, but she and Luke weren't. At first, we thought maybe they'd gone hiking, but that didn't seem right."

"Were there any other vehicles there?"

Jane shook her head. "No."

"Did one of the deputies ride down to the Ramshorn with them?" Becky asked. "Because there was someone else in the truck with June and Luke."

Ben's heart hammered against his ribs, and he couldn't find his voice to ask for more detail.

"Son of a bitch!" Pat snapped. "We have to go. Now."

Ben was already striding into the cabin. First, he

grabbed a backpack and stuffed the first aid kit and several bottles of water in it. Then, he snatched the keys to Luke's and June's dirt bikes, slipped into the shoulder harness and tucked June's .38 revolver in the holster, stuffed his arms into the straps of the backpack, and raced outside. Aaron had already packed his trauma kit, handheld radio, handcuffs, and extra ammo in his backpack. Ben thanked him with a nod and handed him the key to June's bike. Pat climbed on his own bike while Ben straddled Luke's.

"Stay here," Ben told his sister.

"Call my wife, would you, and let her know what's going on?" Pat asked.

Andy and Jane both nodded.

Ben shot off down the hill with Pat and Aaron half a second behind. They stopped at the crime scene, but didn't shut down the bikes.

"He's got them," Ben called to the sheriff.

"What?"

"JP. He got to June and Luke. At the trailhead."

"Christ." The sheriff yelled orders before turning back to Ben. "All right, I want you three to head back to the cabin while we—"

"Like hell," Ben snapped and sped away.

He didn't wait around to see if Pat and Aaron

followed. By the time the town cops got their act to-gether, it might be too late. He took corners faster than he ever had and wove around rock clusters with skill and accuracy owed to the adrenaline coursing through his veins. Somehow, he made it to the trailhead with-out crashing.

"We'll ride up as far as we can," Pat called over the roar of the engines. "Should be able to make it most of the way. Your Forest Service buddy can fine us later, Aaron."

"Since he'd have to fine me, too, I don't see that happening. For this, I think even Jamison will make an exception."

Ben leaned the dirt bike on the kickstand beside June's truck and peeked inside. The gun was gone from beneath the seat and a flood of relief washed through him, followed quickly by another rush of panic. If June or Luke had the gun, there was hope, but if JP had found it, they were in even greater danger.

"The gun isn't there," Ben said.

He climbed back on the bike and barreled toward the hiking trail, praying that JP wouldn't hear the bikes and take precautions to keep himself from being caught. Ben snorted. Jail time was the least of JP's wor-ries if he so much as scratched either June or Luke. Ben would happily drop JP's body in mineshaft where no one would ever find him.

He led the way up the trail, cursing at the rough terrain that kept him to a painfully slow speed. Luke's dirt bike leapt and jerked beneath him over the rocks and tree roots, zigged and zagged around the curves in the trail, and splashed through the narrow creeks that cut across the path, but Ben clung to it, stubbornly refusing to fall off.

They were forced to ditch the bikes where the trail crossed the wider Sawtooth Creek below the switchbacks, but they had under half a half to go. Ben didn't bother following the trail. This was no day hike, and the need for a shortcut negated the desire for an easier climb. He headed straight up the hill toward the lake and slipped the revolver out of the holster, loading it as he climbed. His legs burned and his lungs ached from the thin air, but he pushed on. Fear gnawed at him, but he refused to think about what he'd find… if he found anything at all. For all he knew, JP had driven June and Luke off the trail somewhere far down the mountain. They might not have come this way at all, but he was going with his gut.

They crested the trail, and Sawtooth Lake came into view, glittering serenely like a giant sapphire. Ben paused to listen but heard nothing other than the babble of the outlet stream and the gentle lapping of waves on the shore. Doubt wormed its way into his mind.

"Where are they?" he whispered.

"Look," Pat said, pointing to the trees just to the left of the meadow. "There."

Ben watched for a moment but saw nothing. Then movement caught his eye. He motioned for Pat and Aaron to follow him and set off toward the meadow with his gun at the ready and moving with cautious, stealthy steps.

A gunshot boomed, reverberating like a crack of thunder off the granite walls of the mountains. A second shot followed. Ben abandoned caution and surged forward.

Twenty

LUKE'S MOUTH AND THROAT felt like he'd swallowed fire. Or sandpaper. The heat of exertion burned in every muscle, the grip of the pistol was rubbing a spot raw near the point of his pelvis despite the protection of his t-shirt, and the constant buzz of mosquitoes was maddening. Inexplicably, his mind was sharply clear with all the bitterness, grief, and fear hovering around the edges like the eye-wall of a hurricane, waiting patiently to sweep down and drown him. He couldn't let that happen any more than he could afford to let the weariness get the best of him. He and June had never ascended this trail so quickly, and they both stumbled occasionally in their weariness, but they were both faring better than their captor, who panted and wheezed. The man was in shape—Luke would *not* underestimate that—but he wasn't as accustomed to walking for an hour straight at this altitude, two thousand feet above the floor of the Northstar Valley. Luke just had to figure out how to use that to his advantage without getting himself or June killed.

June glanced over her shoulder at him, and Luke gave her a brief nod to let her know he was okay. For now. Pete's ramblings grew steadily less coherent the higher they climbed, and he coughed a few times. Luke smiled humorlessly, imagining JP was likely feeling a bit dizzy and lightheaded. Good.

"What's wrong, JP?" Luke asked. "The hike a little tough for you?"

JP prodded him in the back with the barrel of his gun. "Keep your mouth shut unless you want to die right here and now."

Luke swallowed the reckless urge to turn around and punch Pete. With a loaded pistol pressed into his back, his chances of succeeding without being shot were nonexistent, so he bit his tongue, ignored the surge of anger and the burning in his lungs, and marched on.

When they reached the log bridge across Saw-tooth Creek, June stepped lightly across it, and Luke followed with a sure and steady stride. JP slipped off the log and didn't even seem to notice when he sank up to his thighs in the icy stream. The uncontained madness gleaming in his eyes made it impossible to see the man Luke had thought of with respect and even fondness for five years. What was wrong with him? There was no trace of the quiet, humble Pete, and surely he couldn't be *that* good an actor. How could anyone effectively hide such a deep rage? How could everyone around him have missed it? How could he kill Carol, the niece he'd helped raise, the girl he adored like his own daughter? Luke gagged and nearly vom-ited when an image of her atop the mine deposits sprang to mind. He forcibly pushed back those ques-tions, memories, and emotions; he couldn't afford to let them gain a foothold on him.

As they neared the end of the main trail, Luke dreaded the view of the lake. If he survived this day, would he ever again be able to look at that glittering jewel without recalling the horror? Then they were at the lake, and it lay before him, promising a peaceful final resting place if he lost this game. With so much ahead of him—Ben and June's wedding, the family that had been denied him for so many years of his young life, graduation, college, and everything else that should follow after—it would be an absolute waste to let JP win.

"Where, June?" JP asked flatly. "Here?"

June scowled. "Here what?"

"Or over there?" He gestured to the meadow across the lake.

"What the hell are you talking about?"

"That son of a bitch, Conner. Did you give yourself to him like a whore in the meadow?"

"Go to hell."

"Keep moving," JP snarled.

June leapt across the outlet stream, but Luke hesitated before he joined her on the opposite bank. He glanced over his shoulder and saw JP's gaze drop to his footing as he gauged the jump. When JP's foot touched the dirt, Luke slammed his elbow into the man's face.

"Run!"

June launched up the narrow trail to the meadow, and Luke dashed after her. Behind them, JP floundered in the creek and scrambled to regain his feet. Adrenaline pumped through Luke. They had to get far enough ahead to hide, though where they would, he hadn't a clue. There was an old, half-built cabin that would hide them from sight, but it was too obvious a shelter. The forest atop the rim of the lake was too open, and there weren't enough bushes or saplings to take cover behind. He glanced over his shoulder to see JP barreling after them and not nearly far enough behind.

June followed the trail around to the camping area and, taking Luke's hand, dragged him into a thick stand of spruce and pines at the edge of the meadow. She collapsed to the ground, gasping for breath. Luke squatted beside her, breathing hard with aching lungs, and let her pull him close. Their respite was short-lived, and they did not even have time to consider their next move before JP reached the thicket.

"I know you're in there," he called. "You can make this easy on yourselves and come out, or I can just start shooting. I'd rather not do that, June."

Luke yanked the pistol out of his waistband and clicked the safety off.

"Luke, no," June whispered.

"What other choice do we have? At least we'll be on a more level playing field now."

He cocked the revolver and hoped JP heard the sound of it. He would need only to squeeze the finger resting against the cool, silky metal of the trigger and this whole terrifying mess would be over. He closed his eyes and whispered a brief prayer that Ben and Pat had realized something was wrong when June didn't call the cabin, and that they could figure out where he and June were. He briefly heard something on the wind that sounded like dirt bikes, but he couldn't be sure. *Please, Ben, find us.*

With a steadying breath, he stepped carefully into the open, keeping himself between June and JP. Despite the throb of adrenaline, his hand was amazingly steady as he aimed his gun.

"Golden boy knows how to play the game," JP remarked. "Bravo, Lukie. I always knew you were cunning."

Blood trickled from the man's nose, and when he sneered, he looked like something out of Luke's darkest nightmares. The outward appearance truly matched the hideous monster within. Luke tightened his hold on the smooth wood grip of the .357.

"The question is… are you cold enough to pull that trigger?"

"You seem to think I am."

"You are selfish and cruel, yes, but that doesn't mean you have the guts to kill a man."

Luke shuddered with revulsion, and his lip curled.

For several agonizing minutes, JP said nothing else but continued to glance between Luke and June.

"Why can't you see it, June? Has this boy so completely infiltrated your heart that you are blind to his lies? No one is as perfect as you think him."

"No one ever said I was perfect," Luke snapped. "Least of all me."

"You… just shut up. She has heard enough of your lies." JP's hand began to shake and righteous fury twisted his face into an even more gruesome scowl. "I'll bet you had her marked from the moment you met her. You played it just right, too, didn't you? Played the wounded little bird who'd lost a father. How could she resist that? You wormed your way into her heart, didn't you, made her believe that you needed her so she would never turn you away."

"I'd be stupid to not want her love. Even you, in your sick, twisted mind—"

"I told you to shut up. I do the talking."

"Be my guest. I'm quite interested to hear what deluded logic drove you to—"

"Silence!" the man bellowed. Veins bulged and his face flushed. "I know exactly what you are. You forced June to choose between you and me, and I didn't see then what I know now. I didn't see how effectively you had manipulated her. I loved her, you know." JP paused and his eyes seemed to lose focus as if he were staring through Luke instead of at him. "She was there to pull me back from the abyss. I found him on the floor of his bedroom with the gun still in his hand and his head half-gone, blown all over the wall. There was so much blood. Ah, Paul…. But you were there, June, my angel in chaos, and you saved me."

An odd vulnerability fluttered across JP's face that reminded Luke strongly of Pete, but between one heartbeat and the next, it was gone. From the corner of his vision, Luke saw June inching away from him, and panic shot through him. He glanced at her and took a step toward her, determined to shield her as best he could, but she twitched her head in a barely perceptible *no*. Tears glittered in her eyes, though he couldn't tell if they were of fear or sorrow, for Pete's tragedy or for him. Terror needled him. What was she doing?

"For that short, perfect time, I was whole again." Venomous hatred dripped from JP's voice, and his gaze refocused directly on Luke. "And then *you*… you came between us. You waltzed into her life and refused to share her."

"I did not—"

"Oh, yes, you did. Don't pretend you didn't know

exactly what you were doing."

"He was only eleven, Pete! For God's sake, leave him alone!"

JP ignored her. "And Carol. You broke my niece's heart."

"*You* convinced her I betrayed her. You and Mike."

"We couldn't have done it without your help."

Luke's eyes stung, and his throat constricted. There was some truth in that, and he couldn't deny it. If he had been more considerate of Carol's thoughts and feelings about Becky, would she have disregarded everything her uncle and Mike told her? Would she still be alive? Would any of this be happening? He flexed his grip on the revolver, and his hand began to tremble as tears flooded his eyes.

"Broken hearts heal," June stated. "Dead ones can't."

JP turned his attention to her. Surprise briefly lightened his ugly sneer when he realized she'd snuck around to the side of him, and he turned the gun on her.

"Tell me, *JP*, why did you kill Carol? Did you kill your own niece only to hurt Luke?"

JP didn't answer and frowned as if confused by

the question.

"And Mike? What about him?"

"You still refuse to see." He took aim at Luke again. "I guess I should just take care of the problem right now, then."

"No!"

"Or…."

Luke shivered when a demonic gleam ignited JP's eyes.

"How to make you suffer most…."

Sheer terror gripped him as JP shifted his aim back to June without taking his eyes off Luke.

"No. Please, God, no." With his thumb holding the hammer, Luke pulled the trigger, and gently eased the hammer down. He held his arms outstretched, offering surrender and a clean shot. "Please don't hurt her. Kill me instead. My life for hers. Please."

"No!" June screamed.

JP glanced at her, distracted.

Luke swung the pistol back in front of him and wrapped both hands around the grip. Before JP could fire at June, Luke aimed and squeezed the trigger. He felt the pistol buck in his hands, heard the explosive crack, and saw the slug tear a hole in JP's shoulder, but JP charged with a wordless bellow, unfazed. Luke launched his pistol toward June just before JP plowed into him. He grappled with his assailant and managed to shove JP back. JP snarled, lifted his gun, and took aim. Luke stepped back, and his heel caught on a root. The bullet sang past his head. When he hit the ground, his head whipped back and struck something hard. Pain exploded as his brain rattled against his skull, and stars blinked and swam in the blackness that enveloped him.

* * *

The scream that ripped from her throat when Luke begged JP to kill him and spare her burned like acid. JP glanced at her, and a gunshot shattered the quiet of the mountain bowl, echoing and re-echoing. She watched, frozen by shock, as the bullet struck JP in the shoulder. The sound that came out of him as he charged Luke was inhuman.

When Luke threw her gun, she jumped toward it and scooped it up as JP aimed and fired. She saw Luke fall, but no scream came. Instead, fear and anger melded into a chilling calm. She didn't see the man she had dated five years ago, the one she called her friend. This was not Pete. He was JP, the fiend who had tormented them, made her doubt her home and her choices, taken away two of her cherished students, and was now poised to kill her son.

As he stepped toward Luke with his pistol aimed and ready, she pulled the hammer back. Her gun was a double action, and all she needed to do to kill him was squeeze the trigger, but the clicks of the firing mechanism seized JP's attention. Without hesitation and with steady hands, she lined up the sights between his stunned eyes. Somewhere at the far edge of her conscious mind, she heard someone running toward them and glimpsed movement to her right, but she refused to be distracted.

"It won't be his life for mine, JP. It will be yours for his."

Her finger twitched against the trigger.

"June, no!"

Ben! He stepped toward her with the .38 gripped comfortably in his hand. Relief flickered through her, but she did not look away from JP.

"Don't do it, June. You don't want that kind of regret. Believe me."

"What regret?" she asked.

With an animal shriek, JP swung his pistol toward Ben, and his finger jerked on the trigger. The shot wailed harmlessly into the trees above them as JP dropped to the hard earth. Ben, Pat, and Aaron piled on him, and he thrashed and flailed, but the three of them were able to restrain him. Ben and Pat rolled him over, pressed his face into the dirt, and pinned him while Aaron cuffed him.

"He's down, June," Pat said. His voice was level, but soft. "We've got him."

"Ben?"

"Not hit," Ben replied.

Slowly, she lowered her gun. The cold determination evaporated, leaving her weak and shaky. She sank to the ground and crawled over to Luke. He still lay on his back, but his legs were turned to the side. It took a moment for her to realize that he'd knocked JP off his feet, and that his action had saved Ben's life. His brows were pinched together and his eyes were closed, but she didn't see any blood. By some miracle, he hadn't been shot.

"Luke?"

"I'm alive." He opened his eyes and winced. Gradually, he bent his legs, and with one hand on his knee and the other holding his head, he sat up. "Ah, that really hurts."

"Lean forward for a minute if you can."

He curled forward and rested his forehead gently on his knees. June parted the hair at the back of his head to check for blood. The blow against the tree root hadn't broken the skin, but when she gingerly prodded the area, she felt a sizeable knot.

"Are you dizzy?" she asked.

"Yeah, maybe a little, and my thoughts are sort of jumbled."

"Did you black out?"

"Not completely."

"You might have a concussion."

"Could've been a lot worse."

"That fall saved your life," she replied, choking on the words.

He turned his head to face her and tried to smile. "I love you, Mom."

His statement was more than a declaration of feelings. It was also an explanation of his actions and the only description she needed. Her tears spilled over, and she wrapped her arms around him, unable to find the words to express her love for him, her gratitude for what he'd done, and her relief that he was alive. Ben knelt beside them, and all she could do was take his hand and pull him into the embrace. Both her boys were alive and safe now. In that moment, that was all that mattered. She would deal with the rest of it later.

She had no idea how long they sat huddled

together at the base of the tree, but when Pat joined them, she wiped her eyes and was absurdly amused that, after their strenuous forced hike, she had enough moisture left in her body for tears. She took several deep breaths and was able to meet Pat's concerned frown with a smile.

"Are you both all right?" he asked.

"For the most part," June replied. "Luke knocked his head pretty hard, but that's the worst of it."

"Concussion?"

"Probably."

"Five years of football," Luke mumbled, "and this is how I get my first concussion."

Ben pulled a couple water bottles out of the backpack June hadn't noticed he wore. She took one gratefully and drank most of it in a swallow. Luke was more frugal with his.

"I brought more," Ben said.

"Pete?" June inquired.

"Well, he'll live," Pat replied. "Aaron radioed down to Sheriff Rogers and briefly explained what happened. The two local EMTs, Rogers, and two deputies are on their way up on four wheelers, and I'm sure they'll have some extra help with them. I gotta tell you, once we got Pete restrained, he just… deflated as if all the fight had left him. He asked what happened like he honestly couldn't remember."

June rose to her feet and wandered over to Aaron. The deputy had JP propped against a tree and was keeping pressure on the cowhand's wound. Pat was right. JP slumped, held upright by Aaron's hand, and she could see no trace of the violent rage. With a frown, she dropped to her knees a few feet back from him to better see his face.

"Pete?"

He sluggishly lifted his head, and she saw confusion and pain in his familiar brown eyes, but again, no sign of the madness that had consumed him so short a time ago. He explored her face for what seemed like minutes before timidly addressing her.

"June?" he asked as if he didn't recognize her. Or didn't expect to see her before him.

She nodded.

"What happened? Aaron won't tell me what happened."

"You don't remember?"

"No."

"What does the name JP mean to you?"

He frowned. "Name? They're my initials… and Jake's. Would someone please tell me what the hell is going on? I've been shot, and I think I'm at Sawtooth Lake, but I don't know why or how."

Could it all be an act? Or did he really not remember? She met Aaron's gaze, and he shrugged, indicating that he was also at a loss to explain it.

"You don't remember forcing me and Luke up here at gunpoint?"

"Careful, June," Aaron warned. He mouthed, *I don't want to set him off again.*

"Gunpoint? What? No, I don't remember." Horror widened Pete's eyes. "I've been… losing time like I did after Paul died."

"What do you mean?" Aaron asked.

"I'll be doing something, and next thing I know, I'm doing something else, sometimes hours later, and I can't remember anything of what happened in between. I don't black out. I just can't remember how I got from one thing to the next. What else did I do?"

"The Hay Fever potluck," June said. "Where were you?"

"Where was I? Isn't it tomorrow?"

June met Aaron's surprised gaze. "Do you think he's telling the truth?"

"It's possible."

"What is going on?" Pete asked again. Hysteria

edged into his voice. "How much did I lose this time? And what happened? What did I do?"

"The potluck was six days ago," Aaron answered.

"I lost a week?" He looked to June to confirm it.

She nodded. If he truly didn't remember anything between then and now, he wouldn't remember killing either Mike or Carol. Pity trickled into her heart. The nightmare he'd put her family through was nothing compared to the hell he would enter when he realized what he'd done.

"I'm so sorry, Pete. After everything that's happened, I don't know how I can be, but I am. Someday, I know I will have to forgive you, and if you really don't remember, I will *want* to. But not today."

She rocked to her feet and turned away. He called her name, but she ignored him. It stunned her, that she had been able to think so clearly, especially to feel that pang of pity for him when, less than twenty minutes ago, she had been prepared—wanting, even—to kill him. She walked back to Luke, Ben, and Pat to find her son on his feet with his hands braced on Pat's and Ben's shoulders as if testing his steadiness. Another wave of relief washed through her when he took a firm step forward. The older men walked beside him toward the lake, ready to assist if needed, but Luke didn't need it.

"Rest for a little bit before we start down," Ben said. "Drink some water and take it easy."

The four of them sat together beneath the shade just a few feet back from the water's edge. Pat was careful to keep Aaron and Pete in sight and got up a couple times to relieve Aaron while they waited for the EMTs to arrive.

"Did anyone give him water yet?" June asked, nodding her head in Pete's direction.

"Yeah," Pat replied. "We had to make him drink."

"How is it possible that I feel sorry for him?"

"Because you are the most compassionate woman I've ever met," Ben answered. "Do you think this losing time thing is genuine?"

"I'd rather believe that than think he killed Carol in cold blood," Luke murmured. "He really loved her, and I can't believe he could fake *that*. I don't know how it's possible, either, but I feel sorry for him, too. Maybe if things hadn't turned out as well as they did, I wouldn't feel this way, but we're all alive."

"Yes, we are," Ben agreed with a sigh. "Thank you, Luke. You saved my life today when you kicked Pete's feet out from under him."

"Guess that makes us even."

Ben tucked an arm around Luke's shoulders and squeezed. "If I ever doubted you were June's son before, I certainly don't now."

June understood that they still had a long road ahead of them and many heartbreaking memories to move past, but they would face them together. As a family.

* * *

Ben stepped out onto the back porch to watch the sun set on the longest day of his life in a spectacular blaze of fiery hues. The cabin was finally quiet. Aaron had departed after chasing Sheriff Rogers out half an hour ago, and Pat and Aeli had left a few minutes later to collect their children from her grandparents. He wasn't sure if he was glad everyone was gone or not. In the tranquility of the evening, he could finally relax, but at the same time, he was alone with his thoughts. He would've been quite happy to have Pat and Aelissm stay for a while longer, but they were nearly as emotionally drawn as Ben, June, and Luke. Ben counted their friendship among his many blessings on this day, and they had already done so much for him that he couldn't begrudge them the need to unwind.

What a day, Ben thought, relieved that it was over. His mind drifted back over all that had happened despite his best efforts to prevent the replay.

An EMT had looked Luke over and agreed with the assessment of a concussion before assisting the other first responder with Pete's gunshot wound. Sheriff Rogers had asked them to walk him through what had happened up at the lake with Aaron standing in for Pete. For the first time since beginning his investigation, Rogers had been satisfied with hearing it once. Afterward, everyone had hiked down to where the dirt bikes and four wheelers had been left.

Pete had been taken to the hospital in an ambulance, and Ben had driven June and Luke into Devyn. Luke's doctor confirmed a mild concussion and sent him home with a prescription for plenty of rest. Upon their return to the cabin three hours ago, June and Luke had promptly retreated to the loveseat and couch and—physically and emotionally exhausted—had immediately fallen asleep, leaving Ben to take the brunt of the questioning.

Inhaling deeply of the cool mountain air, he tried not to think about what he'd nearly lost today, but after reviewing the events at least five times for the sheriff and his deputies, it was impossible. It wasn't his own brush with death that frightened him, although it would have been a pity to have finally forgiven himself for John McKindel's death only to die. It was the thought that he'd almost been deprived of his family before they were officially—and legally—his that scared him.

He had thought he'd known what fear felt like, until he reached June and Luke and seen the teenager lying unmoving on the ground. On the hike down to the bikes, June had painted a picture of Luke throwing his arms wide to offer his life for hers, and Ben could all too easily imagine it. The kid had lightning reflexes, though, and luck had been with him when he'd tripped. What could've ended in his and June's deaths had come to a comparatively peaceful end. Ben could not begin to express his gratitude for that.

"All right, Conner, stop thinking about it. It's over and done."

He heard the back door open behind him. Luke joined him on the deck and lowered himself gently into one of the chairs. For a few minutes, they were content to enjoy the quiet splendor of the blossoming sunset, then Ben turned around to face his companion. He leaned on the deck railing and crossed his ankles.

"Your mom still asleep?"

"Yep."

"How are you feeling?"

"Other than a pounding headache… I guess I'm okay."

"How are you doing with the rest of it?"

The teenager shrugged. "Right now, it's pretty hard to think through the headache… but I can feel it all, hovering around the edges, waiting to close in."

Ben heard the emotions seep into Luke's voice and sat in the chair closest to him. "Don't start thinking about it now. Let it wait until tomorrow. Better yet, let it wait until next week."

"I wish it was that easy."

"And what fool ever said life was easy?"

Luke gave a sniff of laughter, but his eyes saddened when he noticed the thick weathered-wood frame lying on the table. "Is that the amethyst frame?"

Ben nodded. "Aelissm brought it by."

She'd made a beautiful frame, he thought. It reminded him of a shadow box and was about two inches deep with the picture set at the back and matted in navy blue. She had cut a diamond-shaped hole in the frame below the picture for the amethyst, which was suspended by a slender silver chain. The setting she'd used—instead of drilling into the stone—was nearly invisible; four tiny silver prongs. Ben sidled closer and stared at the picture. The picture June and Aelissm had chosen to frame, out of the dozen or so the tourist had taken, radiated love. He missed those carefree grins on June's, Luke's and Becky's faces, and though he hadn't known Carol very well, he lamented the loss of her cautious smile.

"Do you think Pete even understands what he did?"

"I don't know, Luke. I do know there's something wrong with him. Losing time, telling you 'Pete's not here'…. I don't have any answers, and I know you need them."

"She's really gone, isn't she? I didn't imagine finding her. And Mike, too. They're never coming back."

Luke pinched his eyes closed, pressed the inside of his wrists to his forehead, and braced his elbows on his knees. In the warm glow of sundown, Ben saw the tears rolling down the teenager's cheeks. The soft sobs wrenched his heart, but he knew Luke needed to grieve for his friends, and he hadn't yet. Not really.

"It even hurts to cry," Luke murmured.

"I'm sure it does."

Ben scooted his chair closer and rubbed his hand across Luke's back to show his support. When Luke leaned toward him, Ben believed with every beat of his heart that he had made the right decision in returning to Northstar. As strange as it might seem on the outside, this was where he belonged.

By the time Luke's grief had run its course—at least for the time being—the sky had darkened into the blue-green and indigo of late twilight. Stars glittered brightly above them, and Ben allowed their soothing beauty to wash away his worries. Luke straightened and watched the sky with him, silent for a long time, and clearly more peaceful for indulging his sorrow. A meteor shot across the sky in a trail of gleaming white light.

"Hey, Ben?"

"Hmm?"

"I can't wait until December."

Ben smiled, disbelieving for a moment that the son of the man he'd shot five years ago—almost to the day, he realized—would soon be *his* son. It was certainly *not* the outcome he'd imagined when he'd decided to come home, but it was better.

"Neither can I."

Epilogue

"ALL RIGHT, IF WE'RE GOING to get a few shots with the sunlit mountains in the background, we'd better hurry," the photographer said.

Though the sky over the valley and the east peaks of the Northstar Mountains was one of the most brilliant, deep blues June had ever seen, the temperature had dropped easily ten degrees in as many minutes. Cold front indeed. Not that she was complaining. The forecast called for twelve to twenty-four inches of snow over the next two days, and the prospect of it added a new facet to her giddiness. She and Ben were going to have the cabin to themselves tonight—Luke would be staying with Pat and Aeli—and she couldn't imagine a more romantic wedding night.

She handed her coat back to her new sister-in-law and shivered when the cold air hit her bare arms and shoulders. Her dress might not be the most practical for a winter wedding, but it was exquisite. The sweetheart bodice was wrapped in a herringbone pattern of overlapping, shimmery organza and each layer was edged with silvery beads and rhinestones that reminded her of frost. The organza was gathered at a snowflake brooch that rested just above her left hip and laid gently over the full skirt and chapel train. June skimmed her hand lovingly over the smooth material and took in the site of her wedding party.

The bridesmaids, Aelissm and Becky, wore stunning dresses of deep sapphire overlaid with matching organza and sprinkled with beads and rhinestones. Becky had commented that the dresses looked like a winter night sky, and June quite agreed. Ben and the groomsmen, Pat and Luke, all wore midnight blue tuxes. *That* was one idea she had borrowed from Pat and Aelissm's wedding, and she was glad she had because the dark blue really brought out the beauty of their eyes.

"Feeling a little girly, my dear wife?" Ben whispered in her ear.

"Maybe a little." She threaded herself around Ben, ignoring the rapid-fire clicks of the photographer's camera shutter and touched her lips to his. "Mmm. Wife. I think I like it."

"I know I do."

"Congratulations to you both," Luke said. He leaned down to kiss her cheek.

The photographer continued to snap pictures as June pulled her two favorite males close to her. Finally, they got serious about the photos when a few people grumbled good-naturedly about the imminent snowfall. The nippy air gave everyone a very good reason to stand close together, and June managed to not freeze through the dozens—maybe even hundreds—of photos that were taken by the photographer and by wedding guests. Even if she hadn't been warmed by the body heat of her friends and family, the glow of love burned so brightly in her heart that it was hard to let something as insignificant as a snowstorm chill her.

The temperature continued to plummet, and by the time they finished the photoshoot with a few poses—and more than a few candids—with Cheyenne and Casey, the clouds had sailed in from the northwest and thickened from gossamer streamers that thinly veiled the sun into a flat pewter ceiling. June was glad they'd opted for a morning wedding, because the mountains had been an absolutely stunning backdrop, decked out as they were in glittering white finery. Now the peaks were already disappearing behind the first flurries. After the reception, Ben would whisk her away in his truck through a curtain of feathery snowflakes to their cabin. It was absolutely perfect.

"I think those last shots of the three of us and the dogs will be my favorites," June remarked as she headed toward the doors of the dining room.

She gathered her skirts, and Luke and Ben held the doors open for her. They were met with cheers and applause and the blessed warmth of a roaring fire in the hearth. She had managed to hold back the tears so far, but the sight of Pat and Aelissm and their children, her parents and Ben's and Aelissm's, Uncle Bill and Aunt Mary, Ben's former landlady Mrs. Miller, Grandma and Grandpa Davis, Jane, Andy, and Becky, Marvin and Mary Struthers, and every other beloved face set her eyes to burning and the rest of her face to beaming.

Aelissm tapped a fork against her water glass. Expectant silence fell over the room.

"It is my great pleasure to welcome my two best friends and my favorite nephew to the Bedspread for the first time as the Conner family," Aeli said. "Welcome, Ben, June, and Luke Conner, and many congratulations."

Her impromptu toast was met with another round of cheers. A dozen flashes nearly blinded June.

"That's the picture I want, right there," Aeli remarked. "All three of them are grinning like idiots."

"And you want proof," June retorted.

"Yes, I do."

The dining room was packed, and if June had been anywhere else, she might have felt anxious. After everything that had happened with JP, perhaps she *should* feel nervous, since a man she'd considered a friend had nearly destroyed her family. It was all over, though, and she felt nothing but flawless joy.

June's and Aelissm's mothers, with the help of half a dozen other cooks, had roasted the prime rib to perfection. The side dishes of mashed potatoes and gravy, salads and cooked vegetables were wonderful, too. June lingered over her meal and enjoyed the pleasant chatter that filled the dining room.

Luke excused himself to chat with some of the other valley teenagers. June was relieved he and Becky were finally beginning to socialize more comfortably again, but the strained interactions with Shane made her worry that Luke's bond with his best friend had been damaged beyond repair. School had been tough for Becky and Shane but especially for Luke. It made her sick, the cold disdain with which some people treated him, as if they really believed he had been responsible for the deaths of Mike Thompson and Carol Landers. June did her best to protect him, but she knew it would take time before people were able to forgive what had happened. Wrong as it was, with Pete mentally unable to stand trial and currently undergoing treatment several hundred miles away, Luke had become the scapegoat for their anger.

June's gaze drifted to Luke's football coach, Greg Wells, and gratitude rushed through her. He and the football team had sheltered and defended Luke from the worst of the disgusting animosity, and the sport had proven to be effective therapy for him. When Luke had led the team to their fourth state championship in a row just a few weeks ago, June had happily noticed a significant reduction in the hard feelings toward her son. Mike wasn't Devyn's only promising star, and the football team's victory had done a lot to remind people of that.

Northstar was a different story, and for that, she would be forever appreciative. At home in the valley, Luke was welcomed with open arms and treated with the same warmth and love he'd always known here.

"June, Ben," Coach Wells greeted as he walked over with two packages in his hands. "Congratulations, again. It was a beautiful ceremony."

"Thank you, Greg," June replied. "We're glad you came."

"I am, too, but with the weather, I should probably head back into town. I know you're waiting to open your gifts, but I wanted to give you something before I go." He handed her the packages. "One is for Luke."

June called Luke over and, together with her son and husband, carefully opened the gift addressed to the Conner family. In it were an album chronicling Luke's football career in photos and a framed, twelve by eighteen inch photograph of her, Ben, and Luke at the state championship game. June adored the exultant grin on Luke's face and the pride on hers and Ben's. She sat and flipped through the album, reliving the unbelievable changes in Luke from the front to the back of the book. Greg had included portraits, the team pictures, newspaper clippings, and dozens of action shots from games. It was a superb compilation.

"I knew you didn't need any of the traditional house wares, so I thought these would be much more appreciated." Greg explained. "You have a beautiful family, June, but I know you already know that. Luke, here. This one's for you."

Luke tore open the wrapping paper and pulled out two football jerseys, both the white and navy away jersey and the navy and gold home jersey. They were the last Luke had worn in his high school career, emblazoned with his number eighteen. When he unfolded them, June saw the real gift. Coach Wells had had Luke's last name—Montana—stitched onto the back of the away jersey, and on the back of the home jersey was Conner. She pressed her knuckles to her lips and swallowed the lump in her throat.

"Thank you," she whispered and embraced the coach. "Thank you, so much."

When she released him, he turned to Luke and hugged him tightly. "Thanks for the best four years of my coaching career, Luke. I'm really going to miss you next year. MSU for sure, huh?"

"Yeah. I think Mom's right about getting out of Devyn for a little while. Besides, I'm kinda fond of the old blue and gold, so I am naturally drawn to the Bobcat uniforms."

June expected Coach Wells to comment on Shane's decision to take the offer from the Griz, but he didn't, though she saw he also regretted the fracturing of that friendship when he glanced over his shoulder at his other player and sighed.

"All right, folks, I'd best be on my way."

"Thank you, again, Greg. For coming and for the gifts."

After Coach Wells had left, Luke sat down in his chair and stared at his jerseys. "Wow. Coach didn't even give Mike his jerseys when he graduated."

"Goes to show that Coach Wells knows how special you are," June said.

Becky bounced over. "Hey, Uncle Ben, Aunt June, is it time for toasts and cake?"

"I suppose so," June replied. She flipped a ringlet of her new niece's dark hair over her shoulder. "You look absolutely beautiful, Becky."

"Thanks. Oh, wow! Coach Wells gave you your jerseys?"

Luke nodded with a broad smile.

Pat and Aelissm stood together and called for everyone's attention, but before they could begin the toasts, the front door of the dining room opened. A tense silence settled over the crowd. Jake Sterling stood just inside the door, glancing nervously around the room at the unfriendly faces. June had seen him only a couple of times since Pete's arrest, and they hadn't spoken, but she had learned he'd been in Missoula at orientation for college when Carol had been killed. He took a few cautious steps toward the wedding party's table, hesitated, and finally strode forward.

"What are you doing here, Jake?" June inquired.

"I just stopped by to see how Luke is doing."

"Jake, I warned—"

"I'm not…. I really mean it this time. I'm not trying to be a dick."

June sat back, disbelieving for a moment until she noticed the sadness in his eyes. It had completely washed away the arrogant sneer, and she felt a twinge of regret for him. For all his faults, he had loved Carol.

"I want to apologize," Jake continued. "For what Pete did."

"Pete didn't do it," June replied. "JP did. I forgave Pete—we all did—as soon as he was diagnosed."

"But Pete *is* JP."

"No, JP is a separate personality, and Pete had no control over him."

"I keep thinking…. Pete told me he was losing time again. If I'd done something or said something…."

"Don't say that," Luke said quietly. "How could you have known what was wrong? I suppose we owe you an apology, too, because we suspected you."

"I guess I kinda earned it." Jake's eyes glittered with a sheen of tears. "I'm sorry, too, for the way I've treated you. You're a good kid, Luke, and I just couldn't see it."

"Sounds like you've been doing a lot of thinking," June remarked.

"I have been. And I have some issues I've been working on, too. Anyhow, Luke, I'm not saying we're ever going to be friends, but I am sorry for being such an ass. Carol was right about you, and I should've listened to her." The corner of his mouth twitched upward. "Wouldn't have gotten the snot beat outa me if I had. Truce?"

Luke didn't hesitate to shake Jake's offered hand. "Truce."

"Did ya have to pick Bozeman? It's gonna kill me, rooting for the Bobcats."

"Thanks, Jake."

Jake shifted his weight and turned his attention to Ben. "I wanted to congratulate you both, too. June's an incredible woman. Not that I need to tell you that.

Hell, she gave me and Pete a chance even though we didn't deserve it. Don't take her for granted."

"I don't intend to."

"Well, I guess that's all I came to say."

He turned abruptly away and strode out the door. A quiet murmur fluttered through the room, and June found herself staring after him. She'd finally seen something in him to admire. It took guts to stand in front of their neighbors—many of whom were none too thrilled with him or Pete right now—and apologize.

"That was delightfully unexpected," Luke murmured.

"Yes, it was," Aelissm agreed. "Now, can we get on with the toasts? Thank you. I know it's traditional for the best man and maid of honor to give their own toasts, but since we're both friends with both the bride and groom, we decided to share."

Pat tucked an arm around his wife's waist. "For the three of you, today is only a step on a road you began walking years ago and will continue to walk for years to come. June and Ben, your friendship has persevered through many trials. Let it now become the solid foundation upon which you build your life together."

"To June, Ben, and Luke," Aelissm said, raising her glass. "Who prove that second chances can turn into the most beautiful love."

Their toast was met with overwhelming approval.

Luke stood. "To Mom and Dad—and yes, Uncle Bill, to you, too—for my second chance." Bill chuckled and raised his glass to that. "For the first time in my life, I have a complete, loving family."

"You had to go and make me cry, didn't you?" June asked, wiping beneath her eyes.

"Sorry, Mom."

Next, it was Becky's turn. "I worried I'd never get my Uncle Ben back, but now he's happy again—happier than ever—and I have a new aunt and a new cousin in addition. I love you all."

Trisha and Dan Blue and James and Eleanor Conner stood together.

"This one is from all of us, together," Trisha said. "When children find true love, parents find true joy. Here's to your joy and ours, from this day forward."

"Thank you," Ben whispered. More loudly, he said, "All right, it's my turn now. And, I promise, June, I'll do my best to keep it short and sweet. To Luke, you are the best son any parents could ask for, and I doubt I'll ever feel like I deserve you."

Luke didn't reply, but the bear hug he gave Ben said what words could not. By the time they let go of each other, both had tears shining in their eyes. Ben cleared his throat and turned to June.

"To the woman with the most beautiful heart I have ever known, you are my summer angel, because you brought me the warmth of summer to chase away the chill of my darkest winter."

June rose and kissed him and said the only words that seemed powerful enough to properly balance his statement. "With all my heart, I love you."

* * * * *

USA Today Bestselling Author
SUZIE O'CONNELL
Twice Shy
A Northstar Novel

Twice Shy

Five years after his wife died in his arms, Aaron Hammond doesn't think he'll ever be ready to love another woman, but Skye Hathaway's arrival in Northstar will test that theory.

Wounded and wary from walking in on her philandering husband and his mistress and with the ink still wet on her divorce, the last thing Skye needs is to get tangled up with a handsome widower and his charming daughter. And yet…with those sad eyes and a patient attentiveness, Aaron could be exactly what her bruised heart needs.

As Aaron coaxes her out of her painful memories, he finds himself facing an intriguing possibility: life may yet have a lasting love in store for him. But can he let go of his wife and open himself fully to Skye? Because she won't compete with a ghost for his heart. She has been competing with other women for her husband for too long.

AVAILABLE NOW

Visit www.suzieoconnell.com for more information.

About the Author

Suzie O'Connell is the *USA Today* bestselling author of the Northstar romances. The series is the product of a love affair with Southwestern Montana that began with a two-week adventure at her stepsister's rustic cabin in her teens. That love affair shows no sign of abating.

She has been writing stories for as long as she can remember, and her love of writing and of Montana pushed her to earn a Bachelor of Arts in Literature and Writing from the University of Montana-Western. What else would you expect from a self-professed mountain-loving nerd?

When she isn't writing, you'll probably find Suzie in the mountains with a camera in hand and enjoying the beauty of Montana with her husband Mark, their daughter Maddie, and their golden retrievers Reilly and Angus.

Find Suzie online at www.suzieoconnell.com